WINGS

ALSO BY
ELIZABETH RICHARDS

Black City

Phoenix

WINGS

A **BLACK CITY** NOVEL

ELIZABETH RICHARDS

G. P. PUTNAM'S SONS
AN IMPRINT OF PENGUIN GROUP (USA)

G. P. PUTNAM'S SONS
Published by the Penguin Group
Penguin Group (USA) LLC
375 Hudson Street, New York, NY 10014

USA | Canada | UK | Ireland | Australia
New Zealand | India | South Africa | China
penguin.com
A Penguin Random House Company

Library of Congress Cataloging-in-Publication Data
Richards, Elizabeth (Elizabeth Fleur), 1980–
Wings / Elizabeth Richards.
pages cm.—(A Black City novel)
Summary: "In this conclusion to the Black City trilogy, Natalie finds herself separated
from Ash, who is hiding out from the Sentry government. But they'll never give up
their hope of reuniting and their quest to bring an end to the terrible reign
of Purian Rose"—Provided by publisher.
[1. Fantasy. 2. Race relations—Fiction. 3. Drugs—Fiction.
4. Social classes—Fiction. 5. War—Fiction.] I. Title.
PZ7.R37953Win 2014 [Fic]—dc23 2013040025

Printed in the United States of America.
ISBN 978-0-399-15945-9
1 3 5 7 9 10 8 6 4 2

Design by Ryan Thomann. Text set in Sabon.

For my sisters, Genny and Kirsty

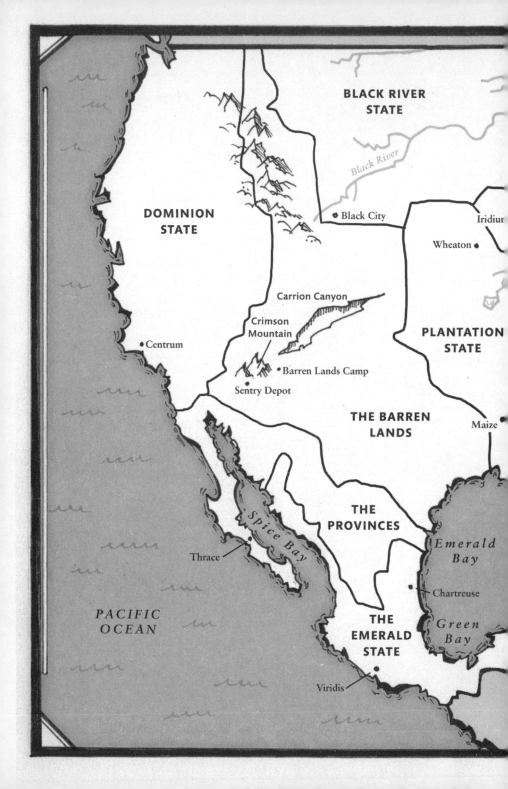

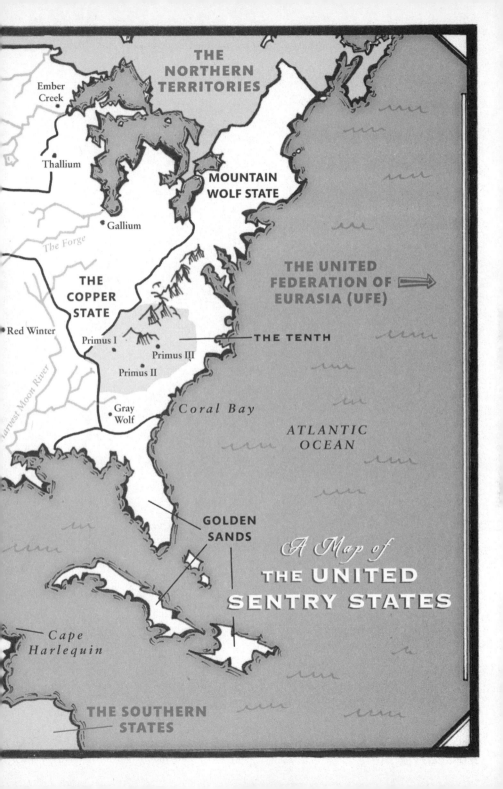

PART 1

CRY OF THE PHOENIX

1.

EDMUND

Amber Hills, Mountain Wolf State
30 years ago

THE CHURCH BELLS CHIME MIDNIGHT, signaling the start of the Watchmen's shift. No one else is allowed out after dark; no one else dares. Night is for the creatures that live beyond the wall. The ones lurking in the shadows of the forest. The ones that are watching me now.

A whisper of wind, as cold as winter's breath, chills the back of my neck. I lift up the collar of my woolen jacket as I patrol the Boundary Wall that encases our compound. What the hell was I thinking of when I volunteered to do this? Well, it's obvious *who* I was thinking of: Catherine. Maybe now that I'm a Watchman, she'll stop seeing me as Best Friend Edmund and more as Potential Boyfriend Edmund.

I'm surprised the Guild allowed me to take the job—it usually goes to the hunters, not the eighteen-year-old grandson of the town minister—but I'm good with a gun . . . well, pellet gun. I can shoot a rat in the eye from thirty yards away. I weigh the rifle in my hands. It's heavier but not too dissimilar.

Somewhere in the blackness beyond the wall a Lupine howls,

the sound echoing across the night. I shiver. Their howls don't bother me so much during the day, when the sun is high and there are hundreds of people milling about, but it's altogether a different matter when you're up on the wall, with nothing but darkness all around you. This was a *really* bad idea.

"All clear," Mr. Kent's gruff voice calls from farther down the wall. He's one of the four Watchmen on duty tonight, including me. He's far enough away that I can only make out his shadowy figure moving about in the night.

I scan the tree line, searching for the Lupine. From my vantage point on the thirty-foot-high wall, I can see right across the Forest of Shadows toward the volcano, Mount Alba, known locally as the Claw because of its talon-shaped peak. I squint at the trees. Their gnarled branches are like witches' fingers, ready to snatch anyone who dares enter the forest.

"All clear," I call back. "No Howlers here."

We nickname them Howlers because of the noise they make when they call to each other. I shiver again. This is going to be a long night.

"Edmund?"

I whip around, gun raised, ready to shoot the frightened brown-haired girl peering at me from the top of the ladder. *Catherine!* A thrill of nervous excitement rushes through me.

"Fragging hell, Caterpillar. Don't sneak up on a guy when he's carrying a gun," I say, lowering the weapon.

"'Hello' to you too," she says, pouting. "And don't call me that. You know I hate it."

She climbs up the rest of the ladder and joins me on the wall. Tucked underneath her arm is a blanket. She's wearing a long red cape over a simple cotton nightdress, which clings to the swells and dips of her newly developed curves. She's no longer plain, skinny Caterpillar, who would happily wrestle with me in the dirt. When she turned seventeen this summer, she started wearing makeup and doing her hair, and now looks like an actual *girl* girl—something all the boys in town have noticed, including me.

She's not the only one who's changed; in the past few months I've shot up another four inches and fill out my clothes much better. I even have a smattering of dark stubble across my jawline, which helps cover some of the scars on my face, so I don't look half bad now. Not *great* but not completely vomit-worthy either.

"What are you doing here?" I say. "Not that I'm complaining, but you know it's after curfew, right?" I glance along the wall, making sure Mr. Kent can't see us. He's walking toward the east corner of the wall. We're safe.

She rolls her eyes. "Since when do you care about curfews? Besides, what sort of friend would I be if I didn't come and celebrate your first night as Watchman?"

"A terrible one," I tease.

"The worst," she agrees, laying the blanket on the stone walkway that runs along the top of the wall. Folded inside the gingham blanket are two red apples and a blue-veined cheese. "I thought you might be hungry."

I catch a whiff of the stinking cheese, and my stomach knots.

Catherine frowns, noticing my reaction. "It's all I could take from the store without my parents noticing."

"It's great, Cater—Catherine, thanks." I join her on the scratchy blanket, sitting close enough to smell her perfume: orange blossom and honey. I lean against the stone turrets and rake a hand through my stubborn black hair. "Pass me an apple, then."

Our fingertips touch as she hands me the apple. Desire aches through me.

"Do you remember that time we snuck up here as kids?" she asks.

When I was twelve and Catherine eleven, we crept up here after curfew to look at the lights coming from Gray Wolf, the city closest to our secluded compound. I remember seeing them glittering in the distance, brighter than any star. Catherine had cried, saying they made her sad. Until that moment, she hadn't realized how trapped we were here.

Neither of us has left the safe confines of our town, Amber Hills—a walled commune built a hundred years ago by the Guild, to allow us to live away from the sins of modern life. *"The world may have fallen to sin, but we don't have to,"* Catherine's father, Mr. Langdon, is keen to remind us whenever we step out of line. I don't usually agree with him, but on this one point we see eye to eye. We all know what's out there. *Demons.* I briefly grip the circle pendant around my neck—a symbol of our religion. Our faith keeps us protected from them. Well, that and this great big wall. Catherine's wearing a similar pendant, although hers is gold, whereas mine is wood.

"I recall your dad sending out a search party for you," I say. *And the beating he gave me afterward, before Grandfather stepped in.*

She frowns, clearly remembering that too. "He's so overprotective; it drives me crazy sometimes. He thinks just because he's the head of the Guild, it somehow gives him the right to control every aspect of my life too."

"I think that's just what dads do," I say, half smiling, although I wouldn't know. I never knew my father.

"I guess," she says, nibbling on her apple. "So how are you finding your first night as Watchman?"

I shrug. "I don't know why everyone keeps making such a fuss about it. It's not *that* scary out here," I lie.

Another Lupine barks, closer this time. Catherine lets out a squeak of fright and throws her arms around my neck. The scent of orange blossom fills my nostrils. I try not to smile.

"Nothing's going to hurt you when I'm on watch," I say. "I can take on a few Howlers. I'm a good shot."

"It's not just them I'm frightened of," she says, pulling away from me. "Patrick says there's"—she lowers her voice—"*Darklings* in the woods."

"Oh, well, if your brother says it, then it must be true."

Catherine scowls at me. "He hunts in those woods all the time with Harriet and Drew."

"Did he see one?"

"Well, no," Catherine admits. "He found a deer with two puncture wounds in its neck."

"Any number of wild animals could've made that wound," I reply. "Besides, have you ever seen a Dark? Has *anyone,* in all the years we've been alive?"

She shakes her head, giving a little shudder. "No, praise be. They scare me more than all those other demons put together."

"Why? A Lupine can tear you to shreds just as easily," I say. "And a Bastet's venom can rot the flesh from your bones."

"I know," she says. "But the Darklings are different. They don't just kill you, they play with you first. They drug you, make you think you're in love with them, so you willingly let them feed on you, until there's nothing left of you but an empty shell. It's sick."

I roll the apple over in my hand. "Well, you don't need to worry. The nippers are long gone," I say, taking a bite. "There's nothing in that forest but man-eating Lupines."

"That makes me feel *so* much better."

I smirk. "I aim to please."

Shadowy rainclouds slowly blanket the sky, blinking out the stars one by one. It begins to drizzle, but thankfully Catherine makes no attempt to leave—in fact she edges closer to me, causing her nightdress to ride up her legs a little. There's a tiny freckle above her left ankle, and another one higher up her calf muscle. I wonder if there are any more hidden underneath the cotton—

"You're staring at me, Edmund," she says.

I clear my throat, embarrassed. "Sorry."

We're silent for a long moment, letting the sounds of the night fill in the blanks: the rustle of the trees, the hoot of Phantom owls, the steady *plip-plip-plip* of rain splashing against the wall. I absentmindedly run my tongue over my top teeth, a habit I formed as a kid.

"I got a new dress for the dance tomorrow night," Catherine says.

My stomach flips. The dance has been on everyone's lips all week. It's been eighteen years since we united with the Lupines and forced the Darklings out of the forest, bringing an end to a period of conflict known as the Misery, and each year the Guild throws a dance for the townsfolk to celebrate. We've had a shaky truce with the Lupines ever since, neither side wanting a return to the violence, but over the past six weeks they've been breaking into the compound, snatching people, and we don't know why. They've already taken three victims, including my predecessor, Mr. Smyth, which is why I'm up here tonight, guarding the wall.

"Are you going with anyone?" I say as casually as possible.

"No." She sighs heavily. "I'd sort of hoped Eric Cranfield would ask me, but I think Patrick scared him off."

My mouth twitches at the thought of Catherine's brother. He's made it his mission in life to make mine hell. Still, I'm glad he's frightened off the competition. I might stand a chance with Catherine now.

"It's so frustrating. Patrick's worse than Father. He thinks he owns me," she continues. "Are you taking anyone?"

"Sure, because all girls are desperate to date the village freak," I mumble.

"Don't call yourself that," she says.

"Why not? Everyone else does."

"You're an attractive guy, Edmund." Catherine lightly rests her hand on my leg. A whirlpool swirls in my stomach. "Any girl who can't see that needs her head examined."

I look down. "We . . . er . . . we could go to the dance together, you know, since we're both free?"

"Sure," she says, removing her hand from my thigh.

I grin. "Really?"

"Why not? It'll be fun," she says. "We can go with Harriet and Drew."

I'd rather poke out my own eyeballs—I hate those two almost as much as I do Patrick—but I won't let them ruin the night.

"It's a date th— Gah!" I grasp my chest as a burning sensation rips through it.

"Are you okay?" Catherine asks, alarmed.

"Yeah." I rub my aching chest, waiting for the pain to subside. What in His Mighty's name was that? "It was just a cramp."

"In your chest?" she says.

I shrug, unable to come up with another explanation. Whatever it was, it's gone now. It's nothing to get worked up about.

There's a sudden roll of thunder in the distance. The vibrations sweep across the sky, shaking the swollen clouds so that they release all the rain at once. It's like someone tipped a bucket of ice water over us, soaking our clothes in an instant. We hurriedly roll the remaining food up in the gingham blanket.

"I'll walk you home," I say. I'm forbidden to leave my post, but I'll be gone only a minute. I toss the bundled blanket over the side of the wall, and it falls to the ground thirty feet below us, hitting the dirt with a soft thud. We head down the ladder, taking it slow, not wanting to lose our footing on the slippery rungs.

My feet eventually touch the wet ground, and I help Catherine down the rest of the way. My hands slide over her trim waist, and I hold on to her for a fraction longer than I should before releasing my grip. Her cheeks turn pink.

A lightning bolt flashes overhead. I glance up. For a split second a shadow cuts across the bleached sky—a Phantom owl? It's impossible to tell in the sleeting rain—before we're plunged into darkness again. Another burst of pain blooms in my chest and I gasp, falling back against the wall, and clutch a hand to my rib cage. *What the hell?*

"Edmund! Are you okay?" Catherine asks as fire rips around my heart.

"I . . . I don't know," I say through clenched teeth. "I'm not feeling so great."

A moment later there's a second flash of lightning, and whatever I saw before has gone. It *must've* been a Phantom owl. There are hundreds of them living in the forest. I lower my hand, the fire in my chest extinguishing as quickly as it came. I straighten up, feeling better.

"Maybe you should ask Mr. Kent if you can go home if you're unwell," she suggests.

"No, I'm fine," I say, which is true. I'm not sick; it just feels like a bad cramp or perhaps a serious case of heartburn. "Come on, let's get you home."

We rush through the village, our boots slapping through the rapidly forming puddles. The cobbled streets are empty, apart from the occasional cat slinking between the thatched cottages. We run past Mrs. Hope's house, a ramshackle building with a green door and circular windows, which are always shut no matter what time of year it is. The old lady is on her porch, watering the already sodden flowers, seemingly unaware there's a thunderstorm. She's tiny—barely five feet tall, with a stooped back, coarse gray hair, and a flowing white nightdress that hangs off her bony frame.

"What is that daft old crone doing?" I mutter.

Catherine slaps my arm. "Be nice, Edmund. You know she hasn't been the same since Dr. Hope died last year. Someone should get her inside." She looks pointedly at me.

I sigh and jog over to the porch, while Catherine waits nearby on the street. Mrs. Hope looks bewilderedly at me when I take the watering can from her, placing it on the ground.

"You need to get out of the rain," I say loudly to her.

Mrs. Hope squints at me with milky eyes. "You're Minister Hector's son, aren't you?"

I nod, although Hector's my grandfather, not my dad.

"I didn't see your sister at church today," the old lady continues. "Is Cassie unwell?"

"She's dead," I say sharply. "She's been dead for almost eighteen years, and Cassie was my mother, not my sister."

"Oh . . . yes," Mrs. Hope murmurs as I usher her inside the cottage. "Yes, that's right. She hanged herself, after dropping that poor little baby into a tub of scalding water . . ."

I stop dead. "What was that?"

She brings her fingers to her lips, like she's trying to remember what she was saying.

"Mrs. Hope?"

She gives me a weak smile. "You're Minister Hector's boy, aren't you?"

I roll my eyes, slamming the door behind her. *Crazy old bat.*

Catherine looks curiously at me when I join her. "I thought your mother fell down the stairs and broke her neck."

"She did," I say. Shortly after I was born, my mom accidentally dropped me into a bath of hot water. In her hurry to fetch the doctor, she tripped down the stairs and snapped her neck. At least, that's what my grandfather told me happened. I glance back at Mrs. Hope's house. Her husband used to be the town doctor and would have been the first person on the scene after the incident. Does she know something I don't?

Catherine takes my gloved hand, drawing me out of my thoughts. We quicken our pace through the dark streets, although we're both already soaked to the bone. At the center of the town is Langdon Square, named after Catherine's family, who run the butchery, general store and boutique. We pass the chapel, where I live. During the day, the spire casts a long shadow across Amber Hills, a reminder that wherever we are, we're always under the watchful eye of my grandfather and the Guild. We pause outside Langdon and Son's General Store, where her family is asleep upstairs, both of us breathless from running.

"Well, good night, Edmund," Catherine says, giving me a shy smile.

"Night, Caterpillar." I hold her gaze, wanting to kiss her. *Just do it!* I lean toward her.

Her hazel eyes widen. "Edmu—"

Her words get lost in my kiss. Her soft lips taste of apples and rain.

"What in His Mighty's name are you doing with my sister?"

I jump at the sound of Patrick's voice, breaking the kiss. He glowers at us from the doorway, his arms angrily folded across his broad chest. I'm usually taller than Patrick, but he's standing on the step, so we're eye to glaring eye. He's the complete opposite of Catherine. Where she's dark haired and petite, he's blond, blue eyed and built like a bear. He's the kind of guy who would've made a great Watchman, but Catherine told me he's afraid of heights.

"He wasn't doing anything," Catherine says.

"He was kissing you," Patrick says furiously.

"That was just a good-night kiss, between friends," she says, looking uncertainly at me. "Right, Edmund?"

I wince at the word. *Friends.* But then realize that *of course* she's going to say that in front of her brother; she doesn't want him scaring me away like he did Eric and all the others.

"Right," I say.

Patrick drags her inside and then turns to look at me.

"I have a good mind to report you for leaving your post," Patrick says.

"And get your sister in trouble for being out after curfew?" I say. "I don't think so."

"Stay away from her, freak," he snarls. "Or else."

"Or else, *what?*"

That was a mistake. Patrick shoves me and I hit the ground, getting mud all over my woolen pants. I catch Catherine's eye just as Patrick slams the door. They're filled with pity. I furiously pick up the rifle and clamber to my feet, roughly brushing the mud off my pants, my mind racing with a million ways to get back at Patrick. I trudge through the town to resume my post on the wall, my head bowed against the lashing rain.

Something flashes across the path in front of me.

What was that? My hand twitches over my rifle. If a Howler's gotten inside the compound, I'm in big trouble. Nearby is Mrs. Hope's cottage. Her bedroom window is wide open, the long metal latch clanking against the wall. *Oh no!* I enter the cottage without knocking.

"Mrs. Hope, it's Edmund," I say, my voice cracking a little.

All the lights in the cottage are off, apart from a single candle that illuminates the hallway. Rows of medical books line one side of the wall. A clock ticks at the far end.

There's a creak of floorboards from the room overhead.

I walk up the rickety staircase, gun raised. Every instinct screams at me to run, but a strange tugging sensation compels me forward, like someone is pulling on a gossamer thread woven to my chest, drawing me farther up the stairs.

I lick my dry lips. "Whoever's here, I've got a gun, so you'd best leave now!"

A dull pain begins to ball up inside my rib cage as I softly tread toward the bedroom.

I open the door.

"Mrs. Ho—" My words get lost in my throat. The old lady is in front of the window, floating several feet above the ground, her long white nightdress billowing in the breeze. A pale arm is hooked around her waist—someone is lifting her out of the window! I take a step toward them, and pain explodes in my chest. I fall to my knees, dropping the gun.

"Help me!" Mrs. Hope cries.

I struggle to my feet and stagger over to the old woman just as she's dragged out of the window. She stretches out her hand, our fingertips touch, and then—

She's gone.

2.
NATALIE

"I DON'T SEE ANY OTHER OPTION. I'm going to steal a Transporter and find Ash myself," I say to Elijah, or more accurately, to his backside. He's currently knelt in the dirt in front of me, pulling up carrots from the vegetable patch. His catlike tail sways happily as he works.

We're in the UG—an enormous subterranean greenhouse lit by ultraviolet strip-lights, thus its imaginatively titled name, Ultraviolet Greenhouse, or UG for short. It's unlike any hothouse I've been in before—equal parts farm, fruit orchard and garden, complete with outbuildings and a water tower. We're gathering supplies for lunch. Well, Elijah is. I'm "supervising" from my spot on the rockery beside him. Colorful primroses jut between the stones, sweetening the recycled air with their perfume.

The UG is definitely my favorite place in the Sentry rebel stronghold—a secret military base that runs under the city of Gallium, the capital of the Copper State—but its beauty is lost on me right now. It's been nine days since Rafe Garrick and his Lupine pack brought us to the compound, and my patience is wearing thin. Ash is somewhere out there, and I'm stuck down here just waiting for any news of him. A radio crackles in my pocket as if to remind me of this point. I have it constantly tuned to Firebird, a pirate radio station run by Humans for Unity, listening for any mention of Ash—thankfully we're able to get a signal down here because of the complex's booster system—but so far there's been no word on Phoenix, the name by which he's commonly known these days.

"That's a great idea, pretty girl," Elijah says, tossing a bunch of carrots into the basket by my feet. "Except for the bit about you flying a Transporter, of course."

I frown. He has a point. I have no pilot training.

"Okay, I'll kidnap Garrick and force him to fly it," I say.

Elijah quirks an eyebrow at me.

"All right, bad idea." I pick up a garden knife lying on the dirt and twirl it between my fingers. "Why did my parents leave Ash behind? If they'd just brought him with us, none of this would be an issue."

"You know why," Elijah says patiently. "They thought you'd be better off without him."

I let out an angry sigh, still mad at my parents. I sort of understand their reasoning—they wanted to bring me and my sister, Polly, to the compound so we could be a family again, but there was no place for Ash in their plan. When I pushed them for an explanation, my mother threw up her hands and finally admitted the truth. *That boy is a bad influence, Natalie. A drug dealer and a wanted criminal, and he's caused you nothing but trouble since you've been together. He's torn this family apart! I don't like the hold he has over you,* she'd said. *It's not healthy. My God, you're just seventeen and you're already talking marriage.*

I turned to my father for support, but he just shook his head slightly. *"We only have your best interests at heart, Talie,"* he said.

My grip tightens around the knife in my hand, frustrated with them. It's always been this way with my parents. They controlled my life as a child and they're still doing it now. I stab the blade into a patch of primroses, beheading a few of the flowers. One of the female gardeners—a pretty brunette named Josie, who always has a smudge of dirt on her nose— gives me a frosty look. I blush. Unlike Elijah, I haven't exactly made a good impression around here, after the "incident" in the Mess Hall.

Shortly after I arrived at the compound, I set fire to the canteen when my father refused my umpteenth request to retrieve Ash. It worked. He sent Beta Squad to Viridis, but by the time they arrived, Ash and two of Elijah's half brothers—Acelot and Marcel—had vanished and Purian Rose's troops were swarming all over the place. Beta Squad barely made it back alive. After that disaster, and two more failed missions to look for Ash in Thrace and our rendezvous point in Centrum, my father was ordered not to send out any more rescue teams. *"I'm sorry, but those are the Commander's instructions. It's out of my hands now,"* he said.

Although my father runs the compound, he isn't the man spearheading the Sentry rebellion. That person is some rich benefactor, known only as the Commander, who has been funding this operation for years, and *he's* the one who makes all the decisions around here. I don't know his real name, as it's a closely guarded secret to protect his identity.

I sink my chin into my hands, wondering what to do about Ash, while Elijah continues to work. The gold bands on his wrists glint as he heaves three bags of fertilizer over his muscular shoulders and carries them back to the vegetable patch. He grabs a fork and begins to shovel the fertilizer over the earth. He briefly pauses to mop his brow, smearing dirt over his face in the process. The effect somehow manages to make him look even *more* gorgeous. A group of nearby women cast appreciative glances his way.

I roll my eyes, laughing. "God, they're shameless." Elijah lifts a brow, and I nod toward the ogling women. "They're old enough to be your mother."

A flash of pain crosses his features.

"Oh, Elijah, I'm so sorry," I stammer. "I didn't think . . ."

"It's okay," he says quietly.

His mother, Yolanda, went missing a month ago, along with Ash's aunt, Lucinda Coombs, and their childhood friend Kieran. They were all members of a terrorist group known as the Four Kingdoms, whose goal was to unite the four races by any means necessary. Before they disappeared, the trio were searching for the Ora—a powerful weapon believed to be weaponized yellowpox, which targets only those with the V-gene, namely the Sentry. Ash, Elijah and I had been on a mission to find them and retrieve the Ora, before we got separated in Viridis.

"We'll find her," I say gently. "Garrick's put the word out in Gray Wolf to look for them. Hopefully his men will turn up something soon."

"Yeah, hopefully," Elijah says, unconvinced. "I wish Esme had been able to give us more details before she was killed."

Esme was Kieran's wife, whom we met in Thrace. She'd told us that the trio had contacted her from Gray Wolf, saying they were heading to a nearby mountain called the Claw, to retrieve the Ora. That was the last any of us heard of them. Before we could question Esme further, we were attacked by Sentry guards and Esme was shot. We've tried to figure out which mountain the Claw is, but it's not on any map that we can find. I thought it might be a nickname, like how Crimson Mountain is also known as the Devil's Fork because of its twin peaks, but the closest mountain to Gray Wolf is Mount Alba, but that has a caldron-shaped crator, so that can't be it, as it doesn't match the description of a claw. So we're back at square one.

My antique watch beeps and I sigh, getting up. It's time for my daily appointment with Dr. Craven Eden. Without needing to be asked, Elijah starts packing away our things. He brings the basket of carrots over to Josie.

"Thanks, kitten," she says, smiling flirtatiously.

He flushes, mumbling, "No worries. Always happy to help out."

I smirk at him when he returns. "Kitten?"

He turns a deeper shade of red. This sweet, blushing version of Elijah is so unlike the arrogant, strutting boy from a few weeks ago—that boy's favorite pastime was flirting with girls, and he wouldn't lift a finger to help out—but then again he was impersonating his spoiled half brother Marcel, so I'm only just starting to know the *real* Elijah. I pull the wood-handled knife out of the murdered primroses and tuck it into my pocket, intending to return it to the toolshed.

We stroll through the tranquil garden toward the exit, taking our time. I'm in no hurry to become Dr. Craven's human pincushion. On top of my heart condition—I had a heart transplant when I was eight—I recently contracted the Wrath virus, after an infected Darkling boy bit me. Since my arrival at the rebel base, the Sentry doctors have been trying to cure me, injecting me with experimental vaccines and drugs. Until I came here, I'd made my peace with dying, but now that there's hope I can get better, I'm terrified the treatment won't work.

Elijah thrusts his hands into his pockets as he walks beside me, the sleeves of his jumpsuit rolled up to reveal the leopard-like spots on his arms. The metal bands around his wrists glimmer in the fake sunlight. Looking at them, you'd think they're just pretty pieces of jewelry, but I know what they really are: shackles. They denote his status as a slave to the Bastet Consul, who also happened to be his father. Elijah's relationship with his father is complicated to say the least. Or *was* complicated, I correct. The Bastet Consul was murdered nine days ago, along with Elijah's half brother Donatien.

"How are you coping?" I say gently.

Elijah shrugs, knowing what I'm talking about. "Fine. Terrible. I miss them, despite everything." He lowers his gaze. "I can't help but feel my dad got what he deserved, though." His topaz eyes flick up to meet mine.

I don't say anything, but deep down I agree with him. The Bastet Consul used Elijah to lure me and Ash to Viridis, under the pretense that they wanted to join the rebellion. However, it was just a ruse to get us to Viridis so they could hand us over to Purian Rose's forces. The plan backfired, as the Sentry double-crossed the Bastets, and his father was killed in the ensuing fight. We only just escaped with our lives.

I should be mad at Elijah for his part in the conspiracy—I *was* angry at him for a few days—but he was only following his father's orders. Besides, when Garrick kidnapped me in Viridis, Elijah risked his life by coming after me. Neither of us knew at the time that Garrick was working for my father, so it was a brave thing for him to do. And now he's a "permanent guest" here, forbidden to leave the compound in case he tells someone about the Sentry rebels. Elijah won't be seeing the surface for a while, at least until I'm able to persuade my father to stop being so ridiculous and let him go. I think that's why he volunteered to work in the UG. It's the next best thing to the outside world.

We pass a bush of bright yellow Pollyanna lilies, and I brush my fingers over the flowers. Orange pollen bursts into the air.

"My sister was named after this flower," I say.

A sad smile passes over Elijah's lips. Polly was murdered a month ago by my former bodyguard and boyfriend, Sebastian Eden, on Purian Rose's orders. Elijah was with me when I found her body. Grief tightens around my throat like a vine, threatening to strangle me.

I slip my fingers into my pocket and find the blade concealed there. I'd made a promise to my sister that day. I told her I wouldn't stop fighting until Centrum was nothing but burning rubble around Purian Rose's feet. And when that moment came, I was going to stride up to that son of a bitch and drive a dagger straight through his black heart. We approach the tool-shed and I walk past it, my hand still clutched around the knife.

3.
NATALIE

THE HOSPITAL IS A LEVEL UP from the UG, next to the main entrance, and by the time we reach it, I'm out of breath. I pause outside the glass doors, steeling myself for what's to come—an intravenous drip to help with the anemia, plus a cocktail of antiviral drugs followed by several excruciatingly painful injections. We've been following this procedure every day since I got here, and although I'm grateful for the treatment, I hate every second of it.

I glance up at Elijah. His Adam's apple nervously bobs up and down in his throat as he stares at the doors leading into the hospital. I gently take his hand.

"You don't have to come in with me," I say. "I know you hate these places."

My mother and Dr. Craven held Elijah hostage in their laboratory in Black City and experimented on him. It was his venom they used to create the Golden Haze, which killed several teenagers in Black City and resulted in my mother being sent to prison, so obviously Elijah's not a big fan of hospitals. Or Dr. Craven. Or my mother.

His gaze drops to my hand, which is still holding on to his. "Anything for you."

Guilt coils up inside me, and I move my hand away. Hurt flickers across his face. Elijah confessed he had feelings for me a few weeks ago, when we were traveling to Thrace, and we've both tried to pretend like he never said anything, but it's always lurking in the corners of our friendship. He holds the glass door open for me, and I enter the hospital.

Everything inside the ward is clinical and white, apart from the green door at the end of the room, which leads into Dr. Craven's laboratory. The ward is filled with all sorts of machines that whir and beep, and whose sole purpose, I'm certain, is to give me a migraine. Rows of metal beds line both sides of the room. Standing by one of them are my parents, who are in the middle of an argument.

"I'm not going to discuss this again, Jonathan," Mother says tersely. She's painfully thin, with sharp cheekbones, pale skin, and black hair that is neatly pinned up into a chignon.

"She was my daughter too," Father says in the stiff I'm-trying-not-to-shout voice that he uses when he's *really* mad. "I raised her as if she were my own flesh and blood."

I'm still caught off guard by the sight of my father. Until nine days ago I thought he was dead, so it's taking a little getting used to, having him back in my life, especially since the man standing here now isn't the one I remembered. Father used to be classically handsome, like a movie star from the old films my sister and I used to watch, with a strong chin, mischievous blue eyes and an easy smile. He never smiles now, although it's probably not easy for him to do after the Wrath mauled his face.

I was with him when he was attacked, and his wounds were so severe that it seemed impossible Dr. Craven would be able to save him. So when my mother told me Father died, I'd *believed* her. I didn't even question her when she refused my request to see his body, saying it would be too traumatic, or why she demanded a closed casket at his funeral. I'd just assumed she didn't want people looking at his mutilated face. In reality, my father had been stabilized by Dr. Craven, and then secretly transferred to this facility to be nursed back to health, while we buried an empty coffin.

It hurts that my parents kept this enormous secret from me, but I understand why they did it. My father was considered a traitor of the state, so it was safer for all of us if he just stayed "dead" while my mother continued working for Purian Rose as if her loyalties were still with him. To a point, they were; I know she agrees with his segregation laws. But my mother's first loyalty is to this family, as I came to realize months ago when she confessed she only agreed to Purian Rose's plan to infect Darklings in Black City with the Wrath virus, because he threatened Polly and me. She'd ally with whoever is most convenient to us at the time. Right now, that's the Sentry rebels.

"Siobhan, we can't keep putting this off. She's not coming back," Father says.

To my surprise, Mother lets out a pained sob and crumples against my father.

"I can't do it, Jonathan, I just can't," Mother gasps between sobs.

Father wraps his arms around her. I'm stunned at how broken my mother looks. I've only ever seen her like this once before, on the day she was sent to prison. She hasn't spoken to me about what they did to her there, but I've heard the rumors: torture, sleep deprivation, starvation, drugs—all designed to break a prisoner's spirit.

The door at the end of the ward opens and Dr. Craven enters the room, clipboard in hand. He's a tall, middle-aged man with vivid green eyes, wiry bronze hair, and half-moon spectacles perched on the end of his long nose. He's wearing a pristine white lab coat over his bottle-green jumpsuit. For twelve years, Dr. Craven worked for my mother in Black City, as the head of the Anti-Darkling Science and Technologies Department. He's also been our family's personal physician for almost two decades—he was the one who performed my heart transplant when I was younger.

Dr. Craven engineered the C18 "Wrath" virus, which was designed as a biological weapon against the Darklings, so he's my best hope of getting cured. My father mercifully didn't contract the disease after he was attacked by an infected Darkling, but I wasn't so fortunate. Perhaps it's because I have a Darkling heart inside me? Or my father's just immune? We're still trying to work it out.

"Hello, pumpkin," Dr. Craven says.

My parents pull apart, and Mother quickly dabs her eyes.

"Hey, Dr. Craven," I say, taking a seat on the edge of my bed. "Long time, no see."

He smirks a little. I've spent most of my time at the hospital since I got here.

The pager on my mother's belt beeps and she checks it. She turns to my father. "It's the Commander. He wants me to call him right away." My dad runs the military operations here, but as the highest-ranking government official in the compound, my mother is technically his boss. She looks at me, uncertain.

"That's fine. You should go!" I say, a little too enthusiastically. I love my mother, but we can't spend more than ten minutes together before we end up bickering.

Elijah gives her a cold look as she walks past. When she's gone, Father plucks a book from his pocket: *The Adventures of Captain Redbeard*. My heart sinks. That's definitely more my dad's taste than mine.

"You don't have to stay here; I know you're busy."

"I'm never too busy for my little girl."

I cringe slightly. That's still how he sees me—as his little girl. Father squashes beside me on the narrow bed, stretching his legs out in front of him, while Elijah sits cross-legged on the bed next to us. They take turns reading the dialogue, putting on stupid voices and making me giggle—Elijah's damsel in distress is hilarious. It's a welcome distraction as Dr. Craven inserts the IV line into my hand and starts the treatment.

Thankfully for me, Dr. Craven is a very cautious man and has been working on an antidote to the Wrath virus since he first engineered it several years ago, on the off chance it might jump species. He was right to be concerned—I'm the living (well, possibly dying) proof of that. But the antiviral drugs have never been tested on humans before, as he didn't get a chance to complete his trials before having to go into hiding after the Golden Haze scandal, so we have no idea if this is going to work.

I try to focus on the story as Dr. Craven draws my blood before starting the intravenous drip. He takes the sample to the lab to run some tests to see if the treatment's having any effect. I'm not optimistic; the last eight results have all come back showing there's been no change in my condition.

"What were you and Mother arguing about?" I ask my father.

Father puts his arm around me. "We were discussing Polly's memorial service. I thought it was time we had one, but your mother doesn't agree. She's not ready for it."

I picture how broken my mom looked earlier, and understand what my father means.

"Do you miss her?" I whisper.

Father gives a curt nod, his jaw clenching. He loved Polly deeply, despite the fact that she wasn't his biological daughter. Her real dad was Purian Rose. My mom had an affair with him early on in her marriage to my father and got pregnant with Polly.

"Why did you stay with Mom when you found out Polly wasn't yours?" I say.

Father glances at Elijah. He pretends to read the book, politely ignoring us.

"I didn't," Father says. "When I discovered the truth, I left her."

I sit upright, surprised. "I had no idea." Although Mother deserved it, I can't help but feel sorry for her. "Why did you come back?"

"Your mother was truly sorry for what she did," Father says. "And I had to accept some responsibility for what happened. My work took me away from her for months at a time. It didn't help that we'd been trying for a family, but it just wasn't happening." His thin mouth sets in a grim line. "It caused a lot of strain between us, and I wasn't there for Siobhan when she needed me," he continues. "So she found comfort in another man."

"Purian Rose," I mutter. *Gross.*

"Was it wrong of her? Yes. But is she totally to blame? No," Father continues. "We saw this as our second chance to be a family, Talie. It wasn't easy, but over time I forgave her. And I'm so glad I did, because we had Polly and then two years later we were blessed with you." He kisses my forehead. "I love your mother. I have no regrets."

I peer down at my engagement ring, thinking about Ash. We've overcome plenty of trials, so I can sort of understand how my father managed to forgive her.

"Dad, I was wondering—"

"We're not discussing this again, Talie," he says, cutting me off.

"You didn't even know what I was going to say," I reply.

"You were going to ask me to send out a search party for Ash," he says.

"If you'd just let me speak to the Commander—"

"He's been very explicit with his orders," Father says, using the curt voice he usually saves for his lieutenants. "He feels we've done enough. We can't spare any more resources on this, Natalie. We have our own priorities."

"And he should be one of them." I stand up and yank the IV line out of my hand. "Ash is a vital part in the war against Purian Rose. He's *Phoenix,* for heaven's sake! Doesn't that mean anything to you people?"

Father leaps to his feet. "Where do you think you're going?"

"To Viridis," I say. "Maybe Beta Squad missed something. Someone there might know where Ash and the others went." I turn to Elijah. "Are you coming?"

He nods, getting up.

"Sit down!" Father commands.

Elijah immediately sits.

"You don't have to listen to him," I say to Elijah, then to my father: "You have no right to keep him prisoner here. We're going."

"And how precisely are you getting to Viridis, hmm?" Father says.

"Stow away on a train, steal a truck, whatever it takes," I

say. It's a risky journey through enemy territory, which is why I've been reluctant to try it, given my already ill health, but my father's left me with no other option.

He blocks our path. "You're not leaving this compound."

"You can't order me about. I'm not one of your lieutenants," I say.

"No, I'm your father," he snaps. "I understand you think you love that boy—"

"I don't just love him, I'm *connected* to him." I press a hand to my chest. "When you took me away, you wounded Ash in a way you will *never* understand. He's hurting, Dad. I can feel it."

"Natalie . . . ," Father says, his voice softening.

"Ash deserves better than this," I continue. "He sacrificed himself for me. He took the blame for a murder that *I* did, and he was literally crucified for it! And this is how you repay him?" My blood boils, furious with my father and the Commander. I'm tired of trying to persuade them to find Ash; it's obviously not going to happen and every day he's out there, he's in danger. If I want this done, I have to do it myself. "I'm going to find him, and nothing you can say will stop me."

I push past my father, and Elijah follows.

"What about your treatment?" Father says.

I hesitate. I haven't thought this through. How long can I survive without my injections? Will it be enough time to find Ash and bring him back here before I get too sick? I'm not so sure.

"Don't do this, Natalie, please," Father pleads. "Your mother and I have been through enough. We can't lose you, and from everything you've told me about Ash, he wouldn't want you to die for him either."

I stop. That did it.

Elijah looks at me. "We're not going, are we?" he says quietly.

I shake my head and return to my bed, defeated.

Just then, Dr. Craven returns from his laboratory, his eyebrows drawn together as he studies the results of my latest blood test on his clipboard. My stomach lurches, sensing something is up. Elijah's fingers slip through mine. His hand is slightly calloused and warm. Comforting.

"So, what's the news, Doc?" I try to sound casual, my fingers tightening around Elijah's.

"Well, I'm sorry to say you're still infected with the Wrath," Craven says, and my stomach twists. "So we'll have to continue with the course of injections—"

"Am I going to die?" I blurt out.

My father and Elijah look at Dr. Craven expectantly. We all hold our breath. It's so silent, I can hear my blood swooshing in my ears. He takes off his glasses.

"No, pumpkin," Dr. Craven says. "Although you're not cured, it looks like the virus *is* going into remission. The treatment's working." He smiles at me. "You're going to live."

4.

NATALIE

MY FATHER AND CRAVEN discuss my results—apparently if we continue with the injections for the next few months, there's a good possibility the virus could go into complete remission—but I'm finding it hard to concentrate. A sound between a laugh and a sob escapes my lips. *I'm going to live.*

Elijah engulfs me in his arms. "I knew you'd be okay, pretty girl." I lean against him, grateful for the support, although a small part of me wishes that it were Ash's shoulder I was resting my head on now. "We should celebrate."

I glance hopefully at my father. "Can we go to the surface?"

He gives me stern look. "No, of course not. We've just been over this."

"Alpha Squad can escort us, so you don't need to worry about us running off," I continue. "We're just asking to go to the surface for a few hours, Dad. It's not an unreasonable request. We've been cooped up here for more than a week; it can't be good for my health."

"A little bit of sunlight might do her some good, Jonathan," Dr. Craven agrees.

I flash a grateful smile at him and he winks at me.

"What if you get spotted?" Father says.

"We'll wear disguises."

He sighs, his resistance melting. "Alpha Squad should be in command central."

Yes!

As its name suggests, command central is in the heart of the compound, at the junction between the hospital, admin offices and Mess Hall. Every minute or so a subway train swooshes past us as we wander down Main Street. The soldiers use the trains to navigate the city-sized military complex, but after what happened the last time Elijah and I were on a train—we were attacked by a gang of Wraths—we opt to walk. The amount of time and money that went into building the compound still astonishes me. I'm even more surprised that Purian Rose knows nothing about it, but it turns out there are more traitors in his administration than he realizes.

The secret compound was built during the first war as a refuge for a bunch of paranoid government officials, who planned to hide here if the Darklings won the war. The Darklings lost, but those same government officials, headed by Emissary Vincent—the former leader of the Copper State, before she was assassinated a few weeks ago—continued to use the base to build an army against Rose, with the support of the Commander. They believed Rose was leading the country into social and economic ruin because of his obsession with the Darklings. It was time for a change. Those officials are here in the base, although I barely ever see them. They prefer to keep their luxury quarters away from the "riffraff."

Soldiers in rust-colored jumpsuits immediately stop what

they're doing and salute my father as he walks past. Even though he's dressed the same as them, he exudes authority. He nods at a few of the soldiers, even attempts the occasional smile with his scarred lips, but there's a cool air around him. The soldiers keep a respectful distance.

Dr. Craven chuckles as Elijah grabs my hand and twirls me all the way down Main Street, both of us laughing. We earn a few odd looks from the passing soldiers, but I don't care. It's nice to have a bit of good news after so much heartache recently. We've all lost people close to us, including Dr. Craven, whose son Sebastian is missing along with Ash and Elijah's half brothers. It's hard to care about Sebastian when he raped and murdered my sister, but he's still Dr. Craven's son; I understand why the doctor is worried about him. Still, the doctor's not going to get any sympathy from anyone around here. If Sebastian turned up right now, he'd be executed on the spot, and Dr. Craven knows it. It might be best for him to stay lost.

There's a lot of hubbub as we enter command central—a circular room filled with military-grade com-desks and glass walls covered in digital screens, which stream live updates of the Sentry rebels' military operations. The soldiers manning the com-desks salute my father as we stroll through the room. On one screen I notice Zeta Squad entering a munitions factory, and on another, Omicron have just destroyed a bridge. They plant a cerulean blue and black flag at the scene—the very flag that Ash designed for Humans for Unity. I furrow my brow. Elijah looks quizzically at me.

"What are they doing?" he says.

I turn to my father. "Are you pinning these attacks on Humans for Unity?"

He nods. "Why draw attention to ourselves if we don't need

to? Humans for Unity are the perfect cover." He smiles, pleased with himself. "I was worried they'd get in our way, but they've proved most useful, keeping Rose distracted while we undertake our own missions."

"We've been doing more than keeping Rose 'distracted,'" I say through gritted teeth. Even though I'm technically a Sentry, I see myself as a member of Humans for Unity first and foremost. "We liberated Thrace two weeks ago."

"And you did a fine job, Natalie," Father says, patting my shoulder. "But we need to focus our efforts on *strategic* targets. Things that might actually help us win this war."

My lips pinch together, annoyed by his patronizing tone. Did he really just say that? Father strolls over to the com-desk while I turn back to the digital screens, needing a moment to calm down before I say something I regret. One of the monitors is broadcasting the latest news from SBN, the government-owned network. A glamorous blond reporter with sea-green eyes, February Fields, is reading the news.

"And today's main story: Darkling Ambassador Sigur Marwick has been found guilty on charges of terrorism, for his role in the Black City bombings in which twenty Sentry guards lost their lives and hundreds of others were injured."

The shot cuts to Sigur as he's being led out of court. He looks malnourished and gaunt, with dark shadows under his eyes. One eye is milky white after he was blinded in it, the other a sparkling orange. He's wearing a gray prison jumpsuit, which hangs off his slim frame, and his rippling ice-white hair twists and swirls around his angular face, sensing the air around him for blood. I knew Sigur would be found guilty, but even so, the news rattles me.

February Fields returns to the screen. "The ambassador's

execution has been scheduled for two days' time. In other news, preparations have begun in every city across the USS for the nationwide Cleansing ceremony next week, the largest of its kind ever to be broadcast live on television. Sentry officials are expecting upward of eighty million Pilgrims to attend the public ceremonies, where Puri—"

"Turn that crap off, will you?" Garrick says from the com-desk in the center of the room. The Lupine is enormous—over seven feet tall—every inch of that packed with thick muscle. He has a mottled gray mane that has been styled into a shark's fin down the center of his head.

Next to him is another Lupine, Sasha, who has a dyed pink mane that matches her neon lipstick. She's got a chunky metal belt around the waist of her jumpsuit, which has been unbuttoned to reveal the top of her cleavage. The Lupines make up two-thirds of Alpha Squad. The final member is Destiny Vincent, a stunning black woman in her early twenties with long cornrows that have been tied back into a neat bun.

Nearly all the men in the base have a crush on Destiny because of her model-good looks—she used to regularly grace the covers of *Sentry Youth Monthly* when she was my age—but underneath that pretty exterior is a woman not to be messed with. She knocked Private Jones out last week during a card game when he accused her of cheating. She was, but that wasn't the point.

She catches my eye and winks. Destiny and I hit it off immediately, as we have a lot in common. We're both from high-profile Sentry families—her aunt was Emissary Vincent—and we mingled in the same social circles growing up, so we have plenty to gossip about.

At the head of the com-desk is my mother. She's deep in

concentration as she gazes at the screen, which casts a bluish glow over her pale skin. Projected onto the screen is a map of Centrum. Five glowing orange dots move about the map. A male voice crackles over the com-desk's speakers.

"This is Omega. We're in position," he says.

Mother lifts her eyes as we approach the com-desk. They widen as she notices the grins on all our faces. She looks hopefully at Dr. Craven.

"The treatment's working," he says.

Mother grips the com-desk, like she might fall over, and lets out a shuddering breath. She doesn't make any move to hug me, but she's not one for public displays of affection. "That's wonderful, absolutely wonderful."

"Natalie and Elijah would like to go to the surface," Father says. "I told them it was okay. Alpha Squad can escort them."

Garrick and Sasha shoot annoyed looks at each other, while Destiny beams. Obviously I'm not the only one who is desperate to get out of here. I grin at Mother.

She sighs, nodding. "All right. Just be back in time for lunch."

Destiny, Garrick and Sasha each collect a gun from the weapons locker and join us by the doorway. Elijah turns to Garrick.

"Has there been any update on my mom?" Elijah asks.

Garrick shakes his head. "Sorry it's taking so long, but Gray Wolf is swarming with Sentry guards right now, as it's the closest city to the Tenth, so my guys are having to keep a low profile." He clamps a hand on Elijah's shoulder. "We'll find them."

Elijah frowns, unconvinced.

The investigation into Yolanda, Lucinda and Kieran's whereabouts would move faster if the Commander would offer some assistance, but he ordered my father not to waste any resources looking for them or the Ora, neither of which he considers of "stategic importance" to the Sentry rebels. Luckily for us, Garrick's pack is based near Gray Wolf, so as a personal favor to us, he asked them to investigate.

Just as we're leaving, Father grips Garrick's arm, holding him back. As I walk off, I hear my father say, "If that Bastet tries to escape, shoot him." A shiver trickles down my spine at my father's chilling words and I hurry after Elijah.

An hour later we're chugging down the river in the *Fogger*— a covered steamboat, with paint peeling off its metal bodywork and a rusting chimney that spews clouds of soot into the resin-brown skies. The *Fogger*'s ugly, but we blend in perfectly with all the other boats on the busy waterway. I gaze down at the river, which is a vivid orange color—a by-product of decades of pollution being dumped into the water by the munitions factories.

The river cuts through the heart of Gallium and is the best way to get around the crowded city. We sail past towering skyscrapers. Their façades are covered in sheets of tarnished metal, creating a patchwork of dirty bronze, verdigris green and gunmetal gray, reminding me of a famous cubist painting that I once saw at Emissary Bradshaw's home in Centrum. The cool spring air whips through the *Fogger*'s windows, and I hug my jacket closer around myself as I sit down on the long wooden seat.

Like many people in Gallium, I'm wearing a respirator mask, which covers my nose and mouth, obscuring the lower part of my face. As well as being a handy disguise, it's also protecting my lungs from the noxious fumes belching out of the munitions factories all around the city. The fumes won't kill you, but I'd still rather not breathe them in, as the air *stinks*. The mask is rather claustrophobic, though, and I adjust the strap, loosening it a little. In addition to the mask, I'm dressed in black leather slacks, with a tight gray vest and hooded tailcoat, which is hiding the gun holstered around my shoulder. Destiny and Elijah are similarly dressed, although his jacket is longer than ours, to conceal his tail.

Garrick and Sasha are in the cockpit, steering the vessel. They're both wearing disguises like ours, even though they're not in much danger. The Lupines are considered allies of Purian Rose, so they aren't on his list of Impurities to be sent to the Tenth—a detention camp the size of a small state—unlike the Darklings, Bastets, Dacians or "race traitors" like me; it's not uncommon to see them walking around the streets. Garrick and Sasha are risking a lot by helping out the Sentry rebels. It's reassuring to know that not all the Lupines are blindly obedient to Purian Rose; some of them disagree with his One Faith, One Race, One Nation policy and want him out of power. It gives me hope.

I cross my legs, and something jabs into my thigh. It's the gardening knife I stole from the UG this morning. I take it out, turning it over in my hands. The whole thing is about five inches long, with a sturdy wooden handle covered in yellow paint. I scratch a word into the paintwork with my thumbnail. When I'm finished, Destiny walks over to me, a little unsteady on her feet as the *Fogger* rocks slightly. She peers down at my handiwork.

"'Polly?'" she says, reading the word I've scrawled into the handle. "Interesting name. My weapon's called Mr. Shooty," she says, patting her holster.

I chuckle, tucking the blade back into my pocket. I pull out the list of supplies that Dr. Craven asked us to get, since we were heading into the city. My parents were initially against us going to the shop, but I reminded them we'd be in disguise. Besides, I've been running a rebellion for the past few months. I can handle a shopping list.

"Where can we go to get all these supplies?" I ask.

"Babbage and Son's in Flux Plaza," Destiny says. "Scott's a friend of mine."

"I'll go tell Garrick," Elijah says.

I watch him as he strolls over to the cockpit, a crease between his brow, deep in thought. I wonder if he's thinking about his mom.

"I hope Garrick's men find Yolanda and the others," I say.

"What good will it do?" Destiny says. "I doubt the Commander will agree to a rescue mission, hon. There's nothing in it for him."

"But they could lead us to the Ora," I say. "We really ought to be looking for it. We can't guarantee the Sentry rebels' weapons will be enough; shouldn't we have a backup?" The Sentry rebels have an impressive arsenal, but it's still no match for Purian Rose's forces.

"Look, you don't need to convince me," Destiny says. "My aunt always told me, 'Have a plan B, Destiny. You never know when you might need it.' But try to see it from the Commander's point of view. If anything happened and the virus got released into the compound, a bunch of people could die. Not me, thankfully. I don't have the V-gene," she adds, laughing a little. "But a good fifteen percent of our soldiers do. So I get why he's being cautious. I think he's *wrong*—we should have every advantage possible—but I get it."

I sigh, knowing it's pointless to discuss it any further. Destiny can't change the Commander's mind any more than I can. The boat goes around a bend in the river, and Destiny peers out the window.

"Man, this city sucks," she says. "I never thought I'd see this stinking place again."

"Why did you come back?" I ask.

"My aunt begged me," she replies. "Things were getting pretty crazy in Centrum. I got mixed up with a bad crowd a few months back, so my aunt persuaded me to come home and join Alpha Squad."

"What sort of bad crowd?" I ask, curious to know more about her life in the capital, where she was working as a model. Polly wanted to do that as a career too. She and Destiny would have gotten on like a house on fire.

"I'd rather not think about it, hon. It's all in the past." Destiny gazes out the window again. "I miss Centrum."

"Speaking of which, what's Omega Squad doing there?" I ask, recalling everyone huddled around the com-desk in command central.

"You know I can't tell you that," she says.

"But—"

She silences me with a firm look. I let it slide, knowing when to push her and when not to.

The *Fogger* slows down as we approach Flux Plaza, the main city square where their Darkling ghetto is located. Or *was* located. The notorious brass gates leading into the ghetto dangle off their hinges, and the place is now empty, all the Darklings having been taken to the Tenth in accordance to Rose's Law. Purian Rose's forces have been sweeping across the country, systematically clearing out the ghettos, city by city. Gallium was targeted a few weeks ago while Ash, Elijah and I were on the run.

Garrick docks the boat beside the jetty next to Flux Plaza and we all climb out, making sure our hoods are up. The city square is jammed with Workboots setting up a wooden stage in the center of the plaza. I vaguely recall February Fields's news report earlier, about a nationwide Cleansing ceremony taking place next week. It's going to be a huge televised event, with millions of people attending ceremonies across the country. I'm guessing the stage is for that.

I watch a group of Pilgrims filtering into the church on the west side of Flux Plaza. They all have shaved heads and a rose tattoo above their left ears—the mark of a follower of the Purity faith, the religion that Purian Rose created years ago. Membership has exploded in the past few weeks, as people clamor to prove their devotion to Purian Rose for fear of being sent to the Tenth. Nothing encourages faith like fear, it seems.

"Babbage and Son's is over there." Destiny points to a shabby store next to the church.

The five of us head through the bustling town square toward the store. I tug my hood lower over my face as a group of Pilgrims walk past, handing out flyers to passersby about next week's ceremony. One of the women thrusts a flyer in my hand and I quickly take it, stuffing it into my pocket as we approach the shop. A tarnished copper sign hangs over the doorway, reading BABBAGE AND SON'S APOTHECARY. A silvery bell rings as we step inside.

The shop is cramped and gloomy with an unpleasant sulfur smell in the air. Glass-fronted cabinets filled with colorful jars of potions and medicines line the side walls, and a large mirror hangs on the back wall behind the counter, giving the impression that the shop is bigger than it is. We head toward the counter. Garrick and Sasha have to bow their heads so they don't bump them on the low metal beams overhead.

Standing behind the counter is a man in his midtwenties with unruly auburn hair and sleepy brown eyes. A brass watch dangles out of the breast pocket of his red waistcoat. I'm guessing this is "and Son's" from Babbage and Son's.

"Hey, Scott," Destiny says, taking off her mask.

A wide grin spreads across his slim face. "Well, aren't you a sight for sore eyes!" He steps down from the platform and gives Destiny a quick hug. "I heard you'd gone on a spiritual retreat or something."

Destiny gives a tight smile. "No. I was just living it up in Centrum."

"I'm sorry about your aunt," he says. "Things have gone to hell around here since she died. At least she could keep those fragging guards under control. Now they keep coming into my store, demanding free this, free that, like they own the joint." Scott turns in my direction and I lower my head slightly, even though I'm wearing a hood and mask, so there's little chance he'll recognize me. "So what are you guys here for?"

"We just need a few supplies," Destiny replies. "Can you put it on my tab?"

He arches a brow. "It's a tab only if you intend to pay the bill someday, Des."

She grins. "True, but isn't it so much nicer for us to both pretend I'm going to do that?"

He chuckles. I raise a quizzical brow at Destiny.

"Scott's father used to work for my aunt," she explains. "During the last war, he let her enemies use the shop to host their cloak-and-dagger meetings so she could spy on them."

Scott walks over to the large mirror hanging behind the counter and hooks his hand around the frame. There's a click as a secret latch unlocks and the mirror swings forward to reveal a hidden room, big enough to comfortably fit one person, two at a push.

"It's a spy room," he explains. "The glass is half silvered, so you can watch what's going on in the shop, but they can't see you."

"Neat," Elijah says, unhooking his mask so it hangs loose around his face. I shoot an angry look at him—we're supposed to be in disguise—and he grimaces apologetically. "Couldn't breathe." Scott's eyes widen sightly as he notices the cheetah-like markings down the side of Elijah's cheeks, realizing he's a Bastet. He casts a curious look at Destiny, but says nothing as he quietly sets about getting our supplies. Destiny trusts Scott, so I probably can too, but even so, I keep my mask on. He places a jar of flaxseeds on the counter and unscrews the lid. The second he opens it, Elijah starts violently sneezing. Garrick and Sasha bark with amusement.

"Id's nod funny," Elijah says between sneezes. "I'm allergic do flaxseed."

Scott puts the lid back on before Elijah has a fit, and starts weighing up the other ingredients. There's a portable digital screen on his countertop, streaming the latest news from SBN. The sound is off, but it's obvious from the pictures that the report is about the bridge that Omicron Squad bombed this morning. Ash's image suddenly appears on the monitor, and I quickly reach across the counter and turn up the volume.

". . . These latest attacks are being attributed to the terrorist organization Humans for Unity, led by wanted criminal Phoenix, whose whereabouts are unknown," February Fields reports over the image of Ash. I stare at the picture. It's been doctored to make Ash look more threatening—they've deepened the hollows in his cheeks, narrowed his black eyes into cruel slits and lengthened his fangs. That's not who he is. That's not my Ash. I reach out a hand to touch the screen, aching to be close to him, then snatch it back when I remember Scott is watching. But it's too late.

He looks from me to Elijah, then to Destiny. "Are you guys with the *rebellion*?"

"We're not here to answer questions," Garrick growls, flashing his canines.

Scott holds his hands up. "Hey now, there's no need for that. I'm on your side." He points toward the Pilgrims outside his store. "Those freaks are scaring off my customers. It's bad for busin—" He frowns. "Great, the Tin Men are coming. I hate these guys more than those weirdos outside."

Tin Men? I turn. Marching across the square is a group of men dressed in metal-gray uniforms. They look like Trackers—the elite police force that specializes in hunting Darklings—but their uniforms are the wrong color. They head straight for the shop.

"Get into the spy room," Destiny says, shoving me and Elijah into the crammed space.

Elijah grunts with pain as my elbow jabs into his stomach. I barely have time to turn around before Destiny slams the door, locking us in. The room is immediately plunged into darkness. It's hotter than hell in here, making it hard to breathe, and I yank off my mask and take a few deep gulps of the musty air.

Elijah fidgets behind me, his hand accidentally running up my back as he tries to get comfortable.

A bell tinkles.

Through the double-sided mirror, I watch five men enter the store. They all have shaved heads and are wearing dark gray garrison caps. The floorboards creak as they walk across the room in perfect unison. They ignore Garrick and Sasha, who are pretending to study the jars on the shelves. Destiny is by the counter with Scott. She stiffens when the squad leader approaches them. He's a middle-aged man with pale skin and penetrating eyes that match the color of his uniform. Pinned to his chest is a silver butterfly medal. Who *are* these people?

"Good morning, gentlemen. What can I do for you?" Scott asks.

"We need a quart of Night Whisper," the man says in a flat voice.

"Gee, sorry, fellas, I don't have any in stock," Scott says. "I'll have to order that from Centrum." He reaches for his notepad and pen, and accidentally knocks over the jar of flaxseeds in the process. The heavy glass jar smashes as it hits the floor, scattering the golden seeds everywhere. Some of them skid under the thin gap at the bottom of the mirror-door, stopping by my feet. *Uh-oh.* Elijah clamps a hand over his nose and mouth, muffling the sneeze. The man's eyes narrow and panic claws up my throat. Did the man hear it?

"I'm such a klutz." Scott chuckles nervously. "How much did you need again? A quart?"

The squad leader ignores Scott and walks around the counter. He stops in front of the mirror. Our faces are just centimeters apart, separated only by the thin sheet of double-sided glass. I don't dare breathe, terrified the smallest thing will give us away. Behind him, Destiny's hand inches toward her gun holster. Light glints in the man's strangely pale eyes. They have an almost metallic quality to them. He shakes his head. "You're imagining things," he mutters to himself, then turns away and addresses Scott. "Make it two. We need it by the weekend."

He joins the four other men and they leave. The instant they're gone, Destiny opens the mirror-door and Elijah and I spill out, both gasping for breath.

Scott stares at me. "It's *you*."

I realize I'm not wearing my mask and scramble to put it back on, but the damage is already done. Garrick and Sasha quickly form a protective barrier in front of me. A low, throaty growl escapes Sasha's neon-pink lips, and Scott wisely backs away.

"You can't tell anyone what you saw," Destiny says to him.

"My lips are sealed." He pretends to zip his mouth closed.

"Who were those guys?" Elijah asks, gesturing toward the shop door.

"Rose's new security force," Scott says. "They've been kicking about the city for the past few weeks, scaring folk into giving them names of anyone suspected of anti-government sentiments." He passes Destiny the supplies we came for. "Use the cellar door. It's safer."

My mind is still on these "Tin Men" as we climb out the cellar door, which leads into a dark alleyway beside the church. A bell lets out a melancholy *dong, dong, dong* from the church's belfry, telling the Pilgrims the morning service is about to start. What does Purian Rose need with a new security squad? It can only mean trouble. Destiny, Garrick and Sasha enter the alley first; Elijah and I follow.

The alleyway is filled with trash cans overflowing with several weeks' worth of garbage, and I cautiously step over the piles of junk. It's nearly all glass bottles. Some of them still have a milky-gray residue in them. They must be some of Scott's potions. I accidentally kick one of the bottles and it rolls across the cobblestones, hitting a pile of rags. The material stirs and a man's craggy face appears between the folds. A gasp escapes my lips. His sallow skin is drenched in sweat and covered in seeping ulcers, which have devoured his face so that part of his nose and eyelids are missing. Even through my respirator mask I can smell the sticky scent of decay reeking off him. He grabs my ankle and I cry out in fright.

"Help me . . . ," he rasps, blood spraying out of his chapped lips.

"Let her go!" Elijah roughly kicks the man's hand away.

We hurry to meet the others, my heart racing. *What was wrong with him?* I haven't seen wounds that bad since the Wrath, but he didn't have any of the telltale signs like yellow eyes and hair loss. So what is it?

"You okay, hon?" Destiny asks as we reach them.

"No," I admit. "That man needs our help."

"Scott can deal with him," Destiny says, taking a firm hold of my arm.

She drags me down the passageway, ignoring my protests to go back. Just before we slip into the crowds, I look over my shoulder. Through the shadows, the homeless man's rotting face peers back at me.

5.

ASH

I STARE AT THE BURNT-OUT RUINS of Black City Zoo, expecting to feel sadness, grief, *something* at the sight. This is where the Darkling assembly used to be. It's where Natalie and I, and so many others, took refuge when Purian Rose attacked the city a month ago. It was our home. But looking at it now, I feel surprisingly empty. Maybe it's because I helped orchestrate the attack on Black City that caused this to happen. Or maybe it's because my real home is where Natalie is and that's not here. I don't know where home is anymore.

I turn my back on the zoo. I knew it would be destroyed, but I had to see it for myself. In the three days since we've been in Black City, I've visited almost every place that was significant to me and Natalie, as if it would somehow bring me closer to her: the bridge where we first met (destroyed); Black City School where my heart activated (rubble); the house where she lived with Day's family (razed to the ground). I've yet to pluck up the nerve to visit my childhood home, the Ivy Church. Maybe some places are best avoided.

The air is crisp as I stroll through the sprawling Darkling

ghetto. Although it's early spring, you wouldn't think it, looking at the cinder skies. My feet stir the ash that has settled on
everything, from the winding cobblestone path to the thousands of cheap metal shacks that once housed my people.

Up ahead, the Boundary Wall splits the horizon. The concrete structure is easily thirty feet high and stretches around
the entire ghetto, dividing Black City in two—the humans on
one side, the Darklings on the other. I frown. Despite a decade
of war, an air raid *and* an inferno, the Boundary Wall is still
standing.

There are hundreds of walls like this one in the United Sentry States, the biggest of them all surrounding the Tenth. I run
my fingers over the rough concrete. Before I met Natalie, I used
to spend hours walking the length of this wall, wondering what
life was like on the Darkling side. Now I know. Famine, disease,
death. What I saw here changed everything; I could no longer
ignore the suffering of my people.

I press my palm against the cold stone.

This wall's not indestructible. It's not an immovable force.

It's just concrete.

And I'm going to bring it down. I'm going to bring them all
down, and free my people.

I drop my hand and head out the nearby gates, which
lead into the town square. The plaza's almost unrecognizable
under the blanket of gray, and it takes a moment for me to get
my bearings. The smoldering pile of rubble at the north side
of the plaza was once Black City School. A few meters to the
east is where Sebastian and I started the fight that ignited a
riot and led to my arrest. My eyes drift to a pile of ashes where
three crosses once stood. That was where Purian Rose tried to
execute me. I briefly shut my eyes, remembering the fire that

ripped over my body, the choking heat that stole the breath out of my lips—

CLANG! My eyes snap open at the sound of metal hitting the ground, followed by a stream of angry curses. Parked in the center of the plaza is a Transporter Mini MV5—a compact version of the tilt-wing aircraft that the Sentry use to transport soldiers and prisoners, more commonly known as a Miniport. The MV5 is the deluxe model, with glossy white paintwork and heated leather seats, and is primarily used by rich Sentry businessmen and politicians to do short hops between cities, although this particular Miniport belonged to the former Bastet Consul and his wife. A deep gash runs down the left side of the aircraft, and the metalwork is badly dented where his brother Marcel crashed it a few months ago while out on a joyride. Jutting out from underneath the aircraft is a pair of leather boots and a long spotted tail.

"Everything okay, Ace?" I ask.

A tall Bastet boy slides out from under the Miniport, his face and green shirt covered in oil. In his hand is a metal disc. He leaps to his feet and grins triumphantly at me, the smile crinkling the corners of his catlike eyes. "I've fixed Alice's oil leak," he says, lovingly patting the Miniport.

We didn't have time to properly mend the aircraft before the Sentry showed up in Viridis, and we had to flee. It was my suggestion to hide in Black City until we could fix the aircraft and gather some supplies, because we wouldn't expect them to look for us here. It's still our intention to get the Ora and then save Natalie and Elijah when we've found out where they're being held captive. My best guess is Centrum, but if Garrick's brought her to Purian Rose, why hasn't her capture been announced all over the news?

"Erm, isn't that supposed to be attached to something?" I say, pointing to the metal disc in Acelot's hand.

He grins sheepishly at me. "Yeaaaah, sorry, I might've accidentally knocked it off. But don't worry; it's not vital," he adds in a rush when he sees the alarm on my face. "I think it belongs to the heat exchanger that controls the seat warmers." He turns it over in his hands and his smile fades. "Unless it's from the engine cooling system. Then we might have a problem."

"What sort of problem?" I ask warily.

"There could be a *tiny* explosion when we start the engine."

"How small?" I say.

"I'm almost certain it's for the seat warmers," he says, dodging the question.

Acelot tucks the disc into his pocket and pulls out a monogrammed handkerchief. He attempts to wipe the oil off his face but doesn't have much luck. There's definitely a family resemblance between Acelot and his half brother Elijah—they both have the same honey-colored eyes and cheetahlike spots on their tanned skin—although Acelot is slimmer, with short brown hair and a long, boyish face that makes him look younger than his nineteen years. Only his eyes look old, ringed with dark circles. With the death of his parents, the welfare of his brothers Marcel and Elijah and that of the entire Bastet people now rests in his hands. It's a heavy burden for anyone to shoulder, let alone a teenager. I know how he feels.

With a defeated sigh, Acelot tucks the handkerchief back into his pocket and nimbly climbs into the pilot's seat. I sit beside him. The windscreen and control panels are badly cracked, and the navigation system keeps going down. Still, it can fly.

"Here goes nothing," Acelot says, punching the START ENGINE button.

I grip on to the control panel and say a silent prayer as the engines roar to life, sending clouds of ash swirling around the aircraft, but mercifully no fiery ball of death. I let out a relieved sigh as the aircraft jerks up and the world (and my stomach) drops rapidly below us.

Acelot smirks slightly. "I told you it was nothing to worry about, my friend!"

"I never doubted you for a second," I say, prying my fingers off the dashboard.

Black City whooshes below us as Acelot confidently weaves the aircraft between the smoldering buildings. Everything is in ruins. The Park is a pile of debris; Chantilly Lane Market is little more than a hole in the ground; the digital screens that once sat upon the rooftops now lie broken on the cobbled streets. We don't need to go near the Chimney to know it's been destroyed, since the Cinderstone plants continue to spew plumes of choking smoke into the sky. A few other civilian aircraft streak across the sky—looters, probably—but otherwise the city is eerily silent.

"I've fixed Alice as best I can," Acelot says. "She should hold together long enough to get to the Tenth and back."

My stomach twists at the thought. I pull out an old photo from my back pocket. It's a picture of my mom when she was younger. We look alike—the same black hair, thin face, and dark eyes. She's standing in a forest glen with Lucinda and my grandparents Paolo and Maria Coombs. Behind them is another Darkling—a stern-looking man with a birthmark on his cheek. I have no idea who he is. In the background of the photo is Mount Alba, the way it looked *before* it erupted, with a claw-shaped peak.

From this photo and an old map I saw back at the Bastet

embassy in Viridis, I figured out that the Claw was Mount Alba. That's where the Ora is and where my aunt, Kieran and Yolanda went to retrieve it. The only trouble is, Mount Alba is right in the heart of the Tenth. I don't relish the idea of walking into the detention camp, but I have a mission to complete. There's no point in putting this off any longer.

"Let's head out today," I say. "What's the time?"

Acelot checks his expensive gold watch. "Just after two."

"Okay, we should get to the station soon," I say, referring to Black City News, on the outskirts of the city. We did a quick sweep of the city outskirts earlier and thankfully the station is still there, having been spared the worst of the fires that swept through the districts because of its remote location. "I want to send out my message before we go."

Acelot turns down Bleak Street and lands the aircraft in an alleyway beside the Sentry headquarters, so it's out of sight from anyone wandering by on the street. Although it was my idea to hide out in Black City, it was actually Sebastian's suggestion we actually set up base in the former Sentry headquarters. I was reluctant at first, given that I distrust everything that comes out of that jerk's mouth, especially since he's our hostage, but it turned out to be a good choice. Not that I'd admit this to him.

The usually white marble building is covered in soot and part of the roof has caved in, but otherwise it's come out relatively unscathed. Which is why I'm surprised when I see dark smoke billowing out of one of the windows on the first floor.

We enter the building via the kitchen and run through the corridors toward the dining room, where the smoke's coming from. I push open the door. Marcel is standing by the window trying to fan the smoke out of the room while Sebastian watches with amusement. He's sitting next to the mahogany table, bound to one of the chairs with rope. The table is covered in piles of guns, tinned food and medical supplies salvaged from the arsenal and laboratory downstairs. On the antique rug next to the table is a smashed oil lantern. A large hole has been scorched into the fabric.

Acelot strolls over to the rug and nudges it with his foot. "I'm pretty certain this didn't have so many holes in it when we left."

Marcel dramatically rolls his eyes. At fifteen, the Bastet boy is only two years younger than me, but he acts like he's twelve sometimes. He's immaculately dressed in a crimson frock coat, black pants and knee-high patent leather boots, like he's attending a state dinner. The fact that we're on the run from the Sentry, and are keeping one of their head Trackers as hostage, doesn't seem to have registered with him at all.

"It wasn't my fault," Marcel says huffily. "I was getting supplies, and when I got back, the rug was on fire. I don't know how it happened."

I can guess. I glare at Sebastian, who smirks back at me. Blond stubble covers his normally clean-shaven head and face, partially obscuring the rose tattoo above his left ear. It was a rash decision to bring him with us, but at least this way I know where he is at all times. I snatch a look at the broken lantern on the rug. He must've knocked it off the table somehow. I presume he hoped it would cause a big enough fire to force Marcel to untie him, so they could evacuate the building.

"Could I talk to you outside, Marc?" Acelot says, nodding toward the hallway.

Marcel sighs and follows Acelot out of the room while I

check Sebastian's binds. Acelot's voice drifts through the open doorway.

"You weren't supposed to leave Sebastian unattended," he says. "What would've happened if he'd gotten loose? He could have killed you."

"I was just trying to help!" Marcel replies. "God, I can't win with you. *Do this, Marc.' 'Don't do that.'* You're worse than Dad."

"Hey! I'm doing my best," Acelot says. "Maybe if you did what I said for once, I wouldn't have to keep nagging you."

"I don't have to do *anything* you say," Marcel replies. "I'm not a sniveling kiss-ass like Elijah."

"Don't you dare talk about him like that," Acelot growls.

"Why do you always take his side?" Marcel says.

Back in our room, Sebastian laughs.

"Such *drama,*" he sneers. I yank the ropes around his wrists, and his green eyes flash with anger. "Watch it, nipper."

"Do you want me to gag you too?" I snap.

He glances down at the binds around his wrists and smiles coldy. "You know, Natalie used to like it when I tied her up like this. She'd make these tiny little moans when I—"

I punch Sebastian in the face. His head snaps back, and blood spurts out of his split lip. He shakes his head, bringing himself back to his senses, then laughs.

"Touched a nerve?" he says, licking the blood off his lip.

I turn away, annoyed at myself for letting him get under my skin. I know Natalie never slept with Sebastian, which is why the jerk cheated on her, but they *did* date each other for a year. The thought makes my skin crawl.

Marcel storms into the room and slumps down on one of the

chairs next to the table. Acelot follows a moment later. His eyes flick toward Sebastian, whose bruised lip has started to swell, and he raises an amused brow.

"Now, now, Ash," Acelot mocks. "What did we say about beating up our prisoner?"

"That it's a good thing, and I should do it constantly?" I reply.

Sebastian scowls. Acelot chuckles and takes a seat beside Marcel.

"Sorry about the rug," Marcel mutters.

Acelot ruffles his brother's hair and Marcel playfully swats his hand away, friends again. The brothers help me make an inventory of the supplies. There's enough to keep us going until we get to the Tenth. Down on the floor is my blue duffel bag. I go through the contents, making sure Marcel hasn't taken anything—he's always nosing around my stuff.

Inside are some rather ripe-smelling clothes, a black headscarf, my mom's diary, a keepsake box, and a few things I managed to salvage from Natalie's and Elijah's bags, which were left behind in Viridis, including Natalie's heart medication and a sheet of paper, which she's neatly folded into a square. I open it, curious to know what it is; we've been so busy, I haven't had a chance to look at it yet.

I'm surprised to discover it's a lab report about something called Project Chrysalis, with all sorts of figures and equations on it that are way beyond my comprehension; science is more Natalie's thing. Stamped at the top of the document are the words BARREN LANDS LABORATORY, and beneath that is a logo of a silver-winged butterfly. I'm not sure what this report is about, but Natalie obviously thought it was important enough to take with her.

I turn to Acelot. "Can you make any sense of this?"

He takes the document, scanning it. Eventually he shakes his head. "Sorry."

I tuck the document in my back pocket. "No, what's far-fetched is you wanting to help me." I turn to Marcel, who is plucking a loose thread off his crimson frock coat, clearly bored. "Help me load these supplies onto the Miniport—then we can get out of here."

He reluctantly picks up a single can of beans. Acelot catches my attention and I roll my eyes. I gather an armful of supplies and Marcel follows me out of the room, holding his can of beans. We head down a corridor lined with portraits of Purian Rose, walking side by side. The boy barely reaches my chest, but I know not to underestimate him; Bastets are much stronger than Darklings.

"You know you're going to get my brother killed, right?" Marcel says when we're out of earshot. "I know you hate me for what happened in Viridis, and I'm sorry, okay, I'm sorry that they took your girlfriend, but Ace is all I have left, so if he dies . . ." Marcel blinks and his golden-brown eyes glisten. "Please don't get him killed."

"I won't," I say, but the promise falls flat. I can't guarantee Acelot's safety.

"Sure," Marcel mutters.

We continue our walk to the aircraft in silence. It takes a good half hour to put all the food and weapons into the aircraft, thanks to Marcel's "help." He's trying his best, but manual labor clearly isn't something he's had much experience with.

We load the last of the goods into the aircraft, kicking them under the leather seats. Marcel slumps down in the pilot's seat, his spotted tail swishing against the metal floor.

"Do you think Elijah and Natalie are dead?" Marcel says. "Sebastian reckons they are."

My fangs flood with venom. "No, I don't."

God, just when I'm starting to warm up to that kid, he says something like that. The hairs on the back of my neck suddenly prickle as a faint, musky smell drifts into the Miniport, stinging my nostrils. I sniff the air again. Marcel scrunches up his nose—he's smelled it too.

"Is that you?" he says, and I growl at him. "What? All you Darks stink to me."

I look outside the open hatch. The street is silent, and yet something doesn't feel right. I can't shake the feeling that something's watching us.

"Let's head back," I murmur.

Marcel lets out a long sigh, like it's the biggest chore in the world, and follows me outside. The instant we leave the aircraft, I know we've made a terrible mistake. A low, throaty growl comes from the roof of the airship. I slowly turn, my pulse racing, to look into the cold, steel eyes of a male Lupine, his silvery hair rippling in the cool breeze.

Behind us, there's a teeth-tingling sound of claws against brick. I risk a glance over my shoulder to see a female Lupine slowly closing in on us. She's dressed all in red. Around her throat is a choker made of Darkling fangs. Bounty hunters used to wear those during the first war. I swallow. The Sentry must've left the Lupines here to keep guard of the city—or what remains of it—and pick up any stragglers.

"I told you someone was staying at the Emissary's old

place, Dolph," she says to the male Lupine. Then to me: "I saw the smoke coming from the window earlier. You ought to be more careful, sweetness. There are dangerous people out here." She gives me a deadly smile.

"Run," I whisper to Marcel, who is frozen beside me. "RUN!"

My raised voice is enough to break Marcel out of his trance, and he bolts for the kitchen door leading into Sentry headquarters just as the male Lupine leaps at me. I manage to dart out of the way of his snapping jaws, but his razor-sharp nails catch my shirt, slashing the material and my flesh underneath. I grunt as a searing pain rushes down my arm, but I don't have time to think about it as the Lupine turns and lunges for me again. This time he catches me, knocking me off my feet. I hit the ground, hard. Nearby, the female Lupine howls, and I get a sinking feeling she's calling out to the rest of their pack, scattered about the city. I struggle against the male Lupine, using all my strength as I try to keep him at arm's length. His canines drip with saliva, and his hot breath stinks of rotting meat.

"Don't bite his face, Dolph," the female says. "We want him recognizable when we claim our reward."

Dolph sneers at me, his face so close, I can see my reflection in his silvery eyes. There's no light behind them, only death and darkness. In the distance I hear the howls of other Lupines as they approach Bleak Street. I should be panicked, but instead a peaceful sensation washes over me. So this is it? After weeks of running, this is how it's going to end?

There's a sudden *pop-pop,* a whimper, followed by the sound of something heavy hitting the ground. The noise distracts Dolph long enough for me to throw a punch, almost breaking my hand as it collides with his square jaw. He falls back, yelping with surprise.

Standing by the kitchen doorway is Acelot, a rifle in his hand. My eyes drift toward the female Lupine splayed on the street, a gruesome hole in her forehead. Her lifeless eyes stare at me, still wide with shock. Dolph lets out a pained howl and rushes over to the dead woman, pulling her into his arms. I'm immediately forgotten in his grief. Acelot aims his gun at Dolph and shoots him twice in the chest. The man slumps over his girlfriend.

"Thanks," I say to Acelot. That's the second time he's saved my skin—the first time was in Viridis when he shot the Sentry guards chasing after me, and now this. The howls of the other Lupines get closer; they'll be here soon. "Start up the Miniport. I'll get the others."

I collect Marcel and Sebastian, keeping the Tracker's hands tied behind his back, then sprint back to the aircraft. Acelot closes the hatch just as the Lupine pack appears on Bleak Street. There are at least ten of them, all baying for blood as they spot us. The engines rumble, and the creatures bound toward us. Several of the Lupines leap up at the aircraft just as we take off, grabbing on to anything they can, trying to drag us back down. The Miniport wobbles, but Acelot guns the throttle and we speed off, the Lupines falling to the ground, *thud thud thud*. One stubborn male Lupine clings on to the roof, his legs dangling in front of the windscreen. Acelot tilts the aircraft, left, right, shaking off the creature.

"I've heard of it raining cats and dogs, but this is ridiculous," he mutters.

I spin around on Sebastian the instant we're clear from Bleak Street and punch him for the second time today, not caring that my knuckles are bleeding from hitting Dolph. It's his fault we were nearly dog food, after that stunt he pulled with the fire. Sebastian falls to the floor, and blood seeps out of a gash on his head—a result of my punch—merging with the red rose tattoo above his left ear. I flex my aching hand and join Acelot in the cockpit.

"Head to Black City News," I say, taking the seat next to him.

Acelot veers the aircraft to the left, flying us to the edge of the city. The broadcast station is a relatively modern-looking building by Black City standards, with BLACK CITY NEWS written in red letters over the entranceway. Acelot parks the ship in the forecourt. It's not ideal being out in the open like this, but I'm hoping we'll be gone before the Lupines catch up with us. We quickly scan the area for any sign of traps or cameras before heading inside the news station. I keep Sebastian a short distance in front of me, so he can't run off.

The studio is deserted, the offices strewn with abandoned paperwork. We hurry through the maze of corridors until we find a voice-over studio. I flick on the light, filling the room with a dull orange glow. I tie Sebastian to a chair while Acelot checks the equipment. Marcel slumps on the battered sofa in the corner of the room and watches us.

"I've programmed the system to broadcast the message for twenty-four hours, then stop," Acelot says. "By the time they trace it, we'll be long gone."

"Okay, let's record it, then get the hell out of here," I say, sitting down at the microphone.

A red light glows, letting me know I'm on air. I just hope Beetle and Roach are listening.

6.

EDMUND

Amber Hills, Mountain Wolf State
30 years ago

I FIDGET ON the hard pew, trying to get some blood circulating back in my bony legs, but it's a lost cause. The church is heaving with people, as the whole town has turned up for Mrs. Hope's funeral. Many have to stand outside and watch the service through the open doors. I'm surprised so many people showed up, but nothing draws a crowd like murder.

Patrick Langdon, and his friends Harriet and Drew O'Malley, discovered her corpse a mile into the woods, lain against a flat rock, like she was sleeping. Her shrouded body now floats in the pool beside the pulpit. Sprigs of lavender bob on the surface of the water to mask the scent of death, but it's not helping. All around me, people delicately cover their noses and mouths with handkerchiefs as they listen to my grandfather's sermon.

He's a grave-looking man dressed in ceremonial robes that match the color of his thick hair and iron-gray eyes. Everybody says my eyes are just like his. It's the only thing we have in common, other than the matching burns on our arms. Grandfather was the one who plucked me out of the scalding water when I was a baby and saved my life.

He's standing at the pulpit—an overly ornate structure made from oak and rosewood, depicting a scene from the ancient scriptures. Carved at the base of the pulpit are a nest of Darklings, their limbs twisted around each other so it's impossible to tell where one Darkling ends and another begins—it's just a contorted mass of naked bodies, their clawed hands outstretched as they attempt to pull innocent girls into their pit of sin.

"It has been a trying time for our community these past six weeks," Grandfather says, his deep voice traveling across the chapel. "Not since the Misery, eighteen years ago, have we experienced such violence and unrest. We have lost family, friends but not our faith."

"So sayeth us all," the congregation murmurs.

The Lupines have claimed four victims now. A kid called Tommy Stevens was the first to be taken, snatched out of his hospital bed in the middle of the night. A week later, they took a crippled woman, Mrs. Summer, then a fortnight after that, the Watchman and town drunk, Mr. Smyth. Mrs. Hope makes number four. What I don't understand is why they're doing it. The Lupines kill only humans who trespass on their territory, so what's changed?

I peer across the aisle at Catherine. She's sitting in the front row with the rest of the Langdon clan, a small frown on her lips. It's no mistake they're at the head of the congregation. The first four rows on the right-hand side of the aisle are reserved for the Guild—the wealthiest or most influential families in the town. Behind the Langdons are the O'Malleys, then the Kents, and finally the Cranfield family. It's the Guild's responsibility to uphold the word of His Mighty and protect our souls from impurity.

Catherine's wearing an expensive blue crinoline dress from her parents' clothing store, and her wavy brown hair has been gently teased up into a chignon, which her mother keeps fussing over. Catherine irritably swats her mother's hand away as Mrs. Langdon attempts to fix another loose curl. I get the sense that Catherine's recent metamorphosis from plain little Caterpillar into this beautiful butterfly was entirely her mother's doing.

Patrick's sitting beside her, his legs hidden by the voluminous layers of Catherine's bell skirt, which is threatening to consume her whole family within its taffeta petticoats. He scowls, shifting position on the pew, clearly uncomfortable, which pleases me. Next to him is his father, Mr. Langdon, who is watching the service with rapt attention. He's a handsome man with sandy-blond hair like Patrick's, brown eyes and a neatly groomed beard.

Catherine senses me looking at her, and turns her head slightly in my direction, offering a sad smile. She gives me a look that says *How are you?* We've known each other for so long, we can communicate in silent shorthand. I frown and shake my head a little. *Not so good.* I can't get the image of Mrs. Hope being dragged out of the window from my mind. She lightly touches her heart and raises a worried brow, referring to the chest cramps I had that night on the wall. I shrug a little. I have no idea what caused them, but they haven't returned. Patrick coughs lightly, and Catherine turns her attention back to the service. He stares daggers at me, and I look away.

"However, we are not without blame for their deaths,"

Grandfather continues. "After almost two decades of peace, we let our guard down, and now we are paying the price."

I gaze at Mrs. Hope's shrouded body floating in the pool. If only I'd gotten there sooner, I might've been able to save her.

"This being said, we must not look upon Mrs. Hope's death as a tragedy, for she was suffering, and now walks in His Majesty's eternal kingdom," Grandfather continues, stepping down from the pulpit to the altar where a goblet and two bowls—one white, one red—awaits. "The Lupines may devour our bodies, but they cannot corrupt our souls, for we are pure of heart and spirit. It is this purity that protects us from the corruptions of evil. So I invite you all to come forward and drink from the sacred cup and be cleansed of your impurities."

The congregation silently files out of their seats and forms an orderly queue down the aisle. I duck into the line behind Catherine. In front of her are Patrick and his friends Drew and Harriet O'Malley. The siblings look very alike, which is unfortunate for Harriet. Although their long slim nose and tapered chin looks noble on Drew, it gives Harriet a shrewlike quality. Harriet turns to look at me. Unlike the other women in the town, she's wearing pants and a boy's shirt and waistcoat. A knife is strapped to her belt.

"Way to go, *freak*," she says to me in a loud whisper. "It takes a special kind of stupid to leave your post on the wall. Are you crazy or something?"

"Like mother, like son," Patrick drawls.

"What's that supposed to mean?" I say, my temper flaring. Patrick's top lip curls up into an amused snarl.

"It's nothing, Edmund," Catherine says, shooting a warning look at her brother. "Just some nonsense Mother was telling us."

"Which was?"

She bites her bottom lip. "That your mother used to hear voices in her head."

"That's not true," I reply immediately, although I don't know anything about my mother. Grandfather never speaks of her, or my dad, but that's only to be expected.

As far as everyone knows, my father was a businessman from Gray Wolf, who wooed my naive teenage mother when she ran away, got her pregnant and then abandoned her to marry another girl. None of it was true, though, apart from the bit where my mom ran away to Gray Wolf, but she was already six weeks pregnant by that point. It was quite the scandal at the time. The townsfolk forgave us only after my mom tragically died and Grandfather was stuck having to raise a deformed, illegitimate grandchild.

"I know my mother's lying," Catherine says, gently placing a lace-gloved hand on my arm. "She still holds a grudge against your mother because she used to date my father when they were teenagers. It's silly. Only my mother can be jealous of a dead girl."

I look at Catherine's mother, who is in the line ahead of us, gazing adoringly at her husband. I had no idea Mr. Langdon used to date my mother. There's so much about her that I don't know. I think back to what Mrs. Hope said last night—that my mom hanged herself—tied with the new rumor that she heard voices in her head, and a terrible, sick feeling starts churning in my stomach. What if these stories are true and my mother really was mad? These thoughts continue to trouble me as the line shuffles forward and Mrs. Langdon steps up to the altar. She dunks the goblet into the white bowl.

"May His Mighty wash away my sins," Mrs. Langdon says, taking the drink. The look of bliss that enters her face is almost instantaneous. She smiles dreamily up at Grandfather as he dips his thumb into the red bowl, which is filled with spring water, and rubs it along her forehead—the "mark of purity" to ward off evil.

"You are cleansed, my daughter," Grandfather says.

Mrs. Langdon moves aside, her movements slightly sluggish, allowing the next person in the line to step up to receive the cup.

"I feel so bad about Mrs. Hope I can't sleep," Catherine says quietly to me as the line moves past the pool. "It's my fault she's dead; if you hadn't left your post to walk me home, maybe the Lupine wouldn't have gotten over the wall."

"It wasn't your fault, okay?" I reply. "There were three other Watchmen on duty that night. We all missed it."

"It's odd how they found her, don't you think?" she says. "Patrick said she'd been bound to the rock, like they wanted the body to be discovered."

That *was* weird. In fact, everything about these attacks feels off.

Grandfather catches my eye, his mouth tightening into a disapproving line. He doesn't like me talking to Catherine. He thinks the Langdons care too much for money, and in his eyes, money is sin, which is why I'm always dressed in these itching, woolen clothes; they're the cheapest suits you can buy from the store. Personally, I think His Mighty blesses those he loves the most with wealth. Otherwise why else would the Langdons get so much—beauty, wealth and popularity—and I have so little? We're the only family belonging to the Guild with barely a coin to our name, but as a preacher, Grandfather was automatically given a seat on the council when he first moved to Amber Hills as a young man. Power and influence is just as important to the

Guild as wealth, and in a religious community like Amber Hills, a preacher has a lot of both.

"I love this part of the ceremony, don't you?" Catherine whispers as the queue shuffles forward. "My spirits always feel lifted afterward. They really need that right now."

I don't say anything. Drew is the next person to take the goblet. He knocks back the drink, then moves aside, allowing Harriet and Patrick to step up to the altar and drink from the cup. I can't believe I have to go to the dance with those jerks . . . that is, if Catherine still wants to go with me. The memory of my brief kiss with Catherine lingers on my lips. I'm disappointed she hasn't brought it up, but we've all had a lot on our mind's with Mrs. Hope's murder.

"Are we still on for the dance tonight?" I ask.

She flashes me a disapproving look. "This isn't the place to be discussing the dance."

"Sorry." I wait a few seconds, then add: "But are we?"

"Yes, of course we are," she says in a harassed whisper as she moves up to the altar.

She accepts the goblet from my grandfather and drinks. I silently watch as she shuts her eyes as he gives her the mark of purity. A joyous smile spreads across her lips.

"You are cleansed, my daughter," Grandfather says.

Her eyelids flicker open and she stares up at my grandfather with unbridled adoration. Everybody looks up to my grandfather, both figuratively and literally—he's easily the tallest man in town. *If only they knew the truth.* Catherine joins the others. Now it's my turn. I take the cup from my grandfather, a knowing look passing between us. Guilt crawls up my throat as I drink the bitter liquid.

"May His Mighty wash away my sins," I say.

Grandfather dips his hand into the red bowl and rubs his thumb over my forehead.

"You are cleansed, my son," he says.

I join the others beside the pool for the final offering to end the funeral. Usually we toss Carrow wreaths into the water, so I'm curious when Patrick heads into the back room with Drew. The congregation starts to murmur. Grandfather looks perplexed.

Mr. Langdon raises his hands and we quiet down. "The Guild has decided to forgo the usual offering, in place of something more . . . *befitting*."

This sparks more excited whispers among the congregation.

"I wasn't informed of this," Grandfather says, drawing his gray brows together.

"Weren't you?" Mr. Langdon says innocently.

Grandfather glances at one of the other Guild members, Mr. Cranfield—a gaunt man with bronze-colored hair like his son, Eric, and dressed in an expensive black suit. The man looks away sheepishly. This can't be good.

Just then, the doors to the back room burst open and Patrick and Drew emerge, carrying a kicking, screaming girl. Even though her head is covered in a burlap sack, it's clear from her size what she is—a Howler. The congregation lets out startled gasps, and several of the women grab their children and rush to the back of the chapel, away from the creature.

"What is this?" Grandfather demands.

Mr. Langdon doesn't respond as he yanks off the Howler girl's hood. My breath gets trapped in my throat as I stare at her. I've never seen a Howler in the flesh before, and she's nothing like the monsters described by the Guild. The girl is dangerously beautiful, with eyes like mercury and a mane of snowy white hair. Her wrists have been bound with rope.

"Patrick found this beast in the woods, beside Mrs. Hope's body," Mr. Langdon says.

There are gasps and jeers from the crowd. We all know how Mrs. Hope was found—tied to a rock—but no one mentioned they'd found a Lupine at the scene!

"Let go of me!" the Howler screams. "Icarus is to blame, not me!"

Grandfather bristles, like he recognizes the name.

"Put her in the pool," Mr. Langdon says calmly. "A life for a life."

"No!" the girl cries out as Patrick and Drew drag the girl toward the water.

"This has gone on long enough!" Grandfather says. "This is a house of worship; I won't allow this." He tries to step in between Patrick and the pool, but Mr. Cranfield and Mr. Kent pull him back, their faces turning red under the strain of holding him.

Mr. Langdon raises his hand in prayer. "And His Mighty spoke to the Pilgrims and said, *'Will thou cast out all the Impurity in the world, for only the Pure shall enter my Kingdom?'* and the Pilgrims cried, *'We will!'*"

"Cast it out! Cast it out!" the congregation chants as Patrick tears off the girl's clothes and drags her into the pool beside Mrs. Hope's body. The congregation pushes toward the water's edge, nearly knocking me and Catherine into the water too. I grab her before she falls in. She buries her face against my chest as the Lupine girl is dunked under the water. Her mouth opens in a silent scream as she thrashes against Patrick, Harriet and Drew, trying desperately to resurface. Tendrils of white hair ripple around her naked body, and for a brief moment she's like a beautiful sea nymph, her luminous eyes gleaming up at us through the water.

"Cast it out!" the congregation chants.

"Stop this!" Grandfather yells.

The Howler frantically flays about under the water. My chest tightens and I can't breathe, like I'm the one drowning. Her silver eyes widen and with a terrified gasp she sucks in a fatal breath. It's over. They pull her out of the pool and dump her body by my feet. Splashes of water drip on my boot. Grandfather stares grimly down at her body.

"Let this be a warning to the Lupines," Mr. Langdon says. "For every life they take, we will take one of theirs."

"So sayeth His Mighty," everyone chants.

Catherine throws a guilty look in my direction. I glance down at the Howler girl, shame squirming in my stomach.

"So sayeth us all," I say.

7.

EDMUND

PATRICK AND DREW PICK UP the girl's limp body and carry her outside while the rest of the congregation files out of the chapel. Mrs. Langdon looks adoringly up at her husband as they walk down the aisle. Tears glisten in Catherine's eyes as she obediently follows them.

Outside, the October air is crisp and fresh, the ground still damp from last night's downpour. Women lift their bustle skirts to prevent their hems from getting muddy as they gossip to their friends about tonight's dance and what they plan to wear, the conversation polite and forced. In the center of the town square is a large wooden cross, more than eight feet high.

During the Misery—a yearlong conflict between the Darklings, Lupines and people of Amber Hills that resulted in hundreds of deaths—any citizens caught associating with a Darkling would be tied to the cross, on the Guild's orders. They'd be left up there for days. Many would die from exposure or starvation. It hasn't been used in almost two decades, until today that is. Patrick binds the dead girl to it as a warning to any more of her kind if they come back here searching for another victim.

Mr. Langdon strolls over to Grandfather, his wife still hanging off his arm. He can't be much older than thirty-six, but his sandy beard makes him look older. All the kids in Amber Hills have young parents, as it's common to marry at eighteen and have your first child at nineteen. I look longingly at Catherine, who is outside her house with some kids from school.

Eric Cranfield—the boy Catherine was hoping would take her to the dance—strolls over to her. He's lanky in a way that's stylish rather than awkward, with a sprinkling of freckles over his nose and auburn hair. He dips his head and whispers something in her ear before placing a consoling arm around her shoulders. Jealousy flares inside me.

"Fine service today, Hector," Mr. Langdon says, drawing my attention.

"Thank you," Grandfather replies coolly. "The ending was certainly eye opening."

Mr. Langdon gives a forced smile. "It's important to show our strength in these terrible times. We can't let the Howlers think they can take our people without consequence."

Grandfather scowls. "Is it really worth starting a conflict between our species over four people?"

"If you ask me, the Howler got what was coming to it," Mrs. Langdon chimes in, ignoring the fact that no one asked for her opinion. She looks just like her daughter, with the same brunette hair, pale skin and heart-shaped face. "If I had my way, we'd put them all down. We have to protect the children, Hector."

Grandfather slides a look at Mr. Langdon. "I always do."

A muscle flexes in Mr. Langdon's jaw.

"Will you be attending the dance tonight?" Mrs. Langdon asks me, her eyes constantly drifting toward the Howler girl. I suspect she wants the girl's long, snowy white hair—Lupine fur is worth a lot of money.

"Yes. I'm taking Catherine, actually," I say.

Grandfather arches a thick brow at me.

"Oh, that's . . . wonderful," Mrs. Langdon replies, clearly disappointed. "You'll have to come by the shop later, so we can fit you for a new suit."

I glance down at my brown woolen pants and jacket. I'd intended to wear these.

"I can't . . . um . . . A new suit would be very expensive," I mutter.

"Don't worry, Edmund. It's on the house," Mr. Langdon says, brushing some imaginary dirt off his own expensive frock coat, which has faint fleur-de-lis pattern on it.

"Thanks," I say, feeling anything but grateful. I hate charity; it's the same thing as pity.

"Will you please excuse us?" Grandfather says.

I reluctantly follow him inside the church, giving Catherine one last, lingering look. She's too busy talking to Eric to notice me leaving. We head upstairs to our living quarters. There are just four rooms in the apartment: a kitchen, a tiny bathroom, Grandfather's bedroom, and the attic where I sleep. The best word to describe our home is *sparse*. The walls are white, the hardwood floors and furniture all the same shade of brown.

There aren't many objects in the kitchen, which is the main room in the house. On the table is a glass jar filled with dead butterflies, while mounted on the wall is a telephone and an old photograph of my mother. We look a lot alike, with matching gray eyes, dark hair and a wide, thin mouth. Did she really kill herself, like Mrs. Hope said?

Grandfather turns to me. "You're not going to the dance

with that Langdon girl. What were you thinking, Edmund? You know it's forbidden for Darklings and humans to date."

"Only because the Guild says so."

"And for a very good reason. You only have to look at yourself to understand why."

I flinch.

"I'm sorry, Edmund. I didn't mean . . ." Grandfather gazes down at me with kind eyes, which are so much like my own. I praise His Mighty every day that I inherited my mother's eyes and not my father's. "I know you're not like the other Darklings; you're a good boy. But His Mighty never meant for our species to be together. That's why their offspring are—"

"'Cursed with a heart of ice,'" I mutter, reciting from our scriptures. "It's not fair."

"I know, Edmund," Grandfather says. "I pray to His Mighty every night to take pity on you and bless you with a heartbeat. It's all I want for you."

I pull away from him and walk to the window. Most people have gone home by now, but a few mill about the town square, including Catherine and Eric Cranfield. They're with her brother and the O'Malley siblings. Patrick is checking his silver dagger while the brother-and-sister act lounge on the steps outside the Langdons' store. I watch them for a moment, imagining what it would be like to be them. They don't need to make excuses when they get invited over for a meal because the food makes them sick, or hold their breath when someone's bleeding because the scent makes their insides tear apart. They didn't have to have their teeth ripped out of their heads when they were babies to hide the fact that they were born with fangs, or lie to their best friend about what they are because if they ever knew, if they ever *knew*. They don't have to do any of these things because they're alive, and I'm . . . I touch a hand to my chest and feel the silence beneath. *A demon.*

Grandfather says I'm not like the other Darklings, that I'm good. But I'm certain that's only because of him and my faith, which keep me on a true path. If I didn't have those things, I'm quite sure I wouldn't have turned out this way. The predator is always there, lurking within me, wanting, hungry. But it's not the only part of me that has desires; the human side of me thirsts for *other* things. I gaze at Catherine for a long moment, watching as she unpins her hair, letting it fall in loose brown waves around her narrow shoulders. Eric smiles.

"You can never be with her," Grandfather says gently. "It's not just your safety I'm worried about, but hers. You know what sinful desires are within you, Edmund."

I look at the floor, ashamed. My father raped my mother, so I know exactly what I'm capable of. I hate the fact that his blood is in my veins. But I would never hurt Catherine!

Grandfather draws me away from the window. "Are you hungry?"

I nod, sitting down at the kitchen table while Grandfather collects a knife and glass from the cupboard. He nods toward the jar of dead butterflies on the table.

"Will you grind some of those up for me?" he asks.

I take off my gloves and unscrew the lid, pouring a few of the silvery-blue-winged butterflies into a stone mortar. I start grinding them into a fine powder with the pestle. My grand-father has been mixing it into the holy water for years, under the Guild's advisement, to keep the townsfolk placid. It's not easy being enclosed inside a walled compound without going stir-crazy after a while, so it's for their own good. I pour the powder into a small pot.

"That should be plenty," Grandfather says, sitting down at the table. He rolls up the sleeve of his dark tunic, exposing his arm. There are slashes all the way up it; some old, some fresh. He slices his arm with the knife and pours his blood into the glass. The rusty scent stings my nostrils. He fills the glass to the brim before passing it to me. I greedily drink.

"Slow down, Edmund," Grandfather says. "That's all you're getting this week."

I force myself to stop guzzling the blood and try to savor it, but it's hard when I'm this hungry. The heat spreads over my tongue, awakening my taste buds. The blood has a slight bitter undertone to it, which I don't like, but otherwise it's good. I place the empty glass on the table and wipe my lips with the back of my scarred hand. They still look hideous, even after all these years. Darklings are meant to have amazing regenerative abilities, and I do to some degree—these wounds would've killed a human child.

"Why did you save me that night Mom dropped me in the bath?" I ask quietly.

"Because there is goodness in you, Edmund. Part of you is human; that part can be saved." He sighs, getting up, and reaches for the phone. "I should call Mrs. Langdon and tell her you're not taking Catherine to the dance. I'll say you're unwell."

"No, wait," I say in a rush. "It'll look weird if I don't go. Everyone will be there."

His hand hovers over the receiver. If there's one thing he hates more than the Langdon family, it's gossip about ours. "Fine. But you're not to see that girl again after tonight."

I nod, not looking at him, knowing it's a promise I can't keep. I'm sick of watching my life from the sidelines. If things go well with Catherine tonight, then I don't care what the risks are; I'm going to ask her to be my girlfriend. I place a hand over my silent heart. For once in my life, I want to know what it feels like to live.

8.

EDMUND

A SWARM OF BUTTERFLIES fill my stomach as I rap on the door of Langdon's General Store. Behind me, in the town square, the dance is already in full swing, with men and women dressed in their finest clothes. Strung from some of the shops is a hand-painted banner, reading CELEBRATING 18 YEARS OF PEACE. Tied to the cross in the center of the town square is the Lupine girl. Her dead eyes stare blankly at the banner.

To the left, a stage has been set up for the band, and to the right is a long row of tables, where an elaborate buffet has been laid out. My stomach roils. I'm not looking forward to eating it later; human food makes me sick, but occasionally I have to swallow it down, to keep up appearances in front of the Guild.

I quickly check my outfit for the umpteenth time, my nerves mounting, as I wait for Catherine to answer the door. Mrs. Langdon could barely conceal her contempt for me when I went to get my suit earlier. She picked out a burgundy velvet frock coat for me, with a cinnamon-gold waistcoat and cravat, dark brown pants and dress shoes. Clutched in my right hand is a purple wrist corsage.

There's a sound of footsteps in the hallway and the door finally swings open. I smile, holding up the corsage.

"This is for you," I say, expecting to see Catherine.

"You shouldn't have," Patrick replies dryly. He's dressed in an expensive ink-blue tailcoat and matching pants. Tucked into his belt is a silver dagger. A lot of people carry weapons these days, ever since the Lupines started snatching people from the town.

I look past him, into the house. "Is Catherine in?"

"She's already at the dance. With *Eric,*" he says, nodding over my shoulder.

I follow his gaze, and my face drops. Catherine's outside Mr. Elwin's curiosity shop with Harriet, Drew and, much to my confusion, Eric. They're studying the macabre objects in the store window: stuffed Phantom owls frozen in midflight, Bastet skulls with gleaming saber teeth and—most disturbing of all—a table with glass jars filled with Darkling hearts.

Catherine's wearing a silk brocade dress in buttercup yellow, with a voluminous bell-shaped skirt and tight corset top that shows off her curves, much to Eric's obvious delight, given the way he keeps leering down her top when he thinks she's not looking.

"Oh. I thought . . . ," I murmur, not quite understanding what's going on.

Patrick looks at my outfit, then the purple corsage, his blue eyes bright with amusement.

"Fragg, you didn't think you and Cat were going on a *date,* did you?" he says.

"No. I thought we were meeting here first," I lie. This would be more believable if I wasn't carrying this stupid corsage. "This is for your mother, to thank her for the suit."

Patrick gives a deep belly laugh before pushing past me, muttering "pathetic" under his breath. I shove the corsage into my jacket pocket and follow him across the square. Grandfather is by the stage with Mr. and Mrs. Langdon. There's a faintly smug expression on Mrs. Langdon's lips. Catherine smiles when she sees me.

"You're here! I was starting to think you weren't coming," she says giddily. *Has she been drinking?*

"Nice suit," Eric says sincerely, sliding his hand down Catherine's back.

Furious, I grab Catherine's arm and lead her away from the group. Patrick watches us, a smirk on his lips.

"What the hell, Catherine?" I snap. "I thought *I* was your date tonight."

"What . . . ?" A small crease forms between her brows, and then her eyes suddenly widen as she catches on. "Oh, Edmund, no, I'm so sorry." She lightly touches my arm. "I meant we'd come together as *friends*. That's why I invited Drew and Harriet too."

"But we kissed," I say.

Color floods her cheeks, and she lowers her gaze.

I think back to the kiss and realize that at no point did Catherine return it. She also told Patrick it was just a good-night kiss between *friends,* because that's all we are in her mind. She was trying to let me down gently, to spare my feelings. It's my fault I chose to ignore the signs. There's a titter of laughter from Harriet, who's clearly been eavesdropping on our conversation. I don't dare look at Patrick's reaction.

Catherine nervously plays with her yellow lace gloves. "I care for you, Edmund, so much. It's just—" She flicks a look at Eric.

"You like him more," I finish for her, letting go of her arm.

"I'm so sorry," she says, her brown eyes brimming with tears. "Please say you forgive me. I couldn't stand you being mad at me, Edmund."

"Don't worry about it, Caterpillar. My mistake. Can't blame a guy for trying." I chuckle slightly, but the sound cracks. "Friends?"

She gives me a grateful smile. "The *best.*"

Catherine takes my hand as we walk back to the others. I want more than anything to go home, but I don't want to give Patrick the satisfaction of knowing how much Catherine's rejection stings. Harriet laughs as we join the group.

"The moron thought you were on a *date?*" she says.

"It's not funny, Harri," Catherine says.

Eric scratches his freckled neck. "Sorry, Ed, I didn't know you and Cat had plans."

"It's fine," I say flatly, dying inside.

Patrick strolls over to me. He dips his head so that his mouth is just millimeters from my ear. "How could you ever think my sister would want to be with you, *freak*?"

That does it. I spin around and shove him. Patrick staggers back, surprised by my unexpected strength. Fury blazes over his face, contorting his features, and he strikes back, his punch landing squarely on my left cheek, sending two teeth flying out of my mouth. They fall into the dirt by Catherine's feet, like a pair of glistening pearls. She gasps. The teeth are neatly attached by a thin steel wire. Drew and Harriet start laughing.

"Oh my God, the freak wears dentures!" Harriet squeals.

The music stops, and a hush falls over the town square as everyone turns to stare at us.

I drop to my knees and frantically gather my dentures,

wedging them into my mouth without bothering to wipe off the dirt. Grandfather was right, this was too risky! What was I thinking? Patrick narrows his blue eyes at me. Catherine pushes past him and sinks down beside me, not caring that her yellow silk dress is getting covered in mud.

"Are you okay?" she says.

I can't look at her. I can't look at anyone, as fear and humiliation burns through me like the scalding water that destroyed my flesh.

"Lots of people have dentures, Edmund," she says kindly. "It's not an issue."

Eric crouches down beside her. "Yeah, really, it's no big deal. My uncle lost all of his front teeth when he was our age. Admittedly, a horse kicked him in the face . . ."

They haven't put two and two together yet, but I can't quell the panic rising in me. It's only a matter of time before they start wondering why a boy my age needs fake teeth. A shadow passes over us, and I glance up to see my grandfather, along with the Langdons.

"Catherine Elizabeth Langdon, you're ruining your new dress!" Mrs. Langdon says.

Catherine rolls her eyes, getting to her feet. Grandfather helps me up.

"Perhaps you should go home?" he says. His voice is tense. *Afraid.*

Mr. Langdon glares at his son. "Patrick, apologize to Edmund."

Hatred simmers in Patrick's blue eyes. "Sorry you're such a freak."

"Patrick!" Mrs. Langdon exclaims.

My heart suddenly cramps and I gasp, clutching a hand to my chest. "Gah!"

"Edmund, what is it?" Catherine says, placing a hand on my arm.

Instinctively I whip my head around, drawn to the Boundary Wall for some reason. I scan the dark, searching for . . . I have no idea what. Something silver flashes across the rooftops.

"Is everything all right?" Catherine asks.

Another streak of silver leaps between two buildings. I get a good look this time.

"Howler!" I cry out.

The town square erupts into screams and chaos as the Lupine springs off the rooftop into the plaza, his long, smoke-gray jacket flaring behind him. The cool night breeze ruffles his snow-white hair, which has been decorated with feathers and bones. I know who he is, based on Grandfather's past descriptions of him: Alaric Bane, the Lupine pack leader.

Behind him, more Lupines leap off the rooftops and surround the plaza, blocking the escape routes. Others hang back on the wall, their faces obscured by shadows. Families huddle together, terrified, realizing they're trapped. One of the Howlers—a vicious-looking man with a speckled-gray mane and a crescent moon tattoo on his neck—stands nearest to us. Catherine lets out a whimper and clings on to Eric, and Mr. Langdon stands protectively in front of his wife. Out the corner of my eye, I notice Patrick drawing the dagger from his belt. Harriet and Drew do the same.

One of the Howlers—a plain-looking teenage girl with short hair and wind-burned cheeks—slowly approaches the wooden cross. Her furlike hair is white, just like the girl on the cross. Given the way she's looking at the girl, I wonder if they were sisters.

"We don't want a fight," Alaric says to my grandfather,

which I find odd, since Mr. Langdon is the man in charge. "I just want my daughter's body back."

"You're trespassing on Guild territory, Alaric," Grandfather says. "You need to leave."

"Not without my sister," the Lupine girl replies.

"Ulrika, be silent," Alaric snarls.

The girl's jaw immediately snaps shut, but her eyes are like flints.

"You kidnapped four of our people and you never returned their bodies to us," Mr. Langdon says. "Perhaps this will be a warning—"

"I will ask you again, please leave," Grandfather interrupts and Mr. Langdon throws him a cold look, his cheeks flushing.

"Not until we get what we came for." Alaric approaches the wooden cross and uses his razor-sharp nails to sever the binds around his daughter's arms. Her body collapses over his shoulder. Ulrika clenches her jaw, visibly holding back her grief, but her father knocks back his head and lets out a pained howl. The other Lupines join him. *Big mistake.*

The second they're distracted, Eric reaches for something in his belt—a dagger—and thrusts it at the Lupine beside him. The blade sinks into the man's flesh, and he howls in pain. Eric pulls out the blade and attempts to stab the Lupine again. This time he grabs Eric and rips out the boy's throat, spraying hot blood into the air. My senses explode as the predator inside me roars with thirst. The Lupine tosses Eric's dead body to the ground.

It all happens in a flash: Patrick lunges for the Lupine and it swipes out a clawed hand to protect itself, accidentally slashing Catherine's neck and chest in the process. She gasps, staggering back, as blood blooms over her yellow silk dress, while Patrick and the Lupine crash to the ground. They roll across the dirt, wrestling for their lives.

Harriet, Drew and Mr. Langdon draw their daggers and plunge their blades into the Lupine's body, stabbing him over and over until the ground is awash with his blood. Mrs. Langdon faints, her blue satin dress pooling around her like an ocean. The town is soon in pandemonium as people push and scream, desperate to get out of the plaza. In the melee, Catherine slips down a nearby alleyway, clearly keen to get away from the Lupines blocking the path to her house. I chase after her.

The winding passageway is cramped and as black as Cinderstone. I follow the trail of Catherine's blood, my hunger igniting with every footstep. I don't feel like a boy looking for a girl; I feel like a hunter stalking its prey. I shake my head, trying to force out these thoughts.

Somewhere behind me, Alaric howls, calling his pack. I quickly scan the rooftops. The Lupines are retreating to the wall, Alaric leading the way. In his arms is his dead daughter. At the end of the pack is Ulrika. There's a pop of gunfire and a bullet whizzes past her, grazing her right arm. She gasps, losing her footing, and falls, unbeknownst to the other Howlers. They keep going without her, leaving her to the mercy of the townsfolk. I don't have time to worry about her now. I rush over to Catherine, who is lying in a ball on the ground at the far end of the passageway, quiet and still. I kneel down beside her.

"Edmund . . . thank His Mighty . . . you're here," she rasps, causing crimson blood to spurt out of the gruesome slash marks on her neck. My insides clench and I shut my eyes, taking a shaky breath, but it's too late. I've smelled her blood. I can taste her in my mouth. My thirst consumes me, touching every nerve, every fiber of my body, demanding one thing: *drink*.

She lets out a startled gasp as I sink my teeth into the open wound on her neck and begin to feed. Unlike my grandfather's blood, hers is sweet and delicious, and a groan forms in my throat. Her fists pound against my arms, trying to stop me, but her struggling just excites the predator in me even more. In my darkest moments I've fantasized about doing this to her, but the reality is so much better than any dream. I don't have to hide what I am now. I can take her, I can have her in a way no other boy can, and she's powerless to stop me.

This thought alone brings me screeching back to reality. I yank my head back, gasping, my mouth dripping with her blood. I'm not a monster; I'm not like my father! I can be pure, I can be good. *Oh Lord, what have I done?* I hurriedly press my hands against her neck, trying to stem the bleeding. The fear and shock on her face makes me feel sick with guilt.

"By His Mighty's name! What are you doing?"

I spin around. Grandfather stares at me, horror-struck. He pushes me out of the way and quickly checks her pulse.

"We need to take her to the hospital," I say.

"We can't," he says quietly. "They'll execute you, Edmund. And me."

Catherine's eyes widen with terror, understanding what this means. "Please don't kill me," she gurgles, rolling her head toward me. "I won't tell, Edmund, I promise . . ."

"I'm sorry, Catherine," Grandfather says. "But I have to protect my grandson."

With a swift motion he grabs her head and twists it to one side. There's a gruesome *crack* as something inside her breaks. The fear immediately fades from her eyes. I stagger back against the building, my hands clamped over my mouth to muffle my scream.

There's a rustle on the thatched rooftop above me, and I gaze up. Ulrika's silver eyes peer down at me, her body pressed flat against the straw. A trickle of blood courses down her bare arm from the gunshot wound. She looks as startled as I feel. How long has she been there? Grandfather hasn't noticed her yet, as he's too busy staring at his blood-soaked hands.

"I saw Catherine come down this way!" Patrick calls from farther down the alley.

Ulrika doesn't wait around to be caught—she leaps onto her feet and springs across the rooftops toward the Boundary Wall. She scales the wall and drops down the other side.

"You need to go, Edmund. I'll tell them I found her like this," Grandfather says.

I give Catherine's body one last fleeting look before racing down an adjoining alleyway that leads home. The last thing I hear before entering the sanctuary of the church is Patrick's guttural cry.

9.

NATALIE

I START AWAKE, wondering what pulled me out of my sleep. I'd been having a nightmare about the homeless guy with the rotting face. He was dressed in gleaming white Pilgrim robes and was chasing me through the streets of Black City. Then he turned into one of the Tin Men from Scott's shop and I was suddenly trapped behind the mirrored door, unable to breathe, as the walls closed in around me. It was terrifying, but something about it triggered a memory . . . *the Pilgrim robes* . . . Then it hits me. I saw a Pilgrim back in Thrace with shimmery gray eyes just like the Tin Man's! I knew I'd seen it somewhere before. It must be some sort of genetic defect, like people with one blue eye and one brown.

I glance about my stark room, which I share with my parents. Their beds are empty. I check the clock. It's barely seven in the morning. Where are they? Footsteps run past my room and I climb out of bed, curious to know what's going on. I inch the door open. Several soldiers rush down the corridor, heading toward the main concourse.

Across the hallway, the door to Elijah's room opens. He's

wearing a loose white T-shirt and a pair of striped pajama bottoms that are slightly too long for him.

"What's going on?" he says, groggily running a hand through his russet hair.

"I don't know. Let's go find out," I reply.

I dart back into my room to slip on my jumpsuit, and then join Elijah in the hallway. He's changed out of his PJs and put on his jumpsuit as well. We head in the direction of the soldiers and find everyone in the main concourse. The place is buzzing with activity. I spot my parents across the hall, greeting five soldiers by the entrance ramp. It's Omega Squad!

Leading the group is Adam Slater. He looks like he belongs on the beaches of Golden Sands, with dirty-blond hair, tanned skin and aquamarine eyes. Two members of Omega Squad are carrying someone on a stretcher. I stand on my tiptoes, trying to see who it is. A gasp gets lost in my throat. He's bloodied and bruised, but there's no mistaking who it is.

"Sigur!" I cry out.

I push my way through the crowd toward him, Elijah hot on my heels. I reach the Darkling Ambassador just as he's being led into the hospital.

"I'm sorry we left you," I blurt out.

He manages a faint smile, showing a glimpse of fang, before he's taken into the ward, followed by my parents. I try to go after them, but Slater stops me.

"I need to see him," I say.

"Not now," Slater replies.

I'm about to protest when I hear a familiar voice behind me.

"Natalie?"

It can't be! I spin around, my heart hammering, not daring to believe.

Standing on the entrance ramp is a pretty, caramel-skinned girl, with glossy black hair tied into a neat side braid, and chocolate-brown eyes. She's dressed in navy blue pants, a vest and boy's black frock coat. Perched on the tip of her long nose is a pair of spectacles.

"Day!" I squeal.

I rush over and throw my arms around her slim body. She hugs me so tightly, it's hard to breathe, but I don't care. She's here, she's really here, beautiful, stubborn, wonderful Day! We're both crying and laughing as we cling to each other.

"Hey, Buchanan, get your hands off my girlfriend."

I let Day go. Walking toward us from the entranceway is Ash's best friend, Beetle. The scar tissue on his cheek puckers as he grins at me. He's handsome in a goofy sort of way, with pale skin, messy brown dreadlocks and a lanky frame. He's wearing an old, battered military jacket, and his black pants are tucked into a pair of chunky leather work boots. Beside him is the head of Humans for Unity, Roach. She looks a lot like her nephew, Beetle, except with freckled skin and garish blue hair. Elijah quickly greets Beetle, doing that awkward half-hug-pat-on-the-back thing guys do, before he embraces Day.

"Hey, spectacles," Elijah says. "It's great to see you."

Day flushes slightly, and Beetle rolls his eyes.

"I'm right here," he mumbles, and Day pecks Beetle on the cheek.

"How did you guys end up here?" I say as we stroll down the entrance ramp together.

"We'd gone to Centrum to rescue Sigur," Day explains. "But just as we reached his cell, those soldiers turned up, guns blazing, smoke bombs everywhere."

"Thankfully Sigur told them to hold fire; otherwise we'd all be dead," Roach adds.

"We had no idea you were here," Day says, then lets out a squeak of delight and embraces me again. "What *is* this place, Nat?"

"Where's Ash?" Beetle interrupts before I can explain, his expression worried.

"We got separated back in Viridis. But I'm sure he's alive." I gesture toward my heart. "I would've felt it if he'd died." During Ash's failed execution in Black City, I'd felt the echo of his heartbeat fading inside me as his life slipped away, so I would know if he were dead.

"Do you know where he is?" Day says.

I shake my head.

"Let's get some chow," Beetle says. "You can tell us everything over breakfast."

Roach heads to the residential quarters to get showered while we go to the Mess Hall. Along the way, I pop into my room and grab the radio, in order to resume my obsessive checking of the airwaves. Day and I walk behind the boys as we head to the canteen. Beetle gestures wildly as he describes an epic gunfight between him and several Sentry guards, while Elijah politely listens, his hands casually thrust in his pockets as he strolls beside Beetle, his tail swaying idly behind him. An attractive female soldier with auburn hair walks by and smiles at Elijah, but he doesn't seem to notice. Day raises a brow at me, surprised.

"Is Elijah feeling okay?" she whispers. "It's not like him to ignore an attractive girl . . . actually *any* girl."

I laugh.

"What's funny?" she asks.

The old Elijah wouldn't have let a beautiful girl go by without some sort of flirtatious comment, but that was when he was pretending to be someone else.

"What's funny?" she asks.

"We have a *lot* to catch up on," I say, looping my arm through hers.

The Mess Hall is jam-packed and buzzing with news of the Darkling Ambassador's arrival. There's still a strong smell of charred wood and metal in the canteen from my recent arson attempt, but I don't mind it so much—it reminds me of Black City.

Destiny is sitting at one of the tables, chatting to a brown-haired soldier. Her black hair is tied back, showing off the angles of her high cheekbones and almond-shaped eyes. She looks a lot like her aunt, Emissary Vincent. She waves us over and the man leaves. I quickly introduce her to Beetle and Day, explaining how they got here.

"Did you hear about Sigur?" I say.

She nods. "I knew Omega Squad was extracting a prisoner from Centrum, but I had no idea it was the Darkling Ambassador. Your dad kept that strictly on a need-to-know basis."

Day whips around to me. "Wait, what? Your dad's here?"

"Yeah, he's alive," I say. "It's a *long* story."

"What do they want with Sigur?" Beetle asks Destiny.

She shrugs. "I'm guessing this is the Commander's way of currying favor with the Darklings," she says. "We need them on our side once we've defeated Purian Rose, so Humans for Unity and other Darkling sympathizers will support the new Sentry regime. Otherwise we'll struggle to stay in power, given how divided the country is right now."

"Hold up, the new *Sentry* regime?" Beetle says.

"Yeahhh," Destiny says slowly, flicking a confused look at me.

"Nat, what the fragg's going on here?" Beetle says.

"It's—"

"A long story," Day finishes for me, smirking slightly.

Destiny makes her excuses and leaves. The rest of us grab some breakfast while I bring Beetle and Day up to speed on everything. The breakfast spread is a strange mixture of oatmeal, fish, fruit and raw meat. The chef unceremoniously dollops some congealed oatmeal on my plate, clearly still mad at me for setting fire to her Mess Hall. Her mood immediately lightens when she spots Elijah. She serves him a generous portion of kippers. Although Bastets are known for hunting Darklings, their staple diet is fish and berries. The Lupines, on the other hand, tend to eat raw beef and venison, although they'll take the occasional human. Thankfully, that's not on the menu today.

"So, let me get this straight," Day says as we take our trays over to the tables. "The Sentry rebels are planning to overthrow Purian Rose's government and put a new Sentry government into power, led by this mysterious 'Commander'? Then they intend to liberate the Darklings, in order to win the trust of Darkling sympathizers, like us, to prevent any further conflict and give the country a chance to rebuild?"

"Yep," I say. "That sounds about right."

We sit down at one of the metal tables. I place the radio on the table but don't turn it on yet, as there's so much we need to catch up on. Beetle immediately tucks into his breakfast.

"Why have they waited so long to strike?" he mumbles through a mouthful of oatmeal.

"They've been building their army," I say. "Plus, they were waiting for an opportune moment to attack. With Purian Rose distracted by Humans for Unity, he's weak."

"Well, that explains a few things," Day says. "There's been a bunch of attacks recently that we didn't do, and we were wondering who was behind them."

"So what's going to happen to the Darklings in the Sentry's new 'regime'?" Beetle says. "What role will they have in the government? Or the Workboots, for that matter?"

"Um, I don't know," I say, flushing.

"How can you not know?" Beetle says. "You've been here for nine days."

"I've been sort of busy . . . ," I murmur.

"Natalie's sick," Elijah explains.

Day's eyebrows shoot up her face. "What's wrong with you?"

"I have the Wrath. I got it from that Darkling bite a few months ago," I say, then add hurriedly, "But I've been getting treatment. Dr. Craven's been working on a cure and it's looking good. I'm heading to the hospital later today for my next appointment, actually."

Day's bottom lip quivers and Beetle comfortingly takes her hand.

"So what's the story with Ash?" Beetle says, diverting the conversation.

I briefly explain what happened—how Garrick had been sent to Black City by my parents to retrieve me and Polly, but when she was killed and the city came under siege, Garrick had to quickly change his plans. He followed me across the United Sentry States, until eventually he caught up with us in Viridis. Elijah winces as I tell them about the massacre at the Bastet embassy, and how Garrick kidnapped me and left Ash behind.

"I'm sorry about your family," Day says, resting her hand on Elijah's. "Have you had any luck finding your mom and the Ora?"

"No," Elijah says. "But we did get a lead in Thrace. Kieran's wife, Esme, told us they'd gone to the city of Gray Wolf."

"Apparently they were heading to a nearby mountain, called the Claw, to retrieve the weapon," I add. "But we can't work out which mountain it is."

"I'll figure it out—don't worry," Day says happily. "They must have some reference books in this place." There's nothing she likes more than sticking her nose into a book.

"So what's been going on with you guys?" I ask. "Have you heard from the others?"

"Mama, Papa and MJ made it to the Northern Territories," Day says, and I let out a relieved sigh. I lived with Day's family for a few months, so I think of the Rajasinghams as my second family. "But we haven't heard from Harold or Martha yet," she continues, referring to Ash's father and my old Darkling housemaid.

I chew on my thumbnail, worried about them.

"Did you hear about Nick and Juno?" Day says.

"We saw it on the news," I reply, remembering the footage of Nick being killed in an explosion during a riot in Iridium. Nick was Ash's decoy and had been traveling with the rebels, pretending to be Phoenix, while we went to Thrace in search of the Ora. Juno Jones, lead reporter for Black City News, was caught in the same explosion that killed Nick, although it wasn't clear if she'd died. "Did Juno make it?"

"No. Amy and Stuart got captured," Beetle says, referring to Juno's younger sister and her cameraman, who were traveling with her. "Stu was executed, along with a bunch of other

Humans for Unity rebels, but we think Amy was sent to the Tenth."

"Oh no," I whisper. Amy is a good friend of ours.

We slowly shift the conversation to more lighthearted topics, not wanting to dwell on these dark matters, and it's like the old times back in Black City. My heart aches, thinking about Ash. I miss him so much. Instinctively, I pick up the radio and turn it on. Static crackles over the airwaves as I tune it to Firebird, having a little trouble finding the signal. I twist the dial another notch to the right, and a voice suddenly rings out through the speakers.

"—local fireworks display."

I drop the radio, my heart racing. It was just three words, but I'd know that voice anywhere.

Ash.

10.
NATALIE

ELIJAH WHIPS OUT a hand and catches the radio before it crashes to the floor. He passes it back to me and I turn up the volume, but all I hear is static. We wait for minute after agonizing minute, listening for Ash. *Talk to me, Ash, please, please, please.* Just as I'm starting to lose hope, the radio sparks to life again:

"Going to the town near here; then checking out the local fireworks display," Ash's voice says again over the airwaves. The last few words of the message are the same as before, so it's clearly a recording, but even so, it's Ash! He's alive! I bury my face in my hands, shaking all over with relief. Elijah gently rubs my back. I knew Ash would try to get a message to us; I could feel it in my heart. I lift my head and take a deep breath. I've been drowning with worry for the past nine days, and now I can finally breathe.

Beetle scratches his scarred cheek. "What does the message mean?"

"He's letting us know where he's going next," Day says.

"Do you think he's looking for me?" I say.

"Maybe," Day says. "But it's more likely the message is about the Ora, since Ash would assume we'd think you and Elijah were still with him, as there's been no news of your capture."

Elijah's eyes light up with hope. "Do you think he's found my mom and the others?"

"It's possible," Day says.

"It's not much of a clue to go on," Beetle mutters. "*Going to the town near here.* Where's 'here'? How are we supposed to figure that out?"

I bite my lip, thinking. "Maybe Ash is expecting us to trace the signal? Perhaps he's going to the town closest to that location?"

"I don't think so," Day says. "It's really hard to trace a radio signal. You need a powerful DF antenna to triangulate the source, and Ash knows Humans for Unity doesn't have anything like that," she explains. "And even if we did, I can't imagine he'll be broadcasting this message long enough for us to trace it. Plus we'd encounter all the same problems the government's been having in locating our broadcasts, like propagation distortions and—" She stops talking when she notices the look of wonder on Beetle's face.

"You amaze me sometimes, babes," he says. "How do you know all this?"

Her caramel skin flushes pink. "It's called *reading*. You should try it sometime."

He grins. "Nah, sounds like a lot of hard work."

I sigh. Ash is giving us a clue and I can't work out where he means! We listen to the radio for another ten minutes waiting for Ash to speak again, hoping to work out the riddle.

"Going to the town near here; then checking out the local fireworks display," Ash says just as my watch beeps. I check the dial—09:30. Time for my appointment with Dr. Craven. For the first time, the thought doesn't depress me. Not only am I getting better, but it's a great excuse to see Sigur.

I push my chair back. "I have to go."

We agree to meet up again in an hour, before I head to the hospital, bringing the radio with me as my mind whirs, trying to work out Ash's clue. I enter the ward. My parents, Dr. Craven and Roach are huddled around Sigur's bed, deep in discussion.

"I overheard my guards at the prison talking about a new security force that Purian Rose has enlisted," Sigur mumbles, his bruised lips making it hard to talk. There are welts all over his bare torso, where he's been tortured.

Father nods. "We've seen them walking around the city."

I wonder if they're referring to the Tin Men I saw in Scott's shop.

"Well, according to the guards, Purian Rose is forcing these men to take a new drug as part of an initiation into the group," Sigur explains. "They're calling the drug Wings."

Father turns to Dr. Craven. "Have you heard of it before?"

Dr. Craven shakes his head.

"What does the drug do?" Roach asks. She's casually sitting at the end of his bed, one scruffy boot propped up on the mattress, her other leg dangling over the side.

"The guards thought it was a performance-enhancing drug," Sigur says.

"Like steroids?" Father says.

"The men who took it were coming back stronger, more aggressive, so it would support the guards' theory," Sigur continues. "But I am not so sure. Perhaps past experiences have made me paranoid"—he turns his good eye toward Dr. Craven, who pretends to clean his glasses—"but I suspect there is more to this drug than people think. Purian Rose has a tendency to disguise one thing with another."

"You mean, like hiding the Wrath virus in the Golden Haze?" Roach says, casting a look at my mother, whose mouth tightens into a thin line.

"I don't see how this drug Wings is a threat to us," Mother says.

Sigur turns toward her. "Perhaps I am being paranoid, but when it comes to Purian Rose, I think it is best to be on guard," he says. "As you know, he used the Golden Haze as Trojan horses, by infecting them with the Wrath virus and then letting my people feed on them, passing it on to us. So who knows what hidden threat lurks in this drug, or who he truly intends to hurt with it? We need to be extra vigilant, Emissary."

Father nods. "I'll put some feelers out, see if we can find out what Rose is really up to."

I cough, letting them know I'm here. "Sorry to intrude, but I have an appointment . . ."

Dr. Craven ushers me over to a bed beside Sigur. I place the radio on the nightstand while Dr. Craven collects a thin black box and places it on the tray beside me. He opens it up, revealing a velvet-lined case filled with four syringes, a pack of needles and four small vials of medicine, each one with a different-colored cap.

"What's that?" I say.

"This is your Wrath medication," he says. "As much as I'll miss your company, pumpkin, I figured you'd want to learn to administer it yourself. There's enough here to last you seven days."

I grin, delighted that I'm not going to have to come to the

hospital every day. Dr. Craven shows me how to fill the syringes, explaining about the dosages, and then teaches me to inject myself. It's painful, and I mess up the first injection, causing blood to squirt out of my vein. Sigur shuts his eyes, his jaw clenching at the smell.

"Sorry," I mutter.

While I'm attempting to do the third injection, the radio crackles and Ash's voice rings out over the airwaves, repeating the same message.

Sigur's head whips around at the voice. "Was that—?"

"Ash, yes!" I grin, briefly explaining everything. My mother's scarlet lips purse together; I think she was secretly hoping he'd stay lost. "I don't know where 'the town near here' is yet, but Day's working on it."

"I want to help." Sigur grimaces as he sits up. "We can arrange a rescue—"

"That might not be possible," my father interrupts.

"What?" Roach splutters. "Why the fragg not?"

Father sighs. "I've been ordered not to expend any more resources searching for him."

"But, Jonathan, he is my Blood Son . . . ," Sigur says.

"You're wasting your breath," I mutter, leaning against my pillow.

Sigur and Roach share a knowing look, their expressions hardening.

"We should let you rest," Father says to Sigur.

He and my mom leave the ward, Roach hot on their heels.

"This is fragging madness!" I hear her yell at my dad just as the door swings shut.

Sigur lies down, wincing with pain. He turns his head away

as Dr. Craven helps me with my last injection. When we're finished, I grab the black syringe case and radio and head to Elijah's room, mulling over what Sigur said about the drug Wings, which Purian Rose is making his men take. I check my watch, wondering if I have time to shower before meeting up with the others. It's 10:20. I could probably— The radio crackles.

"Going to the town near here; then checking out the local fireworks display," Ash says.

My heart aches at the sound of Ash's voice. What does his message mean? There must be a way to work out where he is! *Okay, think, Natalie.* Wherever Ash is, it has to be somewhere Humans for Unity can figure out, based on that clue. So chances are, the place is significant to the rebellion. Black City? No, why would he go back there? Okay . . . erm . . . Centrum? It's possible, but not likely. The only other place I can think of is . . . *Oh!* I pause midstep, making the soldier walking behind me bump into my back.

"Sorry," I mutter as he shoots me an impatient look.

I study my watch, my mind whirring. When I was in the Mess Hall earlier, his message came on at precisely 09:30. And when I checked my watch just now, at 10:20, the message played again. I quickly count how many times the message has played over the past hour, hope building in me. Five times. *Could it be . . . ?* I race through the compound until I reach Elijah's bedroom, barging in without even knocking. He's sitting on the floor with Beetle and Day, a portable com-screen on the ground between them, showing a satellite map of Mountain Wolf State. They must be trying to work out where the Claw is. They look up.

"There's a ten-minute delay between each message!" I say

breathlessly. "That was the clue! They're at the town nearest to the *Tenth*. And you know where that is?" I look at Elijah.

"Gray Wolf!" he answers, recalling what Garrick told us yesterday about Gray Wolf being overrun by Sentry guards, because it was the closest town to the camp.

"Get your things," I say. "We're going to rescue Ash."

11.
ASH

THE MINIPORT SWOOPS dramatically to the left, making me start awake. I run a tired hand over my face. I hadn't realized I'd been asleep. Acelot is beside me, singing very badly to a cheesy song playing over the aircraft's stereo.

"Your beauty is like a priceless work of art; you're the key to unlock the secrets of my heaaaaaaart," he warbles.

"I didn't take you for a Chuck Lazlo fan," I say.

He grins guiltily and turns off the stereo. "It's Marc's album. My kid brother may be a moody brat sometimes, but he's a real softy deep, *deep* down."

I raise a skeptical brow.

"It's not entirely his fault he's like that," Acelot continues. "It's just what happens when you've led a privileged life. You think the world owes you everything."

"You're not like that," I point out.

"I'm older and, well, I wouldn't say *wiser*, but certainly less of a jerk than I used to be," he says. "Although my ex-girlfriends back home might not agree. Elijah's the only one of us who turned out normal."

I furrow my brow. "But Elijah's just like Marcel."

"Are you joking? They're completely different," Acelot says.

It occurs to me that the Elijah I knew was pretending to be his younger brother the whole time I knew him, so I don't actually know the "real" Elijah at all.

"So what's he like then?" I ask.

Acelot shrugs. "He's a quiet sort of person, you know? Hard-working, never complains. And, man, can that kid fish! We used to take my boat out every weekend, and this one time he hooked this marlin, easily a four-footer. Took him three hours to reel it in, but he got it in the end." Acelot smiles at the happy memory.

"Sounds like you two are close," I say.

"Yeah, we are," Acelot says. "Pisses Marc off no end, though. You might not have noticed, but he's a *bit* possessive."

I chuckle and glance out the windscreen. "Where are we?"

"Approaching Gray Wolf," Acelot says.

Through the glass, the historic city looms up ahead. It looks like a fairy-tale town straight from the pages of a children's storybook, with twisting cobbled streets and quaint colonial buildings that remind me of dolls' houses, made from red brick with terra-cotta-tiled roofs and white sash windows, complete with shutters.

A busy railroad is on the east side of the city, and a derelict factory district is on the west side, on the outskirts of Gray Wolf, near a wide canal. I vaguely recall my old history teacher, Mr. Lewis, telling us about the depression that gripped the region around the time Mount Alba erupted. Many citizens relocated to the bigger cities in search of work and new opportunities, which explains why the factory warehouses are dilapidated and overrun with weeds and foliage. Based on the bustling streets below us, the city's fortunes have changed with the arrival of

Purian Rose's troops, who are using the town as a military hub, since it's so close to the Tenth.

The powder-blue skies around us are filled with Sentry Transporters, zooming in and out of the city. Thankfully, because of all the air traffic, our Miniport doesn't look too conspicuous as we fly over the city in search of a place to land.

"Try the warehouses near the canal," I say.

Acelot steers the aircraft in the direction of the factory district. He looks tired, with dark rings under his eyes, but that's hardly surprising; he hasn't slept in more than twenty-four hours. The journey from Black City to Gray Wolf would normally take only about five hours, but because our navigation systems are down, we made a few wrong turns. I check the clock on the cracked dashboard. It's almost lunchtime.

"Do you think Humans for Unity got your message?" Acelot asks, yawning.

"I hope so." I wanted to let them know where I was going, not only to confirm I'm still alive, but to give them a clue to the Ora's location, in case I don't make it back alive. I'm determined to free my people and end this war, even if I'm not there to see it. Ideally Humans for Unity will figure out I'm coming to Gray Wolf, and that the "local fireworks display" is the volcano, Mount Alba, because it looks like a fireworks show when it erupts.

There's a loud snore from the seat behind me, and I glance over my shoulder at our two passengers. Marcel is fast asleep on one of the leather chairs, his tail dangling over the side of the seat. He's using his red velvet frock coat as a pillow, so he's just in a white shirt and dark pants. Tucked into his belt is a small dagger with an ivory handle. Across from him is Sebastian. He's wide awake and citing verses from the Book of Creation, the holy text of the Purity faith. He's been doing it since we left Black City.

"And we shall rid the Darkling plague from His Mighty's green earth, for they are demons sent to tempt us with their opiates and their bodies and their sinful ways. But they are Damned creatures!" he says. "And anyone who lies with a Darkling is Damned as well, cursed to spend eternity in the burning depths of hell—"

"Like you, you mean?" I say, recalling a conversation with Natalie when we first started dating about Sebastian cheating on her with their young Darkling housemaid. Sebastian turns his green eyes toward me. They're filled with hate. "You got her pregnant, right?"

"Shut up," Sebastian snarls.

"You're full of it, Sebastian," I say. "You act so righteous, but I know you've taken Haze, slept with Darklings, and raped and murdered people. Your dad must be so proud of you."

His whole head reddens with anger, highlighting the crimson rose tattoo above his left ear. "My father loves me."

"Sure," I say. "Remind me: when was the last time you saw him?"

A muscle twitches along his jaw.

"No one cares about you, Sebastian," I say. "Not your dad, not Purian Rose. You're nothing but an embarrassment to them. That's why they haven't come looking for you."

Sebastian holds my gaze for a tense moment, then looks away, frowning. I turn around in my chair again and glance at Acelot.

"That was petty of me," I admit.

Acelot shrugs languidly. "Yeah, but he deserves it."

We fly over the abandoned warehouses until we spot one with a roof that's still mostly intact, offering us some cover.

Acelot expertly steers the aircraft through the wide-open doors and lands inside the warehouse. There's a heavy jolt as it hits the earth. Behind me, Marcel lets out a startled cry as he falls off the bench.

"Geez, Ace!" Marcel snaps, standing up. "Who taught you to fly?"

"Hey, at least I didn't crash it. That's one up on you." Acelot winks at his brother and Marcel pouts.

I step off the Miniport to check that our location is secure. Sunlight slices through the holes in the roof, creating a speckled effect on the dirt ground. There's still a few metal shelves running down the left side of the building, and at the far end of the warehouse is a large stack of crates. Dust and cobwebs coat everything, and weeds poke out of the earth. In the rafters is a nest of chirping swallows. There don't appear to be any cameras, and the pathway outside the warehouse is deserted. We should be safe to hang out here for a while.

Acelot strolls off the aircraft behind me, stretching his arms above his head to untangle the knots in his back. Marcel pushes past him, takes one look at the warehouse, curls his lip and then stomps back inside the Miniport.

"So what's the plan, my friend?" Acelot says once we're out of Sebastian's earshot. We've been careful not to discuss anything about our mission in front of him.

"Have some lunch, then do a scout of the city," I say. "We need to find a way to get into the Tenth undetected."

"All right," Acelot says.

I glance over my shoulder toward the Miniport. Marcel's on his hands and knees, searching for something underneath his seat, his tail stuck up in the air. Sebastian watches with amusement.

"You don't have to come to the Tenth," I say to Acelot. "I can't guarantee your safety."

Acelot gazes at his little brother for a moment. "I have to come," he eventually says. "I'm the Bastet Consul; it's my duty to protect my people." He turns his golden-brown eyes on me. "Besides, I owe it to you after what my parents did."

He heads into the Miniport to get some food while I start a small fire. Acelot returns a moment later with a few tins of beans, a glass and a grumpy-looking Marcel. The boy slumps down on the ground and lets out a bored sigh. He draws some swirls in the dirt while Acelot opens up the canned beans and places them on the fire. As they're cooking, he bites his wrist with his saber teeth and pours his blood into the glass. There are several older puncture wounds up his arms where he's done this for me before. I take the glass gratefully, my stomach groaning with hunger, and knock it back in one hit.

"Thanks," I say, wiping my mouth.

Acelot wraps a rag around his wrist. "*Nia probleme,*" he says in his native tongue. "I'd rather not wake up to find you gnawing on my neck. Don't get me wrong, you're a good-looking guy, but I prefer to be taken out to dinner first." He grins at me and I laugh.

Acelot makes sure the beans are cooked and then passes a can to Marcel. The young Bastet curls his lip up at it, in a gesture that reminds me of Elijah. Well, Elijah pretending to be Marcel, anyway. God, it's confusing!

"Don't we have anything nicer?" he sulks. "I don't like beans."

Acelot takes them back. "All the more for me."

Marcel snatches the can, and Acelot musses his brother's hair as he sits down. A beam of sunlight cuts across Acelot's slim face, and he tilts his head back slightly, enjoying the heat. We chat for a while about nonsense, ignoring Sebastian, who is still sitting in the Miniport and complaining about being hungry--he can have some cold beans later, if he's lucky—and for a moment I forget about the rebellion and the Ora, and just enjoy myself. Marcel turns out to be surprisingly amusing as he tells a funny story about Acelot getting caught in a *very* compromising position with one of their maids, by their parents.

"He claimed he was helping her scrub the floor," Marcel says, chuckling. "Father just stood there, utterly mortified! What did Mom say again?"

Acelot puts on a feminine voice. "You've missed a spot, darling."

I belly laugh, and it feels good. I can't remember the last time I did that.

When Acelot and Marcel are finished with lunch, we head back into the Miniport to gather our weapons and hooded jackets. Marcel grabs his dark red frock coat.

"What are you doing?" I say.

He furrows his brow. "I'm coming with you."

"No, *you're* keeping watch over this goon," I say, gesturing toward Sebastian. The Tracker gives me a flinty look. "Just don't let him near any oil lanterns, okay?"

Marcel flushes, remembering the incident back at Sentry headquarters.

Acelot and I put on our jackets, pulling the hoods low to hide our faces, and head into the city.

It takes an hour to walk into the bustling central district, mainly because we're keeping to the winding streets whenever possible, to try to stay out of sight. The town center is swarming with people, and we have to elbow our way through the crowds. The old city of Gray Wolf wasn't designed for this many inhabitants. The narrow roads are gridlocked with military vehicles, the cafés and inns overflowing with Sentry guards, who spill out onto the streets, drinking Shine, smoking and playing cards.

The whole town has been turned into a Sentry stronghold; everywhere I turn, there's another guard or Lupine—the Lupines have long been faithful supporters of Purian Rose, so it's not surprising to see them here—but ironically because there are so many Sentry, it's easier for us to blend in. Even so, I keep my hood low over my face and my hand firmly grasped around the gun in my jacket pocket, *just* in case.

At any other time, the town would be beautiful, but the Sentry guards have already trashed the place, leaving empty bottles and litter on the sidewalks. In all the shop windows there are government propaganda posters. I notice a few posters advertising a public Cleansing ceremony being held next week in Winston Square, with ATTENDANCE IS MANDATORY written in bold letters at the bottom.

I stop dead. In one of the windows is a recent newspaper article. The headline reads DARKLING AMBASSADOR FOUND GUILTY. Someone's drawn a mustache and pair of devil horns on the black-and-white picture of Sigur that accompanies the report. I scan the article, my mind reeling with every word. Sigur's going to be executed this weekend.

The noise around me fades as I stare at the article. *They're going to kill him.* I stretch out a hand and touch the glass that separates me from the photo of my Blood Father. A million thoughts race through my head, trying to work out how to save him. But I know I can't. I won't. I have a mission to complete. I turn away from the window.

"Let's check out the train station. In the Barren Lands I saw a cargo train filled with prisoners," I say. "I'm guessing that's how they're transporting people to the Tenth."

We head down a long road called Colonial Street and emerge in an enormous plaza. In the center of the square is a column, more than a hundred feet high, topped with a bronze statue of Theodore Winston, one of the country's founding fathers. At the base of the statue, a team of Workboots are busy building a wooden platform. My eyes are drawn to the billboard-sized digital screen perched on top of the building to our left. A government commercial is playing on the screen, showing a congregation of Pilgrims during their morning Cleansing. The ritual is fascinating; I've never seen one performed before. I've only ever attended my dad's services, but he was a minister of the Old Faith—the religion the people of the United Sentry States used to follow before the Purity became popular.

The Pilgrims walk up to the altar, one by one, where two bowls are waiting for them: one white, one red. They drink from the white bowl, and then the preacher dips his thumb into the red bowl and draws a mark across their foreheads. They all look serene and blissed out after the ritual. They remind me of my Haze clients—they have that same euphoric, faraway look. The commercial ends with the slogan HIS MIGHTY PROTECTS THE FAITHFUL. I shake my head in disbelief. The government's basically saying follow the Purity faith, or be sent to the Tenth.

Acelot points toward the building on the other side of the plaza. "Well, there's your train station. Shall we take a look inside?"

I nod. It's the only way we're going to know for certain if the trains are running directly into the Tenth. We cut across the square in the direction of the station. It's an impressive Gothic building with a soaring clock tower and arched windows.

The inside of the station is cool and inviting, with marble floors and pillars, and a high vaulted ceiling painted a rich green. A red-and-white Sentry flag hangs down from the ceiling. Like everywhere else in Gray Wolf, the station is heaving with people. I notice a few Sentry guards sitting outside the station's tavern, enjoying their lunch break, and others have gathered around the numerous market tables where vendors sell cheap watches, dirty magazines, playing cards, cigarettes— basically anything they think the Sentry guards will want. The guards jovially barter with the vendors. It's all just a big vacation to them. Venom floods my fangs.

Amid all this, packs of Lupines lug heavy crates of supplies up and down the flights of stairs, which lead to the platforms. We casually stroll around the station, trying to act normal and blend in with the other passengers, although my heart is racing.

"Ash, look," Acelot whispers, subtly gesturing toward a group of Lupines dressed in long burgundy jackets. They're each carrying a crate with THE TENTH stamped on them. They head down the stairs toward platform six. So that's where the trains to the Tenth are running from? One of the Lupines—a female with a snowy-white mane and naturally red lips—glances in our direction. We quickly turn our backs on her.

"Let's get out of here," I whisper, not wanting to stick around any longer.

We hurry back to the warehouse on the west side of the city, taking the same route that we used to get here. I'm relieved when we approach the familiar-looking canal outside the disused warehouses, far away from Sentry eyes.

"I think we should head out at first light tomorrow," I say as we enter the warehouse. "I don't want to wait around here for long—"

We stop in our tracks.

The Miniport's gone.

Tendrils of smoke spiral out of the dying fire I built earlier. Two cans of beans lie abandoned beside it, along with my blue duffel bag. The contents are laid out across the floor—Marcel must've been going through my stuff again. Next to my bag is a bloodstain.

"No," I say. Then louder. "No, no, no, no, NO!"

"Shit!" Acelot rakes his hands through his hair, panicked. "He took Marc!"

There's a groan from deeper in the warehouse. We follow the trail of blood snaking across the ground. The drops of blood get heavier and heavier until it's a steady stream of red, which leads behind the stack of crates.

Marcel is slouched against the wall. By his side is an ivory-handled dagger, covered in blood. The boy's skin is glistening with sweat, his lips ghostly white. There's a crimson stain on his shirt, just above his stomach.

"Marcel!" Acelot pushes past me and kneels down. He gently cradles his brother against him. The younger Bastet looks so small, wrapped in his brother's arms.

"What happened?" I say, pressing my hand against the wound. He's deathly cold.

"I dropped my . . . my dagger in the Miniport . . . when I fell off the bench earlier," Marcel explains between ragged breaths, every word a struggle out of his trembling lips. "I couldn't find it . . . Sebastian . . . he . . . he got hold of it somehow. Cut himself loose."

I can imagine the scene now: Marcel, bored as always, looking through my belongings by the campfire, his back turned to the Miniport, unaware as Sebastian retrieved the dagger from under the bench and used it to sever his binds. The boy had no chance against a skilled Tracker. Based on the blood splatter, Marcel must've been stabbed once near the Miniport, then chased into this corner of the warehouse and stabbed again.

"I'm sorry, Ace," Marcel rasps.

"We're going to get help," Acelot replies, his eyes glistening. "Just hold on, brother."

Marcel's blood seeps through my fingers, stinging my nostrils. I hold my breath, forcing myself not to breathe it in. I can feel the boy's pulse getting fainter beneath my fingertips.

"I'm dying," Marcel whispers.

"No you're not," Acelot says huskily, blinking. The tears finally fall.

Marcel smiles faintly. "You always were a terrible liar, Ace." He glances down at the bloodstain on his top. "This was my favorite shirt too . . ."

He shudders, and lets out a small sigh, the last of his life leaving him. His head droops. A low, anguished wail escapes Acelot's lips as he hugs his brother to him. Grief is such a private thing, and I feel like a voyeur, watching his suffering. I give his shoulder a gentle squeeze, then get up and head outside.

I find a spot by the canal and kneel down, washing my hands in the chilly water. Ribbons of blood lift off my skin and dance about the surface of the deep blue water. The color reminds me of the dark flecks in Natalie's eyes. An aching pain balls up in my chest and I sit back, sucking in a ragged breath, but it barely fills my lungs. I don't know how many more days I can go on without her. If it was Garrick's intention to torment me by capturing Natalie, then it's working. I'm broken. Ready to surrender. I sink my head into my hands.

Where are you, Natalie?

12.
NATALIE

"SO HOW EXACTLY are we going to steal one of those?" Day says.

We're in the aircraft hangar in the Sentry rebel base, where a fleet of Transporters are parked. Several of the Transporters shoot out of the tunnel, sending squads of Sentry rebels on to their next mission, while dozens of soldiers unload crates of weapons from the other aircraft. They've been bringing them in all week.

I considered going to my father and asking for his help to rescue Ash but then quickly decided against it. He'd have to get permission from the Commander, and he's already made his position crystal clear on this particular subject—he doesn't want any more resources "wasted" on finding Ash—and I don't have time to convince him otherwise. We need to get to Gray Wolf before Ash leaves.

"More to the point, who's going to fly it?" Day says. "Does anyone know how to pilot those things?"

"Garrick does, but he won't help us," I say. "He spent weeks trying to get me here; he's hardly going to let me swan off to

Gray Wolf, especially since the place is swarming with Sentry guards. My mother would skin him alive."

"What about Roach?" Elijah suggests.

Beetle shakes his head. "No good, bro. She doesn't know how to fly them."

"Then who?" Elijah asks.

A name suddenly springs to mind, and I snap my fingers. "Destiny!"

We find her in command central, deep in concentration as she types something into the com-desk. She's the only person in the room—I guess the others are still with Sigur. On the digital screen behind her is a map of Centrum. I easily recognize the famous giltstone buildings and the domed roof of the Golden Citadel, where Purian Rose lives. On the map are lots of red dots, plus several areas highlighted in bright green, including the citadel.

"Are you planning an attack on Centrum?" Day exclaims as we enter the room.

Destiny's head snaps up, startled. "Lord above, you guys scared me half to death!" She turns off the screens, looking at me. "You're not supposed to be in here, hon."

"*Is* there going to be an attack on Centrum?" I ask.

"You know I can't tell you that," Destiny says, dramatically nodding her head.

I smirk a little. She's not *technically* telling me if she uses gestures instead of words, so it's not going against her orders. So that's why they're bringing in all those supplies downstairs; they're preparing for an assault on the capital city? It's upsetting that Father didn't mention any of this to me, but then again why would he? I'm not one of his soldiers; I'm just his "little girl."

"When's it going to take place?" Beetle asks.

"I'm not allowed to say," she replies, wiggling five fingers. Five days' time. Wow, all of this could be over in less than a week. It's thrilling and terrifying all at once, knowing the final battle is soon to take place. She looks at me. "Did you want something, hon?"

"I have a teeny favor to ask," I say.

She narrows her brown eyes, flicking a look between me and the others. "Why do I get a feeling I won't like this?"

"We need a ride to Gray Wolf," I say. "Ash is there and I'm going to rescue him."

"You know I can't, hon," Destiny says. "We have—"

"Orders, I know. But here's the thing: I don't take orders from people I don't know," I say. "Do *you* know who the Commander is?"

Destiny frowns, shaking her head. "My aunt wouldn't tell me."

"And yet we're expected to just blindly follow him?" I say. "I know it's a lot to ask, but I don't have anyone else to turn to, Des. Please help us."

"I don't know . . . ," she says.

"If Ash gets caught or dies, just think how much damage it'll do to this rebellion," I continue, trying a different tactic. "I know the Commander doesn't think Ash is 'strategically important,' but he's wrong." Beetle and Day nod. "You said earlier the new Sentry regime needs the Darklings' support. Well, imagine what the Darklings will think—"

"Or Humans for Unity," Beetle adds.

"—if they learn that the Sentry rebels refused to help

Phoenix," I say. "Plus, we think Ash has a lead on the Ora, and I know you agree we should be looking for it."

This seems to pique her interest. Destiny nods. "Okay."

"You'll take us?" I say, grinning.

"It's what my aunt would've done," Destiny says, referring to Emissary Vincent. "She wasn't afraid to break the rules if she believed it was the right thing to do. And personally, I'd sleep better at night knowing Phoenix was here, safe and sound."

I fling my arms around her, giving her a massive hug. "Thank you!"

Destiny chuckles. "Don't thank me yet, kiddo. We have to get out of here first."

On the way back to the hangar, we swing by our rooms to change into our civilian clothes. I grab my heart medication and the black syringe case Dr. Craven gave me, and tuck them into my jacket pocket, thankful that he had the foresight to let me manage my own medication. I suspect he knew I'd go looking for Ash one of these days.

When I'm dressed, I join the others and we make a brief pit stop at the arsenal. We each take a handgun, just in case we get into any trouble in Gray Wolf, and follow Destiny into the hangar. We walk confidently across the forecourt. Destiny nods to a few of the soldiers, acting like nothing out of the ordinary is happening.

I spot the pink-haired Lupine, Sasha, by one of the Transporters, her jumpsuit covered in oil stains. My pulse quickens. If she notices us, then the mission is over before it's even started. Thankfully she's so focused on fixing the aircraft that she doesn't raise her head. We hurry by her and board one of the other Transporters. Inside, the aircraft has that gleaming just-off-the-production-line look. We take our seats.

"I hate these things," Elijah grumbles, nervously playing with his gold bands.

I blush. The first time we were in a Transporter together, I threw up on him.

"I'm sitting up front," Day says, hopping over our legs. "I want to learn how to fly one of these beauties."

Beetle pats her on the butt as she walks past. She takes the copilot's seat while we try to get comfortable, although it's hard when I'm so eager to get to Ash. The engines roar to life, there's a jerk as the aircraft's clamps are released, and soon we're zooming down the tunnel. The aircraft suddenly lifts, Destiny presses a button on the control panel to open the security doors blocking the tunnel exit, and we burst into daylight.

The city of Gallium glints below us, the metal-fronted buildings like coins spilled across the ground. The city isn't as ugly as I first thought. Like Black City, there is beauty here if you look close enough.

"How are we going to find Ash when we get to Gray Wolf?" Elijah says. "His message told us only that he was going to the city, not where he'd be staying. And we still haven't worked out the second part of his message, about the local fireworks display. Where's that?"

My heart sinks. "I don't know," I admit. I'm hoping once we get to Gray Wolf it'll become clear what he meant.

A familiar voice crackles over the cockpit radio. "Destiny, this is General Buchanan. Return to base immediately."

My stomach leaps into my throat. It didn't take them long to realize we were missing.

"Natalie, this is your mother!" my mom's voice shouts from the radio. "You come back this very *minute,* young lady! That's an—"

Day turns off the radio. "Oops, we seem to have lost the signal."

She glances over her shoulder at me and grins.

"Thank you," I mouth back at her. Day's a great friend.

It takes around three hours to reach Gray Wolf, although it feels like a hundred. Beetle and Elijah go over possible places to start searching for Ash, and Destiny gives Day a quick lesson on how to fly a Transporter. She picks it up really fast, but that's hardly surprising. Day's brilliant at everything, except perhaps baking. I recall the lopsided cake she made for my seventeenth birthday. I get up, needing to shake off some of this nervous energy, and join them in the cockpit. The sky fills the windscreen, blistering blue, with clouds like puffs of spun sugar.

"This is so much fun, Nat!" Day turns to grin up at me, accidentally tilting the control stick in her hands in the process. The Transporter lurches wildly to the right and I let out a squeak of fright, clinging to her seat for dear life.

Day grimaces as she quickly corrects the aircraft's position. "Sorry."

"Nice flying, babe," Beetle calls from the passenger section behind us.

"I'd like to see him try it," Day grumbles.

I let go of her leather seat and lean my hip against the control desk. I nervously twist my blue diamond engagement ring.

"You okay, Nat?" Day asks.

"What if we don't find him?" I say.

"We will," she replies gently.

Destiny takes back the controls as we come in to land. The aircraft tilts to the right, and I get a fantastic view of Gray Wolf through the windscreen. Mount Alba is far in the distance, its white snowy cap stark against the robin's-egg-blue sky. She lands the Transporter in an abandoned lot, in the north part of town. We get out. The weather is warm with a cool breeze. We lift our jacket hoods to help hide our faces and head into the city center.

The city is bustling with people, making me feel claustrophobic as they push and shove against me. I start to get a terrible sinking feeling. How am I ever going to find Ash here? We turn a corner and spot a squadron of Tin Men in their coin-gray uniforms, coming from the other way. The crowd parts as they march down the street in our direction.

We dart into a bookstore before they reach us, and take cover behind a rack of books. We pretend to browse the shelves, so as not to arouse too much suspicion from the other customers, while casting surreptitious looks toward the window. It's almost entirely covered by government posters with slogans like ONE FAITH, ONE RACE, ONE NATION UNDER HIS MIGHTY written on them, but through the gaps I can see the men walking by.

Like the guards in Gallium, they're wearing a metal butterfly pin on their chests. They march in perfect unison, their expressions blank. They pass a street vendor who is selling tacky figurines, which are laid out on the sidewalk in front of him. Without breaking their stride, they trample over the porcelain figures, smashing them under their boots. The vendor shakes his fist at their backs. We wait a few minutes, until we're sure they've gone, before heading into the busy street.

"So, where do we start looking?" Beetle says.

I look about me, hoping to get some inspiration, but come up with nothing.

"I don't know," I mutter.

"We can't keep wandering around aimlessly," Day says.

"I know!" I say, getting frustrated. "But I don't know where he is. It's not like I'm psychically linked to Ash."

"Erm . . . actually, you sort of are," Day says, pushing her glasses up her nose.

I blink. I hadn't thought about that, but Day's right—there *is* a special connection between me and Ash. Before we started dating, I would often find myself drawn to the same places as he was, such as the underpass where we first met. At the time I put it down to coincidence, but now I'm not so sure. I think it was our Blood Mate connection luring me to him, like the moon's gravity pulling at the tides.

I shut my eyes and try to drown out the sounds around me, focusing only on the echo of Ash's heart beating inside of me. The sound is faint at first; but like the ticking of a clock, the more I listen for it, the louder it becomes until suddenly it's all I can hear, pounding in my ears. *Ba-boom, ba-boom, ba-boom.* I feel a slight tug in my chest. I open my eyes.

"That way," I say, pointing to a street across the road named Proctor Lane.

Destiny and Elijah share a confused look, while Day and Beetle just grin.

We dash across the busy road, ignoring the blaring horns. Proctor Lane is a winding alleyway, lined by redbrick houses with window boxes blooming with colorful spring flowers. After a few minutes we reach a crossroads and I shut my eyes, waiting for my heart to tell me where to go. There's a faint pull to the left, toward Colonial Street.

"This way," I say.

The others follow without complaint as we weave through a maze of alleyways for more than an hour. I start to feel a little out of breath and dizzy—I probably shouldn't be pushing myself so hard; my treatment might be working, but I still have the Wrath, and my body is aching from the exertion—but I push on, determined to find Ash. Elijah throws me a few concerned glances, so I force a smile, pretending I'm feeling okay.

We walk another mile, and I begin to worry I'm leading them on a wild goose chase when we reach a grand canal near a derelict warehouse district. The deflated look on everyone's face suggests we're thinking the same thing.

"Maybe we should go back to the Transporter, hon," Destiny suggests kindly. "We can regroup, then come up with a better plan."

I sigh, nodding. "Sorry, guys. I really thought—"

"Elijah?"

We all turn. Standing farther down the pathway, outside one of the warehouses, is a tall Bastet boy with ruffled brown hair and a handsomely boyish face, wearing dark pants and a green shirt with the sleeves rolled up to his elbows. There's dirt and blood all over his arms and top. We've only met once, but I recognize him immediately.

"Ace!" Elijah exclaims.

The boys rush toward each other and Acelot roughly picks Elijah up, giving him a tight squeeze, before letting go.

"It's so good to see you, brother," Acelot says.

"You too," Elijah says, looking about. "Is Marcel here?"

The smile slips from Acelot's lips.

"What is it?" Elijah says.

Acelot looks at the blood and dirt on his hands. "Sebastian

stabbed him. He's . . ." Acelot takes a deep breath, clearly trying to hold back his tears. "Marc didn't make it."

Elijah looks down, his jaw clenched. His lashes become slick with tears.

"Is Ash okay?" I ask, panic rising in me.

Acelot nods, ushering us inside the warehouse.

Ash is crouched on the ground, beside a mound of rocks and dirt. Like Acelot, he's covered in dust and blood. A small make-shift cross sticks out of the rocks. I'm guessing Marcel is buried underneath them. Ash suddenly stiffens, pressing a hand to his chest. He whips around. Our eyes meet. Ash blinks once, twice, like he can't believe it.

"Natalie . . ."

"Hey," I say softly. "I got your message."

He sprints over to me, crossing the gap in a few strides, and pulls me into his arms. His lips crush against mine. The kiss is deep, desperate, exquisite, sending little shivers of electricity racing through my veins and into my yearning heart. I run my hands through his rippling hair, which coils and twists around my fingers, while his hands press into my back, drawing me closer. His scent wraps around me: bonfires, musk and rain. *Home.* Ash gently breaks the kiss. His sparkling eyes search mine as his thumb caresses my cheek.

"I thought I might never see you again," he says huskily. "Where have you been?"

"Gallium," I say. "We've got so much to tell you."

"How did you find us?" Ash asks.

I place my hand against his chest. "How do you think?"

"Hey, bro," Beetle says behind us.

Ash looks up. A wide smile breaks out on his lips, revealing his gleaming fangs. I step aside and the boys quickly embrace. Day stands awkwardly nearby. She's never managed to form a friendship with Ash, but they tolerate each other.

Elijah goes over to the pile of rocks while I introduce Destiny to Ash and Acelot. We join Elijah at Marcel's grave, and Acelot performs a short but beautiful remembrance service. I glance at Ash, who gives a faint nod of his head, understanding the unspoken question in my eyes, before I slide my fingers through Elijah's. He clings to my hand as tears slide down his cheeks. It's the first time he's cried since leaving Viridis, his grief finally overwhelming him. I doubt the tears are just for Marcel, but for everyone he's lost these past few weeks. I don't know how he's holding it together.

At the end of the service we each place a trinket on Marcel's grave, as is tradition in Bastet culture. We have to do with whatever's close to hand. Ash leaves his cigarette lighter, while I pluck a dandelion head from the ground and place it carefully on top of one of the rocks. A soft breeze stirs the seeds, scattering them into the air.

The funeral over, Ash grabs his blue duffel bag, which is stained with Marcel's blood, and we return to Destiny's Transporter in the north end of the town. Elijah hangs toward the back of the group. Ash kisses my hand, then walks over to him.

"You okay?" he asks.

"Not really," Elijah says. "Marc and I hated each other, but I never wanted him to die. He was my brother."

Ash places a hand on Elijah's shoulder and gives it a reassuring squeeze. They walk in silence for a few paces.

"Thank you for going after Natalie when Garrick took her," Ash says.

Elijah shrugs. "It was no big deal."

"Yeah, actually, it was," Ash replies. "You could've been killed, but you went anyway."

Elijah gives a faint smile. "I figured I owed you after that whole double-crossing-you-and-nearly-getting-you-both-shot thing in Viridis."

Ash chuckles lightly, rubbing the back of his neck. "Yeah, well. This makes us even. We good?" Ash holds out his hand. Elijah hesitates for a second, then takes it.

"We're good," Elijah says.

On our way back to the Transporter, we catch up on everything that's been going on. Ash holds my hand the whole time, like he's afraid I'll disappear again if he lets it go. His jaw clenches when I tell him about the Sentry rebel base in Gallium, their planned assault on Centrum, and my parents' involvement with my "kidnapping."

"*They* took you away from me?" he asks quietly. "Why?"

"They were worried about my safety. This country is in chaos and they just wanted to protect me in their misguided, controlling way. I'm all they have left, Ash." I lower my lashes. "Plus, they think you're a dangerous influence on me." I look up in time to catch the hurt flashing across his face. "They just don't know you like I do."

He smiles a little. "So they're going to attack Centrum, huh?"

I nod. "In five days' time. The rebel compound is really impressive, Ash—you should see all the weapons they have. Guns, grenades, missiles, a whole *fleet* of Transporters. We could never have dreamed of anything like it."

"We were doing okay," Beetle mutters beside me.

"I'm not trying to diminish what we've done," I reply. "I'm

just saying they have a lot more weapons than we do. We're lucky to have the Sentry rebels."

"So what's Humans for Unity's role in the attack?" Ash asks.

Beetle shrugs. "Like they'd tell us anything, bro. But my guess, we don't have one."

Ash and Beetle share a knowing look, and my cheeks warm up. Why do I suddenly feel like the girl from months ago, stuck in the middle between Humans for Unity and the Sentry?

"Sigur's safe," Day says, quickly changing the subject.

I briefly fill him in on the details, and the tension in Ash's body evaporates.

"Thank God," he murmurs.

"And Natalie's been getting treatment for the Wrath," Elijah adds as we approach the Transporter, parked in the abandoned lot.

Ash's head snaps up, his black eyes sparkling with hope.

I pull out the syringe case from my jacket pocket. "I'm not cured, but Dr. Craven said my prognosis was good. I just have to take these every day."

Ash pulls me toward him and gently cups my face, planting feather-light kisses over my cheeks, lips and eyelids, making my skin tingle wherever his lips have brushed against me. He smiles, showing a hint of fang. "I guess I owe your parents a thank-you. Never thought I'd be saying that."

"How about you guys?" Day asks.

"We've worked out where Aunt Lucinda and the others have gone," Ash says.

"Where?" Elijah says.

"Mount Alba," Ash says. "I worked it out when I saw this tapestry at the Bastet embassy, which showed Mount Alba *before* it erupted, and guess what? It had this talon-shaped peak."

"The Claw!" I say, catching on.

He nods. "Not only was it the right shape, but it's next to Amber Hills—"

"Wait, isn't that where your mother and aunt grew up?" I ask, remembering Ash telling me this a few weeks ago on the train to the Barren Lands.

"Yeah," he replies. "I think Mount Alba's where they've hidden the Ora. It all fits."

"But Mount Alba's in the Tenth," Day says.

"That explains why I haven't heard from my mom in weeks," Elijah mutters. "They must have caught her."

"How will we ever find them?" Day says. "The place is enormous."

"If it's anything like the camp at the Barren Lands, they'll have a registration office with a list of all the prisoners," I say. "It should tell us which barracks they've been sent to."

"Whoa, you guys aren't seriously talking about going into the *Tenth*, are you?" Destiny says.

"Yes, of course," I say. "We have to rescue Elijah's mother."

"And my aunt Lucinda and Kieran," Ash adds. "I'm not leaving them there."

"But you don't even know for certain they're in the Tenth," Destiny says.

"We'll check the registers. If they're not listed, then we'll leave," I say. "The registration offices will be near the entrance gates. We won't even have to venture too far into the camp."

"You're crazy if you think I'm going to allow this," Destiny says.

"I wasn't asking for your permission, Des," I reply firmly.

"We're going in, with or without your help. If you want to leave, I understand."

She laughs. "Yeah right, kiddo! I'm already in big trouble with your parents as it is; what do you think they'll do to me if I go back to Gallium without you? They'd *shoot* me, that's what." She sighs and slides off her chunky black military watch, passing it to me. "This has a GPS tracking chip in it. I'll be able to follow your location on the monitor in the Transporter. When you've got what you need, press this button." She points to a small red button on the side of the watch. "And I'll pick you up."

I hug her. "Thanks, Destiny."

She lets out a heavy sigh, muttering, "I never liked being a soldier anyway."

"So, any suggestions how we get inside the Tenth?" Day says.

"Yeah, the same way as everyone else," Ash says. "We take the train."

PART 2

THE TENTH

13.

ASH

WE WAIT UNTIL NIGHTFALL before beginning our preparations to head to the Tenth. Beetle and Day are sitting on the Transporter's floor, legs crossed, as they clean their guns in silence. Their movements are in sync, their expressions hard and focused—the look of a soldier about to go into battle. Day's tied her long black hair back into a practical braid, revealing the caramel skin on her neck. There's a thin scar on it, like a bullet's grazed her. How close have they both come to dying these past few weeks? Beetle, sensing me looking, smirks.

"Bro, I know I'm pretty, but enough with the googly eyes, okay?"

I laugh. "Someone has a big opinion of himself."

On the bench beside them, Elijah and Acelot talk quietly. Acelot has a reassuring hand on Elijah's shoulder, but he's clearly struggling to hold back his own tears. Elijah nods occasionally, his gaze focused on the gold bands around his wrists.

Acelot glances down at the wristbands. "Why are you wearing those? Dad's gone. You're not a slave anymore."

Elijah shrugs. "Technically, I am. I serve the Consul. That's you now . . ."

"You know, I always thought we had too many servants." Acelot slides one of the bands off Elijah's arm and slips it over his own wrist. He grins and the brothers hug. I turn away and head to the cockpit.

Natalie's got her back to me as she peers at the monitor on the control panel. The Sentry soldier, Destiny, is in the pilot's seat beside her.

"Is that me?" Natalie says, playing with the GPS watch on her wrist.

"It sure is, hon," Destiny replies. "Remember, just hit the red button on the side of the watch when you want me to come and pick you up."

I slip my arms around Natalie's waist, and she lets out a little gasp of delight.

"Do you mind if I steal my fiancée for a minute?"

I lead Natalie into the hull of the aircraft. She leans against the metal wall and hooks her fingers through my belt loops, drawing me near. For a second I forget what I was going to say. I always feel intoxicated around her. She peers up at me. There's still a faint tinge of yellow in the corners of her eyes—a symptom of the Wrath. I can't believe I didn't notice the signs when she first got ill, when it was literally staring me in the face. The thought of her having the Wrath makes the breath freeze in my lungs, my heart stand still. She may be getting treatment, but she's still sick.

"Everything okay?" she says.

"Yeah," I whisper. "You don't need to come to the Tenth with me, blondie. It's dangerous. There's a very good chance we'll get killed."

Natalie half smiles, a cheeky twinkle in her eye. "Since when has that ever stopped me?"

"That's true," I say. "It's one of the many reasons I love you."

Her fingers play with my belt loop. "Yeah? What are the others?"

I hold her closer to me. "Mmm, let me see. You're kind, and brave, and smart, and you hate being told what to do." She blushes slightly. "But most of all, I love this teeny-tiny freckle right here," I say, pointing to the freckle on the side of her throat.

She giggles as I dip my head and lightly kiss her neck. Her pulse flutters under my lips and my poison sacs flood with venom. She sighs as I gently nip her skin, careful not to break the surface. Day coughs dramatically behind us, and we pull apart. Natalie's cheeks are flushed; I'm sure mine are too. I turn to look at the others. Beetle and Day are standing nearby, the small spotlights in the ceiling casting polka dots of white light on their skin. They tuck their newly cleaned guns into their hip holsters. Behind them, Elijah is tying up his bootlace, while Acelot blows his nose on his monogrammed handkerchief. Destiny is still in the cockpit, her hand on her weapon as she peers out of the windscreen for any signs of trouble.

"If any of you want to back out, now's the time to do it," I say.

Beetle chuckles. "Someone needs to watch your back, mate."

"And someone has to watch *his*," Day says. He gives her a lopsided grin.

Elijah stands up. "I'm not staying here when my mom's in the Tenth. She needs me."

I look at Acelot. "I always like an adventure," he says.

"Thanks, guys." It's risky having all of us going, but I'm grateful for their support.

We gather our weapons and sling on our hooded jackets.

Natalie slips her heart medication and black syringe case into one of her pockets. I watch her admiringly. Despite being sick, she still wants to fight. When we're ready, Destiny opens the hatch and we step off the Transporter. The night air is cool and stars shimmer overhead. Natalie takes my hand and nervously looks up at me. I kiss her cheek.

"Let's go," I say.

The station is eerily silent as we creep through the terminal, which is lit only by the pale moonlight streaming through the arched windows. I lead the way as we sneak down the iron stairwell that goes to platform six.

The platform is dark, apart from a few pools of amber light cast by the oil lanterns hanging from a wire overhead. The shadows offer plenty of cover. A train is parked on the rails farther down the platform, the boxcars packed with prisoners instead of livestock. Their hands poke out of the slats in the wood as they beg for water. Toward the far end of the train, a group of Sentry guards load dozens of white bags onto one of the carriages. Printed on the bags is GRAY WOLF LAUNDERETTES. We quickly duck under the stairwell, before the guards see us.

"We need to get onto that laundry carriage," I whisper.

"How are we going to get on there without being spotted?" Natalie replies.

It'll be hard to sneak onto the train now without being seen, since the train is too far away from us and there are no people on the platform to blend in with.

"We'll have to jump on when it passes by us," I say.

Day looks worriedly at Beetle, but he just squeezes her hand.

We linger in the shadows, waiting for our moment. When the guards have loaded all the laundry bags onto the train, they trudge up the stairwell at the other end of the platform. Only the stationmaster is left behind. He blows his whistle and the train starts up. Steam billows out of the chimney spout and I expect the stationmaster to leave, but instead he takes out a packet of smokes and sparks up. The train jerks forward and the prisoners all begin to scream.

"He's not going," Natalie says under her breath.

I stare at the guard. *Leave!* I urge.

He takes a long drag of his cigarette, wisps of white smoke spiraling into the air. The train starts to trundle down the tracks toward us, picking up speed.

"What do we do?" Natalie says.

Just go! I scream inside my head.

The carriages start whooshing by us, stirring my hair. The prisoners' cries become a blur of noise as the train gets faster, faster. The laundry carriage is almost upon us.

Finally, the stationmaster heads into his office.

"Now," I say.

I dash across the platform and leap at the moving train, grabbing hold of the wooden slats. My body slams against the side of the train, and I grunt with pain as I heave myself onto the roof of the carriage. Cold air buffets against me, but I manage to keep my balance. Natalie sprints toward the train and I lean over, grasp her hand and haul her up. She falls into my arms. The carriage rocks wildly and we slide across the roof, but I manage to seize the handle of the escape hatch before we fall over the side and get dragged under the train. I pull us upright just as Acelot and Elijah gracefully leap onto the roof. They don't seem to have any trouble keeping their balance, but their tails must help with that, and they quickly help Day and Beetle up onto the roof.

I open up the escape hatch and we drop inside the laundry carriage, our falls broken by the soft mounds of material. Elijah's the last into the carriage, and he shuts the hatch after him. I rummage around the laundry bags, pulling out the clothes. A lot of them are red-and-white-striped overalls, which must be for the new prisoners. I tear open another bag and let out a triumphant cry. The bag is filled with Sentry guard uniforms. I toss five uniforms at the others.

"Put these on," I say.

The girls go to the other end of the carriage and hide behind a wall of laundry bags as they get undressed. The guys strip down without any embarrassment, although Beetle struggles to put on his pants on the rocking train, hopping comically about on one leg. I change as quickly as possible, ignoring Acelot as he stares at the burns on my upper body. The girls return a minute later, wearing their black uniforms. The disguises aren't foolproof, but it'll still be night when we arrive at the camp, so people shouldn't get a good look at our faces. We settle down among the bags of laundry, and I wrap my arms around Natalie while Day snuggles against Beetle.

Elijah looks warily up at the hatch. "There aren't any Wraths around here, are there?"

The last time we were on a train together, traveling through the Barren Lands, three Wraths—Darklings turned feral because of the deadly C18 Wrath virus—entered the carriage through the escape hatch in the roof and started attacking everyone.

"Only me," Natalie says, smiling slightly.

Elijah winces. "Sorry."

"I thought I heard a crow, though," I tease, remembering he has a morbid fear of birds, recalling how freaked out he was during that same train ride, when something flashed past the window and he thought it was a condor.

"What? Where?" Elijah says, eyes wide with panic.

I smirk.

He frowns. "That's not funny."

Acelot chuckles. "It's a *little* funny, brother."

The laughter quickly dies down as our nerves mount. The only sound is the cold wind whipping through the ventilation slats in the carriage walls. Natalie nudges in closer to me, shivering slightly. I tighten my arms around her.

I don't know how long we're on the train—it feels like hours, but probably wasn't more than forty minutes—before there's a screech of brakes and the train decelerates. I get up and peer through the slats in the wall. All I can see is a long concrete wall, similar to the one in Black City, but this one seems to stretch on for eternity. Written on the wall in big black letters are the words HIS MIGHTY SEES ALL SINNERS. There's a chorus of screams from the other carriages as the train grinds to a halt.

We're here.

Outside the train is a cacophony of noise: the bark of dogs, the pounding of feet, the chaotic sound of Sentry guards shouting orders at each other. Floodlights from nearby watchtowers illuminate the train, but everywhere else is pitch black. If we can get away from the train without being caught, we should be able to walk around undetected.

The guards yank open the train doors and the prisoners literally spill out, the carts are so crammed. Hundreds of Darklings, humans and Bastets all topple to the dirt floor while others stumble over them, not wanting to get shot for lingering in the carriage too long. Everyone looks confused and terrified as they cling to each other.

A young woman with auburn hair falls heavily to the ground. She's dressed in a yellow folk dress, and in her arms is a small boy with curly black hair. He can't be more than two years old. They remind me a lot of Giselle and Lucas, the two Dacians we met in Thrace. Guilt rips through me at the memory of Giselle, the girl I accidentally shot when trying to kill a Lupine named Jared. Based on their appearance, the woman and her son must be Dacians too. I'm not surprised to see them here: the Dacian people are on Purian Rose's list of Impurities, along with the Darklings, Bastets and any other human deemed a race traitor.

"Get up!" a female Sentry guard with black hair shouts, pointing her gun at the young Dacian woman cradling the boy.

The woman is too scared to move, tears streaming down her pale cheeks. "Please, there's been a mistake. He's just a boy, a *baby*. He shouldn't be here."

The guard pulls the trigger once, twice, killing them. I slam my back against the carriage wall, briefly shutting my eyes as the scent of their blood stings my nostrils.

"Everyone grab a laundry bag," I say.

They each pick up a white bag while I peer between the slats in the carriage door. The prisoners are being arranged into two rows: the young and healthy are being put into the first row, and the sick, injured and old are being put into the second row. I can only presume half of them will be going to Primus-Two to work in the factories and the rest will be sent to Primus-Three, where they will be experimented on and exterminated. Now is our best chance to get out before the guards start unloading the laundry carriage and find us.

I quietly slide our carriage door open, then pick up a bag of laundry, lifting it onto my shoulder so that it hides part of my face. I step out of the carriage, my pulse racing, and the others follow. We casually head toward the main gates, passing the black-haired female guard.

"Hey, you," she says.

Ice floods my veins. "Yeah?" I grunt behind the laundry bag.

"Bring those bags *into* the warehouse, okay?" she says. "Don't just dump them outside in the mud like last time."

"Sure," I say gruffly and keep on walking. I risk a look over my shoulder and Natalie catches my eye. She looks petrified. Close behind her is Beetle, Day, Elijah, then Acelot. There's a *pop* of gunfire to my right, making me flinch. Another prisoner hits the earth.

We cling to the shadows as we approach the entrance to the Tenth. The concrete wall is about thirty feet high and topped with barbed wire. At fifty-foot intervals along the wall are watchtowers, each one populated with two guards armed with machine guns pointed at the prisoners who have just gotten off the train. Every minute or so the night sky lights up with a flash of bullets, like shooting stars raining down on the prisoners, killing anybody attempting to run away as they're rounded up to be brought into the camp. I don't look back, not wanting to see the devastation, but the air is thick with the scent of their blood.

A Sentry guard with a German shepherd patrols the wall near the main entrance—an enormous set of wrought-iron gates with thorny metal roses twisting around the bars. It's not what I was expecting at all; they look like the type of gates you'd see at a cemetery. The dog snarls and snaps at Elijah and Acelot as we approach the entrance. Elijah's hand subtly reaches down for the gun on his belt. I reach for mine. The guard yanks on the dog's leash.

"What's gotten into you, Max?" the guard says to the dog, dragging it away.

The gates swing open and we step through. A long cobbled avenue, wide enough for trucks to drive down, leads to a town several hundred feet away. Running down both sides of the avenue are rows of wooden crosses, each ten feet high, just like the one I was pinned to during my failed execution. Bound to the crosses are the rotting corpses of Darklings and humans, their tattered clothes fluttering on the night breeze. The smell is horrific. I can only assume they're here as a warning to the prisoners not to cause any trouble.

"Oh God," Natalie gasps.

I tear my eyes away from the crucifixes as the six of us walk down the avenue toward the town. A painted sign reads PRIMUS-ONE. A month ago, Garrick showed us a satellite map of the Tenth, and if memory serves, the camp comprises three towns: Primus-One, Primus-Two and Primus-Three. Primus-One is the base camp, where all the new arrivals are taken to be registered and evaluated. Those deemed eligible to work are sent to Primus-Two, in the south of the camp. The rest are sent to Primus-Three to be experimented on or exterminated.

Occasionally I risk a look at the watchtowers by the wall, but the guards are focusing on the prisoners by the train, not us. Even though it's nighttime, I can make out the shape of Mount Alba, aka "the Claw," in the distance, silhouetted against the stars. The volcano is easily eight thousand feet high and several miles wide, and its once talon-shaped peak is now a deep horseshoe-shaped crater, thanks to the eruption a few decades ago.

We arrive at a large plaza. In the center of the town square is the peak of a church steeple, the needlepoint poking out of the earth like a modern sculpture. A landslide from the eruption must have buried most of the original town. Surrounding the plaza are several ugly office blocks. A few guards patrol the streets, but otherwise the compound is quiet since the other wardens are asleep and the inmates are in Primus-Two or Three.

"Which one's the registration building?" Beetle asks in a hushed voice.

We look about. Behind us the Sentry guards are starting to bring the prisoners up the avenue. There are horrified sobs from the prisoners as they see the crucifixes. To our right is a large three-story building. The lights are on in one of the rooms on the ground floor.

"That must be it," Natalie says.

We hurry down the alleyway next to building, dumping the laundry bags along the way. At the back of the building is a large parking lot, filled with military trucks. Some have the numeral 2 printed on the side, others 3, which I'm guessing represents the town the prisoners will be taken to after they've been registered. There don't appear to be any drivers in the trucks— they must be inside, keeping out of the cold, until it's time to drive the prisoners to their new homes. Most of the lights in the building are off. We peer through the windows, searching for the records room. Day stops outside one of the windows.

"This room has loads of filing cabinets in it," she whispers.

I carefully open the window and we climb through. There's a long com-desk in the center of the room. I turn it on, but am immediately asked to enter a password. I switch the com-desk off. We'll have to do this the old-fashioned way. I force open one of the locked drawers to find stacks of manila files inside, in alphabetical order. There are thousands of them, which surprises me, considering the Tenth has officially been operational only since the ballot a few weeks ago. Purian Rose must have secretly opened the camp early.

I open up one of the documents. Inside is a photograph of a prisoner—a Darkling woman called Thelma Grieves, thirty-two years old, Nordin species, prisoner number 0000458712, laboratory 6, Primus-Three. The word DECEASED is printed in large red letters across the document. I put the file back and turn to the others.

"We're looking for Lucinda Coombs and Yolanda Theroux—"

"Fillion," Elijah corrects. "Mom was my dad's mistress, not wife. I only took his surname because it's tradition in my culture."

None of us know what Kieran's surname is, so we can't search for him.

"We should look for Amy too," Day says, referring to our friend Amy Jones. "I think the Sentry took her here, after they killed Stuart."

Beetle helps me search the C–D filing cabinets for Lucinda's file, Natalie and Elijah take the E–F cabinets, and Acelot and Day look for Amy's file in the I–J drawers. I have no trouble seeing in the moonlight, but the others are clearly struggling to read the files.

Day lets out a frustrated sigh. "I can't find Amy listed anywhere."

"That's a good thing, right?" Natalie says. "Maybe she escaped?"

Beetle glances at me. *Or maybe Amy died before she got here.*

The sound of footsteps approaches the door and everyone freezes. Beetle reaches for his gun and softly cocks the hammer, pointing it toward the door. I wait, my heart counting the seconds: one, two, three, four. The guard walks past the door. I exhale. We keep searching.

"Here," Natalie says in an urgent whisper, passing a file to Elijah.

"That's Mom!" he says. "She's being held in laboratory seven, in Primus-Three."

Natalie starts closing the filing cabinet, then stops. A crease forms between her brows. She opens the drawer again and pulls out a document.

"Aha!" Beetle says next to me, drawing my attention. He's holding a manila file. "Lucinda Coombs, laboratory seven, Primus-Three."

There's a good possibility Kieran's been sent there too. It's a relief to know they're still alive, although if they're in the science laboratories in Primus-Three, they won't be for long.

"Let's go," I whisper, reaching out my hand toward Natalie.

She's still holding the document, her face ashen. Tears brim in her blue eyes.

"What is it?" I say.

"I'm so sorry," she whispers, passing the file to me.

I open it up. A photo of a gray-haired, middle-aged man stares up at me. The word DECEASED is written across the document. I stagger back, dropping the file to the floor.

The man in the photograph is my dad.

14.

NATALIE

ASH SINKS TO HIS KNEES, the contents of his father's file scattered across the floor in front of him. He clamps his hands over his mouth, trying to contain the howl threatening to escape his lips, knowing he can't make a noise, not here, not now. I know what he's feeling; it's taking all my willpower to hold back the scream that's crawling up my throat like a spider.

I kneel down, crushing the papers beneath my knees, and draw him into my arms. He buries his face into my hair and lets out a pained wail, unable to hold it in any longer, the sound muffled by my curls. He clings to me with desperate fingers, his whole body shuddering with grief.

"I'm so sorry," I whisper over and over, tears spilling down my cheeks.

Beetle picks up the fallen photograph and his face pales. "It's his dad," he murmurs.

Day gasps.

"God," Acelot mutters.

From what I read on the cover sheet, Harold was captured

two weeks ago and taken to one of the laboratories in Primus-Three. He died three days ago from total organ failure. Whatever experiments they were doing to him must've been horrific to have caused all his organs to shut down. *What are they doing here?*

Outside the open window a truck engine revs. The Sentry guards are returning to their vehicles in the parking lot, ready to transport the first batch of prisoners to their barracks.

"We need to leave," Elijah says quietly.

I don't know how we're going to get Ash out of here. I'm not sure he can stand.

"Ash?" I whisper, stroking his silken hair. "Are you going to be able to do this? Destiny can come and get us."

He takes a deep breath, his cheeks glistening with tears. "I need to get my aunt."

Ash gets up and takes the photograph from Day. He tucks it into his pants pocket and climbs out of the window. I hurriedly gather the loose papers on the floor and shove them into the nearest cabinet, and then we follow him. Ash is waiting for us in the alley. About fifty feet away, the back door of the registration office opens and the first prisoners are escorted across the parking lot by several armed guards, to an awaiting truck marked with a numeral 2 at the opposite end of the lot.

"We need to get on one of those trucks." Beetle points to the vehicles nearest to us marked with a 3.

"How will we get on?" Day whispers.

A moment later a plump, middle-aged Sentry guard exits the registration office and strolls over to one of the trucks, twirling the keys around his left index finger while he uses his other hand to smoke a cigarette. He's whistling a jolly tune under his breath. We slink back into the shadows so he doesn't spot us. The chubby guard approaches one of the black vehicles, walking around to the driver's side, which is closest to us.

Before I realize what's happening, Ash confidently strides over to the man. My heart leaps into my mouth. *What's he doing!* Ash taps the guard on the shoulder.

"Got a light?" he says.

The chubby guard turns, smiling. "Sure."

The smile drops off the man's lips. Before he can shout for help, Ash clamps a hand over the man's mouth and pushes him against the side of the truck. He sinks his fangs into the guard's neck. The man struggles against Ash, dropping the keys in the process, but he's no match for a twin-blood. I run over to them and grab Ash's arm, pulling him away from the man before he kills him. Blood oozes out of the puncture wounds on the man's neck, making his black shirt wet like oil. His brown eyes are glazed over from the Haze.

Ash furiously wipes the blood from his lips. "Why did you pull me away?"

"Because it's murder," I say. "I know you're angry; I am too. But you're not a killer."

He lowers his eyes.

The others hurry over to us and lift the drugged man into the back of the truck while Acelot scoops the keys off the ground. He climbs into the driver's seat and starts the engine. Ash and I climb into the back of the truck with the others, and take our seats just as the vehicle lurches forward.

"Any ideas which direction I should head in?" Acelot calls over his shoulder.

"Head east," I say, recalling the location of Primus-Three

from the map of the Tenth we were shown back in Black City, all those weeks ago.

I check out the window to see if anyone is chasing after us, but no one is. I sink back into the seat and take Ash's hand. He shuts his eyes as Acelot drives us to Primus-Three.

The journey takes a few hours, and the mountain roads are bumpy and uneven. The Tenth is enormous, stretching on for hundreds of miles. From our altitude I can see the thin line of the Boundary Wall snaking through the forests below us, cutting off the detention camp from the rest of Mountain Wolf State. Occasionally I notice a house peeping out through the trees. I'm sure most of the former residents of this area were evacuated or rounded up and executed before the Boundary Wall went up, but the area is so vast—the size of a small state— that it's possible a few people slipped through the net and are still living here, unable to escape.

To our left is Mount Alba, its gray, ash-covered slopes stark against the misty yellow skies of dawn. You can still make out the original tracks of the landslides that devastated the area after the eruption, although much of the base of the volcano, where we are now, is lush with vegetation. A lot of the area is covered in Carrow trees, with their famous flame-colored, star-shaped leaves, so the whole area looks like it is on fire.

Elijah is up front with Acelot, chatting to his brother to keep him awake, while Beetle is lounged across one of the benches, snoring loudly. Beside him, Day has just woken up. She rolls her shoulders and head, trying to loosen her stiff muscles.

Lying on one of the seats is the chubby Sentry guard Ash attacked last night. His skin has a nasty gray hue to it, and I don't need to check his pulse to know he's dead. Ash must've injected him with too much Haze. I don't feel any pity for the man, just sad that Ash will have to carry this burden around with him for the rest of his life. Maybe I'm reading too much into it. Maybe Ash won't care. The man drove prisoners just like Ash's father to Primus-Three to be executed. It might be a cold thing to think, but he got what he deserved.

Ash is fast asleep, his head resting on my lap. I stroke his hair, trying not to cry, heartbroken over Harold's death and the knowledge that Ash is alone in this world. Well, maybe not entirely. He has me. I'll take care of him now.

Day pads over to us, sitting down on the seat in front of me. Her usually immaculate black hair is frizzy and tangled from sleep. She wipes her tired eyes, then puts on her glasses. They immediately slide down her nose.

"How's he doing?" she whispers, pushing them back up.

"Not too good," I admit, feeling the echo of his aching heart inside me.

"I'm surprised Harold's capture wasn't announced on the news," Day says.

"The guards mustn't have recognized the name. Harold hasn't been in the papers much, and he's human, not Darkling—so the connection to Ash isn't immediately apparent—otherwise I'm sure it would have been."

Day chews on her bottom lip. "Do you think Logan and Martha are here too?"

I hadn't even considered it, but Sigur's second-in-command, Logan, and my old housemaid Martha were traveling with Harold. Guilt rips through me that I hadn't thought to look for their files back in Primus-One. If they are here, there's a small chance they're still alive, but if they're being experimented on, death might be the preferable option.

"Do you think Amy's alive?" I ask.

Day shakes her head and her eyes glisten. She gazes out of the truck window, studying Mount Alba to our left. "It's a weird place for the Four Kingdoms to hide the Ora, don't you think?" she says, referring to the terrorist organization led by Lucinda.

I shrug. "Not really. It's remote, they know the area, and it's relatively uninhabited."

"Yeah, but it's also an active volcano," she says. "It's not the best place to store weaponized yellowpox. Or to build a detention camp, for that matter."

"Well, I'm presuming it's the only place he could build the camp without rousing too much suspicion, since the area was pretty much uninhabited. Plus, I doubt he cares if prisoners all get wiped out if there is another eruption," I say. "And maybe Elijah got it wrong. Perhaps the Ora isn't yellowpox."

"Then what is it?"

"I have no idea," I say tiredly.

We assumed the Ora was yellowpox, based on old research Elijah found at his mom's laboratory. She's a geneticist, specializing in xenotransplantation—the transplantation of cells or organs from one species to another—but during the first war she worked with the Four Kingdoms in creating weaponized viruses, which would attack only people with certain genes. She had been developing a strain of yellowpox designed to target humans with the V-gene—the gene that helps humans sense Darklings. All the Trackers have it. However, after the Four Kingdoms attempted to poison Black City's water supply, Lucinda was arrested and Yolanda went into hiding, so she never got to finish her work. It's our belief they hid the yellowpox in a secret base on Mount Alba, and have come looking for it so they can finish what they started. A wave of tiredness crashes over me and I wipe my brow. It's covered in a faint sheen of sweat. My skin feels hot, feverish.

Day narrows her eyes at me. "How are you feeling, kiddo?"

"Like I've got the Wrath. Which reminds me . . ." I take the black syringe case out of my jacket pocket, careful not to wake Ash. Day helps me with the injections, which isn't easy when the truck is rocking so much on the bumpy road, but I don't know when I'll get another chance to do this today. The truck hits a pothole just as I put the syringes away, and the boys jerk awake. Beetle bolts upright, the side of his face creased from lying on his jacket, while Ash runs a weary hand over his face.

"Guys, we're here," Acelot says from the front seat.

We approach another Boundary Wall, which surrounds Primus-Three. This one is painted green to blend in with the vegetation. Beetle looks out the back window. From our vantage point we can see for miles down the bending road.

"There are some trucks farther down the mountain," he says. "We've probably got thirty minutes, tops, before they get here."

Acelot slows the truck down as we approach a set of iron gates. They immediately swing open, and we drive along a winding mountain road for a few miles before reaching the heart of Primus-Three. There are eight Cinderstone buildings surrounding an enormous courtyard, which is easily twenty times larger than the plaza in Black City. The medical facilities all look the same: four stories high, flat roofed, with a wide entrance door with a number painted on the front. A road runs around the outside of the buildings.

"Lab seven is over there." Elijah points to the building to our right.

"Bring the truck around the back, mate," Beetle says to Acelot.

He steers the vehicle to the right and follows the tree-lined road around the back of the buildings. There's very little traffic on the road, but it is early. However, I imagine the camp will wake up soon, as the scientists prepare to meet the new arrivals.

Acelot parks the truck close to the back doors of laboratory seven, so we can make a quick escape. It shouldn't rouse too much suspicion, as I see a few other vehicles parked outside one of the other laboratories farther down the road. We hurry off the truck and head to the back door, which has a large numeral 7 painted on it in white. Elijah tests the handle. It's locked. Day points to the keycard scanner mounted on the wall beside the door. I should've figured the laboratories would have tighter security on them than the registration office. Knowing the Sentry, they're developing all sorts of biological weapons in here, similar to the C18 Wrath virus, so the last thing they want is that leaking out into the main population and killing everyone.

"Hold on," Beetle says, jogging back to the truck. He returns a moment later, carrying a keycard. He must have taken it off the dead guard. "I figure he'll have security clearance, since he was bringing the prisoners here." We cross our fingers as he swipes the card through the scanner, and the light flickers green. The door swings open. *Yes!* Beetle draws his gun and enters the building, checking to see if the coast is clear, before the rest of us go inside. Ash stays close to me, his hand protectively on my back.

The building is stark and white, like the hospital back at the

Sentry rebel base in Gallium. Thinking about it makes my insides squirm, wondering what my parents are doing right now. We've been gone twenty-four hours; they must be going crazy with worry. Have they sent a search party after us? I hope not. It's bad enough that I talked Destiny into helping us; I don't want to drag more of the Sentry rebels into this.

"Fragg," Ash mutters under his breath. He points to a security camera at the far end of the hall. It's slowly rotating toward us.

"Leave it to me," Acelot says, walking over to an access panel built into the glossy white wall. It's been screwed shut. "Elijah, give me a hand."

The brothers grit their teeth as they pry the panel off the wall, exposing a network of fuses and wires. The camera keeps turning. It's almost on us. *Come on, come on!* Acelot carefully studies the wires, mutters a prayer and yanks out the blue ones. The camera at the far end of the hall stops moving. He lets out a relieved sigh, then gives a crooked smile.

"I knew they were the right ones," he says unconvincingly. "That should have knocked out all the cameras in this building."

"Let's get going," I say. We probably only have five minutes, ten tops, before they discover why the cameras are out of action and come looking for us.

We quietly walk down the empty corridors. I peer through the glass doors as we pass by. All the rooms on this floor are high-tech laboratories, with gleaming white floors and stainless-steel furniture. In one lab a huge glass-fronted refrigerator runs down the length of one wall. It contains hundreds of vials filled with a shimmering milky fluid. It reminds me of Golden Haze, except it has a silvery hue to it, rather than gold. There are biohazard signs on each door, along with notices warning people to wear their masks "AT ALL TIMES!"

"Let's go up one floor," Elijah says. "They're not down here."

We find the stairwell and go up to the second floor. The rooms up here have solid doors, with just a small viewing window in them. I glance through one of them. The entire back wall is filled with cages crammed with white mice. I shudder. We keep going down the hallway, me leading the way, checking each room as we pass. It's more of the same—mice, rats, rabbits. Bizarrely, one room is filled with caged trees. I round the corner and immediately freeze.

A startled woman dressed in a white lab coat blinks back at me. A faint crease forms between her groomed brows as the others enter the corridor. Her brown eyes flick from me to Ash, and recognition registers on her face. There's no time to think. I draw my gun and squeeze the trigger. The bullet hits the woman in the chest. She gazes down at the red stain blossoming on her white coat, then back up at me. Her mouth is still in a surprised O shape as she hits the floor.

"Oh God . . . ," I gasp, the gun slipping through my fingers. It clatters to the ground. "Oh God . . . oh God . . . oh—" The word gets stuck in my throat as it constricts with panic. I can't breathe. *I killed her.* I shot an unarmed woman. My eyes snag on the gold band on her left hand. I killed an unarmed, married woman. She had a husband, maybe even children, and I—*oh God, oh God, oh God.* Ash pulls me into his arms, holding me against him.

"You had to do it," Ash says into my hair. "She would've alerted the others."

I nod faintly, unable to tear my eyes away from the woman. Her brown hair is fanned around her pretty, slim face. She has deep laughter lines by her pale lips, even though she's probably only in her thirties. She must have smiled a lot. *I had to do it.*

Beetle and Elijah hurry over to the woman and grab her body while Ash picks up my gun, thrusting it back into my hand. My skin feels scorched, like it's holding fire rather than cold steel, and it takes all my strength not to toss it away. Instead, I tuck the gun into my belt.

The boys drag the woman's body to the nearest room—the one with the caged trees in it—and use her security pass to open the door. We follow them inside and quickly close the door behind us. The room is dimly lit and filled with row upon row of cages, each ten feet square, their walls made from a fine wire mesh. Inside each cage is a fully grown Carrow tree, although there's something odd about them. Their bark is a silvery-blue color.

"Put her over there," Acelot says, gesturing to the dark corner behind one of the cages.

Beetle and Elijah haul her body through the forest of caged trees and dump it against the far wall. Her head flops forward, her hair cascading in front of her face. Her lab coat is soaked in blood. I must've hit her directly in the heart to cause that much bleeding. Ash takes my hand, and I look up at him. He's staring at the bloodstain on the woman's jacket, his black eyes filled with longing.

"This place is creepy," Acelot says, glancing around the room.

I release Ash's hand and approach one of the cages. I peer through the wire mesh. There doesn't appear to be anything inside the enclosure other than the Carrow tree. That's weird. Why are the Sentry growing trees inside these cages?

The bark on the tree trunk suddenly ripples. I blink. *What?* I tap the wire meshing, and then step back in fright as hundreds of butterflies swarm into the air, surrounding the tree in a cloud of silvery blue. I know some butterfly species eat tree sap, so that must be why there are so many Carrow trees here. The insects remind me of the butterfly medals I saw the Tin Men wearing in Gallium. One word suddenly pops into my head. *Wings.*

15.

EDMUND

DAWN BREAKS ON THE HORIZON just beyond the mountain, casting a golden hue over the forest so that the leaves look like flames flickering out of the earth. It's the beginning of a beautiful day, but it's wasted on the people of Amber Hills.

The village is silent with grief from last night's violence. All the doors are shut, and the curtains drawn although no one is asleep. I doubt anyone will sleep for days after what happened. The only people up and about are the Guild, plus Patrick, Harriet, Drew and me. We're congregated in the town square by the wooden cross.

Grandfather quietly consoles Eric Cranfield's dad—a thin, handsome man, with long red sideburns and neat mustache. His eggshell-blue eyes are puffy and rimmed red from crying all night. His son's dead body is resting beside Catherine's in the nave of the church, both swaddled in white cloth.

Next to him are Mr. O'Malley and his children, Harriet and Drew. Like their father, they're both bright eyed and alert, their blond hair washed, their faces scrubbed. Harriet has a few scratches on her face from the fight last night, but Drew came out unscathed. Patrick is beside them. His face is ashen and drawn, highlighting the dark purple bruise down the right side of his face where I thumped him last night. He's wearing his hunting outfit: brown leather pants, white shirt and green frock coat. His left hand is thrust into his jacket pocket, and he appears to be clutching something, but I can't tell what it is. He slides a cold look at me, his eyes glistening. I glance away.

Standing apart from the group is his father, Mr. Langdon. His shoulders are slumped as they carry the burden of his sorrow, and I know how he feels. Just thinking about Catherine makes the air heavy, pressing down on me until I'm certain I'll crumple under the weight of it. Every time I shut my eyes, all I can see is the look on her face as Grandfather snapped her neck. I dig my fingers into my thighs, focusing on the pain as I try to hold myself together. But no matter how hard I try, the truth keeps pulling at the threads. *I killed my best friend.* It may not have been me who broke her neck, but it may as well have been. My desire, my hunger, my *impurity* led to her death. Not only that, but I made my grandfather a murderer so he could protect me. I destroyed two souls in one night.

Mr. Langdon strolls over to me. "Thank you for joining us on the hunt, Edmund. Catherine—" His voice breaks on her name. "My daughter was very fond of you."

Guilt twists in my gut. I glance at Grandfather.

"We should go, Father," Patrick says, sliding another cold look in my direction.

Mr. Langdon turns to Mr. Cranfield. "I promise we'll bring back Alaric Bane's head for what his pack did to Eric and my little girl."

"Thank you," Mr. Cranfield says hoarsely.

The Guild members say their farewells and return to their

homes. Only Mr. Langdon, Patrick, the O'Malley siblings and I will be going into the forest to hunt the Lupines, leaving the others to protect the town.

"Good hunting," Grandfather says, squeezing my shoulder. It appears to be a reassuring gesture, but I know what it really is: a warning. He wants me to find the Howler girl, Ulrika, and kill her before anyone discovers the truth about what happened to Catherine. Her murder would have been for nothing if we're caught.

Patrick walks around the group as we check our supplies. We each have enough food and water to last us three days, a rifle, a crossbow and a silver dagger. My fingers fumble as I count out my bullets. Harriet lets out an impatient huff.

"Why does Edmund have to come with us?" she complains to Patrick in a loud whisper. "Can't we just ditch him at the gate?"

"If the freak wants to get eaten by a Howler, I'm not going to stop him," Patrick replies.

I don't say anything, but Mr. Langdon gives me an apologetic look. We pick up our supplies and head to the boundary gates. A thrill of anticipation shivers through me. I've never left the town, and now I'm going into the forest to hunt bloodthirsty Howlers, with a group of people who would happily see me dead. I'm starting to wonder if I'm their bait.

Patrick unlocks the heavy iron gates and we step into the forest. Dawn turns to night as darkness descends over us. Only a few rays of dappled sunlight manage to penetrate the treetops, casting long black shadows across the mossy earth, which dance every time the cool wind stirs the Carrow leaves. The place is unquestionably creepy. I let out a short, nervous breath when something dark flashes between the trees. Harriet laughs.

"Relax, it's just a deer. The Howlers live up on the Claw," she says, gesturing toward the volcano, Mount Alba. "The most dangerous thing down here is Drew."

He chuckles, throwing his dagger at a nearby tree, pinning a squirrel to it. I grimace as he yanks the blade out of the dead rodent and tosses it to me.

"They taste good. Like chicken," he says.

I shove the bleeding animal carcass into my bag, trying to ignore my aching thirst at the scent of the blood. I don't like to drink animal blood, as it's very sour, but desperate times call for desperate measures, and I'm going to get hungry after three days hiking in the woods.

Mr. Langdon stays by my side while the others trek on ahead, expertly navigating through the ferns and overgrown vegetation. He's trying to be kind by staying with me, but it's the last thing I need. I have to find Ulrika and silence her. My hand tightens around the hilt of my dagger.

"Where exactly is the Lupine village?" I ask too loudly, making an animal scurry into the undergrowth. Patrick throws me an impatient look over his shoulder.

"We don't know," Mr. Langdon replies. "Somewhere up on the Claw. Watch it!"

Mr. Langdon shoves me, and I fall to the forest floor with a heavy thud. Harriet and Drew laugh. Mr. Langdon points toward a wire snare on the ground, partially hidden beneath some dead leaves. I notice the other end of the wire is tied to a branch about twelve feet overhead.

"Spring trap," he says. "If you'd stepped on it, you'd be hanging upside down from that tree by now."

Patrick walks over to us and helps me to my feet in an

uncharacteristically friendly gesture. "The Lupines have snares all over the forest to trap deer, so watch where you put your feet, moron."

"Thanks," I mumble, glancing up at the branch above us. "Seems a bit extreme, hanging a deer several meters off the ground."

Patrick shrugs. "It keeps the catch away from other predators."

I look at the snare again, shuddering slightly. If I were out here on my own, I'd be a dead man. The Lupines' main food source might be venison, but they will take the occasional human—as proved over the past six weeks—especially if that human is stupid enough to walk straight into their traps.

Harriet and Drew smirk at me before turning their backs, and continue hiking through the forest. I sigh, dusting myself off, and follow them. A cold wind rustles the leaves, which make a strange whispering sound as the breeze passes over them. I pluck one of the orange leaves off a tree, noticing a damaged white cocoon on it. Inside is a half-formed Night Whisper, its body deformed like mine.

Mr. Langdon takes the leaf from me and turns it over. On the underside are some very thin, tubelike veins. It strikes me that I've never properly inspected the leaves of a Carrow tree before, even though we have them in our garden.

"That's what causes the trees to talk," he explains, pointing to the tubes. "The wind blows through them, making that whispering noise." He lets go of the leaf and it flutters to the moist ground. "Your mother used to love the sound of the trees when we came out here."

My eyes widen. "You came into the forest with my mom?"

He nods, and we keep following the trail marked out for us

by Patrick and the others. They're a hundred feet ahead of us, so they can't hear our conversation.

"Cassie and I used to sneak out here after your grandfather went to bed," he says. I remember Catherine telling me her dad and my mom used to date as teens, so I can imagine what they were getting up to. *Gross.* "She loved it out here. She found life in Amber Hills stifling, trapped within those stone walls, but out here there was freedom and adventure." He sighs, looking at me. "I never shared her enthusiasm for coming into the forest, though. Back in those days, this place was crawling with Darklings."

A shiver trickles down my spine as he holds my gaze. I look away, terrified he'll see through me and discover the secret lurking in the silent space where my heart should be beating.

"Those were dangerous times, Edmund. Your mother wasn't afraid, though." He shakes his head. "She didn't think the Darklings were demons. Cassie wasn't a follower of the faith."

"*What?*" I touch the circular pendant around my neck—a symbol of our faith. My mom wasn't a believer? But she was the minister's daughter; how could she not have faith? I frown. I've heard a lot of terrible rumors about my mom this week: that she was crazy, that she hanged herself and now this? I don't know why it bothers me so much, but the fact that she wasn't a believer . . . well, I'm *disappointed.* My religion has given me so much strength; it's kept me on a true path all these years. I think about Catherine and the sweet taste of her blood on my tongue, and my grip tightens around the pendant. *I won't ever do that again.*

"I couldn't marry a girl who didn't have faith, so we parted ways," Mr. Langdon says.

Ah. So that's how he ended up with Mrs. Langdon? She *was* his second choice.

"I'm sorry," I murmur.

Mr. Langdon shrugs. "Sarah has been a good wife to me, and we have . . . *had* . . . two beautiful children." A sob escapes his lips, taking me by surprise.

I turn away, unable to stand looking at his grief when I'm the cause of it. Patrick snatches a look over his shoulder and notices his father crying. Patrick and the O'Malley siblings race over to us, their feet crashing through the undergrowth.

"What the hell did you say?" Patrick yells at me.

"Nothing!" I reply.

Patrick throws me a hate-filled look before slinging an arm around his father's waist to support him as we continue our hike through the forest toward the Claw. It's much farther away than I realized, and by lunchtime we're still a few miles away from the mountain. I don't mind. The trees, which I once found sinister, now seem beautiful in their dark, unique way. My feet easily navigate the uneven ground, barely snapping a twig. Soon I'm walking ahead of the others. I look back and catch Harriet watching me with grudging admiration.

Somewhere to my right I can hear the roar of a waterfall. I check my canteen. It's empty. I follow the sound of the rushing water until I find a natural pool nestled among the foliage. I'm about to dip my canteen into the water when I catch a whiff of rotten eggs. I scrunch up my nose. It seems to be coming from the pool.

Drew ambles toward me and pinches his nose. "Geez, Edmund, was that you?"

I flush. "It's the water."

Drew smirks. "Sure."

"I think sulfuric gas is leaking into it," I murmur.

"Don't stress about it; the volcano's been dormant for centuries," Drew says.

"Why don't we rest for a while?" Mr. Langdon says, sitting down on the ground.

I don't object. My feet are aching and I'm exhausted from the hike. The others sit down beside the pool while Patrick collects some wood and starts a fire. Harriet cooks some tins of beans over the flames, and everyone heartily tucks into their lunch. I poke my beans around the tin, pretending to eat them. When no one's looking, I toss the food into the nearby foliage.

I pat my stomach, acting like I'm full. Patrick narrows his eyes at me, and doubt starts to niggle at my insides like an itch I can't scratch. Does he suspect what I am? He knows I wear dentures; has he worked out why?

"I'm going to grab an hour's shut-eye, if that's all right," Drew says.

"I'll keep watch," I say.

Harriet snorts, but Mr. Langdon gives me a sleepy smile. "Thank you, Edmund."

"Try not to let anyone get killed this time, okay?" Harriet replies, referring to Mrs. Hope.

I glower at her. Patrick sits down and leans against a tree while the others lie down on the ground beside the fire, using their bags as a pillow. I take a pew on a rock near the waterfall and check my rifle to make sure it's loaded. Patrick silently watches me as the others sleep.

"Your grandfather said a Lupine killed Catherine," Patrick says.

My grip tightens around the gun. I look up, trying not to let my panic show.

"That's what he told me too," I reply.

"So you weren't there when it happened?"

Yes. "No."

He narrows his eyes. "Then where were you?"

I swallow. "At home. I ran home the moment the fighting broke out. I was scared."

Patrick tilts his head, judging whether to believe me or not. "The funny thing is, I spoke to the funeral director this morning and he told me the *weirdest* thing. Apparently, there were bite marks on Catherine's neck."

I clench my hands to stop them from shaking. "The Howler must have done that."

"That's what I said," Patrick replies. "But here's the weird bit: he said the marks looked human. Isn't that strange?"

"Yeah, it's pretty strange."

Patrick holds my gaze for a long, agonizing moment. "I guess he was wrong, though. I mean, why would anyone bite Catherine?"

He gives me a chilling smile, then shuts his eyes. As soon as he's asleep, I take a few deep, ragged breaths, trying to force my panic aside. There's no way he can tie me to Catherine's death; there were no witnesses. *Other than Ulrika.* Reassured by this fact, I start to calm down. I stare at the fire, watching the amber flames dance, finding it soothing. *He has nothing on me; it's going to be fine.* The hypnotic movement makes my lids begin to droop . . .

I start awake. Fragg! How long was I asleep? It felt like seconds, but the flames have died out, and only the glowing embers remain. Mr. Langdon and the others are breathing heavily, deep in sleep. The forest is colder than before, suggesting it's late in the afternoon. We've been asleep for hours. Thank His Mighty everyone is all right. I'd never forgive myself if someone else got killed on my watch. I get up and check our perimeter, wondering what woke me. Then I hear it. *A voice.*

"Kieran!" a girl calls out from the forest, somewhere to my left.

Pain scrunches up in my chest and I wince. Ahh! *What the hell?* It's just like the cramp I felt the other night, when Mrs. Hope was snatched. Not now! I roughly rub my chest, trying to force the pain aside as I grab my rifle. The sensible thing to do would be to stay here and wake Mr. Langdon, but something compels me to follow the voice, like a siren's call. I take the safety off my gun and stalk into woods, ignoring my aching chest. The light instantly dims as I creep through the trees, keeping my footsteps light.

"Kieran?" the girl urgently calls again. There's something familiar about her voice, and yet I'm pretty sure I've never heard it before. "Kieran, where are you?"

My grip tightens around the rifle as I walk farther up the mountain slope, toward the voice. The girl has to be a Lupine, since no one else lives up here. We must be closer to their village than we realized. I pad through the forest, my nerves mounting. Up ahead I notice a clearing between the Carrow trees. A strange tugging sensation pulls at my chest, telling me to go in that direction. I head toward the clearing, despite the voice screaming inside my head to turn back and get Mr. Langdon.

"Kieran! There you are," the girl says from the clearing up ahead. "What on earth are you doing out here with *them*?"

"Relax, T," the boy replies. "Luci and Annora are my friends."

"If your cousin finds out, she'll skin you alive," the girl says.

"I'd like to see Ulrika try," Kieran scoffs. "You won't tell her, though, will you?"

I creep toward the clearing, fear pulsing through me. The pain in my chest worsens with every footstep, and I grit my teeth, trying to force it aside.

"Oh . . . !" The girl gasps.

"You okay?" Kieran says.

"Yes . . . yes, I'm fine. It's nothing."

"Hey, how did you know I was here?" Kieran says. "Were you stalking me? Oh my God, do you have a crush on me or something, T? I *knew* it."

"Ha! In your dreams, dogbreath," a different girl drawls.

"I was *worried* about you," the first girl explains to Kieran. "It's not safe out here. Now I realize why you snuck off without telling anyone. How do you even know these girls?"

I reach the clearing. Through the foliage I see the silhouette of a girl—she's tall, easily six feet, and slim with a long mane of hair. Definitely Lupine. Her back is turned to me.

"I met them a few weeks ago," Kieran replies. "You can trust them, I swear. Just don't tell Ulrika, okay? She won't understand."

I raise my gun, take a step and—

"Argh!" I yell out in surprise as something snaps around my ankle and the world spins upside down. My rifle slips through my fingers and lands on the earth six feet below me. Somewhere in the back of my mind, I realize I've stepped into a spring trap, but it's hard to think straight as pain rips through my ankle and chest, leaving me gasping for breath.

There's a snap of twigs as footsteps pad over to me.

"Don't kill me!" I screw my eyes shut and say a silent prayer.

I flinch as the girl's sweet breath spills over my face. A thrill of pleasure ripples through my body, despite my terror.

"Give me one good reason not to," the girl says, placing a knife against my neck.

I open my eyes. "I—" My words get lost on my lips.

A pair of angry silver eyes glares back at me. They're framed with white lashes that match the girl's snowy skin. Despite the fact that I'm looking at her upside down, I can tell she's beautiful—a heart-shaped face, with full lips and rose-blushed cheeks. We hold each other's gaze for a long moment, neither of us talking. I'm barely breathing. A crease forms in the girl's brow as the expression in her eyes gradually shifts from anger to confusion to . . . something else. Recognition? She blinks, breaking the connection.

"Do I know you?" she says.

"I don't think so." It feels like we've met before, but surely I'd remember *her*. My Adam's apple bobs nervously in my throat, causing the stubble on my neck to scratch against the girl's blade. "I'm Edmund. What's your name?"

"What are you doing here, *Edmund*?" She presses the knife harder against my skin.

"Hunting deer," I squeak. "I got lost."

She narrows her eyes, trying to decide if she believes me or not. Finally, she sighs and lowers the knife from my throat, then slashes the wire tying me to the tree. I fall to the earth with a heavy thump. The Lupine tucks the knife into her belt and gazes down at me.

"It's Theora," she says. "My name's Theora."

16.

EDMUND

"THEORA," I SAY QUIETLY, liking how the word sounds on my lips. "That's a pretty name."

She blushes slightly. "Thanks."

Now that I'm not hanging upside down, I can get a better look at her. She's wearing a floaty yellow dress, strapped at the waist with a chunky belt, and a hunting jacket. Her gray eyes flicker toward something on the ground. I follow her gaze. My gun! Before I can move, she quickly grabs the rifle and takes a cautious step back, keeping her eyes trained on me as I stand up. I should be afraid, but I'm not. In fact, I feel weirdly *excited,* like there are these little shivers of electricity rushing through my veins.

She holds my gaze, her expression an odd mixture of curiosity and anger. It's clear she's just as intrigued by me as I am with her. I've never seen anyone like Theora before. She's obviously a Lupine, but the more I study her, the more irregularities I notice. Her nose is slimmer than a normal Lupine's, her face is rounder, and her eyes are almond shaped. She looks . . . well, she looks a little bit like *me.*

"Thanks for cutting me down," I finally say.

Her brow creases, as though she's wondering why she did it. "I didn't want us getting blamed if you got eaten by a Darkling," she eventually replies.

"We wouldn't have eaten him," a girl says to my right.

I flinch, startled at the sound of the girl's voice. I'd forgotten there were other people here, I was so fixated on Theora. I turn to look at the girl.

If I had a heartbeat, it would've stopped.

Standing a few meters away are a boy and two girls. The Lupine boy, who I presume is Kieran, is about fourteen or fifteen years old, based on his boyish features, although he's very tall. He has a silver streak through his white mane. But it's not the boy who's turned my blood to ice; it's the two girls next to him. The older of the two girls, who looks a year or so older than Kieran, is wearing a green dress, and the younger girl—who is holding Kieran's hand—is wearing boys' pants and a gray top. They both have pale skin, rippling black hair and glimmering eyes the color of onyx. I let out a shaky breath.

Darklings.

A dizzying mixture of emotions races through me all at once; it's hard to grab hold of one and stick with it. It's thrilling to finally meet some of my own kind, but I've been raised to not trust these *demons,* and rightfully so after one of their kind raped my mom.

"How long have they been back?" I growl.

Kieran steps protectively in front of the two Darkling girls. The younger of the two girls—the one wearing the pants and gray top—glares defiantly at me from behind him.

"A little over six weeks," Theora answers.

Six weeks? That's how long the Lupines have been snatching people from our village. It can't be a coincidence.

"What's going on?" I say. "Why are you trying to start a war between our species?"

"We're not. We're trying to *keep* the peace," Theora explains. "I know it sounds like a contradiction, but you don't understand. Icarus is back."

Dread creeps over me. *Icarus?* Why does that name sound familiar? Then it comes to me. He was the Darkling who killed dozens of our people during the Misery.

"When Icarus came back, he started snatching our people to feed on," Theora explains. "There are so few of us left, Edmund, we had to do something—"

"So you offered him *our* people instead?" I can imagine Icarus was delighted with this bargain—from everything Grandfather's told me about the Darklings and what I know from my own . . . *desires*, they prefer human blood over all others, although they will drink Lupine blood at a push.

"We only took the weak and the sick ones, like that old woman I snatched—"

"It was you who took Mrs. Hope that night?" I say.

Theora nods. "We gave them to Icarus as a gesture of goodwill," Theora says. "So far it's kept him happy. He hasn't attacked your town or ours."

That explains why Mrs. Hope was left out on a rock like a sacrificial lamb, because that's exactly what she was.

"Why was Ulrika's sister found with Mrs. Hope's body?" I think about the Lupine girl we drowned.

Theora lowers her pale lashes. "She was guarding it, until Icarus turned up."

I glance at the two Darklings, feeling a surge of anger. The older of the two girls, the one in the green dress, shrinks back, clearly frightened of me. Her angular face has an almost impish quality to it, with a small mouth and narrow chin.

I look back at Theora. "Why didn't you just come to us and tell us all this?"

"We did," she says. "The minister gave us permission to take the victims, as long as we kept Icarus's return a secret from the villagers; he thought it would cause unnecessary panic. That's why he made us snatch the victims at night; he wanted to make sure the villagers blamed us for the kidnappings, so they didn't suspect Icarus had returned." Theora sighs a little. "We thought the rest of the Guild was aware of this arrangement. But they killed Naomi, so I guess not."

I rake a hand through my hair. My *grandfather* was behind the kidnappings? He's been lying to me, to everyone, including the Guild! Why keep Icarus's return a secret from *them*? I ball my hands into fists. This is all Grandfather's fault! If he hadn't gone behind the Guild's back, they wouldn't have gone in search of Mrs. Hope's body, and the Howler girl, Naomi, wouldn't have been captured and executed. Alaric wouldn't have entered the town to retrieve her body, and Eric and Catherine would still be alive. And now Mr. Langdon, Patrick, Harriet and Drew are down at the waterfall, on their way to kill Alaric Bane to avenge Catherine's and Eric's deaths, and I've been sent on a mission to murder Ulrika. There's been so much bloodshed. How could he let this happen? Why didn't he just tell the Guild the truth?

I'm so caught up in my thoughts that I don't immediately notice that the birds have stopped chirping. In fact the whole forest has become deathly silent. Theora gazes up at the trees, clearly noticing the silence too.

"What's going on?" she says. "Why's it so qui—"

She doesn't have time to complete her sentence as the ground begins to quake, knocking us to our knees. Thunder roars beneath the earth, like a Titan awakening. The Darkling girls huddle together with Kieran as pebbles and small rocks bounce down the forest slopes, striking our arms and backs. Around us the Carrow trees start to shake, the vibrations making their leaves scream like banshees, and I'm terrified they're going to crash down on top of us.

"What's happening?" Kieran cries out.

"Earthquake!" I yell over the roar of the ground shaking beneath us.

I duck as more rocks and forest debris bounce over my head, nearly taking it clean off. I've never known anything like this. The whole world is shaking, threatening to tear us apart, swallow us whole. Kieran yelps in pain and the air fills with the scent of blood.

"Kieran!"

I lift my eyes in time to see Theora struggle to her feet. She attempts to run over to the wounded boy, but her feet keep slipping out from under her. She's so focused on reaching him, she hasn't noticed the boulder crashing through the trees, heading straight toward her.

"Theora! Watch out!" I lunge at her, pushing her out of the way just as the rock thunders past, missing us by inches. We both hit the ground hard and I cry out in agony, unable to breathe, unable to do anything but dig my fingers into the dirt as my body rips apart with pain. All I can think is I'm dying, I'm dying, I'm dying, the sensation is so intense. I roll off Theora, gasping for air as shivers of electricity pulse through my veins, rushing toward a single point in my chest. I think the pain is never going to end, and I pray to His Mighty to take me, to let the shaking earth swallow me, anything to end this. Then—

It's over. The forest is still once more.

And through the silence, one sound drums in my ears.

Ba-boom. Ba-boom. Ba-boom.

17.

ASH

"**WHAT DO THEY NEED** with so many Night Whispers?" Acelot says, tapping the cage filled with the large butterflies. Their silvery-blue wings flutter, agitated.

"Night Whispers?" Natalie says, looking at me. "Why does that sound familiar?"

"Giselle was grinding them up in her kitchen, back in Thrace," Elijah answers. "She was putting it in her tea. If you drink it, apparently it makes you really relaxed."

"Maybe they're using it as an anesthetic for the patients here?" Day suggests.

"I don't think they care about hurting their patients," I say flatly, thinking about my dad. My heart pinches and Natalie lets out a small gasp, feeling my pain. That's the only problem with being Blood Mates—when my heart aches, hers does too. She turns her blue eyes on me. They're filled with concern. I look away, trying to hold myself together, but I feel like cracked glass ready to shatter at any moment.

"Purian Rose has been forcing his men to take a new drug, called Wings," Natalie says, gazing up the insects. "I doubt it's a coincidence that the men who've taken it are all wearing silver butterfly medals, which look just like the Night Whisper."

"Do you think that's what they've been developing here?" Day asks, glancing at me.

"I don't fragging know!" I snap, and she flinches. "We're wasting time."

I turn on my heel and storm toward the door. The others hurry after me. Natalie gives me a worried look and I take a deep breath, trying to calm myself down. I check to see if the coast is clear before we enter the corridor again. There's a bloodstain on the floor where Natalie shot the scientist. She gazes at the mark, her face pale. Beetle wipes the stain away with his sleeve before we continue up the next flight of stairs. We approach a single set of glass doors, and it's immediately obvious this floor is what we're looking for as in front of us is a large ward filled with hospital beds. Natalie swipes the keycard down the scanner and we enter the room.

The stench hits us first and we all suck in a startled breath. The long ward is painted white, like the labs downstairs, and is lit only by the misty dawn light streaming through the high windows. Hanging from the ceiling are UV lights, designed to burn a Darkling's skin as a form of torture—we're severely allergic to UV rays. I shudder, even though the lights aren't currently on, remembering the holding cell I was kept in when Natalie's mom questioned me about Chris Thompson's Haze death a few months ago, back in Black City.

There must be more than two hundred beds in the ward. Shackled to each one is a naked human, Darkling or Bastet. There are even a few unfortunate Lupines who must have gotten on the wrong side of the Sentry guards. They're all emaciated and stink of urine or worse, their skin covered in seeping bedsores. The humans look the sickest, their skin sallow and sweating, like they've got a fever. I wince at the sight of the Darklings, who have had their mouths clamped open and tubes attached to their fangs.

"What are they doing to the Darklings?" Acelot whispers.

"Milking them," Elijah replies. "They did the same thing to me back in Black City, to extract my venom to use in the Golden Haze."

Natalie lowers her lashes, ashamed.

"What do they need with so much Darkling venom?" Day says.

No one has an answer for this.

"Come on, we need to hurry. Beetle, Day, you take this side with me," I say, gesturing to the beds on the right. "The rest of you check the others."

We split up into our groups and quickly search the faces of the people on the beds.

"Over here!" Elijah exclaims a moment later.

We hurry over to him. A beautiful Bastet woman is chained uncomfortably to the bed by her skinny arms and ankles. There's only a scratchy-looking blanket separating her gaunt, naked body from the bedsprings and a hard-looking pillow for her head. Asleep on the bed beside her is a middle-aged Lupine with a speckled mane. The word TRAITOR has been carved into his chest. I'm guessing this is Kieran. He stirs, his eyes opening. He looks at me, blinks with surprise, and then gives a lopsided smile.

"You know, you look just like your mom, kid," he says.

"Thanks," I say, removing his shackles and helping him up. Acelot drapes a blanket over Kieran's shoulders, which isn't easy, given that the Lupine is more than two feet taller than he is.

Elijah kneels beside his mother's bed. "Mom, it's me."

Yolanda turns her honey-colored eyes toward Elijah. A look of confusion and then panic enters them. "Eli?" she rasps, her voice hoarse. "What are you doing here?"

"We've come to rescue you." He unties her binds, and Natalie places her jacket around the woman's body.

"Is Lucinda here?" I ask Kieran.

"Over there," he grunts, nodding toward a bed at the end of the room.

Natalie and I follow him over to it. My aunt Lucinda is stretched out on the mattress, her mouth held open with a metal clamp. Like the others, her wrists and ankles are shackled to the bed frame. She doesn't look anything like the plump, smiling girl from my mom's photo. This woman is bruised and broken, her black hair cropped so close to her head that there are several bald patches. Kieran gently removes the clamp from her dry lips, and Natalie unfastens the shackles. Lucinda throws her arms around Kieran the instant she's released.

"Hey, frogface," Kieran mutters against her cheek.

"Hey, dogbreath," Lucinda replies. "Took you long enough to get me. I've been lying here for three weeks, you know," she teases.

He chuckles faintly. "Yeah, what can I say? I got tied up." He releases her and she struggles upright. "You can thank the kid. He came and got us."

Lucinda's black eyes slide toward me, noticing me for the first time. *"Ash?"*

"Hey." I shrug off my jacket and hand it to her. "We're going to get you out of here."

"You shouldn't have come," she says, slipping it on. "It was stupid of you."

I frown. I thought she'd be happy to see me.

Natalie tries to help Lucinda up, but my aunt waves her off.

"I can walk." She shakily gets to her feet but manages only two steps before she stumbles. Kieran catches her. She doesn't object when he slips a supportive arm around her.

The other patients stir in their beds, awakened by our voices. They begin to moan and whimper. I realize we're still wearing our Sentry uniforms—they must think we're here to hurt them. I catch Natalie's eye.

"We can't leave them, Ash," she says.

It wasn't my intention to release the inmates, but now that we're here, I can't let them stay like this. These are people's moms and dads.

"There's too many, bro. We can't take them with us," Beetle says.

"I know," I say. "Untie them anyway."

Elijah helps his mom to her feet while the rest of us hurry to each bed and unhook the tubes and remove their shackles. The freed patients help us release the others. Downstairs I can hear movement—the pounding of feet, the click of doors being un-locked, tired voices wishing each other good morning.

The patients don't wait around for orders; they just stag-ger over to the open door. I notice two familiar faces among the crowd—Pullo and Angel, two of the ministers from the Darkling Assembly in Black City. Like Lucinda, Pullo's hair has been closely cut and he's got some welts on his body, but oth-erwise he still looks as strong as an ox. Angel hasn't fared quite as well. She's beaten and bruised, her lilac eyes swollen, but there's a hard determination in them. They've both wrapped their blankets around themselves. They catch my eye, but don't say hello. They never liked me, and I never liked them. The only acknowledgment I get is a curt nod from Pullo before he sweeps out of the room with Angel.

"Natalie, over here!" Day calls out, running toward one of the beds nearby.

Lying on the bed is an elderly Shu'Zin Darkling woman with graying hair and purple eyes. Like all Shu'Zin Darklings, her feet are clawed. They're the only breed of Darklings with that unique physical feature.

"Martha!" Natalie races over to the bed to help Day untie her. They wrap a sheet around the old woman to preserve her modesty.

"Hello, dears," Martha croaks, standing up. "It's so lovely to see you."

Natalie throws her arms around Martha, holding her tight. The woman winces, obviously in pain, but she doesn't let go. Her legs are shaking, barely able to hold her upright. I jog over to them, and Martha smiles up at me. She used to be friends with my parents and even babysat me when I was a cub, so I have a real soft spot for the old lady. I pick her up and she rests her head against my chest, exhausted.

"We'll get you home," Natalie says, giving Martha's hand a reassuring squeeze.

Downstairs I hear a *pop* of gunfire, followed by screams.

Lucinda struggles down the aisle toward the door. "We need to leave."

Elijah helps his mom as we head to the door. The hallway is in chaos, with humans, Darklings and Bastets running in all directions. We force our way through the crowds and hurry downstairs.

The smell of blood hits my nostrils the moment we reach the second floor. There are screams as the Bastets, Darklings and a duo of Lupines leap on the scientists, ripping out their throats or snapping their necks. I spot Pullo and Angel at the end of the corridor, their faces coated in red. My foot skids on a puddle of blood, and I nearly drop Martha. Someone pulls an alarm and the siren wails around the compound. Fragg! It won't be long before this place is swarming with Sentry guards.

"Head for the truck!" I yell at the others.

They nod, and we push past the fighting Darklings and humans. I hold my breath, trying not to inhale the scent, my thirst mounting. Martha groans, her lips parting to reveal her fangs. This must be agony for her too. I glance at Lucinda. She's got a hand over her nose and mouth as she stumbles down the corridor, hungrily eyeing a bleeding man on the floor.

We reach the ground floor just as the first wave of Sentry guards crash through the front doors and file upstairs, drawn to the sound of screams. Two guards catch sight of us and raise their guns. I skid around the corner just as a bullet smacks into the plasterboard on the wall behind me. We sprint through the hallways, the two guards hot on our heels. Bullets fly and one grazes Day's arm. She grimaces but keeps running, clutching a hand to her bleeding arm, her ebony braid bouncing against her back with each step.

We turn down a familiar corridor and race past the laboratories we passed on the way in. The back door looms up ahead, just thirty feet away. Acelot bursts into a sprint and barges through the door. I'm relieved to see that the truck is still parked outside. He climbs in and starts the engine. Day is the next one out, followed by Lucinda and Kieran, then finally Elijah and his mom. Natalie is almost at the door when she suddenly stops and spins on her heel, running toward one of the labs.

"What are you doing?" I cry out.

Natalie swipes the keycard down the scanner and enters the laboratory. I throw a look over my shoulder. The guards are coming. She sprints across the lab toward the refrigerator at the back of the room and snatches one of the vials of silvery-white liquid. On her way out, she notices something on a workbench and grabs it.

"Stop!" one of the guards yells, shooting his gun. The bullet whizzes past my ear.

Beetle whips around, drawing his handgun at the same time, and unloads his clip into the two guards. They crash to the ground, dead.

Natalie joins us in the corridor. In her hand are the vial and a blue digital disc with PATIENT TRIALS written on it. She thrusts them into her pocket as we run outside. The truck's waiting for us on the road. Beetle leaps into the back of the truck and takes Martha from me. I help Natalie up, then jump in myself just as Acelot guns the engine and we speed down the road. As I shut the doors, I catch sight of groups of Darklings and Bastets spilling out of the lab. Some run down the roads, others scatter toward the forest. In the distance I spot several Transporters heading in our direction. *Reinforcements.* Several Sentry guards rush out of the building, and one of them spots us.

"Get into the forest!" I say.

I fall against a seat as Acelot takes a hard right, getting off the road. The truck rocks wildly as he drives over the bumpy terrain, accelerating up the steep slope. Everyone braces themselves as we burst into the forest. The light immediately dims as the sun is blocked out by the canopy. Acelot expertly steers the truck through the trees and Elijah lets out a whoop, thumping the ceiling, like we're on a roller coaster and not running for our lives. Acelot grins. The brothers are really enjoying this. Yolanda chuckles at her son.

Natalie takes out her black syringe case and carefully places the glass vial of silvery-white liquid inside while Beetle bandages Day's arm. The truck bounds over some bracken, and then we emerge on an old dirt track, which the Sentry must've used during the camp's construction to bring wood down from the forests.

Natalie presses the red button on her watch. "Destiny will be here soon to get us."

"We need to go to Ulrika's first," Kieran says, and Lucinda nods.

"Who's Ulrika?" I ask.

"My cousin," Kieran explains. "She's who we were coming to meet."

I shoot a look at Natalie. She shrugs, as baffled as me.

"Your *cousin* lives here? That's crazy!" Beetle says. "Isn't she afraid of being caught?"

"No," Kieran says. "The guards know she's here. They've been told to leave her alone."

Now I'm really confused. "Why would they do that?"

Kieran turns in his seat, ignoring my question. "Follow the trail for about five kilometers until you meet a fork in the road, then take a right," he instructs Acelot.

"Are we fetching the yellowpox?" Elijah asks his mom.

A crease forms between Yolanda's brows. "What are you talking about, sweetheart?"

"The weapon that you came here to get," Elijah replies. "It's yellowpox, isn't it? I saw your research documents back in your lab . . ."

Lucinda scoffs, and Yolanda throws her a cold look before turning back to her son.

"I abandoned that project years ago, when it became clear to me it couldn't work; even though some of us didn't agree," Yolanda says, sliding a look at Lucinda, whose mouth pinches together. "It would've killed all humans, not just those with the V-gene. That was a line I wasn't willing to cross."

"If the Ora isn't yellowpox, then what is it?" Natalie asks.

"The Ora?" Yolanda quizzes.

"The *weapon*," Elijah says, clearly confused. "Lucinda mentioned it in the letter she sent you. We've been looking for it."

Lucinda laughs. "Oh Lord," she mutters.

Elijah scowls, his cheeks flushing. "What's so funny?"

"It wasn't the Ora," Yolanda explains gently. "It was *Theora*. She's a girl."

"I don't understand," I say. "How is this woman a weapon?"

Yolanda looks at my aunt. Lucinda sighs and begins to speak. "It all began thirty years ago, with a boy named Edmund Rose . . ."

18.

EDMUND

I LET OUT A STARTLED LAUGH, the sound some-
where between hysteria and joy. A heartbeat. I have a heartbeat!
I tilt my head to look at Theora, who is lying on the ground
beside me. The shaking has mercifully stopped and a hush settles over the mountain. Theora's long white hair is strewn with
twigs and forest debris. A hand is clutched to her chest. *Did she
feel something too?* We gaze at each other for a long moment.
My pulse pounds in my ears, the sound deafening after eighteen
years of silence. I have no idea what's going on, but somehow I
know it's connected to her.

"How did you do it?" I whisper.

"Do what?" she says.

I frown, confused. "My heart . . . ?"

Her brow furrows. "What about it?"

I study her for a moment, wondering if she genuinely doesn't
know what's going on, or if she's lying to me, but her eyes don't
give anything away.

"Nothing," I eventually say.

Disappointed, I quickly dust myself off and then help Theora to her feet. My heart clenches as our hands touch—it clenches!—and any tiny niggle of doubt I might have had that Theora wasn't responsible for my newfound heartbeat vanishes in that instant.

"Thanks for saving me, Edmund," she says, shaking the debris out of her hair. Panic suddenly washes over her face. "Kieran!"

We rush over to the groaning boy, who is lying beside the two Darkling girls. The older girl in the green dress is cradling a swollen ankle, and the younger girl is leaning over Kieran. From our angle, it looks like she's feeding on him.

"Get off him!" Theora yells, roughly pushing the Darkling girl out of the way.

"Lucinda was just trying to stem the bleeding," Kieran says, grimacing.

Lucinda shows her blood-soaked hands to Theora, who flushes slightly. The older Darkling girl groans with pain, and Lucinda's head whips round.

"Annora!" Lucinda says, hurrying to her side. She gently inspects Annora's ankle, which is starting to turn purple.

I study the two Darkling girls, Annora and Lucinda, trying to see something of myself in them. They both have narrow black eyes and delicate mouths and chins. It's hard to believe these innocent-looking girls are the demons the Guild makes them out to be, but I suppose that's how they get you to trust them. I must never forget what they are: Unholy. Sinful. Impure. *If Darklings are so bad, then why did that girl help Kieran?* A voice whispers inside my head. *One of their kind raped my mother!* I furiously reply. I'm under no illusion what they're capable of, because their sins are in me too.

I kneel beside Theora. She lifts up Kieran's shirt. He has a nasty gash along his flank and dark bruising around his rib cage. I hold my breath, trying not to smell his blood.

"Is it bad, T?" he asks.

"Well, you'll live, but it's going to leave a pretty nasty scar," Theora says.

"That's cool." Kieran forces a brave smile. "Girls dig scars."

Theora laughs, but there's worry in her silver eyes.

Kieran struggles into an upright position. He eyes Theora's hair, which is covered in twigs and leaves from our tumble on the ground, and bursts out laughing. He immediately winces, but keeps laughing. "You look like a scarecrow."

She blushes and shakes her head in an attempt to dislodge some of the debris from her snowy mane. Most of it falls out, but a stubborn Carrow leaf remains above her left ear. Without thinking I pluck it free.

"Leaf," I say, showing it to her.

"Thanks," she replies, turning pink again. "I must look like a complete—"

A gun clicks behind us.

I whip around, my heart slamming against my chest. Patrick stalks out of the shadows, his gun aimed at us. Instinctively, I move closer to Theora.

"How long have you been there?" I say.

"Long enough," Patrick replies as he slowly walks toward us, his blue eyes fixed on me. Annora grabs Lucinda and pulls her protectively toward her. "I always knew something wasn't right with you, *freak*. I could sense it in my gut. But Catherine kept saying I was just being an overprotective brother. But here you are, helping out a bunch of Howlers and these *nippers,* and I'm starting to think my suspicions about you were right all along."

My throat suddenly feels tight. "And what were they, exactly?"

"That in eighteen years, I've never seen you eat. That you run away at the sight of blood. That you have fake teeth where your canines should be." He slides a look between me and the Darkling girls. "It all makes sense now. You're one of *them*."

Theora shoots a confused look at me.

I nervously lick my dry lips. All these years I thought I was being so careful; I had no idea that while I was watching Catherine, her brother was watching me.

"That's ridiculous," I say. "You're mistaken."

"Yeah? Then explain this." He pulls something out of his pocket and tosses it at my feet. It's a purple corsage; the very one I intended to give to Catherine at the dance. It must've fallen out of my jacket when I attacked her! The fabric petals are covered in dried blood. Fear surges through me. Patrick's handsome face contorts with rage.

"You killed her," Patrick snarls. "You murdered my sister and then got your grandfather to lie about it, you fragging nipper!"

He aims the gun at my head. I shut my eyes, waiting for the bullet, then—

"Patrick! Edmund! Where are you?"

My eyes snap open at the sound of Mr. Langdon's voice. Patrick turns his head, momentarily distracted. It's the diversion we needed. Theora pushes Kieran out of harm's way at the same moment I lunge for Patrick. We hit the ground together, and his gun goes off, the bullet smacking into the tree that Theora was in front of just seconds before.

"Father! Over here!" Patrick shouts as we wrestle. He strikes my cheek with the butt of his rifle, knocking me off him. He scrambles to his feet and points the gun at me.

"Not so fast!" Theora's aiming my rifle directly at Patrick. "Drop it!"

He lets go and his rifle falls to the dirt. I grab it and hurriedly stand up, spinning the weapon around on him at the same time. My finger hovers over the trigger.

"Do it, you *freak*!" Patrick yells. "Murder me like you did my sister."

I lower the weapon. "I didn't mean to hurt her," I whisper.

"Patrick, where are you?" Harriet calls out.

They're just a few meters away; we haven't got much time. I take Theora's hand and the five of us—me, Theora, Kieran, Annora and Lucinda—hurry into the dense woods just as Harriet, Drew and Mr. Langdon enter the clearing.

"Go after them!" I hear Patrick shout.

We race through the forest, following Theora, who expertly navigates the thick undergrowth. Kieran and Annora are at the back of the group, both of them struggling to keep up because of their injuries. I let go of Theora's hand and sling one arm around Kieran, holding my rifle in the other, while Lucinda helps Annora. The older Darkling grimaces with pain as she limps on her sprained ankle.

The farther we go into the forest, the steeper the ground becomes as we start to climb up the side of Mount Alba. Lower down the mountain, Patrick and the others dart through the trees, heading toward us. Drew spots me and shoots. A bullet whizzes by my head, missing me by millimeters. I shoot back, more to scare them than to hurt anyone.

"I'm going to kill you, Edmund!" Patrick cries out, his voices echoing through the forest. "And when I'm done with you, I'm going to pin your grandfather to the cross!"

"Guys, I need to stop," Kieran says. His shirt is slick with blood.

"No time." I grunt as I lift the boy over my shoulder. He weighs almost as much as me, despite being younger—Lupine's aren't exactly small—and I struggle up the steep slope after the girls, my feet slipping on the uneven earth. My boot skids on some loose rock, and I almost drop Kieran. His fingers dig into my back.

I risk a look over my shoulder. Patrick and the others are closing the gap between us. He raises his gun and another bullet whizzes by us. This one hits its mark, landing firmly in Annora's shoulder. She cries out in pain, her legs buckling underneath her, and she stumbles down the slope, dragging Lucinda with her, straight toward Patrick.

"Luci!" Kieran shouts right next to my ear.

Theora spins around on her heel and races after them. She manages to grab Lucinda's hand, but Annora keeps tumbling down the slope, out of our reach.

"Annora!" Lucinda screams as Theora lifts the girl over her shoulder and continues running up the mountainside. She punches Theora's back. "Let me go! That's my sister!"

"We can't go back; we'll be shot!" Theora says.

I snatch another look behind me. Annora is on the ground and Drew's gun is aimed at her head. Her onyx eyes are wide with fear.

"Don't kill her yet," Mr. Langdon orders, his voice carrying on the breeze. "Bring her back to Amber Hills; I want the whole town to watch the demon burn."

Drew and Harriet drag Annora onto her feet while Mr. Langdon and Patrick continue up the mountain toward us. I turn away. There's nothing we can do for her now.

It's hard to keep pace with Theora as we run through the woods, and I stumble more than once on a fallen branch or tangle-weed. This is *her* territory, and she knows it like the back of her hand. She suddenly drops Lucinda on the ground, leaps at one of the evergreen trees, and easily shimmies up it. She pulls herself onto a thick branch, then helps us up after her, and not a moment too soon, as Patrick and Mr. Langdon arrive. Farther down the slope, Harriet and Drew restrain Annora.

"Where did they go?" Mr. Langdon says.

"I'm certain they came this way, Father," Patrick says.

Patrick studies the ground, searching for our tracks. He won't find anything, though—there's too much vegetation for him to spot our footprints. He lets out a frustrated yell.

"They have to be nearby!" Patrick says, his face red with fury.

"Let's go back to Amber Hills," Mr. Langdon says.

"No! Edmund killed Catherine; he can't get away with it," Patrick says.

"He won't." Mr. Langdon tilts his head up and says in a loud, carrying voice, "We have your Darkling friend and your grandfather, Edmund! If you hand yourself over to the Guild, they will be spared. If not, we'll execute them both. You have until noon tomorrow!"

I can't let Grandfather and Annora die for me! I should hand myself over now. I move, and Theora shakes her head.

"They'll shoot them," she mouths, nodding toward Kieran and Lucinda.

I sit back.

Patrick and Mr. Langdon leave. They join the others farther down the mountain and head back to Amber Hills. The instant they're gone, I turn to Theora.

"I have to go back," I say.

"They'll kill you, Edmund," Theora says.

"But we have to save my sister!" Lucinda says. "You heard what they said. If Edmund doesn't hand himself over to them by noon tomorrow, they'll execute her!" Lucinda makes a move to leave. "I need to tell my family what's happened. Fragg, when Uncle Icarus finds out, he's going to be *so* mad. He's only stayed away from Amber Hills because it suits his needs, but this changes everything."

I grab her arm. "He can't find out. If he goes after Annora, lots of people could get killed, including my grandfather," I say. "Most of the folk in Amber Hills are good people. They don't deserve to die."

"Edmund's right; we can't risk any more bloodshed," Theora says.

Lucinda scrunches up her brow. "But Annora . . ."

"We'll save her, I promise," Theora replies. "We'll go to Amber Hills tonight, when it's dark, and get Edmund's grand-father and her. Maybe if we return Annora safely, Icarus can be persuaded not to retaliate. But until then, you should both come back to my village. It's not safe out here, and Kieran re-ally needs to see a doctor."

Kieran groans and clutches his side. Blood seeps between his fingers.

Lucinda looks at me, and I nod. It's the best plan we have. We climb down the tree. Theora and Lucinda gracefully leap off the bottom branch and softly land on the earth. Kieran struggles down, grimacing the whole way, but it's clear he's an expert climber. My attempt is much clumsier, and I fall into the bracken.

Theora grins and stretches out a hand. The instant our fingers touch, a shiver of electricity shoots up my arm and into my chest. Theora inhales sharply, her cheeks flushing. *Did she feel that too?* We hold each other's gaze for a breathless moment. I search her silvery eyes, trying to see any sign that it's not just me who's experiencing *whatever* the heck it is I'm feeling. It's hard to describe. It's like I've known Theora my whole life, which is crazy, because we've just met! I wish I understood what was going on; I've never heard of someone's heart spontaneously activating after eighteen years of silence. How is this even possible?

We hike up the forest-coated mountain, getting as much distance between us and Patrick as possible. Everything around here looks the same; it would be easy to get lost if you didn't know where you were going. Our progress is slowgoing because of Kieran.

"You okay, dogbreath?" Luci says to him.

He attempts a grin. "Yeah, I'm fine. Just taking it slow, so you girls can keep up."

Lucinda rolls her eyes.

"So how did you two meet?" I ask them.

"I got trapped in one of Kieran's deer snares," Lucinda mumbles.

Theora throws an amused look at me. Heat rises up my neck.

I turn to Lucinda. "So where has your clan set up camp?" I'd like to know where I'll be taking Annora later. I'm hoping it's not too much of a hike.

She casts a suspicious look at Theora, which doesn't go unnoticed by Kieran.

"It's okay, frogface, you can trust her," he says. "She won't tell anyone. Will you?" He aims that last part at Theora. She shakes her head.

Lucinda glances back at me. "In the caves, about a mile out-side of Amber Hills."

"You're living in a cave?" I say, surprised.

She shrugs. "It's dry, it's safe and it's secluded from the sun." She peers up at the misty sunlight and winces slightly. "It's perfect, really. It's where Uncle Icarus lived before, well, you know . . . ," she says, referring to the Misery.

"Where have you been living for the past eighteen years?" I ask.

"All over the place," Lucinda says. "We rarely stay in a town longer than a few months. Uncle Icarus causes too much trouble."

The trees suddenly thin out and we reach a vertical rock face, about a hundred feet high. On top of the plateau is the Lupine village. A steep set of stone steps are carved into the side of the rock leading up to it.

"So, did you really kill that boy's sister?" Theora asks as we climb the steps.

"No," I say quietly. "But I was feeding on her."

"Oh," she says, then louder. "Oh! So you're—"

"A twin-blood Darkling," I mumble.

I expect her to gasp, to scream, but instead she just says, "I'm a hybrid too. Half Lupine, half human." The corner of her rosy-pink lips turns up in a smile, and my heart yanks.

"And the Lupines are okay with you being a hybrid?" I ask. It's not something that would be tolerated in my town.

She nods. "Sure. They've taken really good care of me since my parents died."

"What happened to them?"

"Icarus murdered them during the Misery," she says, glancing at Lucinda. The Darkling girl pretends not to have heard that, but her cheeks redden. I don't know how she can stomach being around me and Lucinda, when a Darkling killed her parents. She's a more forgiving person than I am. "Kieran's cousin, Ulrika, and her father have practically adopted me. She's my best friend," Theora explains. My left hand grips around my rifle. "I spend more time at her house than my own."

"I'm so sorry for your loss," I say sincerely.

She shrugs a little, frowning. "So what happened with that boy's sister?"

"My grandfather caught me feeding on her and . . ." I briefly shut my eyes, remembering the sound of Catherine's neck snapping. "He couldn't risk her telling anyone. Ulrika saw the whole thing." I figure it's best to tell her the truth before Ulrika does.

"You weren't hunting for deer in the forest, were you, Edmund?"

I glance down. "The Guild sent us to kill Alaric, as payback for last night."

She stops. "If you hurt any of my people, I'll rip your throat out. Got it?"

I nod, passing her my rifle as a show of trust. "I'm not going to harm anyone."

She studies me for a long moment, then nods, and continues on up the steps, but she keeps the gun safely by her side. We're all out of breath by the time we reach the village. The rocky mountainside has been carved into tiered levels and is connected by a maze of steps and steep pathways. On every level are tall, blocky stone buildings, crammed tightly together.

Lupines race about the village, helping to carry the injured inside their homes, or fix broken windows and fallen doors that must have been damaged in the earthquake. We're in a town plaza, about the same size as the one in Amber Hills, which is surrounded by merchant stalls.

The roof of one of the stalls has caved in. Standing beside it is a middle-aged Lupine with a white-and-black mane, just like Kieran's—the Lupine pack leader, Alaric Bane, and his daughter, Ulrika. She's wearing the same outfit as last night—leather pants and a tight top—and there's a bandage around her arm, where she was shot by one of the townsfolk in Amber Hills. Her cropped hair is matted around her boyish face, and there are dark shadows under her eyes. I doubt she's been to sleep yet.

"We should evacuate the village," the man with the spotted mane says.

"It was just an earthquake, Penn," Alaric says. "We've had them before. There's no reason to believe we're in any danger of an eruption."

Ulrika glances over her shoulder, sensing us.

"Uncle Penn, they're back!" she cries out.

Penn follows her gaze. The look of relief that enters his face quickly fades when he sees Kieran. He rushes over to us along with Alaric and Ulrika.

"What the fragg are they doing here, Theo!" Ulrika says, gesturing toward me and Lucinda. "Did you forget they're our *enemies?*"

"Luci's my friend," Kieran grunts.

"Don't you realize how much danger you've put us in, bringing her here?" Ulrika continues. "What if the other Darklings come looking for her?"

"They won't," Lucinda says. "Not until nightfall, anyway. Annora and I often stay out all day."

"Lucinda will go back to Icarus tonight, after we've rescued her sister," Theora explains.

"Is this girl who you've been sneaking out to see, son?" Penn says.

Kieran grips his side. "Argh, Dad, can we talk about this later? I'm sort of bleeding here." His knees buckle and his father grabs him.

"Take him to my house, Penn. It's closer," Alaric says. "Put him in Naomi's room."

Ulrika flinches at the sound of her sister's name but doesn't protest as her uncle carries Kieran into a nearby house with a yellow door. As soon as they're gone, Alaric turns to me.

"You've got some nerve coming here, boy!" he growls.

"I invited him," Theora explains. "We were being chased by hunters. I couldn't leave Edmund and Lucinda in the woods. It wasn't safe."

Alaric looks questioningly at me. "What's going on?"

"The Guild sent a hunting party to kill you, as payback for last night." I tell them everything, starting with what happened to Naomi during Mrs. Hope's funeral, right through to now, leaving nothing out. Alaric's eyes widen as he learns I'm part Darkling, while Ulrika scowls. "They took Lucinda's sister, and they're going to kill my grandfather."

Alaric pinches the bridge of his nose. "This whole thing has turned into such a mess. I should *never* have trusted Hector to sort this out. He lied to the Guild about our deal, and now my little girl is . . ." He winces. "But I thought he cared about his people."

"He does," I say. "My grandfather's devoted his whole life to the people of Amber Hills . . ."

Alaric furrows his heavy brow at me. "I wasn't talking about them."

"Who did you mean, then?" I say, confused.

He spreads his arms wide, like he's gesturing toward the whole village. I blink, perplexed, and then it slowly sinks in what he means as I stare at the man's silver eyes—*silver,* just like my mom's, like my grandfather's, like *mine.* I stagger back as the truth hits me. I'm part Lupine.

19.

EDMUND

"HOW CAN MY GRANDFATHER be a Lupine? He doesn't look anything like you," I say. Except, I realize he does. He has the same steel-gray eyes as Alaric and he's tall too.

"Hector's a hybrid," Alaric explains. "His father was human."

I furrow my brow. So if my grandfather's a hybrid, like Theora, that means I'm a . . . *what?* They don't even have a word for someone like me: half Darkling, with a generous pinch of human and a dash of Lupine. Blend ingredients together to make Edmund Rose.

"I thought you knew," Alaric says.

"No," I mutter. "Grandfather's never spoken about my great-grandparents, so I had no idea one of them was a Lupine." All I know is that he was orphaned as a baby and raised by an uncle in Carrow Falls, who died of yellowpox when my grandfather was just fifteen. He moved to Amber Hills and worked as an apprentice for one of the original members of the Guild, got married when he was nineteen, then took the preacher's job after his young bride died while giving birth to my mom. And that's everything I know. Why didn't he tell me what he was? My blood simmers, stung by his betrayal, but it also explains why he's been so accepting of me all these years. We're the same. *Freaks.*

"So who was my great-grandmother?" I ask.

Alaric ushers us toward the stone building that his brother, Penn, and Kieran just went into. Ulrika pushes past me, bumping my shoulder—I can't tell if it's on purpose or not; I might be part of the pack now, but that doesn't mean she trusts me—and enters the house before me. Theora gives me a reassuring smile as we follow her.

The hallway is cramped and dark and cluttered with furniture. Alaric slings his jacket over the coatrack by the door before leading us to the living room at the end of the corridor. We pass a reception room along the way. The door is open, and I stop midstride. Lying on the table is Naomi's body, shrouded in a muslin cloth and surrounded by pine wreaths. Ulrika shuts the door, grief burning in her silver eyes.

"We can't cremate her until tomorrow's full moon," Theora says. "It's Lupine tradition."

"I'm really sorry," I mutter, my words falling flat.

Theora frowns. "It's not your fault."

No, it's my grandfather's fault for agreeing to let the Lupines take our people to give to Icarus to feed on. I still don't understand why he felt the need to be so underhanded about this whole situation and hide the Darklings' return from everyone, including me. If he'd just been honest, maybe Catherine and Naomi would still be alive.

We head into the living room. The floors are all made of stone, so there's a cold, damp chill in the air. Old photographs and paintings of Lupines cram every inch of wall space.

"Who are all these people?" I ask.

"Our pack," Alaric says, lifting a pile of books from a chair and indicating for me to sit down. Lucinda plops down in the seat before I have a chance to take it. Instead, I find a place to sit on a striped purple sofa next to Theora. Ulrika takes a seat in the leather chair beside the fireplace and puts her feet up on the coffee table. She pulls a dagger out of her belt and digs it into the armrest, her angry eyes fixed on Lucinda.

Alaric plucks a circle-shaped picture frame from the wall, and passes the photograph to me. The picture is clearly old, with faded sepia tones and mildew beginning to bloom on the decaying paper. A beautiful young Lupine smiles back at me, dressed in a very uncomfortable-looking dress with big ruffled sleeves and a high collar. Her mane has been neatly braided.

"That's Prudence Black. Your great-grandmother," he says. "She was our pack leader, until she died. The position should have gone down to her son, Hector, but he was just a baby at the time and the bloodline ended with him. So he was sent to Carrow Falls to live with his human uncle, and the job of pack leader went to the next family in line. *My* family. We invited Hector to stay with us after we learned his uncle had died, but he refused. He'd moved to Amber Hills by this stage and was happy there."

"What about my great-grandfather? Who was he?" I ask.

Alaric shrugs. "Just some farmer from Carrow Falls. He died of tuberculosis a few months before Hector was born."

I look up. "My grandfather's the rightful pack leader?"

Alaric's mouth tightens. "Yes. But he refused the position when he came of age."

I glance down at the photograph of my great-grandmother. Why did Grandfather choose to stay in Amber Hills, under the

Guild's oppressive regime, instead of returning to his family, here? Then it hits me. He'd met my grandmother. He stayed for love. I wonder if his wife knew what he was. Probably; I can't imagine he could keep it a secret from her. I pass the photograph back to Alaric, and he places it on the wall.

I notice a newer photograph on the mantel above the fireplace. It's of Naomi. She's got her arms slung around Ulrika and Theora. They're all grinning up at the camera. Alaric follows my gaze, and grief crosses his features when he sees the photos.

"Why did Icarus have to come back," he says, his voice broken. "My beautiful girl would still be with us if he'd just stayed away."

"Why don't we ask Kieran's 'friend'?" Ulrika says, sliding a look at Lucinda.

She sinks back in her seat. "He came back for his son. A boy from Amber—oh!" Lucinda looks at me. "It's you."

My heart freezes. Icarus is my father. So that's why Grandfather has been desperate to keep Icarus's return a secret from the Guild? He was terrified they'd find out I'm part Darkling and kill me. I cradle my head in my hands. It's a lot to take in. I'm the reason Icarus has returned and the reason Naomi and all the others are dead.

"Why has he come back for you now?" Alaric says. "It's been eighteen years."

I look at Lucinda, hoping for some answers. "It's custom for the firstborn son of the clan leader to take a blood oath when he turns eighteen, basically promising that he'll lead the clan when his father dies. It's a stuffy old tradition, but Icarus really believes in it. And you're his only son."

"I turned eighteen last month," I mutter.

"He's been trying to see you for weeks," Lucinda adds. "He sent a message to your grandfather when we first arrived, asking to meet with you, but your grandfather refused."

"He said 'it was time,' that's all," Lucinda says.

Ulrika leans forward. "If Icarus is so desperate to see Edmund, why didn't he just go to Amber Hills and talk to him directly, mmm?"

"Uh, because the Guild would try and *kill us*?" Lucinda replies. "Uncle Icarus didn't come back here to start a fight with them, if it could be avoided—our people suffered at their hands during the Misery as much as they did ours. Plus, he wanted his son to come back to him willingly; it's part of the ritual— his son must 'return to the fold of his own free will and accept his burden as leader,' or something," she continues. "He just wanted to talk to Edmund and then we'd be on our way. But his patience is wearing thin; he's *really* mad at Edmund's grandfather."

"And while Icarus was waiting around to talk to Edmund, he was snatching *our* people to feed on, so the Guild wouldn't suspect he was back?" Ulrika throws her hands up. "Nice, real fragging nice."

I glance at Alaric. My grandfather *had* tried to rectify the situation, by allowing the Lupines to take a few sick and elderly people from Amber Hills to offer to Icarus instead. As long as the Guild believed the Lupines were behind the kidnappings, there was no reason for them to know the Darklings were back and question why Icarus was here. My grandfather did all of this to protect me. He probably hoped Icarus would get the hint and leave, but the situation spiraled out of his control.

"You have to believe me; I had no idea about any of this," I say to the group.

"It wasn't your fault, Edmund," Theora says, lightly placing her hand over mine.

Ulrika notices the gesture and narrows her eyes.

Theora turns to Alaric. "What are we going to do about Lucinda's sister and Hector? We only have until noon tomorrow to rescue them."

Alaric sighs. "I'm not so certain we should be getting involved—"

Lucinda flashes a panicked look at Theora. "But you promised! If Annora dies, Uncle Icarus will feel forced to retaliate, that's just how he is."

"It'll be the Misery all over again," Theora says.

"I'll take Annora to Icarus myself and end this," I say to Alaric. "No more people have to die. All I ask is that you let my grandfather stay with you; he'll have nowhere else to go."

Alaric thinks about this for a moment, then nods. "I need to run that past the League first." I'm assuming the League is the Lupine's equivalent of our Guild. "I'll go talk to them now. We'll leave at nightfall." With that Alaric sweeps out of the room.

As soon as he's gone, Ulrika yanks her dagger out of her armrest and tucks it back into her belt. She stands up. "I'm going to check up on Kieran."

Lucinda follows her without asking for permission, leaving me and Theora alone in the dark, cluttered room. A grandfather clock ticks loudly in the corner of the room. I'm suddenly aware how closely we're sitting together on the sofa; there are just a few purple stripes between us. Theora shifts and her knee touches mine. I swallow, unable to focus on anything but that one inch of skin where our legs are pressed together. I lift my eyes and hold her gaze. Blood rushes into her cheeks and she looks away, but a faint smile flitters over her lips. There's an awkward pause as neither of us knows what to say.

"Let's go for a walk," she finally says, standing up.

Outside, the Lupines are still busy cleaning up the mess made by the earthquake, so they don't pay us any attention as we stroll through the village. We pass a house covered entirely in wisteria and Theora brushes her hand over the violet flowers, releasing their sharp honey scent. An old woman with a long gray mane is standing on the front porch, picking up fragments of broken potted plants. Scattered around her feet are hundreds of orchid petals.

"Oh no," Theora says, her lips turning down. "Those were Hettie's pride and joy. She must be devastated."

She hurries up the porch steps while I wait at the bottom, uncertain whether I should join her or not. I watch as Theora quietly offers words of comfort to the old woman. Looking at her now, it strikes me how much she reminds me of Catherine. They both have kind hearts. Theora didn't have to bring me back here; she could have easily left me in the woods, with nowhere to go. But instead she's helping me and Lucinda, despite what we are. The old lady dabs her eyes and smiles at Theora. They briefly hug, and then Theora joins me again. We continue our walk through the village.

"Where are we going?" I ask as we approach the outskirts.

Theora grins. "Are you afraid of heights?"

"No," I say, getting a bad feeling.

She gestures for me to follow her up a flight of stone steps that are carved into the mountainside. We climb the steps for several minutes, walking side by side, despite there not really being enough space for the two of us. Occasionally the backs of our hands brush against each other and my stomach swirls, like I'm going to be sick, but not in a bad way. I desperately want to lace my fingers through hers, but that's insane! I don't even know this girl, yet every part of me is aching to touch her.

I'm out of breath by the time we reach the top of the steps, but Theora's hardly broken a sweat. We're on a rocky outcrop several hundred feet above the Lupine village. Up here, the air is much thinner and I feel dizzy, although that might just be because I'm standing close to Theora. The sky overhead is cloudy and gray, and there's a weird eggy smell in the air like there was at the waterfall where we'd set up camp earlier. It's a little disconcerting, especially after the earthquake, but nobody seems that worried about it, other than me. Maybe it's normal; I don't know. Until today, I'd never ventured outside the walls of Amber Hills, so perhaps the air up here always smells like this? It's crazy to think how much has happened since then: I've met Theora, gotten a heartbeat and now I'm a wanted man.

"This is what I wanted to show you," Theora says, gesturing toward a circular building on the edge of the precipice. The building has no walls; it's just a domed roof held up by several marble columns. "This is our temple."

"Oh," I say, still trying to catch my breath from the hike. "Pretty."

Theora laughs slightly as we enter the temple. From here, we can see right across the Forest of Shadows. In the far distance, I can see the Boundary Wall surrounding Amber Hills.

"You can see where I live from here." I point toward the spire of my grandfather's church, which pokes above the wall. Grief suddenly rips through me as I realize that I can never go back there. I'm homeless. Instinctively, I clasp the circle pendant around my neck. It always gives me comfort when I'm feeling lost or frightened.

"What is that?" Theora asks, pointing to my pendant.

"It's the symbol of my faith," I say. "Everyone in Amber Hills follows the Purity."

"The Purity?"

"We believe that the Darklings are demons sent from hell to corrupt our souls." I attempt a smile, but it quickly fades on my lips.

Theora looks at me, a small crease between her white brows. "You believe that, despite what you are?"

"*Especially* because of what I am," I say. "My faith keeps me pure. It helps me control my urges so I don't hurt people. It works." I imagine the sound of Catherine's neck snapping. "Well, most of the time."

Theora frowns. "I couldn't imagine living like that. Having to hide what I am, for fear of being killed." She takes my hand and my heart stutters. "You must have been very lonely."

She releases my hand and lies down on the marble floor, patting the ground beside her. I lie down. The stone is icy cold against my back, but I don't want to miss this opportunity to be next to Theora. We're lying so close together, my left arm is pressing up against her right one, but she doesn't make any attempt to move hers away. I smile and face the ceiling. The domed roof has been painted like the night sky, with pearls embedded into it to replicate stars. In the center of the roof is a hole, so you can see the actual sky.

"My people . . . *our* people," she corrects, "worship the goddess Luna. And every month, at the full moon, you can see her face perfectly through that hole." Theora tilts her head toward me. Our eyes lock and I get that jittery feeling in my stomach again. Up close, I realize her eyes aren't silver but steel-gray with these tiny metallic flecks in them, like the tinsel we use during Winterfest. "This is my favorite place in the whole world," she whispers.

"Thank you for sharing it with me."

She smiles faintly. "I thought you'd like to know a little bit about your heritage." Her smile fades and she's quiet for a while.

"What are you thinking about?" I ask her.

"Icarus," she says. "You do know when you bring Annora back to him tonight, he's going to expect you to leave with him?"

"I know. But I don't have a choice," I say. "The longer he's here, the more danger the Lupines and people of Amber Hills are in. I can't have any more blood on my hands." I think of Mrs. Hope and Naomi.

We fall into a long silence as we just gaze at each other. Her eyes drift over the old burn marks on my cheeks, along the wide line of my mouth, up my narrow nose, back to my eyes.

"What happened?" she says. I know she's referring to the burns.

"My mom dropped me into a tub of scalding water," I say. "Do my scars bother you?"

She shakes her head.

I prop myself up onto my left elbow. "Why are you being so nice to me?" I ask. "I mean, I'm a Darkling and my father killed your parents. You should hate me. *I* hate me."

"You can't condemn an entire species of people because of the actions of one man." My pulse quickens as she places her hand on my chest. "It's easy to hate, Edmund. The true test of our hearts is to forgive." She frowns slightly. "Why do you dislike yourself so much?"

I roll onto my back. "Because I'm a freak. Until we met, I didn't even have a heartbeat."

Her eyes widen. *"What?"*

"Something happened to me back in the forest," I blurt out. "I was cursed without a heartbeat when I was born—it's just what happens when a Darkling and human mate—but when we touched, my heart *activated*. I don't know what it means, but it's amazing and brilliant and terrifying, because I have these feelings for you, Theora," I continue. "It's like, I feel *connected* to you, like we're meant to be together, which I know is insane, as we've just met, and I don't even understand it, and fragg, please say something! Tell me you felt something too," I gasp for breath. I've never strung so many sentences together all at once.

She looks away.

I sit up. "You felt something, didn't you?"

"I don't know," she finally says. She sits up and looks at me. "Before I saw you in the woods, I felt this . . . this *tugging* . . . in my chest. It was really strange. Then when you fell on me after the earthquake, I . . ."

"What?" I say excitedly.

A tiny crease furrows between her brows. "I felt a sharp pain in my heart. I thought it was just from the shock of you landing on me, but now . . ." She sighs. "I don't know what's going on, Edmund. Something obviously happened back in the woods, but I don't feel 'connected' to you in the way you described. I think you're attractive, but it's not because of"—she gestures toward my chest—"whatever *this* is you're experiencing."

"You think I'm attractive?" I say, grinning slightly.

She blushes. "You really didn't have a heartbeat until we touched?"

"Really," I say.

"Have you ever heard of this happening before?"

I shake my head. "But I've never met a Darkling before today, so I don't know what's considered normal behavior for our kind and what's not," I admit.

She stands up. "Well, let's go ask someone who might know."

20.

EDMUND

WE FIND LUCINDA at Alaric's house, sitting beside Kieran on the wooden bed. He's propped up by several pillows, a hand-sewn quilt pulled up to his slim waist. He's not wearing a top, so I can see the gash on the side of his body, which has been patched up with a few stitches and a foul-smelling ointment. He's pale but seems to be okay. He's certainly enjoying Lucinda dabbing his forehead with a damp cloth, given the grin on his lips.

Ulrika's sitting on a blue chair in the corner of the room. She's gazing out the window, her body language stiff, like she'd rather be anywhere but here, babysitting her cousin and his Darkling friend. She scratches her fingers through her short, tangled hair. She turns her head as we enter the room. Her eyes immediately dart down to our locked hands.

"What's going on, Theo?" Ulrika says.

"Um, we need to talk to Lucinda," Theora says. The Darkling girl glances up at us. "Something a little *weird* has happened. Edmund's got a heartbeat, and he didn't have one before."

I briefly explain what happened. Ulrika's and Kieran's eyes widen with surprise, while Lucinda just nods as she listens.

"Do you know what's going on with me?" I say.

"Yeah. Theora's your Blood Mate," Lucinda says.

"My blood what?" I say.

"*Blood Mate,*" Lucinda repeats slowly, like I'm stupid. "When a Darkling meets their true love, their dual heart activates. Or in your case, your only heart."

"Their *true love?*" Theora says, shooting me a confused look. "But I'm not a Darkling; my mom was a Lupine and my dad a human. So how can I be his Blood Mate?"

"I don't know," Lucinda says. "Maybe it's because Edmund's, like, a mixture of three things—Darkling, human and Lupine—so he can make the connection with any of those species? Or maybe you've got some Darkling DNA in you somewhere? I mean, it's possible, right?" she adds when she sees the uncertain expression on Theora's face. "If we trace our family trees back far enough, I'm sure we've all got a little bit of something in us, somewhere. So perhaps you've got a dormant Darkling gene in you, and it activated when you met Edmund?" Lucinda throws her hands up. "I don't know. I'm just fourteen."

"It's possible," Theora mutters. "I don't know much about my father's side of the family. He could have had a distant Darkling relative."

"But if that's true, how come you were born with a heartbeat and I wasn't?" I say.

"She probably doesn't have any *Trypanosoma vampirum* in her blood," Lucinda says. I raise a confused brow. "Come on, you must know what they are! How do you think you're alive?"

I shrug. Grandfather doesn't know anything about Darkling physiology, and it's not like I could ask anyone in town.

"They're these teeny-tiny creatures that live in your blood," Lucinda explains.

"Gross," Kieran says, curling his lip.

She slaps his arm. "They feed oxygen to your organs, essentially doing the job for your heart, and as a result, it becomes dormant, as it's not needed," she continues. "But when you met Theora, it triggered the Blood Mate connection and zap! Hello, heartbeat."

I look down at my hands, trying to picture these microscopic creatures wriggling about inside me. It *is* gross.

"So, what happens to these *Trypanosoma vampirum* thingies now that I've got a heartbeat?" I ask.

Lucinda shrugs. "I guess they become dormant, like your heart used to be."

"This is twisted," Ulrika mutters from her chair.

"Anyway, I doubt Theora has any *Trypanosoma vampirum* in her system," Lucinda finishes. "If she does have any Darkling in her, which we don't even know for sure, it's far, far, *far* down her bloodline, so they've probably been bred out of her by now. That's why she's always had a heartbeat." Lucinda looks at Theora. "So do you have mushy feelings for Edmund?"

Theora drops her eyes, flushing. I know she's attracted to me, but it's pretty obvious this Blood Mate connection we have is more on my side than hers. Of all the people in the world to form a connection with, my stupid Darkling heart chose a hybrid Lupine, who can't properly form it back.

"It doesn't mean what you're feeling for me isn't real, Edmund," Theora says quietly, taking my hand. "And maybe when we've gotten to know each other better, I'll develop those feelings for you too. I just need time, okay?"

I nod. In truth, I need the chance to digest all this too. It's a lot to take in. But I'm grateful for what's happened. I've spent my whole life wanting to make a connection with someone; I thought it would be with Catherine, but I was wrong. I glance at Theora and she smiles. *Maybe in time . . .*

The bedroom door opens and Alaric enters the room. He nods at me.

"The League's agreed to let your grandfather stay with us," he says, and relief washes through me. "Now all we need to do is get a rescue team together."

"I'm going," Theora immediately says, squeezing my hand.

"And me," Kieran says, throwing off his blanket.

Ulrika leaps up and shoves him down on the bed. "No you're not! You're injured."

"I'm *fine*," he says, then looks at Alaric. "I want to go, Uncle. Annora's my friend."

Alaric nods. I admire how the teenagers here are treated as equals. There's no question about their ability to handle themselves.

"Well, if you're going, numbskull, then I'm coming too," Ulrika mumbles.

"Then that's settled," Alaric says. "We leave tonight."

As soon as night falls, we head to Amber Hills to rescue my grandfather and Annora. Kieran grits his teeth as we hurry through the forest, trying not to let his pain show in front of Alaric and Ulrika. Even though it's dark, we're able to navigate the woods—Lucinda and I have good night vision, while the

Lupines follow their old scent trails from their previous visits to the town. Theora takes my hand as we weave through the trees, her anxious eyes flitting up to meet mine. I give her a reassuring smile, although I'm nervous too. I glance over my shoulder, getting the feeling we're being followed, but there's no one there. It's probably just my imagination playing tricks on me.

After a few hours the woodlands thin out and we reach the meadow separating the forest from the Boundary Wall that surrounds Amber Hills. I always took comfort in the sight of that wall, but from this vantage point I realize how ridiculous it is. The people of Amber Hills have spent their whole lives imprisoned within the confines of that wall to protect themselves from the Darklings. Now I realize it would've made more sense to trap the Darklings inside the compound while we roamed free.

Guarding the top of the wall are Mr. Kent and three new Watchmen. They haven't seen us yet, as we're still hidden in the tree line. Mr. Kent is on the side of the Boundary Wall nearest to us. He silently paces up and down, holding a rifle. From somewhere in the town, a girl wails in pain. *Annora.* Lucinda rushes forward, but Ulrika grabs her and drags her into the tree line just as Mr. Kent turns to look in our direction. He lifts his gun and aims it at the forest. No one makes a sound as Mr. Kent stares in our direction. I hold my breath. Eventually, he lowers his gun and moves on. I exhale.

"We have two minutes before he'll come back," I whisper, recalling the Watchman's patrol route.

Alaric waves at us to follow him. We rush across the meadow and scramble up the wall. The Lupines have no trouble getting up—they've done this a few times in recent weeks—but Lucinda and I struggle to find the handholds. She misjudges a hold and the brick crumbles in her fingers. "Oh!" she gasps as she skids down the wall a few inches before catching herself. Her boot kicks me in the face and I grunt in pain. "Sorry," she whispers. Alaric and Theora reach down for us and pull us up the rest of the way. We drop down the other side just as Mr. Kent turns. He doesn't see us.

The town is silent as we stalk through the cobbled streets. Even so, I scan the alleyways around us, unable to shake the feeling we're being watched, but there's nothing there except shadows dancing in the moonlight.

"Where do you think they'll be?" Lucinda asks.

"The town square," I say, thinking about the wooden cross. "Mr. Langdon will want them on display for everyone to see."

The six of us hurry down the dark alleyways, passing Mrs. Hope's cottage along the way. The flowers on her porch have died and withered. It's after curfew, so I'm not expecting to bump into anyone, but even so, I'm on the alert as we enter the town square.

Everything is the same as it always was: the church dominates the west side of the plaza, the spire casting a dagger-shaped shadow across the moonlit square. Opposite the church is Langdon's General Store, and to the left of the building is the curiosity shop. The taxidermy animals in the shop window watch us with their beady glass eyes. Beside them are the jars of Darkling hearts. I can almost hear them beating: *ba-boom, ba-boom, ba-boom.*

In the center of the town square is the wooden cross. Theora's hand tightens around mine. My grandfather is bound to one side of the cross with silver chains, his body stripped bare. His pale skin is covered in deep purple bruises. Crudely carved into his chest are two words: RACE TRAITOR.

Tied to the other side of the cross is Annora. She's naked, and her thin body is wrapped in silver chains. Like Lupines, Darklings are severely allergic to the silver, and the metal has seared her sensitive skin, which is already red-raw and flaking from being exposed to the sun all day. There's a gruesome hole in her shoulder where Drew shot her. She lets out a wail of pain, her cracked lips splitting over her fangs. It's obvious Mr. Langdon's put them up here as bait, but we sprint over to them anyway.

Lucinda, Kieran and Ulrika tug at the chains holding up Annora while Theora helps me remove the silver chains around my grandfather's ankles, fury and tears blinding me. The chains sting my bare skin as I peel them off his flesh.

"Edmund . . . ?" he whispers, struggling to get the word out through his dry lips.

"I'm going to get you out of here," I say.

"Go . . . ," he says. "Not safe . . ."

"I'm not going anywhere without you," I say firmly.

He groans as I remove the last of the chains and he falls heavily into my arms. We crash to the ground. *Oooph.* All the air leaves my lungs as my grandfather's head slumps against my chest. He shakily struggles upright and notices Alaric.

"What are you doing here?" Grandfather asks, confused.

"You're coming back with us," Alaric replies. "Edmund's agreed to—"

His words are cut off as the door opens to Langdon's General Store. Patrick appears at the doorway, holding a rifle.

"Well, well, well, the nipper's returned," he says loudly.

He steps out of the building, followed by Harriet and Drew. As if on cue, the doors open in the buildings around us and the townsfolk spill out into the plaza. They must have been waiting for us, listening for Patrick's signal. They look furious, their eyes cruel slits, their lips snarled. Leading the mob are the Guild members: Eric's father, Mr. Cranfield; Mr. O'Malley; and Mr. Langdon. His wife lingers behind him, his constant shadow dressed in black, her brown hair braided and tied with a blue ribbon, like the one Catherine used to wear.

I edge closer to Theora, and Alaric and Ulrika protectively surround Kieran. Lucinda cradles Annora, who is kneeling on the cobbled ground, weeping with fear. Grandfather attempts to straighten up, his chin lifting as Mr. Langdon approaches us. It's hard to look defiant when you're naked, but somehow he manages it.

"I hoped the boy would return for you," Mr. Langdon says to Grandfather. "I wanted you to watch him die. Then maybe you'd understand *my* pain."

Mrs. Langdon sniffs, dabbing her puffy, tear-stained eyes.

"Edmund had nothing to do with Catherine's death," Grandfather says. "He's innocent."

"Innocent?" Patrick yells. "He's a fragging nipper!"

The townspeople all murmur, agitated, angry. I hear the names Catherine, Eric, Mrs. Hope, Mr. Smyth spread through the crowd, like a war cry. They start to converge around us. I sling my arm around Grandfather's waist, while Alaric helps Lucinda drag Annora onto her feet. We frantically look about for a way to escape, but it's no good. Everywhere we turn, neighbors crowd the side streets, blocking our escape routes. They close in around us, backing us up against the curiosity shop on the east side of the plaza.

Someone throws a rock and it misses my head by a hair's

breadth, smashing into the shop window. Theora presses her face against my chest as the glass rains down on us, nicking our skin. The rock crashes into the table holding the jars of Darkling hearts, and they tumble down. A few shatter, splashing the putrid fluid everywhere. The glistening hearts lie on the ground like dead fish. One jar remains on the table, unbroken.

Right then, there's a bloodcurdling scream from the east corner of the town, then another from the west, followed by several pops of gunfire from the south. Everyone looks about, confused, wondering what's going on.

"Darklings!" Mr. Kent cries from the north end of the wall. There's more gunfire, and then a man's scream, followed by something hitting the ground with a crunch.

People start running in a blind panic, bumping into each other, not knowing where to go, reminding me of the time a bull escaped the paddocks on the outskirts of town. Then I see them—dozens of shadows spilling from the alleyways and over the rooftops slowly take form as they step into the moonlight: pale skin, glittering eyes, hair like black fire.

I realize now we were being followed earlier, but not by Patrick and the others. It was by the *Darklings*. They must have been out looking for Lucinda and Annora and saw Lucinda with me, and followed us here. The townsfolk scurry out of the way as a tall Darkling stalks through the crowd. He's dressed all in black, the tails of his frock coat fluttering behind him.

His dark, penetrating eyes slide over Patrick as he passes by. The boy stiffens, his hand tightening around the rifle, but he's too scared to use it. Harriet and Drew keep their knives held out in front of them, but they too are frozen in fear as the Darkling approaches us.

"Icarus," Grandfather exhales, his voice shaking.

"Hello, Hector," Icarus drawls, turning his black eyes on me. "So . . . this is my son."

I flush but hold his gaze. Around us, shadows move about the rooftops, closing in on the townsfolk. A few of them silently drop down into the plaza. There must be fifty Darklings, if not more. One approaches us. He looks similar to Icarus—narrow face, sharp cheekbones and thick brows over ebony eyes—so much so that I'm guessing they're brothers.

"Girls!" he cries out, ushering Lucinda and Annora over to him.

"Dad!" Lucinda replies, a look of relief entering her pretty, elfish face. She shrugs off her jacket, gently wrapping it around her sister's skinny body, and helps her over to their father. Kieran makes a move to follow them, but Ulrika grabs his arm and shakes her head.

Nearby, Mrs. Langdon angrily tugs on her husband's arm. "Do something, Christopher."

Mr. Langdon steps forward and nervously clears his throat. "You're breaking the terms of our treaty. I must insist that you leave, or—"

Icarus turns, a terrifying darkness entering his eyes, silencing Mr. Langdon.

"Or *what?*" he says softly. "You broke the treaty when you captured my niece Annora. That makes our deal null and void. We're perfectly within our rights to seek retribution."

"Father!" Patrick yells.

We all whip around. A male Darkling has grabbed Patrick. Two more have Harriet and Drew. They snap the O'Malley siblings' necks in one swift movement, and Harriet and Drew crash to the ground, the light in their blue eyes extinguished. From somewhere in the crowd their father, Mr. O'Malley, screams, a guttural, animalistic sound.

The two Darkling girls, Annora and Lucinda, look on, horrified. There's a big difference between feeding on a human and killing one. It's a fine line, but it's one I wasn't willing to cross with Catherine. The Darkling holding Patrick yanks his head to one side, baring his fangs, about to plunge them into the boy's neck.

"No!" Mr. Langdon cries out. "Not my son! Please!"

Icarus flicks his hand. "That'll do. We've made our point."

The Darkling closes his mouth, but he doesn't let go of Patrick.

Icarus takes a few paces toward Mr. Langdon, his eyes narrowing. "Haven't we met before?" The Darkling studies him for a moment, and then a smile spreads across his pale lips. "Yes, I remember. You were Cassie's boyfriend. And if memory serves, one of my best customers too."

There are stunned gasps from around the plaza. *Mr. Langdon was a Hazer?*

"Christopher?" Mrs. Langdon says quietly, her brow puckering.

"It's not true," he replies.

"Yes it is," my grandfather says, leaning against me, clearly struggling to stand. "You, Cassie and these two"—he gestures toward Mr. Cranfield and Mr. O'Malley—"frequently went into the forests to meet with these *demons.*" He practically spits the last word. "And then Cassie went and got herself pregnant. Why do you think we had to force the Darklings out of the forest eighteen years ago? Your parents and I did it to protect you from *them.*"

"*You* started the conflict between our people and the Dark-lings?" I say, my head spinning with the revelation that my grandfather started the Misery. At least now I understand how he was able to persuade the Lupines to join us in the fight—as their rightful pack leader, I'm guessing, he still must have some sway over them. I shoot a look at Alaric. His face is grim.

"I'm the minister of this town, Edmund," Grandfather says. "It's my duty to guard people's souls from impurity."

Icarus gazes at me. "You seem surprised, Edmund. Didn't your grandfather ever tell you how he led the hunting party that slaughtered ten innocent Darklings in their sleep?"

"No," I whisper.

Icarus slides a look past me toward the curiosity shop window. I follow his gaze. He's looking at the remaining jar of Darkling hearts.

"Didn't you ever wonder how they got those hearts?" he says, turning his attention back to me. "They were trophies your grandfather took from his victims that night. Two of those hearts belong to my parents."

I wince, looking at my grandfather, struggling to take this all in.

"I only did it to protect Cassie's soul," Grandfather says. "They're *demons*, Edmund. The world will never be a safe place until they are all destroyed."

Icarus takes a step toward us, and instinctively I move in front of Theora. Her hand tightens around mine. The gesture doesn't go unnoticed by Icarus. He arches a curious brow.

"Could it be . . . ?" He places a hand on my chest, and I shudder. A look of surprise briefly flitters across his features. "How is this possible?"

I slap his hand away and he growls at me, flashing his long

fangs. He digs a finger under my chin, tilting my head up so I'm looking into his black eyes. Up close, I realize I have my father's wide lips, his long nose and his square chin. Another shiver runs through me.

"You have your mother's eyes," he says. "Cassie always did have the most beautiful eyes. I must admit, I rather enjoyed seducing her."

Fury burns through me. "Is that what you call rape these days?"

"Rape?" He laughs. "I didn't attack Cassie. Where would the victory have been in that? I had no real interest in hurting her." His gaze shifts to my grandfather. "It was Hector I wanted to destroy, after what he did to my parents. I wanted to take away everything he loved the most, and what better way to do that than to corrupt his precious daughter's soul?" A cruel smile plays across his lips.

"It had only been my intention to get Cassie pregnant. I knew once everyone saw her bastard child, she'd be shunned from the community and Hector would be disgraced. I couldn't have dreamed she would try to drown you and then hang herself, but I can't say I'm disappointed at how it turned out."

I whip around on my grandfather. "Tell him that's not true! Mother dropped me in the bathwater!"

Grandfather lowers his eyes. "I'm sorry, Edmund," he says quietly. "Cassie was heartbroken when he rejected her. She couldn't live with the shame of what she'd done."

His words are like a freight train hitting me in the gut, and I sink to the stone steps in front of the curiosity shop. *My mom tried to kill me?* Theora kneels down and puts her arms around me.

Icarus unfurls his hand, stretching it toward me. "Join me, Edmund."

"No!" Grandfather says. "You took Cassie from me. Isn't that enough?"

Icarus's face hardens. "I gave you eighteen years with Edmund—the same amount of time you got to share with Cassie. I've been more than generous. But now it's time for my son to take his place in our clan."

My whole body begins to shake as I'm consumed with rage. Icarus toyed with my mom's heart and brought about her suicide, and now he's trying to take me away, all to punish my grandfather—the man who has spent his whole life protecting me, guiding me, even *killing* for me. I won't let this happen.

Before I realize what I'm doing, I lunge at my father. Icarus is so surprised by my sudden attack that he doesn't block it, and we both fall to the ground, me on top of him. My fist connects with his nose and there's a snap of bone breaking. Icarus grunts and grabs my hair, yanking me off him, his fangs bared. Blood streams out of his nose. He clamps his strong hands around my throat, his fingers digging into my flesh, and drags me up onto my knees so I'm staring at him. There's nothing but hatred in my father's eyes as he glares down at me.

"I will only ask you this once," he says darkly. "Leave with me tonight and take your rightful place by my side, son."

"I will never live with you demons!" I spit.

Icarus's mouth twitches. "Have it your way."

I claw at his hands as he slowly, deliberately, begins to squeeze my throat. Black spots start to form in front of my eyes as the air is forced out of my windpipe. In my peripheral vision, I spot something white flash past. Icarus suddenly releases me. I crash to the ground, gasping for air. Chaos immediately breaks out around me.

The Darklings surge forward, the humans try to flee. Bodies drop to the ground; blood flows between the cracks in the cobblestones. Mrs. Langdon's lifeless body hits the earth. Her husband is next. Ulrika holds Kieran back, keeping him out of the throng, while Alaric fights a group of Darklings. They swarm over him until he's swallowed by their bodies. A moment later the scent of Lupine blood bursts into the air.

"Dad!" Ulrika screams.

All this is background noise to the fight happening in front of me. Theora is on top of Icarus, her white hair flowing wildly around her as they brawl. Her gray top is torn, there's blood on her lips, but she doesn't stop, her silver eyes glinting with fury. They roll across the ground, wrestling with each other. She tries to pin him down, but he smacks her across the face and she falls to the ground, stunned by the blow. He stands up. Theora tries to crawl away from him, her fingers clawing at the stones. Her panicked eyes snag mine as Icarus looms over her. It all happens so quickly, I don't even have time to cry out as his hands clamp around her head and twist.

I gasp, clutching my chest.

My heart clenches, there's a stab of pain, and then:

Silence.

21.

EDMUND

SILENCE. IT SITS INSIDE ME like a physical thing, cold, unbreakable, everlasting. It can only mean one thing. My heart has stopped beating, because Theora is dead. The grief, the loss, is sudden and sharp, paralyzing me. I want to die. I am dead. Lucinda was right; Theora was my Blood Mate. But now she's gone, she's gone, she's gone . . .

Icarus lets her go, and Theora flops to the ground like a rag doll. Somewhere to my left Ulrika wails with grief. The fighting continues around us, but I barely notice it. Ice already begins to form in my veins. Lucinda rushes over to Theora's body, checking her pulse, but it's no use, I know she's gone. Grandfather puts his arms around me, holding me close.

"Why did you do it?" Lucinda shouts. "Theora saved me and Annora! She was kind and—"

"A mongrel," he interjects. "Just a mongrel."

My blood boils. "She was my Blood Mate!"

Icarus turns toward me.

"I had a heartbeat and you took it from me. You—" My words get trapped in my bruised throat as the loss consumes me again. Grandfather's grip tightens around me and I can hear him crying too. Icarus got his wish without even realizing it; he destroyed my grandfather by taking away the one thing he wanted the most for me.

"Didn't I tell you, Edmund? Darklings are demons," Grandfather whispers in my ear. "This is what they do; they take everything you cherish."

Icarus's eyes drift toward something in the shop behind me. He steps over Theora's body to retrieve it and returns a moment later, carrying a jar of Darkling hearts. He scoops the organs from the jar, carefully placing them on the ground, then kicks Theora onto her back. I'm too horrified to move as he leans over her body, blocking her from my view. There's a crack of bones, the scent of blood, the *plop* of something dropping into fluid. A moment later Icarus stands. He strolls over to me, a sadistic smile twisted on his lips. Clutched in his bloodied hands is the glass jar. Floating inside it is Theora's heart.

"It's tradition in our culture to harvest your Blood Mate's heart after they die," he says tauntingly. "This is my gift to you, son. A *token*, just like your grandfather took from my people." He gestures toward the pile of hearts on the ground before passing the jar to me.

I stare at it, revulsion crawling through me. This isn't a gift. It's a cruel reminder of everything I so briefly had but will never experience again.

He killed her.

The shimmering fluid in the jar begins to vibrate, and for a moment I think Theora's heart is beating inside the glass container. Then I hear the thunder deep within the earth, slow at first, then growing, growing, like the anger boiling up inside me.

He took her from me.

Houses begin to shake, the bell chimes in the church spire, glass shatters. The fighting in the square stops as the earth violently quakes. All around me people cry out in terror. Kieran grabs on to Ulrika while Lucinda scrambles back to Annora and her parents. Tiles slide off the curiosity shop roof, smashing around us. Nearby, Patrick struggles against the Darkling still holding on to him, but the creature refuses to let go.

Right then, there's a low, ominous rumble in the distance. Everyone turns to look at Mount Alba, silhouetted against the stars. The trees growing up the mountainside start to tremble. There's a moment of silence, like the world holding its breath, then:

BOOM!

The force of the blast knocks everyone onto their backs. Plumes of ash and smoke spew into the sky, forming a mushroom cloud miles above Mount Alba, where its claw-shaped peak once stood. The heat is intense, singeing my eyebrows and lashes. My ears throb with the roaring, churning, belching sound of the volcano as it disgorges the earth's innards.

Everyone begins to scream, even the Darklings. Grandfather lets me go. I look about me. To my left, Ulrika is beside Kieran, close to Alaric's mauled, lifeless body; to my right, Grandfather has his arms thrown over his head; in front of us, Icarus just stares up at the sky in awe. Nearby, I spot Annora and Lucinda being led out of the plaza by their father and a pretty female Darkling I hadn't noticed earlier. The other Darklings scatter, including the one who had held Patrick hostage. Patrick scrambles to his feet and takes a few steps toward me, when something bright orange shoots through the sky—a volcanic bomb! The molten rock crashes into the town square.

Boom!

There's a tremendous explosion, sending stone and debris into the air, making the glass jar in my hands rattle. Patrick lies on the ground, groaning with pain. Nearby, the enormous cross that my grandfather was recently strapped to starts to teeter dangerously, the damaged frame creaking loudly.

"Look out!" Ulrika shouts.

Icarus whips around, his eyes widening as he notices the shaking cross. Grandfather and I scramble to our feet just as the wood splinters and the cross falls. It's going to hit us! Grandfather pushes me out of the way a split second before Icarus grabs him and pulls him into an embrace. The cross lands on them, crushing them both under its weight.

"No!" I scream. "NO!"

I thrust the glass jar into Ulrika's hands and attempt to lift the cross off Grandfather's body, but it's too heavy. I push it, kick it, but it just won't budge. Ulrika tugs at my arm.

"Edmund, stop!" she says. "He's gone! We have to get out of here!"

Tears slide down my cheeks. *Gone*. First Theora and now my grandfather. Everyone I've ever cared about, gone. My eyes shift to Icarus's dead body. It's his fault. He took them both from me. His last act on this earth was to murder my grandfather and leave me alone in this world. My father's soulless black eyes stare up at me, blank, hollow, but there's a mocking smirk on his frozen lips.

Another volcanic bomb lands in the town, toward the east, making the ground shake. Thankfully most of the townsfolk are running toward the north end of the town, near the paddocks. There's a second gate there, which leads out to the main road that connects Amber Hills to the nearest city, Gray Wolf.

"Edmund, we have to go!" Ulrika says, blinking rapidly as ash settles on her eyelashes.

"We have to get Dad first," Kieran says, pointing toward the mountain. "Our whole pack is up there, we—"

The ground shifts again. Ulrika falls against me, nearly dropping the glass jar in her hands. There's another roar of thunder from the volcano as a scorching torrent of rocks and mud slides down the mountainside like a river, drowning the forest, destroying everything in its path, including the Lupine village. It's heading straight for Amber Hills!

"Dad!" Kieran screams as if his voice could somehow carry across the miles. There's nothing we can do but watch as the forest is shrouded by clouds of molten ash.

"We need to leave!" Ulrika shouts over the roar of the landslide.

I give my grandfather's and Theora's bodies a final glance, knowing it's the last time I'll ever see them, before we race through the crowds and join the throng of people trying to escape. I shoot a look toward Mount Alba. The landslide is getting closer, closer, tearing up the earth. The Boundary Wall will slow its progress for a short while but I don't know for how long. Ash and small rocks rain down on us, cutting our skin, burning our clothes, but we don't slow down. The smell of rotting eggs fills my nostrils and I gag.

We leap over the dead bodies. Something grabs my ankle and I nearly lose my footing. I look down. Patrick's hand is gripped around my leg. There's a large gash in his thigh.

"Help me," he begs.

I could leave him. I *should* leave him. He tried to kill me. But it's not like I'm blameless. If I hadn't fed on Catherine, my grandfather would never have had to kill her.

I look up at Ulrika. "Head to the paddocks! Just follow this path—it'll take you there."

She leaves with Kieran, the glass jar tucked under her other arm, while I help Patrick up. He briefly looks back at his parents' lifeless bodies in the plaza, and then we're hurrying through the streets as fast as we can with his injured leg, toward the gate beyond the paddock. It's hard to see as volcanic ash rains down on us, scorching my throat with every breath. Through the gritty fog, I notice the Boundary Wall looming up ahead. The gate is already open, and people stream out of the narrow entrance to the world beyond. We run toward the gate, but halfway there Patrick yells out in pain as his injured leg buckles beneath him.

"Leave me," he gasps.

"No." I grit my teeth as I lift him over my shoulder.

I carry him out of the gate and run down the main road as fast as I can, putting as much distance between us and Amber Hills as possible. Along the way we pass the townsfolk who managed to escape the town. I spot Ulrika and Kieran among them.

"You made it!" Ulrika says breathlessly. She's still carrying Theora's heart in the jar.

The four of us keep running, running, running. I run from the landslide, I run from Amber Hills, I run from the life I once had. I don't stop until my legs burn and my lungs are unable to take another breath. I drop Patrick on the ground and collapse, panting, heaving, throwing up bile and ash. He groans, but manages to sit up, clasping his bleeding leg.

Kieran collapses on the ground beside him. "I think we're safe."

I look down the road. It's hard to see through the smog and ash, but I think he's right. The Boundary Wall must've slowed the landslide down just enough to keep it from coming this far.

"Thank you," Patrick says.

I glance at him. His whole body is covered in ash, so he's gray from head to toe. So am I. So is everything. The sky. The ground. Our faces. *Gray.* Everything is the same.

"No problem," I say flatly.

Ulrika hands me the glass jar. It's covered in soot. I wipe away the black dirt, revealing Theora's heart inside. Grief spills over me, thinking about the life we might have had together. I'll never get the chance to love her or have her fall in love with me. I'll never feel my heart beating again. Icarus stole that from me. I want Theora back, but not in this way.

I thrust the jar into Ulkira's hands. She doesn't say anything as she accepts it.

"What do we do now?" Patrick says.

I look down the road. There's no point in going back to Amber Hills; there's nothing there to go back to. I turn my head. The road on this side leads to Gray Wolf, then beyond that . . . *freedom.* I can go wherever I want to go. Be whoever I want to be. My options are unlimited. But there is one thing I am certain of: I will make the Darklings suffer for what they've taken from me. I clutch the circle pendant around my neck as a plan starts to formulate in my mind. The future stretches out before me, and I see it how I want it to be:

A world without sin.

A world in her image.

A world united.

So sayeth us all.

22.
ASH

"**SO NOW YOU KNOW** the truth about Purian Rose," Lucinda says tiredly.

Everyone is silent. I sink back in my seat, trying to wrap my head around everything I've heard. Purian Rose is related to me? No wonder my mom never spoke about her family. Who wants to admit that their cousin is the man responsible for leading a war that killed millions of Darklings? She must have been so ashamed, and frightened too—being related to Purian Rose would've put our family at terrible risk during the war.

"Ulrika and I lived with Edmund and Patrick for a while in Gray Wolf," Kieran says. "But it didn't work out. They became fanatical about religion, spending day and night rewriting the Guild's scriptures that were lost in the eruption and tweaking it to suit their own beliefs—"

"The Book of Creation?" Day interjects, referring to the holy text that the Purity faith is based on.

Kieran nods. "During that time Edmund's hatred of the Darklings got worse. He blamed them for everything wrong in his life." He sighs, rubbing his head. "He blew his top when he found out I was still in touch with Luci and Annora, so we parted ways. Ulrika came back here while I went traveling with Luci and Annora, attending civil rights rallies across the country, and Edmund and Patrick moved to Centrum to make a name for themselves in politics."

"When he came into power a few years later as Purian Rose, we knew we had to stop him," Lucinda adds. "That's why we formed the Four Kingdoms."

Elijah turns to his mom. "How did you get involved in the group?"

"I met Luci and the others at a rally in Thrace," Yolanda answers. "We were all staying with Esme at the Moon Star tavern."

Kieran smiles at the mention of his wife and home. Natalie flicks a guilty look at me. Neither of us has had a chance to tell him that Esme's dead. Now's not the right time.

"Why didn't the Four Kingdoms reveal Edmund's true identity?" Day asks.

"Because we didn't have any evidence, just our word," Lucinda says. "And who would believe *us,* especially since Edmund looks human. We tried to hunt down some of the former residents of Amber Hills, but many died that night of the eruption, and the rest were unwilling to talk."

"We approached a detective with this information years ago," Yolanda adds. "We think the detective got close to something once. He said he was following a lead—something about an illegitimate child"—I shoot a look at Natalie, who has turned pale—"but he died in a house fire before he could pursue it any further. The fire was set deliberately."

"Sounds like something the Sentry would do," Day says fiercely.

The Sentry guards burnt down her house after the ballot a

few weeks ago. Her younger brother, MJ, was still inside at the time, although Natalie and I managed to save him.

"But you said Purian Rose doesn't have a heartbeat?" Elijah says from the front seat. "How come no one's noticed that?"

Lucinda gives a bitter laugh. "Oh, I'm sure Purian Rose has bribed or threatened his doctor to keep his mouth shut."

"Guys, we're here," Acelot says from the driver's seat.

The truck sways as we drive over the bumpy dirt track toward a run-down log cabin, hidden among the lichen-covered trees. It's very dark both inside and outside the vehicle, since barely any sunlight penetrates the forest. Sinister shadows lurk between the trees like stalking wolves, making me shudder. I can see how the Forest of Shadows earned its name.

Acelot parks the truck outside the cabin and we get out. We're in a forest glen. The air smells like pine needles, rain and sap. My boots sink into the lush, mossy earth as I jump out of the vehicle and help Martha down, then Natalie. Her hand is soft and warm in mine. She smiles at me, and for a second I return it, before guilt and grief come crashing down on me. I shouldn't smile, shouldn't feel any happiness when my dad is . . . he's . . . I swallow a painful lump in my throat. Natalie's brows draw together and I look away. Now isn't the time to break down.

Kieran strides up to the cabin and raps loudly on the door, knocking three times, then twice, then four times. The house looks abandoned—the walls are covered in ivy, the windows are dirty, and the yellow paint on the door is cracked. I'm starting to think Ulrika isn't here, when suddenly the door opens. A middle-aged Lupine stands in the entranceway, dressed in leather pants and a tight black top and frock coat. She's thin but athletic, with weather-chapped skin, short cropped hair and dirt under her nails. She immediately pulls Kieran into her arms.

"Fragg, I thought you were dead. You were due here weeks ago," she says, then adds dryly, "You could have called."

"Yeah, you know me, cuz. Always like to be fashionably late," Kieran says. "We got caught sneaking around Primus-One."

They pull apart, and Ulrika nods politely at Yolanda and Lucinda. She notices us for the first time.

"This is my nephew, Ash," Lucinda explains.

"I know who he is," Ulrika says, ushering us inside. "Everyone's heard of 'the boy who rose from the ashes.'" Did I detect a note of sarcasm in her voice?

The inside of the cabin is cool and dank. The main source of light in the kitchen/living room comes from the amber flames flickering in the stone hearth to my left, which casts a deep orange glow over everything in the dingy room. Shelves line the peeling walls, which are crammed with warped, mildew-covered books. Perched on a rickety cabinet nearby is a portable TV and a dust-covered telephone. There's a simple pinewood table in the center of the room, and a few mismatched chairs. To the right, there's a single work surface, stove, fridge and a couple of cupboards. Several dead rabbits hang from hooks above the sink, their fresh blood dripping into the porcelain bowl.

"We can't stay long," Kieran says to his cousin. "Do you have it?"

Ulrika nods. She walks over to the cupboards at the kitchen side of the room, while Natalie and Day clear a seat for Martha and help the old lady sit down. Beetle does a quick check of the house to make sure it's secure. Ulrika angrily purses her lips when he goes into her bedroom.

"You won't find anything suspicious in my panty drawer," she calls to him.

Beetle exits the bedroom, the tips of his ears bright pink. He's carrying some cotton slips.

"I thought the ladies might want something better to cover themselves with." He passes them to Yolanda, Martha and Lucinda, who put them on underneath their blankets and jackets. Ulrika sighs but says nothing as she starts looking through the cupboards.

"Kieran said the guards know you're living up here?" Day says.

Ulrika throws her an impatient look. "Of course they do. Edmund came to visit me when they started putting the wall up, giving me the opportunity to leave."

"And you deliberately *stayed*?" I splutter.

"Why not?" she says. "This is my home. And at least here I'm safe. There are a lot of Lupine haters out there at the moment."

"I wonder why," Beetle mutters.

"It doesn't bother you that millions of people are being killed just a few miles down the road?" I say.

"Of course it bothers me, but what can *I* do about it?" she says.

My fangs throb with venom and Beetle frowns, making the scar tissue on his cheek pucker. There's plenty she could do, if she wanted.

"If you don't mind my asking, why is Edmund still protecting you?" Natalie asks. "I thought he was mad at you and Kieran."

"Kieran more than me. He's the one who wanted to stay in touch with Lucinda and Annora," Ulrika says, casting a cold look at Lucinda, who returns her frosty gaze. "Besides, Theora was my best friend. That still means something to him." Ulrika closes the cupboard door and checks the unit above the sink.

Beetle turns to Lucinda. "Do you think Rose knew you were being held prisoner?"

Lucinda sits at the table. "I doubt it. He probably would have let Kieran go at the very least, if he'd been told we were there."

I think about the fact that no one knew my dad had died at the camp—something that would have been all over the news if they had—and figure she's right. With the huge amount of people flowing into the Tenth each day, it must be hard for them to keep track of all the prisoners. The registration department probably hasn't had time to cross-check the names to make sure no one is there who shouldn't be.

"Ah, here it is," Ulrika says, pulling a dusty jar out of the cupboard. She places the glass jar on the table in front of us. It's filled with a sickly yellow fluid. Floating inside it is Theora's heart.

"Aw, gross," Beetle mutters.

"Why did you keep it all these years?" Day asks.

"Theora was like a sister to me, and we lost our whole pack in the eruption the night she died," Ulrika says. "I wanted to keep part of her, part of *them*, alive, I guess."

"How is this going to bring down Purian Rose?" Elijah asks his mom.

I'm curious to know this too.

"We were going to transplant it inside someone," Yolanda explains. "Our hope was that if we could get this person to Purian Rose, his heart might reactivate, creating a Blood Mate connection, and she'd be able to persuade him to stop the war."

Beetle and Day share bemused looks.

"Utterly insane," Ulrika mutters under her breath. "There's

no guarantee it would work, even if you could get the heart transplanted."

The plan *is* crazy, but if anyone in this room understands the strength of the Blood Mate connection, it's me and Natalie. If she asked me to end a war, I would, in a heartbeat.

"I think it's a fragging brilliant plan," I say.

Lucinda grins. She looks a lot like my mom when she does that; my mom always had a wry smile on her lips.

"But isn't the heart *really* old?" Day says. "Not to mention it's been in embalming fluid all this time. You won't be able to transplant it inside someone without killing them."

"We could if they were a twin-blood," Lucinda says, sliding a look at me.

My stomach knots as it dawns on me that Lucinda intends to use *me* as the vessel. It makes sense. Twin-bloods don't need their hearts to live, so I won't die, even if the organ fails. I'm immune to most toxins, so the embalming solution the heart has been preserved in won't poison me, and I have the power to regenerate dead tissue. Lucinda's thought of everything, except one thing: I don't want to do it. I don't want someone to rip my heart out and replace it with another one. Not to mention, I'd be Purian Rose's Blood Mate! That's twisted on *so* many levels. I don't care so much about the guy-guy thing; I've had plenty of male Haze clients in my day, and things often got steamy—my "added extras" were why clients came to me instead of buying vials of Haze from the human dealers—but Purian Rose is the butcher of the Darklings, not to mention we're *related*. That's . . . urgh! Just, *urgh*. Natalie takes my hand, sensing my discomfort.

"It's a Lupine heart. Surely Ash would reject it," Day says.

"Not if he had a geneticist who specialized in xenotransplantation," Yolanda replies.

So that's why Lucinda needed Yolanda's expertise. It wasn't anything to do with her research into yellowpox; it was because of her work with cross-species transplants. I can't believe we didn't pick up on this earlier. What better way to bring down Purian Rose, without risking anyone's life?

"This is all assuming Ash is okay with you cutting out his heart," Acelot says distractedly from the other side of the room. He's peering out the dusty window, checking our perimeter. He's left his Sentry guard jacket in the truck, so he's just wearing a white vest, black pants and boots. His speckled tail sways rhythmically behind him, stirring the dust on the floor. He glances at me. "Lucky for you, my friend, we don't need to go ahead with this *fukaka* plan, huh?"

I give him a grateful smile, feeling secretly relieved. I'm not sure I'd be able to do it if push came to shove. Lucinda shoots a quizzical look at me and at Natalie, who briefly explains about the Sentry rebel stronghold in Gallium.

"And you trust those people?" Lucinda asks.

"Those *people* are my parents," Natalie replies tersely. "So, yes, I trust them."

"They do have an amazing arsenal of weapons," Elijah says to his mom. "Not to mention a whole fleet of Transporters, which have all been weaponized. It's very professional. They're planning an attack on Centrum in four days."

"And then what?" Lucinda snarls. "We'll replace one fragging Sentry for another. How will things be any different?"

Natalie looks at me, uncertainty sliding behind her blue eyes. Lucinda has a point. If the Sentry rebels take control of

Centrum, then it's not going to improve our situation much. It'll still be a Sentry government, filled with people who will put their needs above ours. At least if Humans for Unity and the Four Kingdoms took control, they would try to create a fair and representative government.

Natalie's watch suddenly beeps. "That's Destiny."

"I see the Transporter," Acelot confirms, stepping away from the window.

Ulrika opens her arms to Kieran. "Well, I guess this is good-bye, cousin."

"You won't come with us?" he asks.

She shakes her head. "This is my h—"

Her words suddenly cut off. The lines in her forehead deepen with confusion. She opens her lips to speak, and a bubble of blood pools out of a small bullet hole in her throat. There's a matching hole in the windowpane that Acelot was standing in front of moments before. Ulrika crashes to the floor.

"GET DOWN!" I yell just as the back windows shatter in a rain of bullets. They thump into the wooden walls, tear up books, smash glasses.

Elijah shoves his mom to the ground just as a book explodes above her head, sending a confetti of words into the air. Everybody hits the floor. Kieran lands beside me. Part of his face is missing.

"Kieran!" Lucinda's wail pierces my eardrums. "Kieran, KIERAN!"

Natalie is a foot away, lying facedown, her hands clasped over her head. I grip the back of her jacket and drag her toward me, and shield her with my body. Her pulse is racing. A shadow blocks out the dim light from the front window, and there's a loud hum of engines. Another burst of bullets punctuate the room as Beetle crawls across the floor toward the front door. He inches it open and checks outside.

"Destiny's landing the Transporter! We can make it if we run," he says.

There's another round of gunfire, and Natalie flinches. Day leaps to her feet and helps Martha up. They hurry out the door, followed by Beetle, Elijah, Acelot and then Yolanda. Lucinda is under the table, frozen with fear, her eyes fixed on Kieran's destroyed face.

I look down at Natalie. "Go."

"Not without you!" she says.

"I'll be right behind you."

Natalie quickly kisses me, then scrambles to her feet and darts out the front door, her blond curls fanning behind her. A bullet slams into the wooden doorframe, missing her by an inch. My heart clenches. There's no time to panic. I turn toward my aunt.

"Lucinda, we need to go," I say, stretching out a hand toward her.

Something else in the room shatters and Lucinda cowers.

"Take my hand!" I demand.

She blinks, coming back to her senses, and takes my hand. We clamber out from under the table. I grab the glass jar containing Theora's heart—we came all this way, and I'm not leaving without it—and we dash outside.

The aircraft is about fifty feet away, the engines roaring, making the trees sway and their leaves stir. Beetle is by the hatch, his gun raised toward the trees. "Hurry up, mate!" he says. The others are already inside.

Above the tree line, I hear the telltale hum of more Transporters approaching.

"Over there!" a voice shouts from the trees to my left.

A Sentry guard emerges from the gloom, his gun poised. I steer my aunt to the right just as he pulls the trigger. The bullet grazes my arm and I grunt with pain. There's a *pop-pop-pop* of retaliatory gunfire from the Transporter as Beetle unloads his weapon, giving us a few vital seconds of cover. I force myself to run faster, my lungs burning with the effort. Lucinda barely manages to keep pace, her feet stumbling on a fallen log. I drag her upright as another bullet whizzes by us. We reach the Transporter just as more Sentry guards race around the cabin and start shooting. Beetle grips Lucinda's hand and helps her on board. I leap onto the aircraft, landing heavily on the metal floor, and nearly drop Theora's heart.

"Go!" I shout to Destiny as Natalie rushes over to me, helping me to my feet.

Destiny yanks on the control stick and the Transporter lurches up.

The hatch begins to close, but it's not fast enough. A Sentry guard aims his gun at the aircraft and pulls the trigger. Two bullets hit the metal frame, but one makes it through. The Transporter suddenly dips wildly. Natalie lets out a cry of panic as she stumbles against me, and we slam into the right wall.

In the cockpit, Destiny is grimacing with pain as she attempts to keep control of the aircraft, blood seeping out of the wound in her shoulder. Acelot, Beetle and Day race over to the cockpit. Acelot takes over the controls, stabilizing the aircraft, while Beetle lifts the Sentry woman out of the pilot's seat and lays her down on the empty bench. Day slides into the copilot's seat. A stream of curse words spill out of Destiny's lips as she clutches her bleeding shoulder.

The aircraft levels and Acelot boosts the engines. The

Transporter rushes upward, the sound of the tree branches like rats scratching at the metal walls. We break through the tree line, and immediately the aircraft is flooded with brilliant white light. There's a *rat-a-tat-tat* of machine-gun fire, and bullets thud into the armored walls and crack the windscreen.

"We have company!" Acelot says.

Out the splintered windscreen I notice three Transporters. They're heading straight at us.

"Hit the green button!" Destiny says through gritted teeth.

"Which green button?" Day replies, panicked. There are several on the dashboard.

"The one next to the orange switch," Destiny grunts. "The missiles automatically lock on the closest target, unless you aim them elsewhere."

"I see it!" Day says, slamming her hand on the green button.

A missile flashes across the sky, and a second later the nearest Transporter explodes into a ball of fire, sending metal and debris raining down on the forest. Day punches the switch again. The second missile hits its target and the aircraft's wing rips off. The vehicle spirals down to the ground. There's a terrible explosion, followed by shock waves that buffet our ship, making everyone jerk in their seats. The third Transporter veers off, knowing it's vastly outgunned, the guards wisely trying to escape before they're shot out of the sky too. We zoom over the detention camp, flying over Primus-Two, then One. Several new trainloads of prisoners are being led up to the registration office. The Boundary Wall looms up ahead. An idea hits me.

"You got any more missiles?" I say.

She checks the monitor. "There's three left."

"See that wall?" I say, pointing toward the concrete structure. "Aim them all at that."

Day grins. "Yes, sir."

She aims the controls and punches the green button, once, twice, three times. The missiles all hit their targets. Dust and debris fly up into the air as the wall is blasted apart, leaving a hole about a mile wide across it. The startled guards aren't quick enough to react as the prisoners swarm to it, spilling through the gap toward freedom. *One down.*

Acelot and Day fly us away from the Tenth, and soon Mount Alba becomes little more than a pockmark on the landscape. I return to the main cabin. Beetle and Natalie are tending to Destiny's wounds, while Elijah rests his head on his mom's lap. I quickly check the wound on my arm—it's just a graze—then take a seat beside Lucinda on the metal bench, the glass jar in my hands. It weighs so little. It's hard to believe this small object was the catalyst that started Edmund Rose's campaign of terror against the Darklings. Now it's time to end it.

23.
NATALIE

THE SUN HAS STARTED TO SET over the city by the time we reach the Sentry rebel stronghold in Gallium, so the bronze-fronted buildings glow like candlelight. It's only been a little over a day since we left here, but it feels like a lifetime, so much has happened. Through the windscreen, I watch the city swoosh past us in a blur of copper. Transporters zoom across the sepia skies, carrying cargo to and from the munitions factories. I don't think we were followed out of the Tenth—I haven't seen any aircraft. Acelot's an incredibly skilled pilot, expertly weaving the Transporter between the skyscrapers and industrial buildings. Day is chatting happily to him, enjoying her impromptu flying lesson.

Ash sits silently beside me, his jaw clenched. He hasn't said a word since we left the Tenth, and I haven't pushed it. He's trying so hard to keep it together. His hair stirs gently, sensing the blood around us. We all have cuts and scrapes from the shoot-out, and Destiny's shirt is stained with dry blood. Her wound has finally stopped bleeding; Beetle did a great job on the bandage. He patched up Ash's arm too. Beetle's now asleep on the bench between me and Destiny.

She glances at the glass jar on Ash's lap. "I can't believe we did all that for a *heart*." She sighs. "Well, it wasn't a total bust. At least we got Ash."

I smile, my hand tightening around his. Getting him back was my priority, so I'm not too disappointed the Ora didn't turn out to be yellowpox, although it's going to be hard explaining to my father why we risked our lives to retrieve a thirty-year-old Lupine heart.

I check my jacket pocket, remembering the vial of silvery-white liquid I stole from the laboratory in the Tenth. I take the vial out of my syringe case. Thankfully it hasn't broken. There's a small label on the glass tube with F-09 WINGS written on it.

"That looks suspiciously like a Haze blend," Ash says, glancing at the vial.

"Yeah, that's what I thought too." I've had enough experience with the Golden Haze—a mix of milky-white Haze, which has a distinctively gluey consistency, and glimmering gold Bastet venom—to recognize a blend when I see one. The mix is just milky-silver instead of milky-gold. "It's the silver stuff the Haze has been combined with that I'm curious about. Maybe it's Night Whisper?" I muse, recalling the butterflies we saw on the laboratory. Their wings are silvery in color. But why would Purian Rose add them to the Haze?

I lift it up to the overhead light. The liquid glints, drawing Yolanda's attention.

"What's this?" she asks, taking it from me.

"A drug called Wings. It was in the Sentry lab back at the Tenth, along with this disc," I say, retrieving a blue disc out of my pocket with PATIENT TRIALS scrawled on it. "I want Dr. Craven to run some tests on the drug, to see what's in it."

"I'd like to help with that," Yolanda replies, passing the vial back.

I tuck it into my pocket and go up to the cockpit.

"Which way?" Acelot asks me. The cheetahlike markings down the sides of his handsome face are more pronounced in the gold light of sunset.

I point toward a smelting works on the west side of the city, which conceals the tunnel leading into the Sentry rebels' stronghold. From an onlooker's perspective, it just looks like we're flying into the factory's warehouse, which won't rouse suspicion—it's common to see Transporters flying in and out of factories around here as they transfer cargo. Acelot steers the vehicle through the open factory roof, and Day punches a button on the control panel. The warehouse's false floor opens, revealing the tunnel entrance, and we fly down into the rebel compound. I return to my seat and buckle up as we land inside the aircraft hangar.

"Home sweet home," Elijah says, giving me a tired smile. He seems exhausted but happy. Then again, why shouldn't he be? He's got his mother back.

The hatch door lets out a hydraulic hiss as it opens. Waiting for us on the other side is my mother, father, Garrick and Sasha. They all look furious. *Uh-oh.*

"What do you have to say for yourself, young lady?" my mother shouts.

I glance sheepishly at my father, who looks angrier than I've ever seen him before, his scarred face twisted into a fierce scowl.

"You've got a *lot* of explaining to do, Natalie," he says through clenched teeth.

Ash grabs his blue duffel bag from under the bench, which Destiny had been storing for him while we were in the Tenth, and takes my hand. My mother's icy blue eyes narrow with disapproval, but I ignore her. I don't care what my parents think of Ash, it's not going to change my feelings for him.

Garrick and Sasha help Destiny off the Transporter, while the others assist Martha, Lucinda and Yolanda. They're able to walk, but they're all shaky on their feet. Mother gives Martha an awkward hug, which surprises the old Darkling woman as much as it does me.

We head to the elevator, my mother muttering angry words at me the whole way. I chew on the inside of my cheek, accepting the barrage of abuse. She has every right to be mad at me. Occasionally I flick a look at my father, but he refuses to meet my eye.

"I'm sorry I worried you," I say, unable to stand his silence any longer. "But I'm not sorry for what I did. Ash needed my help, and I couldn't wait around for you to ask the Commander if we could send a rescue mission, only for him to say no anyway."

Father's scarred lips tighten, but he doesn't say anything. He knows I'm right.

The elevator doors slide open and we enter the compound. Ash's eyes widen as he takes it all in: the zooming subway trains, the bustling sidewalks, the metal buildings—it's a lot to digest. He whistles through his teeth.

"You weren't exaggerating," he murmurs.

We head straight for the hospital, where Dr. Craven is waiting for us to tend to our wounds. Sigur is lying in one of the hospital beds, still recovering from his own ordeal. He struggles into an upright position when he sees us. A muscle in Ash's jaw tightens as he looks at his Blood Father. Sigur's long ice-white hair has been pulled back, revealing the full extent of the wounds on his muscular torso. There are lacerations and UV burns on his alabaster skin, plus a patchwork of bruises where the guards have kicked him. On his back are two pink nubbins where his wings used to be, before Sebastian cut them off.

"Son," Sigur says, opening his pale arms wide.

Ash places his bag and Theora's heart on the sideboard, then sinks down on Sigur's bed and allows himself to be folded into his Blood Father's embrace.

"I'm sorry I left you," Ash whispers, his voice pained. "I should never have let them hurt you. I should have saved you, I'm sorry, oh God, oh God, I'm so sorry . . ."

Sigur catches my eye.

"Harold's dead," I say quietly.

Grief flickers across Sigur's features and he tightens his hold on Ash, realizing the apology isn't aimed just at him. Lucinda sits beside them and gently strokes Ash's hair.

Across the room, Elijah, Acelot and Yolanda are in their own huddle, their arms around one another as they cry for their lost family. If this war ever ends, I want to go back to Gray Wolf and retrieve Marcel's body, so he can be buried with the rest of his family in Viridis, where he belongs, rather than underneath a pile of stones in some abandoned warehouse, with nothing but a few trinkets and dandelion seeds to mark his grave.

I turn to my own father and wrap my arms around him. He doesn't say anything, just holds me close. My mother lightly places her hand on my back. I'm so lucky to have them. I briefly gaze up, noticing Martha lingering nearby. Father stretches a hand out to her. She takes it, and joins the group hug. My family is finally back together again . . . almost. My insides ache at the thought of Polly, missing her desperately. I think about the knife back in my bedroom—the one I stole from the Ultraviolet Greenhouse—with her name etched into the handle. I haven't forgotten about my promise to my sister. I'm going to kill Purian Rose.

I eventually pull away from them, dabbing my eyes. Garrick and Sasha have brought Destiny in. She's being tended to by Dr. Craven and a few of the nurses farther down the ward. They've taken off her jacket so that she's wearing just her bloodstained vest, which shows off her toned arms and enviable figure. Dr. Craven rubs some numbing gel on her skin, then sews up the wound.

I glance up at my father. "What are you going to do to Destiny?"

"We'll discuss her punishment later," Father replies.

"Please don't be too harsh with her," I say. "She was just being a good friend. And she's a great pilot; you'll need her if you're planning an attack on Cen—" I cut myself off, realizing I've put my foot in it. I'm not supposed to know about the planned assault on the capital city. Father gives me a hard look and I grimace. "Don't be mad at Destiny. I accidentally walked in on her when she was looking at the attack plans in command central."

Father's brow creases. "When was this?"

"A few days ago," I say. "Why?"

"No reason," he says, glancing at Destiny.

Dr. Craven finishes suturing her wound and comes over to us.

"Hello, pumpkin," he says, giving me a warm smile, although his eyes scan the faces of everyone in the room. I wonder if he's searching to see if Sebastian, his son, is with us.

"Sebastian's alive. He murdered Acelot's brother and stole

their Miniport; he's probably in Centrum by now." That's the
most likely place Seb would've gone.

The doctor takes off his glasses and rubs his tired eyes. "I just
don't understand that boy anymore," he says quietly. "My son
was never perfect, but he was a good boy until he got caught up
in that Purity nonsense. It breaks my heart he's turned out this
way. I'm just glad I never told him about this place."

That makes two of us.

"I have something for you." I pass Dr. Craven the vial of
Wings, briefly explaining how I got it. "I'm pretty certain the
milky stuff is Haze, given its gooey consistency, but I'd like to
know for certain what it's been mixed with. It's possible it's
Night Whisper."

"I'll run some tests," he says, taking it to his laboratory at
the end of the ward.

Ash gets up from Sigur's bed and collects his duffel bag and
Theora's heart. He looks exhausted, his cheeks gaunt, his dark
eyes shimmering behind his long black bangs.

"There's a spare bunker three doors down from ours," Father says. "Ash can stay there."

"Thanks. I'll collect my stuff from our room," I reply. Mother
flashes a worried look at Father, and I sigh. "Mom, Ash and I
are *engaged*. I'm staying with him."

"I'm not sure how comfortable I am with that," Mother
replies.

I kiss her cool cheek. "I love you, Mom. But this isn't up for
debate."

Mother frowns. "But—"

"Siobhan, let them go," Father says gently, silencing my
mother. I smile at him and he hugs me. "When did you get all
grown up, huh? I'm not sure I like it," he whispers in my ear,

then releases me. He stretches out a hand to Ash. "You treat my girl right. She's the most precious thing in the world to me."

"That's how I feel about her too, sir," Ash replies, shaking his hand.

Father nods curtly and lets go of Ash's hand. We head to our bunker, stopping off at my old room along the way to collect my belongings, including the yellow-handled knife. Ash notices the writing on the handle.

"'Polly?'" he says. "As in your sister?"

I tuck the blade into my pocket.

"What are you planning to do with it?" he says, eyes narrowing.

"You know what I'm going to do," I say. "The day I found Polly's body, I told you that I was going to kill Purian Rose. Nothing's changed."

A muscle twitches in Ash's jaw but he doesn't push the matter, not wanting to start an argument. I take his hand and lead him to our new bunk.

Our room is smaller than the one I shared with my parents, with a double bed, two nightstands, a small desk and a cupboard built into the white, glossy wall. Ash places the glass jar on the desk and quietly shuts the door. We're alone at last.

He crosses the room in two strides and pulls me into his arms, his lips crushing against mine. The kiss is both urgent and tender; he's wanting to savor the moment but barely able to hold himself back. Yearning aches through me, and I press my body against his, my fingers tangling through his hair. I suddenly taste salt on my lips and immediately break the kiss.

"Ash?"

He fixes his eyes on a point on the floor, his jaw clenched tight, as tears snake down his cheeks. I take his hand and we lie down on the bed, both fully clothed. I softly kiss him, opening a channel between us, known as Soul Sharing—something that only Blood Mates are able to do with each other—allowing his emotions to flow into me. My heart swallows his grief, his guilt, his pain, trying to take away some of his suffering. Tears spill down my face. His sorrow is almost too much to bear, but I hold on to him until eventually he severs the connection. He gently wipes the tears off my face with his thumbs.

"I love you, blondie," he whispers.

"I love you too," I say, wrapping my arms around him.

He rests his head on my chest, and we stay like this for the rest of the night.

24.

ASH

IT TAKES ME A LONG TIME to fall asleep, despite how exhausted I am. When I do drift off, my dreams are haunted with nightmarish visions of starved bodies chained to hospital beds, their jaws clamped open. I pull back one of the blankets to reveal my dad lying on the soiled mattress. His body is gray and sunken, his bones jutting out of his ulcerated skin. He grips my arm, and flames erupt from his fingers and lick up my sleeve until I'm engulfed in fire, just like the day I became Phoenix—

I bolt up in bed. My throat is raw from screaming.

"Shh, it's okay, it's okay," Natalie says, drawing me into her arms. I cling to her, trying to catch my breath as a wave of grief crashes over me when I remember my dad's dead. I focus on breathing, *in out, in out, in out,* until eventually I calm down.

After a few minutes, I reluctantly pull away from Natalie and check the clock on the nightstand. It's already eleven in the morning. We get out of bed and shower and change. I empty the contents of my duffel bag onto the bed and start putting a few things away. A folded piece of paper flutters to the floor. Natalie picks it up.

"What's this?" she says.

"Some lab report you got from the Barren Lands about Project Chrysalis," I say.

She unfolds the document and scans it. Her eyes widen with surprise. She twists the paper around to show me the gray butterfly emblem printed at the top of the page. "Look familiar? This is about Wings. I can't believe we've had the information all this time! We should give this to Dr. Craven; it might be important."

We head into the main compound. The Sentry stronghold is even bigger than I first realized. Subway trains filled with soldiers swoosh by us at regular intervals while other Sentry rebels march past us, talking in hushed, excited tones about the "upcoming assault."

We pass command central—a glass-walled room filled with high-tech digital screens and a massive com-desk. Standing around the desk are Natalie's parents, a younger man with sandy-blond hair and green eyes—his name tag reads Adam Slater—Roach, Acelot and the Lupines Garrick and Sasha. Next to them are Destiny and Sigur. I'm surprised to see them out of their hospital beds. Sigur's slightly hunched over as he stands, but otherwise alert and focused as he studies the holo-map projected above the com-desk's screen. It looks like they're having an important meeting and I wasn't invited! I angrily push open the door and Natalie follows.

"We'll take out targets here, here and here," General Buchanan says. "That will block off access to the city."

"What's going on?" I say.

They all look up.

"Good to have you back, Phoenix," Roach says. Her blue dreadlocks have been tied back, showing off her freckled face. She looks a lot like Beetle.

I turn to Sigur. "Why wasn't I invited to this meeting?"

"I thought you should rest, son," he says.

"Is this the attack plan?" Natalie says, studying the map.

General Buchanan quickly runs through their plan of assault on Centrum for us. It'll be in three phases. We'll attack Port Cassandra first. It's on the outskirts of the city, where the main fleet of Destroyer Ships are docked. They'll then blast all the bridges and connecting roads, isolating the walled city from the outside world, and strike strategic targets, including the Fracture—a shard-shaped skyscraper—where Sentry headquarters are located in Centrum. Finally, the ground troops will take over the city.

"When is this taking place?" I ask.

"Tomorrow, at oh-seven-hundred hours," General Buchanan replies.

I gaze at the attack plans. Tomorrow the war could be over. I should be delighted, but I'm not. Something doesn't feel right. Destiny suddenly winces with pain.

"Excuse me, General. I think my sutures are coming undone," she says.

Natalie's dad excuses her and she leaves.

I turn my attention back to the map. "What do you want me to do?"

"Nothing," General Buchanan says. "You and Natalie are going to stay here."

Natalie's mouth drops open. "You can't be serious."

"I'm deadly serious," he says. "There's no reason for you to come. We have it under control. We'll come back for you once the Commander is in power and the dust settles."

Anger boils up in me. I shoot a look at Roach, who frowns back at me, clearly as unhappy about this as I am.

"So let me get this straight. The Sentry rebels are going to take down Purian Rose and put this Commander guy in power instead?" I say. "And where does that leave the Darklings *when the dust settles*? What plans do you have for us in your new regime?"

"They'll be taken good care of, Ash, you have my word," General Buchanan says.

"Will we have a voice in the new Sentry government?" I say.

Natalie's mom, Emissary Buchanan, is the one to answer. "Sigur has been invited to join the council."

"And what about the Bastets and Lupines?" Acelot asks.

This piques Garrick's and Sasha's interest. I'm sure the Lupines are keen to know where they stand in the new Sentry regime.

"We expect a place on the council," Garrick says. "We've risked a lot to support you, Emissary."

Roach snorts. "The Lupines are *collaborators*. Why should they be rewarded?"

"We don't all blindly follow Rose," Sasha snaps. "Many of us believe what he's doing is wrong. We've put our lives on the line to help the rebellion. We deserve a voice too."

"*Everyone* will be represented," Emissary Buchanan interjects.

"But the Sentry will remain in charge?" I say. "You'll still be the ones calling the shots?"

She narrows her cool blue eyes at me. "Yes."

"This is bullshit," I mutter, storming out of the room. Natalie chases after me.

"Ash—"

I spin around on her. "What was the fragging point of any of this? I've spent months campaigning against Purian Rose, fighting him, trying to unify the species, and tomorrow the Sentry rebels are just going to swoop in and . . ." I grind my fangs together.

"What? Steal your thunder?" Natalie says.

I glare at her. "No. God, you know I don't give a crap about that. I never asked to be Phoenix; I'm not interested in being some hero."

"I know you're not. Sorry," she says. "Then what's bothering you? This is what we wanted—to bring Rose down. I'm not going to lie, it's frustrating we're not the ones who get to do it, but really, does it matter in the grand scheme of things?"

"Yes, it does!" I say. "I didn't want to replace one Sentry government with another. How can we be certain things will get better after tomorrow's attack? We don't even know who this fragging 'Commander' person is. He could be worse than Purian Rose!"

Natalie's mouth tightens slightly. "I trust my father. I *sort* of trust my mother. They won't let things continue on as they are."

"But will it be enough? Will it be what *we've* been fighting for?" I take her hand and gently rub my thumb over her palm. Her blue diamond engagement ring sparkles in the fluorescent light. "I don't want it to be illegal for us to be together. I want to be able to marry you one day," I say quietly. "I want our kids to be able to get into the Fast Track programs, to have jobs, to be accepted. I want them to have all the opportunities I never did. But in my heart, I don't believe that will ever happen if the Sentry remains in control."

"But Sigur will have a say in what happens," Natalie replies.

"Sigur is just a token, don't you see that?" I say, getting frustrated. "You heard your mom; the Sentry will be calling the shots. He's been brought in as a spokesman for the Darklings, so when he tells them to support the new Sentry regime, they will. But it won't be any different from before. How can it?

Until the Sentry are gone, nothing will ever change. Your parents are bullshitting you, Natalie."

She snatches her hand away, her cheeks flushing. "That's not true. I think you're letting your feelings about the Sentry color your opinion of my parents."

"No, I think the fact that your dad worked in the Barren Lands camp and that your mom tried to frame me for Chris Thompson's death 'colored my opinion' of them," I retort. "Oh, and not to mention the fact that they tried to *split us up*. So forgive me for being the tiniest bit suspicious about their motives."

Natalie blinks and tears darken her lashes.

I rake a hand through my hair. "I'm sorry. That was out of order," I mutter.

Natalie bites her lip, shaking her head. "No . . . no, you're totally right. *I'm* the one who's being blind. It's been so wonderful having my parents back, I've not been pushing these questions hard enough with them, and I should have been. I'm sorry, Ash."

I kiss her tears away and hold her against me for a long moment.

"Holidays with the in-laws are going to be interesting when we get married," I murmur, and Natalie laughs.

We head into the hospital in search of Dr. Craven. Martha is propped up in bed. Her graying hair is loose around her bony shoulders and her wrinkled skin is ghostly white, but there's a youthful sparkle in her lilac eyes. She gives me a gap-toothed grin. I try not to wince at the sight of her missing fangs. All domesticated Darklings have their fangs removed for safety reasons. She shakily attempts to drink a glass of Synth-O-Blood, splashing it over her nightgown. Natalie rushes over to her and perches on the edge of Martha's bed, then holds the glass up to the woman's withered lips.

"Thank you, dear," Martha says.

Natalie gives her a loving smile.

"Where are Lucinda and Yolanda?" I ask, looking about the near-empty ward. I'm confused to see that Destiny isn't here; I thought she was coming to get her stitches redone. Huh. She must have already been and gone.

"Yolanda's with Dr. Craven, and Lucinda went to the Mess Hall with your friends, Day and Beetle, and that nice Bastet boy," Martha says in her quivering voice, taking another sip of blood before passing it to Natalie.

Natalie places the glass down on the nightstand. "Try to get some rest. I'll come read to you later, okay?" She kisses the Darkling woman on the cheek, and then we go in search of Dr. Craven in his laboratory at the back of the hospital.

The laboratory is a large room with white walls and furniture, and gleaming silver medical equipment. The doctor is peering through an electron microscope. He's tall with brassy-blond hair that curls around his ears, and spectacles perched on the end of his long nose. He looks a lot like his son, Sebastian, with the same green eyes and narrow face. Sitting at the com-desk beside him is the Bastet woman Yolanda. She's got on a white lab coat over a green jumpsuit, and her brownish-red hair is swept back into a functional bun, highlighting her beautiful face.

Dr. Craven looks up from the microscope and smiles at Natalie. "Hello, pumpkin."

"Hey, Doc. Have you had a chance to run those tests on Wings yet?" Natalie asks.

"I have. Like you suspected, the base component of the drug is Haze and we found traces of Night Whisper." He gives me a proud look, the kind a teacher gives his student. Once upon a time I *was* going to be his lab assistant, before I met Ash and my life changed forever. "However, we found something else mixed with it." He punches in a command on the com-desk, and a holographic projection of a double helix immediately appears above the screen. "It's a retrovirus, designed to alter DNA."

Natalie shoots a worried look at me.

"Why in hell is Purian Rose trying to change his men's DNA?" I say. "What's he turning them into?"

Dr. Craven takes off his glasses. "From what we can tell? Lupines."

"*What?*" I splutter.

"Well, to be more accurate, hybrids," Yolanda corrects. "Half human, half Lupine."

"Like Theora," Natalie whispers. "And Edmund's grandfather."

My stomach twists. "He's trying to make everyone like them. One race—"

"One faith," Natalie continues.

"One nation, under His Mighty. Fragg . . . ," I mutter.

We're all silent for a moment, letting this revelation sink in. This has been Purian Rose's plan all along: to create a new world in his Blood Mate's image, where everyone follows the same religion. This is why he's been rounding up the Impurities and sending them to the Tenth, because only those who are "pure" in his eyes deserve to be transformed into this new race, made entirely of human-Lupine hybrids.

"Why is he only giving the drug to the Tin Men, though? You know, those guys walking around in those gray uniforms with the butterfly pins?" Natalie says. "If he truly believes in 'one race,' then why are they the only ones being given the retrovirus?"

Dr. Craven shrugs. "He has to start somewhere, and I suppose a small group of test subjects wouldn't rouse too much suspicion."

"He's rewarding them," I say darkly. "He thinks he's giving them a *gift* by being the first people to be turned into his new, purer race."

"The retrovirus doesn't work, though," Yolanda adds. "We've run numerous simulations, and the results were worrying, to say the least." She punches another button, and the double helix disappears to be replaced with a glowing blob, which I assume is a representation of the retrovirus. "In *very* basic terms"—she looks at me, and I smile appreciatively; science was never my thing—"when working correctly, the retrovirus produces DNA from its RNA genome, using its reverse transcriptase enzy—"

I raise a brow. I'm already confused.

She smiles apologetically. "It converts RNA to DNA. This new DNA is then incorporated into the host's genome and replicated, successfully altering the host's DNA without any harm to the host."

I nod, sort of understanding. Natalie peers at the holographic projection.

"But it isn't working?" Natalie asks.

"Errors are occurring during the reverse transcription process, causing mutations—"

"Because there's no proofreading ability?" Natalie says.

Yolanda nods. Now they've completely lost me.

"What's the result of these mutations?" Natalie says.

"Death," Dr. Craven replies simply. "You need to watch this." He opens a drawer under the workbench and takes out the blue digital disc that Natalie recovered from the Tenth, and slots it into the com-desk. The hologram of the retrovirus disappears, and a video starts playing on the screen. It's footage taken inside the hospital ward where Yolanda and Lucinda were being held captive. The patients are all chained to their beds, emaciated, terrified. I scan the faces, searching for my dad, barely able to breathe. He's not there. I'm both disappointed and relieved. Natalie's hand grips around mine when a woman appears on the screen—it's the scientist Natalie shot. She walks down the aisle, injecting the human patients with Wings, including a young girl no more than twelve years old with brown hair and hazel eyes.

"When I first got taken to the Tenth, three weeks ago, the Sentry scientists used to come into my ward every day and inject something into the human patients," Yolanda says. "They claimed it was a vaccine against Myra fever."

"Myra fever?" I ask.

Dr. Craven is the one who answers. "It's a particularly nasty virus that spreads in places like prisons and hospitals. It was common for Sentry guards to fall sick with it at the Barren Lands camp during the last war. It would make sense to vaccinate the human patients against Myra so that the Sentry staff didn't contract it."

The video footage cuts to a long shot of the ward. The date stamp indicates that a few weeks have passed. The Sentry doctor walks down the aisle again, checking the human patients. Most seem fine, except they now all have eerie, shimmering gray eyes. The camera stops on the young brown-haired girl. Her skin is sallow and rotting. She coughs, spewing up blood. Natalie winces. Dr. Craven turns the video off.

"I thought it was a little odd that only the humans were getting vaccinated, since Bastets carry the Myra virus too, but I wasn't going to complain," Yolanda continues. "A week after they were injected, about a fifth of the human prisoners started experiencing flulike symptoms—sweating, vomiting, fever, that sort of thing—then over time their organs failed and they died. I thought it must be the Myra fever, even though that's rarely fatal. I realize now they'd been infected with Wings."

So that's how my dad died? "It isn't killing everyone, though?"

Yolanda shakes her head. "Not based on what I saw at the Tenth. Whatever these mutations are, it's killing only certain humans, but we don't know what it is about their genetic makeup that puts them at risk and not others."

Natalie digs around in her pocket and pulls out the document she found in the Barren Lands. "Maybe this can help."

"Project Chrysalis?" Yolanda says, scanning the document. A grin breaks out on her lips as she passes the document to Dr. Craven. "It's the results from the first clinical trials of Wings."

Dr. Craven pushes his glasses up his nose as he reads it. "Thank you, pumpkin. This will be very useful," he says distractedly, already turning back to his microscope.

"We'll leave you to it," Natalie says.

We head out of the hospital and go to the Mess Hall, since that's where Martha said Lucinda, Day, Beetle and Elijah had gone. We bump into Acelot just as he's leaving command central and tell him where we're heading.

"Mind if I join you? I'm *starving*," he says, patting his flat stomach.

I look sideways at him. "Don't get any ideas." Bastets have been known to eat Darklings.

Acelot grins. "I can't make any promises. You're looking particularly tasty today, my friend."

The canteen is bustling with activity as the soldiers arrive for the first lunch shift. We grab some trays of food and find everyone at one of the tables in the far corner of the room. Beetle's got his foot up on a seat, his arm draped around Day's shoulders. As always he's a total mess, his brown hair more tangled than ever, his jumpsuit already creased and covered in blobs of gravy. How does he do it? Day, on the other hand, looks pristine, her jumpsuit neatly starched and pressed, her glossy black hair tied back into a braid.

Opposite them is Lucinda, who is stirring her glass of Synth-O-Blood. She sniffs back tears, and I wonder if she's thinking about Kieran. Beside her, Elijah is chatting to a pretty brunette soldier at the next table. She whispers something to him, and his cheeks turn bright red. He looks up as we approach. He glances at Natalie, then quickly lowers his eyes. It can't be easy for him, seeing Natalie and me together. As much as I hate the fact that another guy has a crush on my fiancée, I've given up being jealous. It just leads to heartache and misunderstandings.

I toss a chicken leg onto his plate as I sit down. "Thought you might like this. I know how much you *love* birds," I tease.

"Ha-ha, very funny," he says, rolling his honey-colored eyes.

Acelot smirks at me, and steals the chicken leg off his brother's plate. We quickly fill them in on everything we know about the attack on Centrum tomorrow and Wings. Everyone has turned a shade paler by the time we've finished.

"That's so messed up, bro," Beetle says, shaking his head.

Natalie glances at something in the center of the room. "What's Destiny doing?"

I turn. Destiny is on top of one of the tables, dressed in white Pilgrim robes. People's looks of confusion quickly turn to fear as she speaks.

"His Mighty has looked into your souls, and He has seen

your impurity," she says vehemently. "You will be cleansed from this earth for your sins, to make way for the new order. One faith! One race! One nation, under His Mighty! So sayeth us all!"

The glasses on everyone's tables begin to rattle as a low hum reverberates through the compound. Natalie throws me a panicked look. I know that sound.

Destroyer Ships.

25.

ASH

I PULL NATALIE under the table just as the first bomb drops. Plaster shakes off the ceiling, and metal trays clank to the floor as the bomb hits the compound. The scent of blood hits my nostrils—warm, delicious, intoxicating. Screams tear through the canteen. A second later the lights blink off, replaced by the red emergency lights. Alarms blare throughout the compound *wharp-wharp-wharp-wharp*. There's a hiss as the sprinklers turn on, putting out the fires that are already sweeping through the Mess Hall.

Natalie's panicked eyes catch mine. The others are under the table with us. Beetle's holding Day, and Lucinda covers her head with her arms. Lying next to them are Acelot and Elijah. The older Bastet boy is covering Elijah with his body, shielding him. A glistening shard of metal is jutting out of Acelot's back. Blood pumps out of the wound.

"Ace!" I cry out, dragging him off Elijah.

Acelot flops into my arms, his lifeless eyes gazing up at me. A trickle of blood seeps out of his parted lips.

"Ace, oh God . . . ," I say, my throat tight.

Elijah stares at his brother. "No," he says, shaking his head. "No . . . no . . . no . . . NO!"

There's a terrifying screech of bending metal overhead, and I glance up. The beams holding the concrete ceiling won't last much longer. The whole room is going to cave in.

"We have to get out of here, bro!" Beetle shouts over the noise.

I place Acelot's body on the ground. Elijah blinks and tears stream down his cheeks. I lay a hand on his arm.

"We have to go," I say.

Elijah sniffs and nods. He gives his brother one last pained look, and then we're scrambling from under the table and leaping over the injured, the dead, not stopping to help. I briefly register Destiny's twisted, broken body strewn in parts across the floor. I feel nothing. The six of us make it out of the Mess Hall just as the ceiling collapses, sending up a plume of dust. The shock waves knock us off our feet. I skid across the floor, smashing against the wall. *Oooph!* The air is knocked out of my lungs, but there's no time to stop; I have to get everyone out of here. I scramble to my feet and help Natalie up.

All around us there's a tremendous *thud-boom-thud-boom-thud-boom* as more bombs rain down on the compound in an endless barrage, making the whole building rattle. I feel like we're in a snow globe, being tossed about and showered with debris.

"We need to get to the Transporters," Day says.

"I have to get my mom!" Elijah says.

"My parents," Natalie replies. "Martha! Oh God, Ash!"

"Where's Roach?" Beetle says.

Roach was in command central with Natalie's parents and . . . My stomach lurches. *Sigur.* I can't lose him and my dad in the same week. I can't. I can't. I can't. We race down the sidewalk leading toward command central, which is on the way to the hospital ward. People are running in every direction. Some seem to be following an emergency protocol, but everyone else, us included, is just racing to find their loved ones. Everywhere I turn, walls are crumbling; subway trains have slid off the tracks and their cables drag across the railways, sparking blue with electricity.

There's a *pop* of gunfire as we turn the corner. Slater races down the sidewalk toward us, his gun raised. For a terrifying, heart-twisting second I think he's going to shoot us, but then he aims his weapon over our shoulders and shoots the people behind us. I whip around. Sentry guards swarm into the compound from the nearby entrance, led by a teenage boy dressed in a gray uniform with a gleaming butterfly medal on his chest. *Sebastian.* Even from here I can see the metallic glint in his newly silver eyes.

"Ash, his eyes," Natalie gasps.

"I see them," I reply.

He spots us and points in our direction. "Over there!"

Elijah pushes me out of the way as a bullet whizzes past my ear.

"Thanks!" I say in a rush.

"Anytime," he replies.

Natalie grabs my hand and leads us down a side alley, away from Sebastian. The sidewalk ahead is blocked with rubble. To my left is a subway track, where a road would typically be, and on the opposite side is another pathway. That one is clear. We drop down onto the twisted rails and hurry over to the platform edge. Elijah gracefully leaps onto an empty sidewalk a few feet above us and helps everyone up. We keep on running, our only thoughts on saving our family.

Thud-boom, thud-boom, thud-boom. More bombs drop on

the compound, shaking the walls, making us stumble. A chunk of concrete lands a few inches away from Day, and she screams in fright.

"There!" Natalie says, pointing toward command central. The glass is still intact—it must be designed to withstand explosions. Garrick and Sasha are positioned outside the doors, shooting at any passing Sentry guards. Natalie's parents are inside, along with Sigur and Roach. Relief crashes over me. They're alive.

We sprint across the bustling street, avoiding flying bullets and cracked pipes pumping out steam. All around us is the deafening *wharp-wharp-wharp-wharp* of the alarms. Garrick shoves us inside the room, slamming the door behind us. Instantly, there's silence. Sigur hurries over to me, pulling me into his arms, while Natalie's parents embrace her.

"We were just coming to look for you," General Buchanan says to Natalie.

"We have to get to the hospital," I say, pulling away from Sigur. "Yolanda, Martha and Dr. Craven are there."

"We can't," General Buchanan says, pointing toward the digital screens on the wall, which are streaming live closed-circuit footage of the compound. On one of the monitors I spot Sebastian storming down a sidewalk, his eyes predatory, searching for us. "There are hostiles swarming all over that place. Our priority is getting you kids out of here."

"I'm getting my mom," Elijah says.

"We can't leave Martha!" Natalie adds. "I'm not leaving without her."

"Fine," General Buchanan replies, knowing he's not going to change Natalie's mind. "Grab a weapon from the locker."

He points toward a cupboard I hadn't noticed earlier, on the opposite side of the room. We race over to it and each grab a handgun. I pass one to Natalie, and Beetle hands one to Day. She checks to make sure it's loaded, a hard look in her eyes. This isn't her first firefight. Elijah takes two—one for him, one for his mom, when we find her. General Buchanan and Roach take the semiautomatics, while Emissary Buchanan slings a gun belt around her slim waist and slips a handgun into the holster.

"Let's go," she says.

The moment we step out of command central, our ears are assaulted by the cacophony of sounds: alarms, bombs, screams, gunfire, crashing concrete, exploding gas pipes. General Buchanan taps Garrick on the shoulder and the Lupine takes the lead, while the pink-haired Lupine, Sasha, brings up the rear. Every few seconds there's a *rat-a-tat-tat* of gunfire as we make our way to the hospital ward. I keep Natalie close by me. Beetle raises his gun and squeezes the trigger, *pop-pop-pop*. Three Sentry guards fall off the sidewalk ahead of us and onto the rails.

"To your right!" Day shouts as a couple of Sentry guards appear from a side street.

Beetle swings his gun around. *Pop-pop*. Two more dead.

We reach the hospital. The glass doors have shattered, and our boots crunch over the crystal droplets. Lights hang from their fixtures, equipment lies broken on the tiled floor, and beds are covered in dust and plaster. Thankfully the hospital was nearly empty earlier.

"Martha! Martha!" Natalie shouts.

She pushes past me and sprints over to Martha's bed. The old Darkling woman is hunched on the ground, huddled between her bed and the dresser. Natalie helps Martha to her feet, slinging an arm around her waist. The old lady struggles to walk, dragging Natalie down with her. Sasha strides over to them and picks up Martha in one easy movement, like she weighs nothing more than a pillow.

A door to the laboratory opens, and Dr. Craven and Yolanda emerge. She's holding a scalpel, and Dr. Craven has his leather medical bag clutched to his chest. It's stuffed with papers and bottles, which clank when he runs over to us. Elijah quickly hugs his mom.

"What the blazes is going on?" Dr. Craven asks.

"Destiny gave up our position," I reply. "She was working for Rose."

"Sebastian's here; he's leading the assault," Natalie adds, and Dr. Craven blanches.

"We have to get to the hangar," Emissary Buchanan says. "Come on!"

Garrick leads the way as we race out of the hospital. We hurry down the sidewalks, dodging the bullets flying in every direction. *Thud-boom-thud-boom-thud-boom.* Explosions rip through the compound, tearing up the underground city. The sprinklers can't cope with the fires blazing in every room; it's out of control. The choking smoke fills the passageways, making us cough and splutter. It's hard to tell where we are, but the Sentry rebels don't have any trouble navigating the city. They know the place inside and out. All around us I see flashes of black and red—the Sentry guards are closing in on us, sweeping throughout the compound, taking everyone out.

Pop-pop-pop.

A bullet slams into the wall by Beetle's head. He doesn't even flinch.

"This way!" Garrick calls over his shoulder.

We weave through endless passageways, passing offices and dormitories. We head down a familiar-looking corridor, and I spot the bunker I share with Natalie.

"Wait!" Natalie cries out. "I need to get something."

She sprints away from me and is soon swallowed up by the dust and debris.

"Natalie!" I shout, chasing after her, ducking as more bullets whizz by my head.

Natalie emerges from our room. Her pocket is bulging with objects—I'm guessing her medication—and tucked under one of her arms is the glass jar with Theora's heart in it. She races over to me and we join the others. Garrick pushes open a heavy door, and we head down a flight of steel steps toward the hangar deck, leaping over a dead body—it's the blond soldier Slater. The back of his head is missing. The walls around us start to crack, the ceilings groan. If we don't get out soon, we'll be trapped inside it like a tomb.

Pop-pop.

Sasha cries out in pain. She tumbles down the steps with Martha, hitting the landing wall. My head snaps up toward the source of the gunfire. A Sentry guard is on the landing above us. General Buchanan lifts his gun and squeezes the trigger just as the man shoots at him. The guard slams against the wall, his blood splashing across the paintwork. I cover my nose and mouth, trying to block out the tantalizing smell.

Natalie thrusts the glass jar into Day's hands and runs down the steps with Garrick toward Sasha and Martha, who are sprawled on the landing below. Garrick checks Sasha's pulse, although it's obvious from the unnatural position of her head that her neck has broken. Natalie rolls Martha onto her back. There's a neat circle of blood on the woman's chest where the bullet pierced her heart.

I grab Natalie around her waist, lifting her onto her feet.

"I can't leave her!" she wails.

"She's dead!" I say, dragging Natalie kicking and screaming down the rest of the stairs. I don't let go of her until we reach the hangar deck.

The place is in chaos. Bodies are strewn across the floor, their blood pooling around our feet. Most of the Transporters are on fire. There's a burst of gunfire as a group of Sentry guards spot us. Roach and General Buchanan take them down with their semiautomatics.

"That one!" Garrick says, pointing toward a Transporter nearest the exit. It's one of the few aircrafts that isn't ablaze yet.

We sprint across the hangar.

Pop-pop-pop.

Garrick grunts and stumbles, nearly falling over. He clutches his stomach. Blood spurts between his fingers. I wheel around. Sebastian is standing in the control room at the end of the hangar.

"I knew you'd come down here!" Sebastian shouts, pointing his gun at us.

"Sebastian, *son,* please don't do this! Think about what you're doing!" Dr. Craven says.

Sebastian's silver eyes narrow. A snarl crosses over his lips. "I know what I'm doing. Cleansing the world of Impurities, like *you.*"

He squeezes the trigger. The bullet grazes Dr. Craven's arm, ripping his jacket. The doctor is so stunned, he doesn't move when Sebastian pulls the trigger again. I knock the man out of the way just in time. The bullet brushes past my cheek, scorching my skin.

General Buchanan and Beetle shoot at Sebastian, covering us, while we race toward the Transporter. Natalie's mom punches a button on the outside of the aircraft, and the hatch opens. Lucinda and Elijah help Garrick onto the aircraft. He grimaces in pain, clutching his stomach. He's left a bread-crumb trail of blood in his wake. We all stumble onto the aircraft and quickly close the hatch behind us.

"Can you fly the ship?" General Buchanan asks Garrick.

The man grunts, shaking his head. His skin is slick with sweat.

"Don't *you* know how to fly it? You're in the military," I say.

"I'm army, not air force," General Buchanan replies.

Bullets hit the outside of the aircraft, *thwamp-thwamp-thwamp*. Sebastian is returning fire. Without saying anything, Day places the glass jar containing Theora's heart on one of the metal benches and marches over to the pilot's seat. She sits down and turns on the engines. They whir into life. She mutters under her breath as she flips a few switches and buttons, running through the commands.

"Buckle up," she calls over her shoulder.

We all take out seats, hurriedly putting on the harnesses as Day takes the controls. Lucinda grabs the glass jar, holding it close against her. There's a *thunk* of metal as the clamps are released, then a bone-shuddering jolt as the Transporter jerks forward. We speed through the access tunnel, accelerating at an alarming rate. Natalie grips my hand. Elijah screws his eyes shut. Beetle just grins. The others mutter a prayer under their breath.

Day yanks on the controls and the aircraft lurches upward

so fast, my ears pop. There's darkness, darkness, darkness, and then brilliant light as we burst out into the blue skies. We're going so fast, I think we're going to crash into the Destroyer Ships hovering a few hundred feet above the compound. The airships are easily five hundred feet long and painted white with a red rose on the side: the emblem of Purian Rose. They get closer, closer, closer, filling the windscreen, so close I can see the screws holding the metal sheets together.

"Day!" Natalie screams.

Day yanks the controls to the right, and the aircraft tilts. We zoom through a narrow gap between two of the Destroyer Ships, darting between them. The ships drift closer, threatening to crush us. Fragg, fragg, fragg! I clutch on to the bench. Day punches a few buttons and unloads the missiles into the sides of the ships as we pass. Fire blooms across their surfaces, creating enough force to push the airships apart a few meters, giving us space to fly through. She pulls up on the controls again and the aircraft rockets up, up, up, so high that pressure balls behind my eyes, until we're flying *above* the Destroyer Ships. We're soon swallowed by the clouds. *Good luck finding us,* I think. I suspect this aircraft can't be easily detected on radar.

"Nice flying, babe!" Beetle shouts.

Day doesn't say anything, but I know she's grinning.

General Buchanan unfastens his seat belt and gets up, pressing a hand against the metal wall to brace himself as the Transporter bumps up and down on the rough air.

"Is everyone all right?" he says.

Dr. Craven clings to his medical bag, his face pale. I'm not sure if he's feeling sick from the turbulence or because his son just tried to murder him.

"His eyes were silver," Dr. Craven mutters. "Did you see?

He's not my boy anymore, Jonathan, he's . . . he's—" The doctor buries his face in his hands.

Elijah is sitting opposite me, his eyes shut. Tears slide down his bloodstained cheeks. I look away, unable to take any more pain. My heart feels bruised from so many blows. Natalie rests her head against my shoulder. There are soot smudges on her cheeks.

"I'm such an idiot," Natalie says. "I trusted Destiny; I thought she was my friend. But she just wanted to retrieve you and the Ora, then get us all back into one place so she could blow us up." She looks up at me. "Ash, what are we going to do?"

I stiffen, saying nothing. I have no idea.

Dr. Craven wipes his red-rimmed eyes, then picks up his bag and tends to Garrick's wounds.

"Where are we going?" Day calls from the pilot's seat.

"Centrum," Mother says. "I have friends there who will hide us."

This is met with a mixture of complaints and murmurs of assent.

"We should go to the Northern Territories," Dr. Craven says. "There's no reason for us to stay here and die, Siobhan."

Beetle scowls, his brown eyes flaring with anger. "We still have a duty to bring down Purian Rose! This isn't over yet." He looks at Sigur. "Is it?"

I glance at him too, hoping for some guidance on the matter. I'm so out of my depth.

Sigur sighs, a heavy, defeated sound. "We do not have any weapons. The Sentry rebels are dead, my people are in the Tenth, and most of the Humans for Unity have been captured or killed," he says. "I am struggling to see what the thirteen of us can do."

My fangs pulse. That's not what I expected him to say. I know the situation is dire, but I never in a million years thought he would suggest that we surrender!

Beetle looks challengingly at me. "Is that what you think too, mate?"

Natalie sits up. Everyone turns their attention to me, waiting to hear what I have to say; even Natalie's mom seems eager to know, and it suddenly hits me: they're expecting me to lead them. What I say next will change everything. So the question is, Do we stay and fight, even though in all likelihood we'll die, or do we go to the Northern Territories and live?

There never was a choice.

"No, that's not what I think," I say fiercely. "Purian Rose has tortured us, killed our loved ones and torn our families apart, and now he's infecting people with a deadly retrovirus. He needs to be stopped, and we're the ones who are going to do it. He needs to learn we will never give up. We will never back down. We will not be governed by fear!"

"NO FEAR!" Beetle chants.

Roach pumps her fist. "NO POWER!"

Day punches in the coordinates for Centrum.

PART 3

THE
GILDED CITY

26.
NATALIE

THE TRANSPORTER DIPS through the billowy white clouds and we emerge above the city of Centrum, the capital of the Dominion State. I gently move Ash's arm from my shoulders, and get up. Everyone is asleep, all of us physically and emotionally exhausted. I stretch my legs, which are achy from the eight-hour flight, and join Day in the cockpit.

"I'm sorry about Martha," she says.

"Thanks," I murmur, too tired right now to feel anything but numb.

Day turns the control stick to the left and we swoop over the city. The soaring giltstone skyscrapers glimmer gold in the sunlight, and the streets and sidewalks sparkle like they're coated in diamonds. An enormous turreted wall made from glossy marble and giltstone encases the whole city, topped with thousands of orange trees and rosebushes.

Built into the walls of the skyscrapers are vast digital screens, easily ten times bigger than the ones in Black City. Some stream the latest news from SBN with February Fields, others display advertisements for the upcoming public Cleansing ceremony on

Tuesday, and the rest show a constant loop of government propaganda messages: ONE FAITH, ONE RACE, ONE NATION UNDER HIS MIGHTY! HIS MIGHTY SEES ALL SINNERS! We fly over the unmistakable gold dome of the Golden Citadel, where Purian Rose lives. Down in the enormous plaza outside the citadel, Workboots are busy erecting a large stage, similar to the one I saw being built in Gallium.

Footsteps approach the cockpit, and I turn to see my mother. Her hair tumbles in loose black waves around her narrow shoulders, and her normally flawless skin is scratched, her jumpsuit covered in soot. Even so, she looks beautiful. Slung around my mother's narrow hips is a black leather gun belt. The handgun's grip pokes out of the holster.

"Head toward Catherine Street," Mother says, giving Day the coordinates. "You'll see a round building with a Transporter pad on the roof."

"But that's where Emissary Bradshaw lives," I say, and then my eyes widen. "Oh! *He's* the Commander?"

Mother nods. I now understand why they had to keep his identity a closely guarded secret. Emissary Bradshaw is in charge of the Dominion State, which is the most coveted of all the emissary positions. He's second only to Purian Rose in terms of importance in the government, and—I thought—a loyal supporter of the dictator. We stayed with him last year, after we were evacuated from Black City during the air raids.

"I can't believe he's been working against Purian Rose all this time," I say.

Mother gives me a wry smile. She types something into the com-screen built into the control panel. A moment later a message appears on the screen. "The Commander says it's safe to land."

The others awaken as Day dips the Transporter to the left. It rapidly descends as we reach a familiar round tower, fifty stories high, each and every one of them belonging to Emissary Bradshaw. He has everything he needs at his disposal in the building: numerous apartments, offices, a spa and gymnasium, a fancy restaurant to wine and dine his guests, and even a private doctor's office for any secret nips-and-tucks he wants done. This isn't even the Sentry headquarters, which is an intimidating building shaped like a shard of glass, more than two hundred stories high, like a dagger piercing the heavens.

"Guys, I've never landed a Transporter before," Day says nervously.

The Lupine, Garrick, grunts as he gets up from the metal bench nearby. He's pale and sweating, his furlike mane matted from sleep. He staggers over to the copilot's seat, gripping his injured side. He flicks a few switches and starts grunting instructions at Day. Her knuckles turn white as her hands tighten around the controls.

"This is going to be bumpy," Garrick says as the building rushes toward us.

Ash grabs the jar with Theora's heart while everyone else grips their seats. Day approaches the landing pad a little too fast, and we thump down on the roof. The aircraft judders, and I bump my head against the metal wall and let out a groan, my thoughts spinning. There are a few cries of panic from the others, followed by a smattering of nervous laughter when the aircraft doesn't erupt into a ball of flames. Day turns off the engine and grins at me, pushing her glasses up her nose. I smile, rubbing my bruised head.

We head out of the aircraft, all of us a little shaky on our feet after the dramatic landing, and cross the breezy roof. The air is warm and fresh, and smells like roses. We enter the access stairwell, which leads us down to a wide corridor outside a penthouse apartment.

The plush white carpet is spongy underfoot, and the walls are gilded with gold leaf. Modern art hangs on the walls. They're by some renowned artist and worth millions, but they just look like splashes of blue and red paint to me. Memories come flooding as I take in our surroundings. My mother, Polly, Sebastian and I lived in this building last year, although our apartment was on the thirty-eighth floor. It's weird being back here.

Mother presses the bell outside the white double doors, making a tuneful *ding-dong* sound, and a moment later we're buzzed inside the apartment. It's decorated in a similar fashion to the hallway, with pristine white carpets and gold walls. We're in an enormous living room, with curved windows that overlook the glimmering city. In the middle of the room is a circle of white leather chairs. On the opposite side of the room are a set of gold doors, which—if memory serves—leads to numerous bedrooms, a dining room, a bathroom, a library and a kitchen.

To our right is a marble fireplace. Hanging above the mantel is a huge portrait of Emissary Bradshaw—a bloated man with ruddy cheeks, thinning blond hair and pale blue eyes. He was probably a handsome man in his youth, but years of attending lavish state banquets have taken their toll on him. The gold doors open, and the real Emissary Bradshaw sweeps into the room, dressed in a midnight-blue frock coat, dark pants and a patterned waistcoat that stretches over his large belly. He spreads his arms wide and smiles.

"Siobhan. So lovely to have you back in my home."

Mother embraces him. "Thank you for having us."

Father gives a curt nod. "It's very generous of you, Commander."

Emissary Bradshaw puts his hands on my shoulders, inspecting me up and down. "My dear, haven't you grown up?"

"That tends to happen," I say, a touch harsher than I meant. Emissary Bradshaw is a close friend of my parents, and I can't help but shift the feeling that they were conspiring together to keep Ash away from me. He probably thought he was helping them, but he was hurting me in the process.

Emissary Bradshaw's ever-smile wavers. "Well, yes, I suppose it does." His blue eyes slide past me, and his grip tightens painfully on my shoulders. "What are *you* doing here?"

I turn, wondering who he's talking to.

Lucinda snarls back at him, her black eyes burning with hostility. "Long time, no see."

"You know Lucinda?" I ask Emissary Bradshaw.

He lets go of my shoulders. "Lucinda and I go way back, don't we, sweetheart?" She looks daggers at him. "I don't suppose there's any point trying to hide it; I presume Lucinda's already told you everything. When we were teenagers, we met in the woods outside Amber Hills."

"Wait . . . what?" I say, putting two and two together. "You're Patrick *Langdon*?"

He nods.

"Why did you change your surname to Bradshaw?" I ask, confused.

"Oh, Edmund insisted on it. The Langdon name brought back too many bad memories for him," he says, strolling over to a cabinet near the fireplace. "Can I get you a drink? I would normally have my Darkling servants do this, but they were all sent to the Tenth last week. Edmund promised to send me some more Workboots, but they haven't arrived yet. This war is so inconvenient."

"That's one way of describing it," Ash growls.

Emissary Bradshaw casts his gaze toward Ash, properly noticing him for the first time. "Ah, and this must be the infamous Phoenix."

"In the burnt flesh," Ash quip. "How come you're working against Purian Rose? I thought you two were best buddies after he saved your life in Amber Hills."

Emissary Bradshaw makes a scoffing sound. "I owed Edmund a debt of gratitude and we shared the same thirst for power, but friends? No. I've never forgotten what he did to my sister. Catherine was my whole world." A dark emotion flitters over his features, and for a brief moment I see the boy he was back then: angry, vengeful, hurt. "Besides, Edmund has no head for business. He's running this country into the ground with these damned wars. It's time we replaced him with someone else."

"And that person's you?" Ash says flatly.

"I'm the most qualified man for the position," Emissary Bradshaw says.

I catch Ash's eye and he frowns. I know what he's thinking: Emissary Bradshaw might have the most experience, but that doesn't mean he's the right man for the post. Can we really trust a man who helped write the Book of Creation, which claims Darklings are demons? Is he honestly the best person to lead our new government? I don't think so.

"Well, now that we're all caught up, let me show you to your rooms," Emissary Bradshaw says.

We find a room for Garrick and lay the injured man down on the bed. Dr. Craven changes his bandages while the rest of us find places to sleep. We're not short of options—there are easily fifteen bedrooms in the lavish apartment. Ash and Beetle stay in the living room, and Emissary Bradshaw escorts me and Day to our bedrooms, which we'll share with the boys. Tucked under my arm is the glass jar with Theora's heart. Day smiles wistfully as we stroll down the wide corridor. She brushes her fingers over the expensive gilt wallpaper and antique furnishings.

"If Mama could see me now," she mutters. Not so long ago, it was Day's ambition to become the emissary of the Dominion State—a dream her mother, Sumrina, actively encouraged, as she wanted a better life for her daughter. "Well, at least I made it here, albeit as a wanted criminal hiding from the law."

I laugh, nudging her with my hip, and she grins.

Emissary Bradshaw shows Day to one of the standard guest rooms and then leads me to the plush suites farther down the corridor. On the way to my room we pass a white door with a blue glass doorknob. The door is ajar, and I hear a girl crying inside the room. The sound is muffled, like she's sobbing into a pillow. Emissary Bradshaw closes the door and gives me an apologetic smile.

"That's my maid. The poor girl isn't feeling well," he explains.

"I thought your servants had gone," I say.

"Just the Darkling ones. Don't worry, my maid's very loyal. She won't tell anyone you're here." He places a hand on the base of my spine, a little too low for my liking, as he ushers me away from her room. We stop in front of a door with a red handle. "Here we are, sweetheart." His hand skims over my left butt cheek, and anger flares through me.

"What do you think you're doing?" I say.

He raises his hands in a placating gesture. "My dear, it was an *accident*."

I narrow my eyes, not believing him for a second. "Well, accidents will happen. Just not twice," I say firmly. The message is clear: don't touch me again.

Emissary Bradshaw's mouth tightens. "Enjoy your room."

He turns on his heel and strides down the corridor.

I enter my bedroom and slam the door behind me. The jerk! I place the glass jar on the nightstand, then go to the bathroom and splash some cold water over my face, muttering curses under my breath. I debate whether to tell anyone about what happened, but decide against it. My parents would be furious, and let's not get started on Ash. I'd hate to think what he'd do to Emissary Bradshaw if he knew he'd copped a feel, after everything that happened with Sebastian back in Black City. No, as much as it grieves me, we need Emissary Bradshaw's help right now, so I'll keep the incident to myself. But if he ever, *ever* tries a stunt like that again, I'll rip his damn hand off.

Once I've calmed down, I pull out the items from my jumpsuit pocket—the black syringe case, a bottle of heart medication and the yellow-handled knife I stole from the UG—and place them carefully beside the sink.

I take my medication, then head back to the living room. Lucinda is curled up in one of the leather chairs by the fire, and Yolanda is in the seat beside her. Their faces have been scrubbed clean, but they're both still wearing their dirty jumpsuits. Sitting by his mother's feet is Elijah. Yolanda is stroking his russet hair while he plays with the single gold band around his left wrist. He lifts his topaz eyes when I enter the room, and there's a deep, aching sadness in them. I give him a small smile and join Ash on the sofa, nuzzling up against him. I can hear his steady heartbeat beneath his jumpsuit. *Ba-boom, ba-boom, ba-boom.*

He plays with one of my curls. "You okay, blondie?"

"Mm-hmm," I say noncommittally, still mad at Emissary Bradshaw.

I gaze about the room. Sigur and Roach are playing a game

of chess at the small table nearby, bantering with each other, while Beetle and Day share one of the leather seats to our right. They giggle and whisper to each other.

The gold doors open and my mother, father, Dr. Craven and Emissary Bradshaw enter the room, deep in discussion. They sit down. The chair creaks slightly under Emissary Bradshaw's weight. It's hard to picture him as the handsome, ruthless hunter Lucinda described him as, but the steely look is still there in his blue eyes. We all turn toward him. It's time to talk business.

"So here's the situation. We have to bring down Purian Rose, but our soldiers are all dead and we have no weapons," Emissary Bradshaw says. "Any ideas how we do it?"

Mother nods. "We'll tell the world what Edmund really is. Under Sentry law, no nonhuman is allowed to take office; he'll have to step down."

Lucinda lets out an impatient sound. "We already tried that. We don't have any proof."

"That's not strictly true," Emissary Bradshaw says, glancing at Mother.

She nods, and he hauls himself out of his chair and walks over to the self-portrait above the fireplace. He removes the painting to reveal a safe inset into the wall behind it. He opens it. Inside are numerous folders, wads of cash, and some jewelry. He passes a red folder to me.

Ash and I flip through the file, looking at the charts and photographs. It's a file on my sister, Polly. Everything about her is here: her birth certificate, DNA reports, a lock of her hair in a vacuum-sealed bag, another lock of black hair in a second bag labeled EDMUND ROSE, photographs of Polly's injuries after she was tortured the night my father faked his own death. My heart cramps. There's a digital disc too.

"What's on here?" I ask.

"Recordings of my . . . er, *meetings* . . . with Edmund." Mother looks nervously at my father.

His head snaps up. "What? You *recorded* them?" His face turns bright red, and we all shift uncomfortably in our seats. "I don't . . . I can't . . . I have no words! How could you?"

"It was insurance!" Mother replies. "I was worried about my job, Jonathan. Office romances rarely end up well for the employee. I wanted to have a bargaining chip, in case he tried to fire me."

Father shakes his head in disbelief.

"Oh, Mother," I mutter, disappointed in her. It's so typical of her to always be thinking about her career, even when it comes to having a torrid affair, but I guess we should be grateful for her scheming nature. It's all the evidence we need to hang Purian Rose.

"I'm sorry, Jonathan," she says.

Father turns his back on her and stares at the fire roaring in the hearth, his hands balling into fists. Lucinda and Roach read the file and their expressions harden.

"Did you know what Purian Rose was, when you were with him?" Day asks in her typically blunt fashion.

Mother flushes, but to her credit she answers. "Not at that time, no. It was only during the pregnancy that Dr. Craven and I figured it out. There were a few rather obvious signs that Polly wasn't human."

Before I can push her to give details, Roach slams the file on the table.

"Why the hell didn't you release this years ago?" Roach demands.

"Because I didn't want the world to know that my eldest daughter was . . ." Mother cuts herself short and takes a shaky breath.

"What? A *nipper*?" Ash says.

"No," Mother replies tersely. "I didn't want the world to know she was Purian Rose's child. Don't you see, either way, she was at risk? If the Sentry won the war, they would crucify her for having mixed blood. And if the Darklings won, she'd be killed for being his daughter. I was trying to protect her."

I don't doubt she was trying to protect Polly, but I suspect she was protecting herself too. If the truth ever came out that she had borne a child with a man who had Darkling blood in him, she would've been labeled a race traitor by the Sentry government and executed. Mother takes the file from them and lightly traces her fingers over a photo of Polly.

"When I joined the Sentry rebels last year, I realized there was no need to make this information public, since we had so many weapons at our disposal. We could take down Purian Rose through force, and I could protect my family *and* my reputation in the process." She shuts the file. "It doesn't matter now. Polly's dead and my career is in tatters anyway."

"If this fails, the Sentry will hang you for being a race traitor," I say quietly.

She laughs. "If this fails, we'll all be executed. We have nothing to lose."

Except our lives, I think grimly.

My parents and Emissary Bradshaw discuss how they're going to release the information to various news outlets across the United Sentry States. Once it's released, as the most senior emissary in the government, Emissary Bradshaw would automatically be put into power. As they speak, Roach's foot keeps bobbing up and down irritably, while Sigur quietly takes it all in. Lucinda and Yolanda share a disapproving look with each other.

"What about the Wings plot?" I say. "When are we releasing that information?"

Emissary Bradshaw smiles patronizingly at me. "I think it's best we sit on that information for now, sweetheart. The evidence on Polly is enough to remove Edmund from office and put me in power." He folds his hands over his large stomach. "It's not going to be easy winning over the existing cabinet— things would've been much simpler if we'd seized power by force and replaced the cabinet with men loyal to me, like we originally planned—but since that's not an option now, we have to play this very carefully."

Ash stiffens beside me.

Mother nods. "If we release the Wings evidence, it'll cause a lot of unrest in the cabinet and with the people of this country," she adds. "We want a smooth transition into power. Once Patrick's in office and has won the trust of both the cabinet and our citizens, he can start making preparations to end the war. It might just take a few more months than we originally planned."

"*Months!*" Roach says, her freckled face turning red. "That's not good enough!"

I glance at Day and she frowns at me, shaking her head slightly in despair. I rub the Cinder Rose tattoo on my wrist. Ash was right; this isn't what we've been fighting for. I don't want to replace one Sentry government for another, but what choice do we have? Ash looks down at me and nods toward the hallway door.

"I need a break," I say, getting up. Mother lowers her lashes. Father is still by the fireplace, refusing to look at her.

Day, Beetle and Elijah follow us without needing to be asked. We head to Ash's and my bedroom. Once we're all in the room, Ash furiously slams the door, making the glass jar on the nightstand rattle. We find places to sit on the plush carpet or king-sized bed, except Ash, who paces up and down the sizable room.

"I don't trust that guy," Ash says. "He only cares about ending this war because of the damage it's doing to the economy. He doesn't give a fragg about making things better for the Darklings."

"Then what do we do?" I say.

Ash slumps down on the bed. "I don't know."

Elijah slides a look at the jar on the table. "There is one thing we could try."

"Lucinda's plan," I say, catching on. "You think it could work?"

Elijah shrugs. "It's worth a shot, pretty girl. Rose made a Blood Mate connection with Theora's heart once. It could work again."

"Dr. Craven could perform the operation on Ash," Day says.

"Whoa! Wait! I'm not doing it," Ash says. "There is no way in hell you're ripping out my heart so I can become Purian Rose's boy toy."

"You said you wanted us to take down Purian Rose, whatever the cost," Elijah says.

"That's not what I meant!" Ash looks pleadingly at Beetle. "Back me up here, mate."

"It is pretty fragged up, bro," Beetle admits. "But if we could end the war, shouldn't we try? It's what we've been fighting for."

Ash turns to me. "Natalie?"

"It won't be forever," I say gently. "We can implant your heart back into you afterward . . ."

Hurt flashes across his face. "And what if that doesn't work? I thought you of all people would understand why I can't do this."

Before I can say another word, he storms out of the room, slamming the door behind him.

27.
ASH

BLOOD POUNDS IN my ears as I march down the corridor and head out a set of glass doors leading onto the balcony, needing some fresh air. The balcony is massive—easily thirty feet deep and loops around the entire circumference of the tower like a ring. You could walk around the whole building if you wanted to. Giltstone tiles line the floor, and ornate trees grow in terra-cotta pots and rosebushes climb up the balustrade.

I walk around the balcony, trying to let off steam. Natalie knows how long I craved a heartbeat, so how can she consider letting someone take that away from me? I know we can implant my heart back into me, but there's no guarantee it'll work again. Our Blood Mate connection will be severed, and I won't be hers anymore, and she won't be mine.

And it's not just that. I'm really not comfortable with being Theora's vessel. I don't want Purian Rose making a Blood Mate connection with me, no matter how brief a time it's for. How can they even suggest this? I'd rather die! I furiously kick over one of the potted plants, and the terra-cotta pot smashes against the ground. A door slides open behind me.

"Is everything all right, son?" Sigur says.

I turn. I realize I'm in clear view of the living room.

"How are the discussions?" I say with a note of bitterness.

Sigur sighs deeply. "I do not believe that Emissary Bradshaw is the answer we've been looking for. My gut tells me we cannot trust him, and I sense Roach feels the same way."

"That makes three of us then."

We wander over to the balustrade and stare across the city. In the distance, church bells chime, letting the Pilgrims know it's time for the day's Cleansing. The city is joyous and at peace. The war hasn't touched the lives of anyone here. It's a different world. I can see how the Sentry citizens could easily turn a blind eye to the suffering of others, as long as they continue living their happy lives in their golden city.

"Beetle and the others want me to try out Lucinda's plan," I mumble. "They want me to be the vessel. Natalie agreed with them."

"Ah. That explains the broken pot," Sigur says.

I rub the back of my neck, sighing. "What if they put my heart back in me and it doesn't work? How can Natalie be so willing to risk everything we have together?"

"What you and Natalie share is more powerful than any Blood Mate connection," he says. "Love does not vanish once a heart stops beating. I will forever love your mother, and Natalie will always love you. And Purian Rose clearly still cares for Theora, or he wouldn't be trying to transform people into her image," he continues. "But you already know your love for Natalie isn't just based on your Blood Mate connection. So what is really bothering you?"

"What if I lose my heartbeat forever?" I gaze at the Golden Citadel in the distance. "They don't understand what it's like not to have a heartbeat. I was a ghost walking among the living, never really part of this world," I say. "It was hell. I can't go through it again."

Sigur puts a hand on my shoulder. "We'll figure something out."

With that, he heads back inside. I lean against the balustrade and shut my eyes briefly, listening to my heart beating rhythmically inside my chest. Am I willing to lose that sound, when I spent a whole lifetime searching for it? It would destroy me.

So imagine what it would feel like to get it back.

I open my eyes. Returning Purian Rose's heartbeat is the most powerful weapon we have at our disposal. So I'm going to do it. I'm going to let them take my heart.

28.

NATALIE

"**WE SHOULD NEVER HAVE ASKED** Ash to do it," I say, warily eyeing the glass jar on the bedside table, like it's a coiled snake. "It's the worst thing anyone could do to him. It was cruel of us to even suggest it." *It was cruel of me.*

"Yeah, you're right." Beetle sighs, scratching his scarred cheek. "I remember how Ash was before he met you. He was in a pretty dark place. If there's even a small chance he won't get his heartbeat back, I'm not sure I can do that to him."

"We should apologize," Day says.

"What are we going to do, though?" Elijah says. "We still don't have a plan to bring down Purian Rose."

"We'll think of something. I'm going to look for Ash." I stand up and Beetle gets up too. "Can I talk to him alone first?" I suspect it's going to require a lot of groveling on my part to get him to forgive me.

"Let him know I'm sorry, okay?" Beetle says.

"We should probably find out what the 'grown-ups' have been plotting," Day says, rolling her brown eyes.

We go into the hallway. Elijah, Day and Beetle head toward

the living room while I stalk the corridors in search of Ash. I pass the white door with the blue glass doorknob. It's open. I peer inside the bedroom, curious to know if the maid who was crying earlier is feeling any better.

A teenage girl is sitting by the window, wearing an elegant yellow bustle gown with an orange sash around her waist that matches the color of her flame-red hair. She has pale, freckled skin and sky-blue eyes that are heavily rimmed with Cinderstone powder. Her lips have been painted the color of copper, like the Dacian girls in Thrace.

I let out a startled breath. "Amy!"

She looks up. "Natalie! Oh my God, is it really you?" Amy rushes over to me and flings her arms around my neck. She smells of expensive floral perfume.

"I thought you were dead," I say, releasing her.

Amy shakes her head. "After Juno and Nick were killed, Stuart and I ran away. We tried to escape over the border," she explains. "We got as far as the Steel Sea before we were caught. They shot Stuart, and I was brought up to one of the Destroyer Ships. They were intending to send me to the Tenth."

"Then how did you get here?" I ask.

Amy lowers her lashes. "One of the Sentry guards sent me here. A man named Victor."

My heart seizes. I know Victor. During our failed mission to rescue Polly a few weeks ago, we boarded a Destroyer Ship, which was holding hundreds of people captive, ready to send them off to the Tenth. While on that airship, I met Victor—a vicious man who threw a hysterical woman out of the Destroyer Ship's air lock, letting her plunge hundreds of feet to her death. I discovered he was selling young boys and girls to businessmen in Centrum, who wanted the children to satisfy their own deviant desires. The man running the operation in Centrum was called . . .

Patrick.

"Oh God," I gasp. "Oh, Amy . . ."

She falls against me and starts crying. "I wish they'd sent me to the Tenth."

I hold on to her for a long time, letting her cry. I can only imagine the horrors she's had to endure these past weeks, under Emissary Bradshaw's "guardianship." There's no way we can allow that man to take power. He's a monster, worse than Purian Rose in many ways.

I tuck a strand of auburn hair behind Amy's ear. "I'm going to get you out of here."

She timidly takes my hand, and we head toward the living room. When we get there, my mother and Roach are in the midst of a heated debate. Like everyone else, Mother is still wearing her jumpsuit, the gun belt slung around her boyish hips, where her hands are angrily placed now.

To my relief, Ash is by the fireplace, talking to Beetle. Everyone else is there, including Dr. Craven, having dealt with Garrick. He's sitting in one of the leather chairs. Emissary Bradshaw occupies the seat next to him. Amy's hand tightens fearfully around mine as her eyes flitter toward him.

"We're leaving," I say. "Right now."

"Amy!" Day exclaims when she sees us.

Mother stares curiously at me. "What are you talking about? We can't leave."

"That *monster*," I say, pointing toward Emissary Bradshaw, my hand shaking with rage, "has been selling children to the highest bidder. He's been holding Amy hostage, for himself."

Father spins around on Emissary Bradshaw. His scarred face is twisted with fury. "Is this true?"

A hard expression enters his eyes. "I needed to make a profit somehow. How did you think we were paying for all those Transporters and weapons?"

Mother blanches. "You were selling children?"

Before I realize what's happening, Amy rushes forward and grabs the gun from Mother's holster. There's a *pop* of gunfire and Emissary Bradshaw's head snaps back. Blood splashes on the gilt wall behind him.

Everyone is too stunned to move, too stunned to speak. Amy's hands shake as she continues to hold the gun out in front of her, clearly in shock. I know how she feels, my mind flashing with images of the scientist I shot in the Tenth. I rub my clammy hands against my pants, trying to wipe off the imaginary blood on them. Ash strides over to her and takes the gun, placing the weapon on the mantel, before gently pulling her into an embrace. She stiffens at first and then collapses against him, sobbing. He cradles her head with his hand, whispering soothing things in her ear. Lucinda covers her nose and hurries out of the room, the scent of blood clearly overwhelming to her. Yolanda chases after her.

"What are we going to do now?" Mother mutters as she paces around the room. "Our plan won't work without him."

I turn my gaze back at Emissary Bradshaw's body. His lips have started to turn a grisly shade of gray. There's a neat bullet hole below his left eye. A lucky shot—well, not so much for Emissary Bradshaw. The living room doors creak open and Garrick enters the room, looking pale and exhausted, his hand clutching his wounded stomach. He's still wearing his bloodstained jumpsuit, but he's lowered the top to reveal the white vest underneath, which clings to his lean, muscular frame.

"You should be in bed," Mother says.

"I heard gunshots. What's going—oh," he says as he spots the slumped body in the leather chair. "He was an ass anyway." Garrick staggers over to one of the other chairs and sits down, grunting. "Do we need to worry about security hearing those shots?"

"I don't think so," Mother replies. "The guards are placed at the main entrance, fifty floors below us. They don't start their rounds for another"—she quickly checks her watch—"twenty minutes."

I remember walking past the security guards each morning when we used to live here. If I recall correctly, there were four men posted in the foyer and that's it. Every three hours one of them would patrol the floors, but they were so lazy they rarely went beyond level twenty, where Emissary Bradshaw's private restaurant is located to entertain VIP guests, before stealing a beer from the kitchen and heading back down again.

"We'll have to deal with them," Father says quietly to Mother, who nods. I don't like the sound of that. He goes over to Emissary Bradshaw's body. "Would someone help me get him out of here?"

Sigur, Dr. Craven and Roach join my father. They each take one of Emissary Bradshaw's fat limbs and heave his bloated body out of the room, leaving a red stain on the leather chair. I don't know where they're taking him, and frankly I don't care. I hope it's to the trash compactor. It's where garbage like him belongs.

I go to the kitchen and retrieve a cloth and bowl of water, and head back to the living room. Ash and Elijah help me as we silently wash the wall. The red water drips down the gold leaf like tears. Beetle mops up the stains on the leather chair and white carpet, trying to scrub away the last traces of Patrick Bradshaw from this earth, but it's no good—his blood has already stained the furniture. Day and Amy are kneeling by the fireplace, staring at the flames, their hands clasped together. All the time my mother is muttering to herself: "What are we going to do now?"

"I'm going to do it," Ash says quietly to me and Elijah. "I'll be the vessel."

I stop scrubbing. "No, Ash. You don't have to; it was wrong of us to ask."

"There's no one else," he says. "We don't have any other option."

"I don't want you to," I say.

Ash tucks a finger under my chin, tilting my face so I'm looking up at him.

"I love you," he whispers. "That isn't going to change, you know that?"

"I know," I say. "But this is your heartbeat we're talking about; I couldn't live with myself if you lost it again. And it's not just that. The more I think about it, the more messed up it is. You'll be his Blood Mate." I shudder.

The front-door bell chimes, startling everyone.

I shoot a panicked look at Ash. Is it possible one of the security guards decided to do his job and actually came up here, and heard us moving about?

Ash turns to Amy. "Get rid of them."

She nods and hurries over to the front door, while we all hide behind the furniture. Those who have weapons draw them. Amy opens the door.

"Can I help you?" she says.

"I'm here to see Sigur," a girl's voice replies.

Sigur stands up and smiles. "Ah, that will be my guest. Let her in, Amy." He turns to the rest of us as we come out of our hiding places. "I hope you do not mind, but I took the liberty of contacting a good friend of mine, who I think can help us."

Amy stands aside, letting in the guest. A girl sweeps into the room, wearing a long blue robe. She lowers her hood, revealing waist-length black hair that ripples like the surface of the oceans, and sparkling eyes the color of the night. She fixes her gaze on Ash, and my heart cramps.

"Hello, Ash," she says.

He lets out a breath of surprise. "Evangeline."

29.

NATALIE

JEALOUSY SNAKES THROUGH ME as Evangeline and Ash embrace. They look so perfect together—both tall, dark and devastatingly beautiful—but that's hardly a surprise. They were supposed to be Blood Mates, but when I was a child, I needed a heart transplant, so Dr. Craven ripped out her heart and gave it to me, and as a result Ash and I formed the connection instead.

Even though Ash loves me, it still hurts knowing he was destined to be with another girl, especially when that girl is five feet eleven inches tall, with pouting rose-blushed lips, flowing ebony hair, alabaster skin and sensuous curves. I wrap my arms around myself. I have curves too, but because of my height— or lack thereof—I don't carry them off as well as Evangeline. I suddenly wish I'd brushed my tangled hair. Day looks at me anxiously. She knows how deadly Evangeline is. As if sensing us staring at her, Evangeline's black eyes shift in our direction. There's a chilling, dangerous edge to them.

"Hello, Natalie," she says coldly.

"Hi," I reply, equally stiff.

When we were living in Black City, Evangeline stalked me for a while. She murdered my bodyguard and my cat, ripping out their hearts, and she threatened to rip out mine too. I have to admit, I wasn't sad to hear she'd left Black City. I secretly hoped she'd never come back. Looking at the delighted look on Ash's face, he obviously doesn't feel the same way. I glance down at his hand, which is gently resting on her narrow hip, and jealousy flares inside me again.

"My beautiful Evangeline," Sigur says, opening his arms wide.

She races into them and Sigur spins her around. The Darkling Ambassador raised Evangeline after her parents were killed during the war.

"I was so relieved when you called me," Evangeline says when he puts her down. "I'd been following your trial on the news. I didn't know what to do; I had no idea how to save you. Then I'd heard rumors you'd escaped, but I wasn't sure." She throws her arms around him again. "I'm so happy to see you."

He kisses her forehead. "Me too. Thank you for coming."

"Anything for you," she replies.

"How did you get past security?" Ash says.

Evangeline laughs. "Those *goons*? Pur-lease, Ash," she says arrogantly. "I was able to sneak around Black City all the time without getting caught, so I know what I'm doing. I've been in Centrum for weeks, and no one's spotted me yet."

Sigur briefly introduces her to everyone as we take our seats. Elijah leans against the fireplace and idly scratches his fingers through his wavy hair, his topaz eyes following Evangeline. She catches him watching her and he flushes, looking away. Evangeline smiles a little. Dr. Craven and my mother wisely keep their distance from Evangeline as she sits down on the rug—they were the ones who took her heart, after all.

I slump down on one of the chairs and Ash sits on the floor in front of me, leaning against my legs. I gently stroke his hair. Evangeline shoots an icy look at me, and I stop. It's not fair to flaunt our relationship in front of her, despite everything she's done. At that moment Lucinda and Yolanda enter the room again. Lucinda stops in her tracks when she sees Evangeline and looks quizzically at Ash. He explains who she is, and the women embrace.

"I thought you were searching for more twin-bloods," Ash says to Evangeline.

"I was," she says, playing with a strand of her black hair. "I've been traveling all over the country in search of them."

"And did you find any more like us?" he says tentatively.

Evangeline frowns. "Not yet, but there are still plenty of places to look."

Ash turns toward Sigur. "How did you know Evangeline was in Centrum?"

"Before I was captured, Evangeline and I had been keeping in touch," Sigur replies.

"Why didn't you tell me?" Ash says, clearly stung.

"I asked him not to say anything. I thought things would be less confusing if I wasn't in your life," Evangeline says, flicking a look at me. "So why was I summoned here?"

Shadows from the fire dance across her pale skin as we tell her the story of Edmund Rose and Theora and our plan to transplant his beloved's heart inside a twin-blood. Anger darkens Evangeline's beautiful face as I explain our theory about Rose's plot to convert everyone to human-Lupine hybrids using the drug Wings. This gets a few surprised looks from my parents and Garrick—we were all so exhausted and in shock after the attack on the Sentry rebel stronghold, we fell asleep in the Transporter, so I never got a chance to tell them. Father grips my mother's hand, and she passes him a worried look.

"But why hybrids?" Evangeline asks.

"His grandfather and his Blood Mate, Theora, were hybrids," I say. "He loved them more than anyone."

"He's trying to bring his family back," Evangeline says quietly, catching on.

When we're finished telling her everything we know, the sun has started to set over the city, turning the sky a brilliant orange and making the giltstone buildings shimmer gold. I've missed Centrum. It really is beautiful. Evangeline takes a deep breath, digesting everything.

"So you want me to be the vessel. Will it work?" she says, directing her question at Dr. Craven. It's the first time she's acknowledged his existence. I can't imagine how hard it is for her being around him, when he's the man who ripped out her heart while she was still conscious and gave it to me.

"I honestly don't know," he says. "The heart is very old, and may be too badly decayed even for a twin-blood to regenerate the tissue. Not to mention, it's a Lupine heart."

"I can help with that," Yolanda adds. "Our main issue is getting access to a hospital."

"There's a private doctor's office downstairs, below the gymnasium," Amy says shyly. "Patrick had heart troubles, because of his weight, so there's all sorts of equipment down there."

Sigur turns to Evangeline. "I know it is a lot to ask. But will you consider it?"

Evangeline sighs. "Yes, I'll do it."

Ash leans over and gives her a hug. Her arms linger around him for a heartbeat longer than I'm comfortable with. I tear my eyes away. *He loves me.* We spend the next hour discussing what to do next, while Beetle and Lucinda head into the kitchen and prepare some food for everyone. They bring back plates of ripe fruit, even riper cheese and some glasses of Synth-O-Blood. Emissary Bradshaw must've had some left over from when he had Darkling servants. Everyone hungrily tucks into the food while Amy flicks on the large, wall-mounted digital screen. It immediately turns on to SBN news.

February Fields smiles back at us in that blank way of hers as she reads the headlines: a reminder for people to attend the Cleansing; Purian Rose's upcoming birthday banquet being held in the Golden Citadel; a devastating "explosion" at a smelting works in Gallium, which they're blaming on Humans for Unity (Ha! So typical of the government to twist the story to suit their agenda); plus there's been a "reorganization" of the Sentry cabinet. Reading between the lines, I'm guessing that reorganization involves the execution of several ministers that Rose suspected were involved in the Sentry rebellion. The streets of Centrum will be running red tonight.

Elijah leans down to get some grapes from the tray, his hand brushing against Evangeline's as she reaches for the Synth-O-Blood at the same time. She looks up and their eyes meet. They both flush, quickly glancing away. A small smile plays across Evangeline's lips. Our conversation eventually turns toward Wings.

"So let me get this straight," Evangeline says. "Purian Rose has been making his men take this new drug Wings, which is a combination of Haze, Night Whisper and some retrovirus that turns people into hybrid Lupines?"

Dr. Craven nods. "But the formula's not stable. Some people are dying."

She frowns. "If Purian Rose intends to turn everyone into hybrids, how's he planning to do it?"

"He'll have to infect everyone with Wings at the same time," Garrick says, grimacing slightly. He's still slouched in his seat, gripping his injured stomach.

"How could he do that?" my father says.

"Water supply?" Lucinda suggests.

Sigur's and Yolanda's mouths twitch. I remember Sigur telling us a few weeks ago how Lucinda attempted to poison Black City's water supply during the first war, before Sigur and my father stopped her. Shortly afterward, Lucinda was sent to the Barren Lands camp and the Four Kingdoms disbanded.

Mother shakes her head. "The waterworks are designed to immediately shut down if they detect any viruses. We had to add that feature after your failed sabotage attempt."

"You're welcome," Lucinda replies dryly.

"Besides, the water would weaken the effects of the Haze and Night Whisper in the drug. Rose has added them to Wings for a reason, so it would seem to defeat the object to dilute it," Dr. Craven says. "No, the drug needs to be delivered in its concentrated format to be effective."

As the former head of the Anti-Darkling Science and Technologies Department, and the creator of Golden Haze, he knows a thing or two about delivery systems. He takes off his glasses and wearily rubs his eyes. It catches me off guard sometimes how much he looks like his son, Sebastian—they have the same wavy hair, the same olive skin and slim face, the same green eyes—except, I recall, Sebastian's eyes weren't green when I saw him at the rebel base. They were silver, just like the Pilgrim in Thrace, and the men I saw in Scott's shop in Gallium.

The memory of that visit sends shivers down my spine as I recall the homeless man I saw outside the chapel next to Scott's shop, with his rotting face and . . . Oh! I bolt upright, startling Ash, who is sitting beside me. The homeless man had been surrounded by glass bottles with a milky-silver residue in them. Just like Wings! I'd thought the bottles were Scott's garbage, but I realize now they weren't. They belonged to the church next door. I recall the sound of the church bells chiming as the Pilgrims were being called in for—

"The Cleansing ceremony!" I say excitedly. "The public Cleansing ceremony! That's how Purian Rose is going to infect everyone. He's making them drink it as part of the ritual."

I briefly explain my theory to the others, telling them about the Pilgrim in Thrace with the silver eyes, and the homeless man in Gallium.

"Yeah, I remember him," Elijah says, shuddering.

"The homeless man was really sick," I say, turning toward Dr. Craven. "Just like the girl from the patient-trials video you showed me back at the rebel base. He must have drunk some Wings without realizing what it was, and got ill."

Roach sinks back in her chair, her blue dreadlocks falling around her freckled shoulders. "Fragg, millions of people are expected to attend that."

"How did that Pilgrim in Thrace get infected?" Day adds. "I thought Rose had only given Wings to his own men."

Dr. Craven is the one who answers. "I'm sure Rose would have wanted to do some trial runs to make sure his plan worked, before trying it out on the national stage. It's what I would have done, anyway," he says. "Chances are he sent vats of Wings to a select number of churches across the country, like the one in Gallium, and ordered the Pilgrims to take it during their daily Cleansing ceremony. That's probably how that poor Pilgrim in Thrace got infected too. He was a lab rat."

"Wouldn't the Pilgrims have noticed they were drinking a blend of Haze?" Beetle says.

"Not everyone knows what Haze looks like," Ash says quietly. "They probably thought it was milk mixed with some other harmless ingredient."

"Here's what I don't get about Wings," Evangeline says. "I understand why Purian Rose wants to give people the retrovirus, but why did he add Haze and Night Whisper to it as well? Where do they fit in?"

"Drinking crushed Night Whisper puts people into a hypnotic state," Elijah says quietly. "They'd do whatever Purian Rose says."

"Unless they happen to be a Dacian," Ash adds darkly. "Didn't Giselle say her people have a natural tolerance to Night Whisper, so it wouldn't work on them?"

"That's probably why he sent them all to the Tenth," I say.

"But why does he need to use a mind-control drug on the Pilgrims? Those creeps already do everything he says," Beetle adds.

"Many people attending the public ceremonies won't be Pilgrims; they're just regular citizens," Mother says. "In order for his One Nation plan to work, he has to get the citizens thinking like his truly devoted followers."

Roach sits back in her chair. "It's cunning. People will get addicted to the Haze, so they'll keep going back for more."

"The retrovirus will change them into hybrids," Day says.

"And the crushed Night Whisper will make them mindless puppets, willing to follow his every command," Elijah adds.

"Everyone would think the same, look the same, a whole country in his image," I say. "One faith, one race, one nation, under His Mighty."

"Fragg," Ash says.

"When's the ceremony?" Evangeline asks.

I look at the digital screen, which is running a report on the ceremony. "Two days."

We all look at each other, letting it sink in. Two days until Purian Rose unleashes the retrovirus onto the population. Two days to transplant Theora's heart into Evangeline and somehow get her to the Golden Citadel. Two days and the victors of this war will be decided.

Two days.

I stand up. "What are we waiting for? Let's get prepared."

30.

ASH

THE ELEVATOR DOORS SLIDE OPEN and we step into Emissary Bradshaw's private operating room. Amy quietly moves about the room, turning on the lights. The room is surprisingly small but well equipped, with all the latest gadgets and machines. There's an unpleasant antiseptic smell, which stings my nostrils.

Day and Natalie assist Dr. Craven and Yolanda as they prep for surgery, and I place the glass jar on a nearby counter. Evangeline lies down on the operating table and anxiously plays with her hair. Everyone else is upstairs, waiting for us in Patrick's penthouse. I sit beside Evangeline and take her hand in mine.

"You don't have to do this," I say to her.

"Yes I do." She gazes up at me with glimmering black eyes. Her dark hair is pooled across her pillow, framing her beautiful, angular face. "I want to help, Ash, and I have less to lose than you."

She lightly presses a hand to my chest and my heart tremors under her touch, my stomach clenching. Desire aches through me, and I quickly force it deep, deep down inside me. Evangeline's the only person in this room who truly understands what it's like not to have a heartbeat; she knows how it would destroy me to lose mine again. Natalie looks at us and smiles, but there's worry in her blue eyes. I gently remove Evangeline's hand from my chest. Dr. Craven and Yolanda stroll over to us.

"Are you ready, Evangeline?" Dr. Craven asks.

She nods confidently, but her hand finds mine again.

"There's no guarantee this is going to work," Yolanda says. "Even if the heart isn't rejected, the only way we'll know for certain it's worked is when Purian Rose touches you."

I recall the moment, several months ago during history class, when Natalie and I accidentally bumped heads when we bent to retrieve her dropped pen. The brief touch was all it took to activate my heart.

"I understand," Evangeline says.

I lightly squeeze her hand. "I'll see you when you wake up."

She gives me a nervous smile. I head over to Natalie, quickly kissing her on the forehead, before heading upstairs with Amy. Natalie and Day stay in the hospital to assist Dr. Craven and Yolanda.

We find everyone on the balcony outside Patrick's penthouse. Elijah is sitting precariously on the narrow balustrade, his tail hanging lazily over the side as he gazes across the city. From here I can see the famous domed roof of the Golden Citadel and nearby the shard-shaped building that's currently home to the Sentry government. A million voices ring out in prayer across Centrum, all in worship of Purian Rose, the sound reverberating through my bones. It's easy to see how people become intoxicated by it. It is comforting. On the billboard-sized digital screens built into all the skyscrapers are commercials for the Cleansing ceremony in two days' time. Two days. Fragg. Two days and this will be over one way or another.

Elijah rubs a tired hand over his face. He looks exhausted, and I know it's not just from a lack of sleep. Grief is taking its toll too. It's exhausting being sad all the time. I know how he feels. I could happily crawl into bed and never wake up again, given half the chance. I don't want to constantly remember why my heart hurts so much.

It appears Lucinda feels the same way, given the fact that she's curled up in a ball on one of the plush balcony seats, fast asleep, the cool breeze rustling her cropped black hair. Garrick is slumped in one of the other leather chairs, clutching his stomach. Nearby, the adults talk quietly to each other. Occasionally, Sigur glances toward the door, as if expecting Dr. Craven to walk through, but the operation will take a few hours. Beetle is leaning against a gold pillar, smoking a roll-up. Amy and I join him.

"You're not going to watch the operation?" he says.

"I've seen enough blood for one day," I reply, plucking the cigarette from him and taking a puff before giving it back.

"What are we going to do about Emissary Bradshaw?" Beetle says. "People will notice he's missing."

I glance at Amy.

"I'll tell the guards he's sick, then make a few phone calls and cancel his appointments," she says. "I was Patrick's personal assistant, among other things; it won't seem suspicious that I'm calling them."

"That should keep the guards off our backs for a few days," Beetle says, taking another drag of his cigarette. "So how exactly are we going to get Evangeline and Purian Rose together in the same room?" The question is pitched to everyone on the balcony.

"How about the Cleansing ceremony?" General Buchanan suggests. A light breeze drifts over the balcony, ruffling his wavy blond hair. "Purian Rose is supposed to be attending the event in Rose Plaza."

"The place will be swarming with guards," Roach says.

"Patrick was in charge of organizing the security. I can get you the files," Amy says.

She heads inside and returns a few minutes later with a portable com-screen, placing it on the table next to Sigur. We all converge around it. On the screen is a map of Rose Plaza, with green, yellow and red lights blinking on it.

"The green dots on the roofs must be MGTs. Machine gun turrets," General Buchanan explains when we all look blankly at him. "We had those in Black City to shoot down any Nordins who tried to fly over the wall. Garrick and I can override them."

Natalie's mom points toward the yellow dots. Her black hair has been swept back into a tight bun, highlighting her painfully thin face. "The yellow dots must be where the Sentry guards will be positioned around the plaza. But I suspect there will be a separate squad roaming through the crowd."

"If things kick off, we'll just use the MGTs to take them out," Garrick says.

"You can't go shooting into a crowd of innocent people," I reply. "Purian Rose might not care about their lives, but I do."

General Buchanan nods. "I agree with Ash. We can't do that."

"Yeah, our best bet is to use disguises," Beetle says. "We'll blend in with the other citizens. There's going to be a crapload of people there. The guards can't keep tabs on everyone."

"What about the red dots on the stage?" I say.

"They're Purian Rose's bodyguards," Amy says.

"They're going to be the biggest problem," I say. "They might recognize us when we're up on the stage."

"It's risky, mate, but we don't have many other options," Beetle says. "All we have to do is get Evangeline to Purian Rose before they stop her."

"You make it sound so easy," I drawl, and he smirks.

We discuss our plan for the next few hours, working out the details, although the whole time my mind is on Evangeline and the operation. Everything rests on its success.

"It's not enough to get Purian Rose to declare a cease-fire; we have to get the country to turn against the Sentry government so they don't put another one of those assholes in power," Roach says, glancing at Emissary Buchanan, who ignores the jibe.

"We'll tell them about Wings," I say. "But we'll need to get the evidence to the news stations. Who can we trust?"

Emissary Buchanan sighs, relenting. "I have contacts at SBN news. We can trust them."

The balcony door slides open, and everyone stops talking. My heart leaps up into my mouth. Natalie and Day step onto the balcony. Their clothes are covered in Evangeline's blood, their hair glistening with sweat.

"Well?" I say.

Natalie gives a small nod. "It seems to have worked, but Yolanda said the next twenty-four hours are crucial. Evangeline could still reject it."

"Can I see her?" Elijah asks.

Natalie nods. "She's conscious."

Elijah leaves the balcony and Natalie turns to me, a mischievous look in her eye.

"Someone has a crush," she says.

A knot of jealousy twists in my gut at the thought of Elijah and Evangeline together, but I force it aside, knowing it's stupid to feel jealous. I have no claim over Evangeline. Besides, I'd rather Elijah focus his attention on her than on Natalie.

The rest of us head inside. I follow Natalie to our bedroom and slump down on the bed while she takes a quick shower. I close my eyes for what seems like a second, but when I open them, it's dark outside. Natalie isn't in the room.

I rub the sleep out of my eyes, then go in search of her. I find her in the library with her parents. It's an oval room, the walls covered floor to ceiling with books. General Buchanan is by the open window, smoking a cigarette, and Natalie and her mom are sitting in the red leather chairs beside the white marble fireplace. On a table between them is Polly's file, the photographs scattered across the mahogany table. Natalie turns, sensing me. She waves me over, and I take a seat beside her.

"It didn't really sink in earlier, with everything that was going on. But Polly was like Purian Rose, right?" Natalie says to her mom. "She had some Darkling and Lupine in her?"

Emissary Buchanan nods faintly. Flames dance in her pale blue eyes from the fire roaring in the hearth. "We realized it at the first ultrasound. Dr. Craven couldn't find a heartbeat, and I thought . . ." She sighs sadly. "But then he spotted her fangs."

"*What?*" Natalie splutters.

"They develop in utero in the first few weeks after conception," Emissary Buchanan explains. "It was apparent then that she wasn't normal."

I wince at the word. *Normal.* Natalie's father stares out the window, one hand thrust in his pocket, the other holding the cigarette.

"Craven ran some more tests after she was born and confirmed what she was," Emissary Buchanan continues. "Thankfully, because she was predominantly human, we could pass her off as one of us, with a few moderations."

"Moderations?" Natalie asks.

"You neutered her," I say.

Emissary Buchanan nods. "She wore veneers. No one suspected a thing. Lots of Sentry girls have cosmetic dental work done at a young age."

"Did Polly know what she was?" Natalie asks.

"She didn't know she was different until you were born," Emissary Buchanan says. "She thought every little girl didn't have a heartbeat and craved blood. But then you came along and she realized there was something wrong with her. Your father and I explained to her what she was, and who her real father was, but that she had to keep it a secret."

"So she always knew?" Natalie sinks back in her chair, her blond curls framing her face. "What about her heart? Surely someone noticed she didn't have a heartbeat."

"You didn't," Emissary Buchanan says.

Natalie flushes a little.

"People generally don't go around checking each other's pulses, Natalie. Why would they? Besides, she *looked* human," Emissary Buchanan says.

"And we made sure Craven did all her medical examinations, so he could fake the results," General Buchanan says from across the room. "No one suspected a thing."

"Did Purian Rose know she was his daughter?" Natalie says.

"I told him she was Jonathan's," Emissary Buchanan replies.

Over by the window, General Buchanan's expression hardens. He takes a drag of his cigarette. Smoke spills out of his lips in a long, twisting ribbon.

"Why didn't you tell me what she was?" Natalie says. "Why didn't she?"

"She was afraid you wouldn't accept her," Emissary Buchanan says.

Natalie flinches. "Why? She was my sister! I loved her."

"I know," Emissary Buchanan says. "I tried to make Polly feel part of the family. I doted on her, lavished her with gifts and affection. I did everything I could to make her feel special, beautiful, *accepted,* but she never did. She always felt like an outcast."

"Yeah, well, that tends to happen when you make people like her live inside walled ghettos," I mutter.

Emissary Buchanan's thin lips pinch together.

"How can you justify what you did to my people, when your own daughter was one of us?" I say, anger boiling up inside me.

"She wasn't one of you," Emissary Buchanan says harshly. "Polly was mostly human. She was a good girl; she posed no threat to anyone, unlike the Darklings."

I ball my hands up into fists and Natalie shakes her head in disgust.

"How could you let Purian Rose torture her the night they came for Father?" Natalie says. "She must have been heartbroken that you chose me over her and allowed her own father to do that to her."

"I picked Polly because she was physically stronger than you, Natalie," Emissary Buchanan says. "Those wounds would have killed you. I explained this to her afterward, and she understood. She forgave me."

Natalie blinks rapidly. "You didn't deserve her forgiveness. You should have told me what she was. I could have been there for her, but you never gave me the chance."

Natalie gets up and leaves the room. I follow her, shutting the door behind me, blocking out the sound of Emissary Buchanan's sobs. We go to the balcony. At night the city has a different sort of beauty, like jewels glittering under dark waters. On the digital screens across the city SBN news continues to run reports of the upcoming Cleansing ceremony. Pilgrims have already started to enter the city from all over the state, wanting to be blessed by Purian Rose himself. From up here I can see the outline of Rose Plaza in the distance. In a little over a day, we'll be there for the Cleansing ceremony. Nerves bubble inside me, but I push them down. I draw Natalie into my arms, and she buries her face in my chest.

"I never knew what Polly was going through," Natalie says, her voice muffled. "All those years I was jealous of her, wishing I had her life, wishing I could *be* her. I didn't know how much she was hurting. Can you imagine what it must have been like for her, to be tortured by her father and betrayed by her mother? No wonder her mind was never the same after that." I hold her close as she cries, running my hand down her back. "How could Polly forgive my mother after what she did to her?"

"I didn't know Polly for long, but I could tell she had a good heart," I murmur. "She didn't seem like the kind of girl who could hold a grudge against someone."

"She wasn't," Natalie admits. "Polly tried to see the best in people; she thought everyone deserved a second chance. She was a better person than me." Natalie pulls away, wiping her eyes. "I'm going to apologize to my mother."

"Do you mind if I check on Evangeline?" I ask.

Natalie shrugs a little. "I don't mind."

I kiss her forehead and then go down to the hospital where Evangeline is recuperating. The ward is quiet and all the lights

ASH

are off, except for the one above Evangeline's bed. She looks very pale but otherwise happy. A half-empty glass of Synth-O-Blood sits on her dresser. It shouldn't take long for her to recover from the surgery, which is lucky since we don't have much time; we need her up and walking about in—I check the clock hanging on the wall—*fragg*, thirty-six hours! She's wearing a pale green hospital gown, which is open at the front, although bandages are wrapped around her chest, preserving her modesty. Elijah is with her. They're chatting with each other, laughing. Occasionally she touches his arm. His cheeks flush, his smile widens.

"Hey," I say, and they turn to look at me. "I just wanted to check how you were."

She shrugs. "It feels like someone's stuffed me with a pound of potatoes. Ash, do you think this is going to work?"

"Yeah. Don't worry, everything's going to be okay. I promise."

"You're not scared?" she says.

I give a lopsided grin. "Nah. Purian Rose is the one who needs to be afraid, not us."

She bites her lip. "Do you think my new heart might activate when I touch Rose?" She looks hopefully at me. "Dr. Craven wasn't certain, because it's a Lupine heart, but Lucinda said Theora felt a spark in her chest when they touched, so . . ."

"Yeah, it's possible," I say, smiling reassuringly. I know how much she's longed for a heartbeat. "I'll leave you guys to it."

I head to the elevator and jab the button a few times. There's a *ping* as the elevator arrives, and I enter. The walls are covered in sheets of gilded metal, warping my reflection so I'm just a dark shadow among a sea of gold. I sink down onto the floor and bury my head in my hands. I lied to Evangeline when I said I wasn't scared. *I'm terrified.*

31.

EDMUND

Centrum, Dominion State
Today

I STEP ONTO THE BALCONY of the Golden Citadel, which overlooks Rose Plaza, and rest my gloved hands on the balustrade. All around me the city of Centrum glints in the moonlight, the towering skyscrapers the perfect combination of beauty and power. Down in the square below, a large platform has been erected in preparation for the public ceremony, happening the day after tomorrow. Everything is falling into place. Thirty years of preparation is finally about to pay off. I should be happy. But for some reason, I feel empty.

A sudden cold wind blasts over the balcony, sending a chill down my neck. I sense someone beside me, and turn. Standing a few meters away is Theora. She's wearing a primrose-yellow dress and hunting jacket—the very outfit she wore the night my father murdered her. Her snowy-white mane stirs in the breeze. A few strands of hair fall into her silver eyes.

"*Hello, Edmund,*" she says.

I exhale, grief ripping through me. I know she can't really be here—it seems I've started hearing voices in my head, like

Patrick claimed my mother used to do—but seeing her makes all those memories come rushing back. She looks over the balustrade at the Cleansing pool in the square below.

"Are you really going to go ahead with this, Edmund?" she says.

I place my gloved hand next to hers. Every part of me aches to touch her, but I know it's impossible. She's just a figment of my mind.

"I'm doing all of this for you," I say.

"Is this really what you think I'd want?" she replies.

"It's what *I* want. You and Grandfather were the only people who accepted me for what I truly am." I sigh. "I miss you."

A sad smile flitters over her lips. *"So this is your solution? To make everyone like us?"*

"If we're all the same, then there will be peace at last," I say.

"You're wrong, Edmund." Theora turns her face up to look at the moon. The iridescent light makes her pale skin glow. *"Do you remember when I took you to the Lupine temple on Mount Alba?"*

"I think about it every night," I whisper.

"You asked me how I could be so kind to you, after what your father did to my parents," she says. *"Do you recall what I said?"*

"You can't judge an entire species by the actions of one man."

"And what else?"

I briefly shut my eyes. "It's easy to hate. The true test of our hearts is to forgive."

"Precisely," Theora says, turning to me, her silver eyes sparkling. "Forgiveness *is the only way you will ever find peace, Edmund."*

"That will never happen," I say bitterly. "You need a heart

to forgive, and Icarus took that from me the night he murdered you."

"Your Excellency?" a worried voice says behind me.

I turn to see my servant Forsyth standing by the doorway. He's dressed in long white Pilgrim robes. His head is shaved, and he has a red rose tattoo above his left ear, like all my faithful followers. He studies me with anxious, newly silver eyes.

"Sebastian Eden is here, as you requested," he says.

I glance toward Theora, but she's gone.

"Thank you, Forsyth," I say, moving away from the gold balustrade. I have nothing to fear about Forsyth repeating what he just saw. He's devoted to me.

"I have other news, Your Excellency," Forsyth says as we walk back inside the building. "The bodies of the Lupine woman Ulrika and her cousin Kieran have been brought to Centrum, as instructed. What would you like me to do with them?"

I run my tongue over my top teeth, feeling the rough edges of my veneers. I was furious when I found out they'd been shot, particularly Ulrika. She was like a sister to Theora.

"Have them cremated at the next full moon," I say as we enter my office.

My grandfather would have hated this room, with its lavish furnishings, marble floors and gilt walls. Patrick thought it gave the right air of authority, but I'm not so sure. I miss the whitewashed walls of the church I grew up in. The boy Sebastian is standing by the large fireplace, looking at the photographs on the mantelpiece. He's dressed in a gray uniform, his head cleanly shaven, like Forsyth's. He spins around when he hears me approach, and bows.

"Your Excellency," Sebastian says. There's a long gash down

the side of his cheek, which I presume he got during the siege on the rebel compound. It seeps when he talks. *Disgusting.*

I turn to Forsyth. "Prepare another seat at the dining table for Mr. Eden. Put him beside Patrick."

"Emissary Bradshaw won't be able to attend dinner tonight, Your Excellency," Forsyth says. "His servant girl called a short while ago. Apparently he's had a bad reaction to a"—he lowers his voice—"*procedure.* He's going to be bedridden for at least a week."

I sigh impatiently. For a man as grotesquely fat as Patrick, he's surprisingly vain, just like his parents. It's typical that he won't be there to support me on the most important day of my life; he will be punished for this.

"Fine," I say. "It's probably best he doesn't come to the Cleansing ceremony if that's the case. I don't want him scaring people."

"Very well," Forsyth says. He bows and humbly walks backward toward the door.

"Oh, and Forsyth?"

"Yes, Your Excellency?"

"Find the squad responsible for killing Ulrika and Kieran and have them shot," I say.

"The *whole* squad, Your Excellency?" Forsyth says uncertainly.

"Yes, all of them," I reply. "I won't tolerate incompetence. I gave them strict instructions, and I expected them to be followed."

The boy Sebastian blanches.

"As you wish," Forsyth says, shutting the doors behind him.

I stroll over to Sebastian. There's a slight sheen of sweat on his upper lip, giving away his nerves.

"I hear you were in charge of the attack on the rebel base in Gallium," I say. "Congratulations. You did a fine job."

"Thank you, Your Excellency," the boy replies, his shoulders squaring with pride, making the butterfly medal on his chest glint. "I live to serve you."

I study the medal, then the boy's silver eyes. He's taken the retrovirus, but based on his pallid complexion, he's not reacting well to it. Shame. It's hard to find good employees. I place my hands on the boy's upper arms, and he flinches slightly.

"So did you kill Ash Fisher and Natalie Buchanan, like I asked you to?" I say.

The boy's Adam's apple bobs up and down in his throat. He blinks rapidly. "Yes, Your Excellency."

I release his shoulders. "Good. I can't afford anything to go wrong at the ceremony."

For the first time in weeks, I feel happy. With Ash Fisher and Natalie Buchanan dead, there's no one left to stop me.

32.

ASH

THE NEXT DAY IS SPENT PREPPING for the Cleansing ceremony. Beetle and Roach are on the balcony, their heads newly shaved, chatting to Amy as she practices painting fake rose tattoos behind their left ears. Beetle carries off the shaved-head look well, but Roach seems utterly miserable about her new haircut, given the way she's scowling.

I run through tomorrow's plan in my head again. First thing in the morning, General Buchanan and Garrick will head to Rose Plaza and take out the soldiers manning the MGTs on the rooftops. Beetle and Roach will blend into the crowd on the ground, in case there's any trouble from the Sentry guards positioned there, and Natalie and I will bring Evangeline up to the stage. The others will go in the Transporter, flown by Day, and hide in the clouds above the city. If we need to make a quick exit, Natalie will hail them, using the GPS watch Destiny gave her. I turn to Day, who is sitting with Garrick on the sofas.

"You good for tomorrow?" I ask.

"I think so," she says. "Garrick's been telling me how to land the Transporter; we'll go up to the roof in a minute and run through the aircraft's controls."

I nod, pleased. It's all coming together. The last part of the plan is down to Emissary Buchanan and Dr. Craven. They're currently gathering all the evidence we have against Purian Rose, which includes the file on Polly, plus the lab report Natalie found in the Barren Lands, and the blue digital disc and sample of Wings we took from the Tenth, which Dr. Craven had the foresight to slip into his medical bag while the Sentry rebel compound was under attack.

I pick up the disc, my stomach clenching. It's a vital part of our plan that this video be shown during the Cleansing ceremony tomorrow. Emissary Buchanan takes it from me.

"Are you certain you can trust your contact at SBN news?" I say. "We need them to override the live television feed so that the whole country sees it at the same time."

"Have a little faith in me, Mr. Fisher. This isn't my first rodeo," she replies.

I smile a little. It's hard to trust a woman who tortured me and then tried to frame me for Chris Thompson's death from Golden Haze, but now's a good time to start. I return to Natalie and stay by her side all day, wanting to take advantage of every second we have together. I idly play with the ends of her blond hair; she keeps her hand in my back pocket. Neither of us says it, but we both know this could be our last day together. I suddenly pull Natalie into my arms, catching her off guard, and kiss her. I don't care that there are other people in the living room with us. A few people lift their eyes, but nobody says anything. She grips my shirt, holding me close to her, letting the kiss linger, before we eventually break apart. Her hand slides into my back pocket again.

The apartment door opens and Elijah enters the room with Evangeline. They've been down in the hospital level all night. We kept an eye on the security cameras to make sure no one entered the operating room while they slept, but we needn't have worried. Patrick owned this whole building, so apart from the Sentry guards that were down at the main entrance—they're currently tied up in a supply room—there's no one else here.

Evangeline is shaky and pale, but otherwise appears okay. Her inky-black hair has been washed and brushed, and she's wearing a pretty blue bustle dress, with a low neckline, revealing her surgery scar. It looks gruesome, the flesh raw and red and held together with metal staples. Elijah's got his arm protectively around her waist and keeps fussing over her, making sure she's comfortable as she sits down, giving her extra pillows. Natalie glances at me, her eyebrow raised. I shrug slightly.

Dr. Craven checks Evangeline's vitals while Elijah sits crosslegged by her feet. His tail very lightly brushes against her legs, rubbing his scent on her, claiming her as his. I scrunch my nose up at the smell, but Evangeline doesn't seem to mind it.

"How are you feeling?" I ask her.

"Sore," she admits. "But I think I'll be okay for tomorrow. Elijah's been letting me drink his blood; it's really helping with the healing process."

My fangs pulse, thinking about how his blood tasted when I drank from him in the Barren Lands: sweet, delicious, intoxicating. He catches my eye and a smirk tugs at his lips, reading my mind.

"Don't get any ideas, Darkling," he says.

"In your dreams, catboy," I reply, grinning.

As the hours slowly melt away, the tension in the group mounts. Laughter fades and the conversation diminishes, until everyone is communicating with just nods and shakes of the head. By the evening we're all silently sitting around the fireplace, frightened, anxious. Day is on Beetle's lap, seemingly reading a book, although she hasn't turned a page in more than an hour. Evangeline is curled up on the sofa with Elijah. He runs his fingers up and down her bare arm. Natalie's parents hold hands, and Roach quietly strokes Amy's hair.

The others are out on the balcony, drinking Sanguis wine as they watch the city below them. The seconds tick away on the clock above the mantel, counting down our last moments together. Natalie sits on my lap, her head pressed against my chest, listening to my heart.

Sleep doesn't come to any of us that night; we're all too pumped full of adrenaline to drift off. Besides, I'm not sure I want to sleep anyway. These could be my last moments on earth with my family, my friends. I don't want to waste them.

Beetle catches my eye and gives a faint nod of the head. I can't believe how far we've come. Just a few months ago we were a pair of goofballs hanging out on his barge in Black City, smoking, drinking and talking halfheartedly about revolution. Now here we are in a penthouse apartment in Centrum, just hours away from facing Purian Rose, the fate of the nation in our hands. I never thought I'd say this, but I sort of miss school. I miss the teachers, the students. I miss being a kid. And tomorrow I'm probably going to die. The thought terrifies me. My arms tighten around Natalie.

My skin starts to prickle as golden rays of sunlight spill into the room, slowly lifting away the shadows of night. Sigur and the others come in from the balcony. Everyone sits up, alert, our minds already focused on the day ahead. On the digital screen, a blond and bubbly February Fields is already reporting on the day's events. The ceremony is due to start in two hours' time, so thousands of Pilgrims are already streaming into the city, heading toward Rose Plaza. Aerial footage shows the crammed streets and avenues, a sea of rolling white, interspersed with pops of color where citizens have opted to wear their normal clothes instead of the white Pilgrim robes.

"Pilgrims from across the state have been flocking to Centrum all night to take part in today's historic event," February says. The footage cuts to the Golden Citadel, where Purian Rose is standing on the balcony, staring down at the thousands of Pilgrims already congregated in the plaza. "In two hours' time, Purian Rose will address the nation before holding the first televised Cleansing ceremony, here, in Rose Plaza . . ."

I turn down the volume, my nerves on edge.

General Buchanan and Garrick grab their guns. Emissary Buchanan shakes Garrick's hand, and then hugs her husband. He tenderly kisses her.

"See you soon," he whispers, smoothing down her hair where he's mussed it up.

She nods, her hand brushing against his. "I . . ." She can't say the words.

"I know," he says. "Me too."

Natalie climbs off my lap and rushes over to her dad, flinging her arms around his neck. He holds her close, pressing his face into her shoulder.

"Take care, Dad," Natalie says.

"You too, Talie," he replies, kissing the top of her head. "Love you."

He gives his family a lingering look before he heads out of the apartment with Garrick. The door shuts behind them. Now it's our turn. We go to our rooms and get ready.

I have a lengthy shower, the hot water beating off my back, trying to scorch away my nerves. It doesn't work. I turn off the water and wrap a towel around my waist and enter the bedroom. Natalie sits on our bed, wearing a simple white vest and underwear as she injects herself with her Wrath medication. Venom floods my fangs at the sight of her bare legs and the curve of her breasts. Natalie catches me looking and laughs.

"Ash, we haven't got time," she says.

"I know," I say, kissing her shoulder, forcing down my frustration. *Gah!*

She tugs at my towel as I walk by, and it slips off my hips.

"Natalie, we haven't got time," I tease.

She laughs but it quickly dies on her lips. We're both trying to pretend everything is normal, but I'm nervous as hell. We get dressed in similar outfits, which we found in the wardrobes around the apartment: black pants, gray tops and black hooded tailcoats with bright orange lining—Patrick liked the finer things in life. Natalie spins her hair up into a bun and pulls up her hood. I lower mine over my head, checking my reflection. Shadows cut across my eyes, disguising their distinctive glimmer, and as long as I keep my mouth closed, no one should see my fangs. I'm used to blending in and acting human; I've been doing it all my life.

We go back to the living room where the others are waiting. Evangeline, Beetle and Roach are dressed similarly to us, although under her tailcoat Roach is wearing a cerulean-blue top—the color of the rebellion. I can't help but grin. She smiles back at me.

"Okay, we ready to go?" Roach says, checking the fake rose tattoo on the side of her shaved head in a nearby mirror.

No. "Yup," I say.

Beetle grabs Day and dips her, kissing her hard. When he breaks the kiss, they're both breathless and flushed. Beetle gently cups her face with his hands.

"Take care, babe, okay?" he whispers.

She kisses him again. "You too."

Elijah takes Evangeline's hand and draws her to the side of the room. He whispers something to her and she blushes, biting her lip. Her eyes flick up and hold his gaze for a long moment. I look away. It's not my business. Sigur strolls over to me.

"I will see you soon, son," he says. "Good luck."

Lucinda hovers behind him. She gives a faint nod of her head. I get the sense she's not one for good-byes. Natalie quietly says farewell to her mom, before hugging Day.

"Just hit the button on your watch if you need me," Day says.

Natalie wipes the tears from her eyes before taking my hand. The five of us—me, Natalie, Evangeline, Beetle and Roach—go out into the hallway, and Beetle calls the elevator. The doors *ping* open a moment later. Natalie's hand tightens around mine.

"No fear," she whispers to me.

We step into the elevator.

33.

NATALIE

THE NEWS REPORTS didn't do the crowds justice, as we find when we push and shove our way down Catherine Street, toward Rose Plaza. The noise is unreal—people chanting, praying, talking. Some are excited, but many others are sour-faced and grumbling about having to come in the first place. I keep peering up at the rooftops of the giltstone buildings, wondering if I'll spot my father or Garrick. I pray they're safe, and that they've managed to take control of the manned MGTs around the city square. Otherwise we'll be gunned down before Evangeline can touch Purian Rose.

"I don't see why we have to go to this stupid event," I hear a woman mutter to her friend. They're both dressed in elaborate black gowns with voluminous tulle skirts, just like the dress I wore when I first met Ash, under the canal bridge in Black City. "I'm not one of those Pilgrim freaks. I don't even follow the faith."

"Shh! Do you want to end up in the Tenth?" her friend says, glancing about with anxious brown eyes. "It doesn't matter that we don't follow the Purity—I doubt half the people here do either—we just have to *pretend* to go along with it, okay? So just suck it up; it'll be over in an hour."

I'm tempted to warn them that it's a trap, that Purian Rose intends to infect them all with a retrovirus, but I can't risk revealing myself. Not now, not when we're so close to finishing this. I look at Ash. Most of his face is concealed by his hood, but I can see the determined set of his mouth. His fingers are laced through mine, making sure I stay close to him as we're jostled by the people around us. Day and Beetle are to my left, and Evangeline and Roach are to Ash's right. Evangeline seems nervous, and her hand keeps touching her chest. *Oh God, please let this work.*

Digital screens on all the buildings show a live feed of Rose Plaza. People are already lining up into rows in front of the giant stage. Guilt weighs heavily in my stomach at the thought of all those people who are going to take the Wings before we can stop them. Ash peers up at the screens, then quickens his pace, obviously thinking the same thing.

My heart trembles as we enter Rose Plaza. At the head of the enormous city square is the Golden Citadel, a palatial-looking church where Purian Rose lives. The domed roof reflects the sunlight so it glitters, casting a warm light over everyone standing in the square below. I used to feel amazed when I saw the Golden Citadel, but now it just makes me shudder. To our right is the Fracture—a skyscraper in the shape of a shard of glass—where the government headquarters are located. I scan the rooftops of the other buildings. I can just about make out the black dots of the MGTs. I don't see anyone near them. Relief floods through me; my father and Garrick were successful in taking out the guards manning the weapons.

Hundreds of Sentry guards patrol the city square, getting

people lined up in rows in front of the stage. They're carrying guns or swords, but they all look weary. It's too early in the morning for them to muster up any enthusiasm. It's just turned eight o'clock—the ceremony is about to start.

Set up on the stage is a long bench, and fifty white bowls. Based on everything I know about the ceremony, we're meant to walk up to the stage, then kneel in front of the white bowls, which are filled with Wings, and drink from them. Purian Rose will then mark our foreheads with water—the mark of Purity. That's the moment he'll touch Evangeline and ideally his heart will activate.

Around the square, digital screens set into the buildings show the live footage. It's strange seeing everyone in the plaza up on the screen as well. I tug at my hood, keeping it lowered as a camera pans past us.

"Get into rows," a bored Sentry guard calls out. People start to form into long rows, one behind the other. We push through the crowds, getting as close as we can, but we're still about twenty rows back.

"We need to get nearer the front," Ash says.

"Leave it to us," Beetle replies, grinning.

We follow him as he snakes through the crowd, leading us toward the first row, ignoring the outraged cries from the Pilgrims who have been patiently waiting there probably since yesterday, given the bags under their eyes. He and Roach head down the line, deliberately standing near a few of the Sentry guards.

"Hey! She's trying to push in!" Beetle says loudly, pointing a finger at Roach. The guards turn, drawn by his shouts.

"I was not!" Roach says.

"You were; I saw you!" Beetle shoves her, hard, and she falls against some of the people waiting in the front row. They all crash to the ground. The Sentry guards rush over to Beetle and Roach and drag them away. Everyone's attention is on them, giving Ash, Evangeline and me the opportunity to merge into the front row, undetected by the Sentry guards. The people around us get to their feet and dust themselves off. If they've noticed we've snuck into the line, they don't say anything, clearly not wanting any more trouble. I'm on Ash's left, and Evangeline is to his right. Ash looks at the stage, his face hard. I take his hand and he glances at me, his expression softening for a moment.

Just then, the doors to the Golden Citadel open. A hush descends over the plaza as a squadron of gray-uniformed guards file down the giltstone steps. They each wear a butterfly medal on their chest and have a ceremonial sword strapped around their waist. Even from here, I can see the silver glint of their irises. They're carrying large steel kegs, like the kind they use in taverns, although I suspect these are filled with Wings instead of ale.

They step onto the stage and my heart freezes. Sebastian is at the far end of the row, to our left. There's a gash down his cheek, perhaps an injury from the attack on the Sentry rebel stronghold, and his olive skin looks waxen, but he's still disarmingly handsome, drawing admiring looks from the females in our row.

"Ash," I say.

"Yeah, I've seen him," he says.

Panic spills through me and my legs feel numb. If Sebastian recognizes us, then this is all over. Thankfully, we're in the middle of the row and he hasn't looked in our direction yet. His gaze is fixed on one of the large digital screens on the edge of the plaza. The cameras have all turned to focus on the center of the stage.

He's just out of shot. A scowl passes over his lips. He loves the limelight; he always has.

Ash grips my hand as a figure appears at the doors of the Golden Citadel, dressed in a long red robe and white gloves. Around his neck is a circle pendant. His black hair is swept neatly back, and his pale skin has a strange, waxy sheen to it. I realize now he must be wearing thick makeup to hide his burns.

Excited whispers spread through the crowd as Purian Rose walks down the steps, commanding everyone's attention. The hairs on the back of my neck prickle; I can practically feel the millions of eyes across the nation watching him approach the stage. The guards salute Rose as he strolls over to the microphone at the front of the platform. When he speaks, his voice is amplified by the microphones hidden in the rigging around the stage. His face is projected on all the monitors around the plaza, and I know the live footage is also being broadcast in every city square across the country, as others attend their own Cleansing ceremony.

"Loyal Pilgrims, I am honored that you have joined me today to take part in this momentous event," he says. "The Cleansing is not just about committing yourself to the Purity faith, or proving your devotion to the Sentry government." I look at Ash. His lips are pressed together so hard, they're white. "It is about cleansing your mind, body and spirit of sin. It has always been my dream to have a nation free from impurity, a world where we are all united, and today that dream will be fulfilled."

"So sayeth us all," the crowd chants in unison.

Purian Rose smiles, reveling in this moment. Victory is within his grasp. The gray-uniformed guards fill the white bowls with Wings. The opaque liquid shimmers in the sunlight as it is poured from the kegs.

"First row, step up," says a guard from the stage, ushering us forward.

This is it. Ash's hand tightens around mine. Evangeline takes his other hand as we walk up the steps leading onto the stage, along with the rest of the first row. When we reach the platform, we kneel down and bow our heads. I surreptitiously look to the left. Sebastian is gazing at the digital screens again. He seems frustrated.

Purian Rose heads to the right-hand side of the stage, and the ceremony begins. One of the guards hands Purian Rose a red bowl filled with water. Rose approaches the first person in the row—a middle-aged woman with a shaved head and a rose tattoo above her left ear. She picks up the white bowl in front of her and brings it to her lips. A cry bubbles up in my throat. I want to yell at her to stop, but I clamp my lips shut, forcing the words down as she drinks the Wings. The look of bliss that enters her face is instantaneous as it courses through her veins. Purian Rose dips his gloved hand into the red bowl and swipes his wet thumb across her forehead.

"You are Cleansed, my daughter," he says.

Ash nudges my shoulder, then nods to the other side of the stage. I follow his gaze. Sebastian has left his position and is slowly walking toward us, his hands behind his back. He's timing his footsteps so he'll be in the middle of the platform at the same time as Rose, who is approaching us from the opposite direction, so they both will appear in the close-up camera shot. At this pace, he'll reach me at the precise moment Purian Rose reaches Evangeline.

"What are we going to do?" I whisper, my mind racing. I could try tackling Sebastian when he nears us, but I'm not sure I'd be able to hold him back long enough for Evangeline to grab Purian Rose's hand and activate his heart, before the other guards kill her.

I shoot a look to my right. Purian Rose is now fifteen people away, fourteen, thirteen, Sebastian is matching his stride, getting closer and closer to me, twelve, eleven, ten—*oh God, oh God, what are we going to do?*—nine, eight, seven—my palms start to sweat—six, five, four—Ash's muscles coil, ready to strike, three, two, one—

Purian Rose reaches Evangeline just as Sebastian stops in front of me. He's looking at Purian Rose—he hasn't seen me yet. Evangeline picks up the white bowl and pretends to drink. My heart is beating so hard, I think it's going to burst out of my chest. Evangeline lowers the bowl just as Sebastian's head turns. His eyes snag on mine.

Purian Rose dips his hand into the red bowl . . .

Sebastian's lips twist into a snarl . . .

Rose touches his thumb against Evangeline's skin . . .

Sebastian draws his sword, and—

34.

EDMUND

I GASP, FALLING TO MY KNEES, as pain blooms inside my rib cage. Tremors rush through my body, surging toward a single point in my chest. There's a burst of fire and then:

Ba-boom.

The boy Sebastian turns, alarmed, as confused murmurs spread throughout the crowd like wildfire, their voices muffled by the sound of my beating heart.

It can't be . . .

"Your Excellency?" he says.

I ignore him as I stare at the girl in front of me.

How . . . ?

Beside her, the boy in the black coat stands up and lowers his hood, revealing an angular face with fierce ebony eyes, wide mouth and ink-black hair. There are stunned gasps from the crowd and the word *Phoenix* hisses across the city. The girl beside him gets to her feet and lowers her hood—blond curls, blue eyes, stubborn mouth. Undeniably Natalie Buchanan. Anger burns through me. No! They were supposed to be dead. I shoot a look at Sebastian. All the blood has drained out of his face.

Flustered, the boy quickly raises his sword and swings it at the Darkling girl in front of me. Panic grips my heart.

"Stop!" I command.

The blade stops an inch from the Darkling girl's neck. I stagger to my feet.

"Drop your sword," I demand.

Sebastian's brows draw together. "Your Excellency?"

"Do it!" I say.

The boy drops his sword, and it lands near my feet. My other bodyguards throw confused looks at each other, uncertain what to do as I stretch out my hand toward the Darkling girl. She takes it. The second our hands touch, a jolt of electricity darts up my arm and into my chest, and my heart clenches. I exhale, disbelieving. How is this possible?

I gently sweep a strand of hair away from her eyes, and my fingers linger on her cheek. A blush enters her pale skin. My eyes drink her in, tracing the contours of her face—glimmering black eyes, sharp cheekbones, rosy lips that are slightly parted to reveal her fangs. I can't stop looking at those lips . . .

"Edmund," she whispers. Her voice is like a siren's call, wrapping itself around me, commanding me to listen. "I need you to do something for me."

"What?" I say.

"Stop this war," she says.

Darkness descends over my heart like a shroud. This is a trick! I release her hand.

"Why would I do that?" I snap.

"Because it's over, Rose," Ash says. I turn toward him, fury burning through me. "We know about Wings and your plan to infect everyone with it at today's Cleansing." My stomach twists as he lifts the white bowl in his hands. "You've been making people drink it!"

There are confused murmurs from the audience. The Pilgrims kneeling at the foot of the stage stare at the white bowls in their hands, their brows furrowed.

"Lies," I growl.

The Buchanan girl lifts her chin. "Samples of the retrovirus have been sent to news stations all across the country, along with evidence that it's been killing people!"

"That's not true," Sebastian says uncertainly. His upper lip glistens with sweat. "Wings is a performance-enhancing drug to make us stronger, better, that's all."

Natalie looks at him. "He lied to you, Sebastian. He lied to *all* of you. It's a retrovirus and a lethal one at that. Unexpected mutations have been occurring in some of the patients."

"I don't believe you," he says.

At that moment, the digital screens around the plaza flicker and a new image appears on the monitors. It's video footage taken inside a hospital. A female Sentry doctor with wavy brown hair walks down the ward, passing emaciated Darklings, Bastets and humans who are chained to the beds, their naked bodies dark with bruises and welts. The camera pauses on a girl, about twelve years old, her brown hair slick with sweat, her ulcerated skin oozing with yellow fluid. She stares fearfully up at the camera. Her eyes are an unnatural shade of silver. She coughs, spewing up blood, painting her face and chest in red. There are horrified gasps from the crowd.

"Patient seventy-six was injected with the F-09 Wings virus two weeks ago and is now displaying signs of liver failure," the doctor says, turning back to the camera. She rolls her eyes. "That's the tenth one this week. Back to the drawing board, huh?"

The man behind the camera chuckles.

The video footage cuts off and the live feed returns. The Pilgrims at the base of the stage drop the white bowls and stagger back in horror. Sebastian looks at me. The gash on his cheek is oozing, just like the girl's in the video.

"You told me it was safe," he says. "You promised me."

"A new world cannot be built without sacrifices," I reply harshly. "I felt it was an acceptable risk; most of the patients lived."

There are outraged shouts from the crowd. Cries of "murderer" and "traitor" fill the air. I take a few steps back as people start throwing things at the stage, almost hitting me. I glare at them, furious. How dare they? Several groups of men surge toward the platform. They're held back by the Sentry guards, but I'm not sure how long they can hold them off.

The Darkling girl turns to me. "Edmund, stop this! Our people have suffered enough!"

She grabs my arms and a strange sensation grips me, like a pathway opening between us and all her emotions flow into me. I feel every moment of heartbreak in this Darkling girl's life, as if I were living it myself: the time her parents were murdered in front of her by a Tracker; her terror as her heart was torn out by a Sentry doctor; her grief at being trapped behind the Boundary Wall. Her life is full of suffering and sorrow; it consumes me until I'm drowning in it. And it's my fault. I did this to her, just like my father did to me. It's too much!

I strike the girl, knocking her off the stage into the crowd below. She hits the cobblestones with a thud. Ash turns, distracted by the Darkling girl's fall, and I take my opportunity to attack. I swipe Sebastian's sword off the ground and grab Ash by his hair, yanking his head back. He grunts in pain as I force him to his knees in front of me. His skin sizzles as I press the silver blade to the side of his throat.

"Get off him!" Natalie rushes forward, but she's stopped by the boy Sebastian. She bites his arm and he grimaces, but doesn't let her go. I turn my attention back to Ash. He stares up at me defiantly, a cold wind stirring his black hair.

"This has gone on long enough, Mr. Fisher," I snarl. "I should have done this months ago, when I had the chance."

"Go ahead." Ash spits the words at me like bullets. "It doesn't matter now. Everyone in the country knows you betrayed them. I did what I came here for, so I'm not afraid to die!"

"No fear, no power!" Natalie cries out.

Panic surges through me as the chant gets picked up by the rest of the crowd. Their words spread down the streets and alleyways, crawling through every door, every window, until the whole city is united in one furious, defiant voice:

"NO FEAR! NO POWER!"

There's a clatter of swords as my bodyguards drop their weapons and run off the stage.

"Get back here!" I yell, but my command falls on deaf ears. I whip around to Sebastian. He's still holding the Buchanan girl. "Control your men!"

A muscle twitches in his jaw. Without a word he releases her and calmly walks off the stage, following the rest of my bodyguards. The Buchanan girl snatches one of the abandoned swords off the stage and points it at me.

"Let him go!" she commands, her blue eyes blazing.

My heart clenches as it experiences something I've not felt since the night Theora died.

Fear.

And if I'm afraid . . .

I look down at Ash, and a hint of a smile spreads across his lips.

He has the power.

Terror wraps itself around my racing heart, squeezing it with a viselike grip. I'm unable to move, paralyzed by this new sensation, as Ash grabs my arm. I lose my grip on the sword, and it clatters to the ground. He holds my gaze as he stands up. As he does so, a gust of wind catches his black coat, flashing its vivid orange lining, so he looks like he has wings made of silken fire. I stumble back, falling to my knees. Phoenix towers over me, his body silhouetted against the golden sun, so all I can see are two glinting eyes staring down at me, hard and unforgiving.

"It's over, Rose," he says. "Surrender."

"Never!" I spit.

He nods at Natalie, who presses something on her watch. Almost immediately, a shadow blocks out the sun. I glance up. A Transporter appears out of the clouds and rapidly descends. Air whips around my face as the aircraft approaches the stage, stopping a few feet above the platform. It's hovering so close, I can see the teenage girl waving at me from the cockpit, a smirk on her lips.

The girl expertly turns the aircraft 180 degrees, and the back hatch hisses open. Standing in the cargo hold is Siobhan Buchanan, along with a Bastet woman and boy, a red-haired girl and a middle-aged Darkling woman. It takes a moment to register that this gaunt, broken woman is my cousin, Lucinda. They all point their guns at me. I'm trapped.

"Edmund Rose, you are under arrest!" Siobhan Buchanan says.

I shift my gaze to Lucinda.

"This has to end, Edmund," Lucinda shouts over the roar of the aircraft's rotors. "It's not what Theora would have wanted, and you know it!"

I look back at the teenage Darkling girl, who is watching me from the foot of the stage. Her hands are clutched to her chest, and she looks pleadingly back at me. I close my eyes and listen to my heartbeat, remembering Theora's words. It's easy to hate. The true test of our hearts is to forgive. I should have listened to her.

Forgive me, Theora.

I open my eyes. "I surrender."

35.

NATALIE

Two weeks later, Centrum

ROSE PLAZA IS BUSTLING with activity. I squeeze
through the crowds, my head covered by my hooded jacket, as
I make my way toward the Fracture—the shard-shaped building where the new coalition government headquarters is based,
which was formed within hours of Purian Rose's surrender. A
few eyes slide toward me, and people begin to whisper excitedly to each other. I'm quite the celebrity these days, but I really don't want the attention. *Especially not today.* My hand
slips into my jacket pocket, finding the yellow-handled knife
concealed there. I trace my fingers over the word etched into
the wood. *Polly.* We held a memorial service for my sister last
week but it wasn't the closure I needed. I still have one thing
left to do.

Camera crews are placed around the plaza, and workmen
dash about as they erect a large wooden cross in the city square.
They're preparing for Purian Rose's execution in fifteen minutes, under my father's watchful eye. Rose's televised trial two
weeks ago lasted just one day. It didn't take long for the courts
to come back with a verdict of guilty for his war crimes, and

sentence him to death. Ash was dead set against the execution, saying it made us no better than the former tyrant, but he was outvoted by the rest of the coalition government. I'm against it too, but for a different reason. My stomach knots, my fingers tightening around the knife.

A middle-aged Darkling man with violet eyes and ebony hair bumps into me, knocking me out of my thoughts. He mumbles an apology and hurries toward the stage with a beautiful, flame-haired Dacian woman, their heads bowed. It's obvious from their thin bodies and hard expressions that they were prisoners in the Tenth. They've traveled a long way to witness Purian Rose's execution at noon. Before they can reach the stage, a group of tough-looking men with shaved heads and rose tattoos behind their left ears block their path.

"Go back to the ghetto, nipper," one of the men says, spitting at the Darkling. "We don't want your kind in our city."

The Darkling flashes his fangs in response, and the people around them fearfully back away. Before a fight breaks out, several armed coalition guards in cerulean-blue uniforms race over to them and usher the tattooed men away. A few guards stay with the Darkling man and Dacian woman, their message clear: there will be no violence today . . . other than Rose's execution, of course. I frown. It's going to take a long time before the tensions between our races goes away. To be honest, I'm not sure they ever truly will, but we have to keep fighting for peace. Otherwise, what was the point of all this?

I enter the Fracture. The lobby is an enormous space, with a twenty-foot-high gold statue of Purian Rose at its center. It's due to be removed next week, but in the meantime a blue flag has been draped over his head. In fact, everywhere I look, the once red-and-white Sentry banners have been replaced with

cerulean-blue flags with four interlinked black rings on them—
the symbol of the coalition government, each ring representing
one of the four races: human, Darkling, Bastet and Lupine.

A few coalition guards—some human, others Lupine—nod
at me as I walk by. I give them a polite smile, trying to ignore
the twisting feeling in my gut. I slide a finger down the blade in
my pocket. I need to get to the basement, where Purian Rose is
being detained in the cells. I promised my sister I'd kill him for
what he did to her, and that's exactly what I intend to do. It's
been impossible to get to him these past two weeks, as he was
hidden in a secret location to stop people—like myself—from
taking matters into their own hands. But he was moved here
this morning in preparation for his execution. This is my only
chance to get to him.

On my way to the elevator, I pass the council chamber where
the coalition government has congregated. The doors are wide
open, as they nearly always are—a symbol of the "openness
and transparency of the new alliance." I hear Ash's angry voice
spilling out of the room and pause briefly by the doorway. He's
pacing up and down the oval room. He's dressed in a luxurious
black frock coat with orange silk lining, tailored black shirt and
pants, and expensive leather jackboots. It's a more chic version
of what he wore the day of the Cleansing ceremony, which is
no mistake; the whole outfit has been carefully put together
especially for Purian Rose's televised execution. Ash tugs at his
collar, clearly uncomfortable.

"We can't go ahead with this execution," he says. "It's bar-
baric. I know what it feels like to be pinned up to one of those
crosses; I can't condone this."

"The Workboots need to see him executed, Ash," Roach says.
She's sitting at a long mahogany table with the other members

of the cabinet. Her scalp has a smattering of ginger fuzz on it, where her hair has started to regrow, and she's wearing tight pants, a white vest and a long black frock coat similar to Ash's. "They won't feel safe until they know he's dead."

"The Sentry will think we're weak if we don't execute him," Mother adds.

Sitting next to them are the Lupine ministers: Garrick and a woman named Cassandra, who has vivid purple hair and matching lipstick, reminding me of Sasha. To my right, the new Bastet Consul winks at me. I smile back at Elijah. As the last surviving son of the Theroux family, he inherited the position and he's doing an amazing job under the guidance of his mother, Yolanda, who is his official adviser. He's cut his russet hair short, emphasizing his topaz eyes and high cheek-bones, and he's dressed in a dark green frock coat, with matching pants and waistcoat. Around his left wrist is his gold band. Unlike Ash, he seems comfortable in the elegant clothes. They suit him.

Opposite them are Sigur and Lucinda, the Darkling representatives. Sigur's white hair is loose around his shoulders, which is stark against his violet Ambassador robes. It's good to see him back where he belongs. Ash and Evangeline have been nominated to represent the twin-bloods. I don't see her anywhere, but that's not surprising. She's been locked in her room since the day of the Cleansing ceremony, refusing to see anyone except Ash and Elijah. We weren't certain it would happen, but when she touched Purian Rose, her heart activated. She's refused to let Dr. Craven remove Theora's heart, saying she wants to feel it beating inside her for as long as she can. I can't imagine what she must be going through right now, knowing that in fifteen minutes her heartbeat will be snatched from her again.

"Our people deserve retribution," Sigur says, gesturing toward the com-desk in the center of the room. Projected above the com-desk is a map of the Tenth. The camp was immediately shut down after Purian Rose's surrender. Even so, there were hundreds of deaths, as some of his devoted followers executed whole barracks of prisoners before we were able to stop them. Those men will be facing their own trials soon enough.

Right now, the government is in the process of trying to re-home all the Darklings. Many have stayed in the Tenth, because they have nowhere else to go. Understandably, they don't see the point of leaving one ghetto just to return to another, and the human citizens are still nervous about having them integrated into the cities, as I saw outside earlier. For the past week, the co-alition government has been finalizing documents to officially give the land over to the Darklings, so they can build a perma-nent home there. The Tenth will no longer be a detention camp, but the first official Darkling nation. Personally, the thought of living where so many people were slaughtered makes me shud-der, but then again, there isn't anywhere in the country where Darkling blood hasn't been shed. No matter where they go, they'll be haunted by the ghosts of their dead loved ones.

Besides, they won't be building their homes in the actual camps. The coalition intends to rip down Primus-One, Two and Three, and turn them into memorial parks. Then surround-ing the parks, where there are currently forests and wilderness, they'll build four new towns a safe distance from Mount Alba, called Jana, Martha, Zanthina and Annora.

Ash notices me by the doorway and stops pacing. I smile at him, trying to act casual, my hand shaking slightly around the knife in my pocket. His brows inch together as he lightly touches his chest. He must be feeling the echo of my erratic heartbeat inside him. His eyes flick toward my pocket. I quickly turn away.

"Natalie," he calls out.

I hurry to the elevator and jab the B button. The doors slide shut just as Ash races into the corridor. I take a few deep breaths, readying myself for what I'm about to do. *I can do it. I have to do it, for Polly.* The doors *ping* open.

I'm in the basement where the holding cells are. Like everywhere else in the building, the corridor is sparkling white and gold, with chandeliers lighting the way. Even the cell doors look more like the ones you'd see in a plush hotel than a prison. I don't think the inmates deserve such luxuries, but I don't suppose it matters at the end of the day. Everyone here is a dead man, and a prison is still a prison, no matter how pretty it looks.

I reach a gilt door at the end of the long corridor, which is guarded by two members of Humans for Unity, both of whom are wearing the new cerulean uniforms with the four-ring emblem on their chests. They salute me.

"I've come to see Rose," I say.

"He has company," one of the men replies apologetically.

At that moment the cell door opens and Evangeline comes out, her face ashen, her onyx eyes glimmering with tears. She glances up at me. I'm guessing she's just said her good-byes to Purian Rose. Even though he's a monster, she's still connected to him. She hurries past me, saying nothing. The guards step aside. I suddenly feel light-headed, my stomach sick with nerves. Can I really go through with this? *Yes.* I promised my sister. I enter the cell.

Rose is sitting on a narrow bed, dressed in a simple gray tunic top and pants. Around his neck is a circular pendant. His usually immaculate hair is unkempt, and his skin is makeup free, revealing the true extent of his old scars. On the dressing table beside his bed is a set of expensive dentures, with two gleaming white canine teeth to replace the fangs that were so cruelly ripped from him as an infant.

His hands rest on his lap. I've never seen him without his gloves. His fingers don't have any nails on them and the flesh is puckered—the result of his mother trying to drown him in a bath of scalding water when he was a baby. How different this world would be if she'd succeeded.

"Come to gloat, Miss Buchanan?" he says, not looking up.

"No," I say, trying to keep my voice even as I take the dagger out of my pocket.

His eyes slide toward me. They rest on the weapon. He doesn't seem surprised.

"Ah," he says. "I see."

"You murdered my sister," I say, and my voice finally cracks. "She was your *daughter*. How could you do that to her?"

"I didn't know she was my daughter until the news broke," he says.

SNB news revealed the information shortly after Purian Rose's arrest, along with the Wings evidence.

"Would it have made a difference?" I say, tears welling up in my eyes. "Would you have stopped them from raping her and cutting her up like a piece of meat?"

"No," he says flatly.

I blink, momentarily stunned by his response, and then the fury sets in. My hand tightens around the knife. He's just made this a lot simpler. I step toward him and—

The door bursts open and Ash enters the room, followed by the two guards.

"Natalie, stop!" he says, locking his strong arms around my

waist and dragging me away from Rose. I struggle against him, punching his arms, kicking my heels into his legs. Ash grunts with pain but doesn't let go.

"He murdered her!" I scream.

"Natalie, stop! You don't want to do this." His arms tighten around me. The two guards look at each other, uncertain what to do. "It's okay, I've got this. You can go."

They hesitate.

"That's an order," he barks.

They obediently back out of the room, closing the door behind them.

"Your girlfriend has quite the temper, Mr. Fisher," Purian Rose says, a cold smile spreading across his lips. He knows Ash won't let me kill him. The thought makes me even madder. This is my last chance to avenge Polly's death!

"You promised me, Ash!" I yell. "You promised I'd be the one who gets to do it."

"You're not a killer, Natalie," Ash says.

"I shot that scientist woman in the Tenth," I say, kicking his shins.

"That was self-defense; this is murder," Ash grunts, his voice strained with the effort of holding me.

"He deserves it," I yell, tears streaming down my cheeks. "You weren't there; you didn't see what they did to her."

I picture a red room and Polly's frozen body curled up in a ball on the metal floor.

They cut her up.

I remember the bruises on her thighs.

He deserves this.

I can still see her empty gray eyes gazing up at me. Eyes the same color as his.

He's her father, a softer voice whispers in my head.

He tortured her! He forced Mother to choose between us!

And Polly forgave her for doing that, the voice replies. *She didn't hold a grudge. That wasn't her way.*

I release the knife and it clatters to the ground. I stop struggling, and Ash lets me go.

Rose quirks an eyebrow at me.

"This isn't what my sister would have wanted," I say. "Unlike you, she had a good heart. She believed in forgiveness. So that's how I'm going to honor her memory." I hold Purian Rose's gaze for a long moment and try to see the boy he once was. Things would have turned out so differently if he'd been more like his daughter. "I forgive you, Edmund."

His mouth twitches slightly.

There's a knock at the door, and one of the guards enters.

"It's time," he says.

I look at my watch. It's nearly noon. I take one last look at the man on the bed. He glowers at me, then turns his gaze toward the blank wall. His hand grips the circle pendant around his neck.

Without another word, I take Ash's hand and we leave the room. Day, Beetle and the others are waiting for us in the lobby. Everyone is somber as we walk outside and join the chanting spectators in the plaza. The air is electric as we take our place beside the stage. Ash's fingers tighten around mine. I glance up at him. His sparkling black eyes are focused on the cross in front of us, his lips a pale line. I know he's thinking about his own crucifixion a few months ago. His gaze shifts toward me and I squeeze his hand reassuringly.

The crowd suddenly erupts into boos and jeers, and I peer over my shoulder. Purian Rose is being brought to the stage by a group of guards, his hands bound in front of him, his chin defiantly lifted. He catches my eye as he's led up platform steps. There's no remorse in them. Only fear. He turns to face the cross.

Purian Rose died at exactly 12:08. The execution was swift, his death mercifully quick. It's over. I turn away from the cross as his burnt body is removed, and look up at Ash. His expression is blank, unreadable.

"What do we do now?" I say.

Ash gazes down at me. "We go home to Black City."

36.

NATALIE

A FEW HOURS LATER we're on a luxury Miniport
back to Black City, along with my parents, Dr. Craven, Day,
Beetle, Evangeline and Elijah. Roach, Sigur, Lucinda and
Yolanda stayed in Centrum to deal with any coalition business during our absence. Evangeline's head is on Elijah's lap.
She's been silently crying the whole way here, mourning the
loss of her heartbeat and Blood Mate for a second time in
her life, but even so, she's holding up better than I thought
she would. I suspect Elijah's had something to do with that.
They've been getting close these past two weeks. It's not a
combination I would have put together, but looking at them
now, I realize it's a good fit. Elijah smiles softly down at her as
he strokes her black hair.

Our plan is to set up the new regional office in Black City
where the Sentry headquarters used to be. A crew of builders has
already been sent ahead of us to start renovations. My parents
will stay for a few weeks to oversee the project, then return to
Centrum while the rest of us stay here. Once we're settled, we'll
send for Day's family—Michael, Sumrina and MJ—who are in

the Northern Territories, and bring them back to Black City. It'll be hard to see my parents go, but I know they're needed in Centrum, and I don't want to live there. This is where I want to build my life with Ash. I take his hand and smile at him. He rubs his fingertip over my blue diamond engagement ring.

The Miniport swoops over the remains of Black City, following the path of the Boundary Wall, which slices through the city like a concrete spine. We're flying so low, I can make out the tattered posters on the wall—they're all pictures of Phoenix, the boy who rose from the ashes.

All around us the Cinderstone buildings glow like embers in the fire. The giant digital screens that once adorned the rooftops now lie broken on the cobbled streets, which are coated in a thick layer of ash. Black smoke spirals into the gray sky. I glance at Day and Beetle, who are sitting opposite me. They're grinning, and I know how they feel.

We're finally home.

The pilot lands the aircraft on Bleak Street, outside the former Sentry headquarters, where I used to live with my mother. It's an elegant, white marble building—at least, it was. Part of the west wing has started to collapse and is being held up with scaffolding, but the builders assured us it's safe to live in. We all go inside. Everything looks familiar and yet different. I think it's because there aren't any guards marching about, or any Sentry ministers scurrying to meetings with my mother. The place was always heaving with activity. Or maybe it's because Polly and Martha aren't here, and without them, it doesn't feel the same.

"I'll quickly check the rooms," Father says, heading down the corridor.

"I'm going to the laboratory," Dr. Craven says, a flicker of excitement in his eyes. The laboratory is his pride and joy, and the place he probably thinks of as home more than any actual house. It's the first time I've seen him happy since his son tried to kill him.

The rest of us go to the dining room—a warm, red room with a massive oak table, a huge fireplace and stuffed animal heads adorning the wall.

"Who wants some supper?" Mother says.

My eyebrows shoot up. That's the first time she's *ever* offered to make dinner.

"I happen to be a very accomplished cook," Mother says, clearly offended.

She sweeps into the kitchen and we all take our seats at the table. Father joins us when Mother returns a short while later with some sad-looking sandwiches, a few apples, and glasses of Synth-O-Blood for Ash and Evangeline.

"The rooms are all clear. I found a sleeping bag, but the squatter's gone. We should probably get the alarms up and running as soon as possible, though, just to be safe," Father says, sitting down and warily eyeing Mom's dinner. "This looks wonderful, dear."

I cough, trying to disguise my laugh. Father shoots me a warning look, which only makes me laugh harder. We heartily tuck into our meal, the conversation flowing. Dr. Craven pops in briefly to get a bite to eat before hurrying back down to the laboratory. During dinner, Ash takes my hand under the table, giving it a squeeze, as Father regales us with funny stories about his childhood. It's so strange and wonderful being here. I look at all the smiling faces around me: Sentry, Workboot, Darkling, Bastet. A few weeks ago we were enemies, and now we're having dinner together. I never thought this would be possible in my lifetime. I wish Polly were still alive to see this. Grief spills through me. I scrape back my chair.

"You okay?" Ash asks.

I nod, kissing his cheek. "I just need to use the bathroom."

I head upstairs. The sound of everyone's laughter fades away the higher up I go, muffled by the soundproofing between the floors. It's completely silent in the penthouse. Eerily so, in fact. I wrap my arms around myself, holding back a shiver as I stroll down the hallway. I walk past my mother's office, then by Sebastian's bedroom—he used to live with us, since he was my bodyguard. I reach the white door leading into Polly's room and turn the handle.

I'm disappointed to see that her room has been completely emptied. No furniture, no paintings, no rugs. Every last memory of my sister has been wiped from this place. All that remains are the dimples in the carpet where the furniture once stood. I recall seeing Sebastian and Garrick loading a bunch of antiques onto the train that Ash, Elijah and I escaped on during the evacuation of Black City, and realize that's what he was taking. I didn't recognize the furniture at the time, but I *was* running for my life.

I pad toward my bedroom, although I don't know what I expect to find. The door creaks as I open it. Surprisingly, my bedroom is the same as it always was, apart from the cracked plaster on the walls—the only sign of damage from the explosions that ripped through the city.

All my white furniture is still in place, the gilt-framed mirror still hangs above the dresser, and my cat-scratched rug is still on the plush carpet, hiding a bloodstain where Evangeline killed my kitten, Truffles, several months ago. Why did he leave my belongings and take everyone else's? Maybe he didn't want my things. I frown, a little offended. My stuff isn't *that* bad. I run my fingers over the soft sheets that cover my double bed. A floorboard creaks behind me.

I turn, expecting to see Ash. He probably sensed I was feeling blue earlier and came to comfort me. "Hey, I was just taking a look around—"

My words get trapped in my throat.

Standing in the doorway is Sebastian.

I'm too shocked to scream. His condition has deteriorated since I last saw him. His skin is sallow and slick with sweat, his lips are pale, and his eyes are bright silver. He's holding a sword in his shaking hand.

"I wondered if you'd come back," he says.

"What are you doing here?" I say, my eyes fixed on the weapon.

"I came to die, of course. This is my home," he says. "By the way, the next time your father searches a property, he should really check the roof as well. He's losing his touch."

So that's how my dad missed him. Sebastian must have seen us arrive and snuck up onto the roof, knowing my father would search the rooms. He moves closer and panic bubbles up inside me. I try to think of ways to get out of here since he's blocking the doorway. My best chance of escape is via the balcony.

"You're ill, Sebastian. You need help," I say, taking a step back.

"I'm beyond help," he replies, edging closer.

"Your father's downstairs," I say, trying to keep him distracted. "He can fix you."

"No one can fix me!"

I take another step back, and my legs hit the bed. I'm trapped.

"Ash!" I yell.

"He can't hear you," Sebastian replies in a singsong voice. "No one can."

"I can take care of you," I babble. "You don't have to go through this alone—"

"Don't act like you care!" he yells, thrusting the sword at me.

I flinch and fall back against the bed, landing heavily on the mattress. Sebastian's on top of me before I can blink, the blade pressed against my throat. He stinks of body odor, decay and Shine. Memories of the last time we were together on this bed flash through my mind. He tried to rape me then, and I won't let it happen this time. I bring my knee up, catching him in the groin. He gasps, rolling off me, and I scramble toward the door.

I've barely reached the corridor before he catches up with me and grabs me around the waist. I cry out as he slams me face-down into the floor. The weight of his body crushes me, pinning me to the ground. It's impossible to move. Terror rushes through my veins.

"Ash, help me!" I scream.

"He's not coming," Sebastian taunts. "He can't hear you."

Tears stream down my cheeks, knowing he's telling the truth.

Sebastian presses the tip of the sword between my shoulder blades.

"No! Oh God, please don't do this," I beg. "Please let me go, please, please, please."

"You sound just like Polly," he whispers into my ear. "Right before I killed her."

No! "ASH! HEL—"

He plunges the blade into my back.

37.

ASH

I DROP MY GLASS of Synth-O-Blood as a sharp pain rips through my chest, like a knife piercing my heart. The blood splashes over the oak dinner table. Everyone stops talking, startled.

"Mate, you okay?" Beetle says.

I shake my head, gasping for breath. My heart is stuttering erratically.

Ba-boom, ba-boom, ba-boom.

Only one thing could be causing this. *Natalie.* I groan, pushing back my chair, and stumble out of the dining room in search of her. Beetle and Day catch up with me halfway up the stairs.

"What's up?" Beetle says.

"My chest hurts," I grunt.

Day's eyes widen with alarm, understanding.

I groan and clutch my chest as another sharp pain slices through my heart.

"Natalie!" I cry out.

Ba-boom . . . ba-boom . . .

We reach the top of the stairs. The scent of blood hits me

first. Hot, fresh, tangy. The blood stretches across the floor, a crimson streak, reaching out to touch my boots. I try to rein back my panic. We follow the trail around the corner and that's when I see her, facedown on the floor, her blond curls spilling around her shoulders. Sebastian Eden is straddling her back, his hands clasped around the hilt of a sword. The blade is buried deep between her shoulders.

"No . . ." I exhale. "No . . . no . . . no . . ."

"Natalie!" Day screams at the same time Beetle yells, "Get away from her!"

Rage floods through me, and I lunge at Sebastian. We crash to the floor.

"I'll kill you!" I yell. "I'll fragging kill you!"

He laughs, the sound mad, frenzied—a man who doesn't care. His cold eyes are like silver coins; the infection has spread right through him.

"Natalie, oh God, oh God," Day sobs behind us.

Ba-boom . . . ba-boom . . .

I punch Sebastian, over and over. Blood seeps out of his bruised lips, but he doesn't stop laughing. Panicked voices cut through the air as the others arrive:

"Oh God, my little girl—" General Buchanan.

"Where's Craven—" Natalie's mom.

"In the laboratory—" Elijah.

"We need to get her downstairs—" Beetle.

"Don't take the blade out—" Evangeline.

"She's dying! Oh God, oh God. Natalie—" Day.

Ba-boom . . . ba-boom . . .

No! NO! NO!

There's a crunch as I break Sebastian's nose.

"Don't die, Natalie, please don't die—" Day.

"Put pressure on the wound—" Beetle.

Ba-boom . . .

NO!

I shoot a look over my shoulder. Natalie's struggling to breathe. I whip back around on Sebastian, pain, anger, terror shredding my insides. Hot tears stream down my cheeks.

"I'll fragging kill you!" I scream.

"Go ahead!" he spits. "The whore got what she deserved, just like her sister."

I yank his head to one side and plunge my fangs into his neck, not caring about the risks of infection. Venom pulses out of my fangs, flooding his body with Haze. He flails, his fists pounding against my chest, but I refuse to let go, even when his body becomes limp and my fangs are drained. I don't stop until I know for certain Sebastian Eden is dead.

I rip my fangs out of his neck and wipe my bloodied mouth, tossing his body aside, then race over to Natalie and carefully pick her up, the blade still buried deep in her body. We dash down the stairs to the laboratory.

Her heart, my heart, is just a faint whisper inside my chest.

Ba . . . boom . . .

Natalie is like a rag doll in my arms, her blood seeping over my hands, dripping over my boots. Her usually peach-blushed skin is a pale gray color, her soft lips parted like she's awaiting a kiss. Her breaths come in slow bursts. Everything is just a blur. I can't think straight. All I can focus on is the ice creeping into my heart.

No, please, no. Don't let Natalie die, please, please, please . . .

We enter the laboratory. Dr. Craven's eyes widen with shock when he sees her.

"What happened?"

"Sebastian stabbed her—" Natalie's mom.

"He's here?"

"He's dead." General Buchanan. "Help her, please."

Dr. Craven lets out a broken breath, then nods. "Put her on the gurney."

I place Natalie on her side on the steel gurney while everyone rushes around, getting all the equipment set up. This is where Natalie had her first emergency heart transplant when she was eight years old, so the laboratory is well stocked. I stroke Natalie's ashen face. She's so cold. Her lips are blue. She has just minutes left.

Ba . . . boom . . .

"You have to save her," I plead, my voice choked. "Please, don't let her die."

Dr. Craven pushes me aside. I step back as he removes the blade and begins the operation, with the help of Day and Evangeline, who pass him the tools. There's a crack of ribs. I look on, helpless, as I watch the life slip out of Natalie's broken body. Everyone is shouting, crying, barking instructions at each other, but their voices sound muted and far away, like I'm sinking deeper under water. Memories of my first weeks together with Natalie flash through my mind, with every beat of my heart:

A pair of cornflower-blue eyes lit by the headlamps of a passing truck.

"Can you fix her—" Emissary Buchanan.

"The valves are badly damaged—" Dr. Craven.

The touch of her fingertips against my lips during Tracker training.

"You have to save her—" Natalie's father.

"The damage is too severe—"

Lying side by side on Beetle's barge, the stars glinting above us.

"We're losing her!—"

"Please, Craven! Do something. She's our little girl—"

The fierce look on her face as she announced to the whole world that she loved me.

"I can't save the heart—"

"Take mine!" I cry out, ripping off my shirt. "Give her my heart!"

Beetle doesn't hesitate—he wheels over another gurney, placing it beside the operating table. I lie down. Evangeline hurries to my side.

"Are you sure, Ash?" she whispers, taking my hand.

I nod.

"There's no time for anesthetic," Dr. Craven says.

"Do it," I reply.

I stretch an arm across the two gurneys as Dr. Craven makes his first incision. My fingertips find Natalie's. Warmth seeps out of her skin with every passing second.

Please let there be time.

There's a moment of resistance, then my skin splits. Cold air rushes over parts of my body that were never meant to feel it. I grit my fangs as my nerve endings blaze like fire.

Just hold on, Natalie.

There's a crack of bone followed by stomach-churning, head-swimming pain.

I love you . . .

Viselike hands squeeze around my heart.

I love . . .

My vision blurs as Dr. Craven lifts something glistening out of my chest.

I . . .

38.

ASH

SILENCE.

That's the first thing I notice when I wake up. A deafening stillness that trickles through my veins, where my blood once rushed with life. The blood is still there, but now it's just a stagnant soup for the *Trypanosoma vampirum* to thrive in. I can almost feel them squirming about inside me. I'd forgotten what it felt like; they've been dormant for months. My heavy lids struggle to open, my lashes tangled together like the ivy that once crept over the church where Dad and I lived. Light pierces my sensitive eyes and I immediately close them again, groaning.

My head feels foggy and it hurts like hell, like I've got a killer Haze Headache, but it's nothing compared with the searing pain in my chest. I lift a sluggish arm—How long have I been asleep? All my muscles feel weak—and press my hand against my bare chest. Beneath my fingers are the rough edges of metal stitches holding together pink, puckered skin, and below that . . . nothing. Just deep, endless emptiness.

Natalie! I bolt upright in bed, nearly passing out from the sudden burst of pain. Gah! It feels like I've been cracked open like an egg and scooped out, but I realize that's pretty much what happened. Blood trickles out of my stitches as I gingerly climb out of bed. My bare feet touch the cold floor. I'm in a bedroom, although I'm not sure whose. It's sparse, with white walls, marble floors and a double bed covered in white sheets.

I'm wearing only black pajama pants, so I grab the blanket and drape it over my shoulders, then head to the door. My hand hovers over the handle, unwilling to turn it, suddenly gripped with fear. What if I was too late? What if Natalie died? As soon as I step over that threshold, I'll know. But if she's dead, I don't *want* to know.

I consider going back to bed, so I can hold off finding out the truth for a little while longer, but that's all I would be doing: delaying the inevitable. Natalie is either dead or alive. No amount of time is going to change that, so I might as well find out now. I turn the handle.

The corridor is empty. My eyes instinctively drift toward two bloodstains on the carpet. One belongs to Natalie. The other belongs to Sebastian. I'd been dreaming about him. In my nightmare, he was sitting in a rocking chair, laughing manically as he metamorphosed from a human into a wolf, then back to a human again. I rip my eyes away from the bloodstains.

I hear Beetle's and Day's voices coming from the room at the end of the hallway. I tentatively pad toward the white door and place a shaking hand on the doorknob. I shut my eyes. *Do it.* I enter the room. Beetle is standing by the balcony at the far end of the bedroom. He's holding a black-and-white kitten, which playfully paws at his top.

Elijah and Evangeline are standing beside him. Elijah has his arm casually looped around Evangeline's waist. She warily eyes the kitten in Beetle's hands. Day is perched on the end of the double bed, wearing a simple teal dress, her silky black hair tied into a long braid. She's got a new pair of glasses—these have fine metal rims—although they still stubbornly slide down her long nose. Next to her is her younger brother, MJ. He's twelve years old, with dark skin, chocolate-brown eyes and thick black hair. His gray shirt is ill fitted because of his hunched back—MJ was born with a condition that causes curvature of the spine.

He looks up and beams at me. "Ash!"

"Hey, squirt," I say, my voice croaky from lack of use.

"Ash?" a soft voice says to my right. I glance toward the bed. Natalie is lying on top of the blankets. She looks very tired and pale, her blond curls hanging in loose waves around her heart-shaped face, but she's alive. She's alive!

I rush over to her, ignoring the pain in my aching body, and gently pull her into my arms. I kiss her softly, tentatively, not just because I'm worried I'll hurt her, but because I'm afraid she'll push me away. We no longer share a Blood Mate connection; there's nothing binding her to me. She may not want me anymore. As if reading my thoughts, Natalie's fingers twist through my hair and she draws me closer. All my doubt vanishes as I sink into the kiss, and for a moment, just a fraction of a second, I swear I feel a heartbeat echoing inside me.

Natalie pulls away, biting her lip. She's crying. I cup her face in my hands and gently rub her tears away with my thumbs.

"What's wrong?" I whisper.

"I thought I'd lost you," she says.

"Me?" I say, confused.

"You've been unconscious for nearly two weeks," Beetle says.

"What?" I say, flabbergasted.

"You nearly died, Ash," Natalie says quietly. "The *Trypanosoma vampirum* in your blood didn't immediately kick in, because they'd been dormant for so long. You weren't getting any oxygen to your organs."

"Dr. Craven had to give you a transfusion of Evangeline's blood," Day adds.

I glance at Evangeline and give her a grateful smile.

"You were brain dead for a few minutes," Beetle says. "Of course, nobody noticed any difference at first . . ."

"Hey!" I say, and everybody laughs.

"Then there was the *other* thing," Beetle says. "You might want to look in the mirror."

I wander over to the mirror and look at my reflection. It takes a moment to realize that the boy I'm staring at is me. Black hair. Gaunt face. Pale lips. Silver eyes.

Silver.

"You got infected with the retrovirus when you bit Sebastian," Natalie says. "Thankfully, you didn't have a bad reaction to it, like he did."

I study my reflection, trying to get used to my new look, the new me. I turn to Natalie.

"Were you infected too, when I gave you my heart?"

"The Wrath in my system killed the retrovirus before it could do anything," she says. "I guess I got lucky."

I smirk and she laughs, realizing the irony of that statement.

"So you're still sick?" I ask quietly.

She nods. "But I've been taking my medication." She points to the black syringe case on her nightstand. "Dr. Craven is optimistic I'll be better in a few months."

The black-and-white kitten wriggles out of Beetle's grasp and bounds onto Natalie's bed.

"Who's this?" I say.

"Mittens," Natalie replies. "My parents got her for me to replace . . . erm . . . *you know.*"

Day narrows her eyes at Evangeline, who flushes slightly. I reach out a hand to pet the new kitten, but it hisses, giving me the stink-eye. Natalie giggles.

"We should probably give Ash and Natalie some alone time," Day says, standing up. "I'm sure they have plenty of catching up to do." She starts walking to the door with Beetle and MJ, then sharply turns and rushes over to me, flinging her arms around my neck. I grunt with pain, but let her hold on to me. "Thanks for saving Nat. You're a good guy, Ash Fisher."

I grin as she pulls away and hurries out of the room.

"Roach and Sigur need to see you as soon as you're up to it," Beetle says. "There's a lot of business to attend to."

I groan, rolling my eyes. "Can you tell them I'm still unconscious?"

Beetle smirks. "Sure thing, bro." He leaves the room.

Elijah pads over to the doorway. He leans against the door frame while Evangeline sits down on the edge of the bed. Natalie holds Mittens close to her chest.

"How are you?" I ask Evangeline.

"There's good days and bad. I miss Edmund terribly, but then I remember it wasn't real." She sighs. "It hurt losing my heartbeat again, but not as much as I thought it would." Her glittering black eyes flitter toward Elijah, and he smiles. "I can live without it."

Evangeline stands up and kisses my forehead, then plants a

soft kiss on Natalie's cheek. She walks over to Elijah and takes his hand. They leave the room, shutting the door behind them. Natalie and I are alone. Mittens leaps off the bed and paces over to the balcony.

"I could use some fresh air," Natalie says.

I help her to her feet and shrug off the blanket around my shoulders, placing it around Natalie's, exposing the scar that zigzags down my chest.

"Is it terrible?" she whispers, and I know she isn't referring to my scar, but the emptiness that lies beneath.

"No." I place my hand over her chest, feeling the thrum of my heart beating inside her. "I will always be a part of you. That's pretty amazing, if you ask me."

She beams up at me, and I quickly kiss her.

"I don't know what to get you for our anniversary now," I say. "How do I top giving you my heart?"

She giggles. "I like candy."

I grin. "Candy it is."

We head outside. The air is cool and crisp, giving me goose bumps, but I like it. It reminds me of being in my bedroom in the Ivy Church. Grief grips me and I suck in a ragged breath, thinking about my dad. Natalie takes my hand and gazes up at me. I smile softly.

A gust of wind stirs the ash clouds overhead, and for a brief moment I catch a glimpse of cornflower-blue skies peeping between the gray. I hold Natalie closer to me as Mittens leaps about the balcony, chasing the flakes of ash as they dance and twirl on the breeze.

The street below us is buzzing with activity. Trucks roll down the roads, and coalition workers dressed in cerulean-blue jumpsuits mill about the sidewalks, cleaning up the debris. They've already started to rebuild the city. Instinctively I look toward the Boundary Wall.

Natalie follows my gaze. "The government wanted to bring it down, but I asked them to wait until you'd woken up. I thought you'd want to be there when it happened."

"Thanks," I say.

Bringing down the ghetto wall in Black City is vitally important to me. This is the city that first stood up to Purian Rose; this is where the rebellion began; so this is where the first wall *has* to be torn down, and I want to be there to see it. It's what I've been fighting for. And when the Boundary Wall is demolished, I'm going to make sure they tear down each and every other ghetto wall in the country. Natalie leans her head against my shoulder.

"There's been some resistance from some of the states," she says quietly. "It's going to take a long time before this country is united."

"I know," I say, staring across the smoldering city. "But I'm ready for it."

It's not going to be easy. There may be more blood spilled, perhaps even another war, but there will never be a return to the old ways. Our enemies know what they're up against now. Something that cannot die. Something more dangerous than any weapon. Something like me. I stand up and reach out my hand to Natalie.

"Let's go bring down that wall," I say.

ACKNOWLEDGMENTS

It's such a bittersweet feeling to reach the end of a series. Ash and Natalie have been in my life since 2009, when one summer evening Ash's character burst into my head: a vision in tight jeans, a black shirt and a green military jacket, a cigarette dangling between his lips. That night, my dual heart was awakened and I have been lost to them since. But while I'm sad to say good-bye, it's with a warm heart, knowing they got their happily ever after. It was a little touch-and-go there for a while . . .

One of the greatest parts of this journey has got to be all the amazing people I've gotten to know in the YA community over the past few years. They're the most welcoming, enthusiastic and supportive bunch of people you're ever likely to meet. I'd like to do a special shout-out to the Apocalypsies, The League of Extraordinary Writers, Damaris (Good Choice Reading), Casey (Dark Readers), Nikki (Fiction Freak), Kate (The Bookaholic Blurbs), Christina (Ensconced in YA), Stacee (Adventures of a Book Junkie), Kristie and Julia (Lost In Ever After), Lívia (Nem harap a . . .), Ryan (Empire of Books), Brad (Book YA Review), and to my guys and gals in the Philippines! The Book Owls say hello! And big squishy hugs to everyone I haven't mentioned, but who I hope know how much I adore and appreciate them.

Of course, I can't talk about the YA community without mentioning my partners in crime, Jessica Spotswood and Paula Stokes. Thank you for your funny and sanity-saving e-mails, and for your friendship over the years. You guys are the best.

I am eternally grateful to Amelia Vincent for our long chats over coffee (and your awesome Photoshop skills), and to my critique partner, Tracy Buchanan, for your wise words of advice and friendship. I love you both.

My heartfelt thanks also go to:

The team at Penguin, especially Stacey Barney for your unwavering support, hard work and amazing editorial advice, and Jessica Shoffel, for organizing the kick-ass Breathless Reads tour. I'll be talking about that for years to come!

My awesome agent, Ayesha Pande, for always being there for me and for your kind words of encouragement, and my film agent, Rich Green, for getting us across the finish line.

Mum and Pops, for your belief in me. I couldn't ask for greater parents.

My husband, Rob, for your endless love.

And finally, a special thank-you to you, my readers, for joining me on this journey. It was a fragging awesome ride!

ELIZABETH RICHARDS is an award-winning journalist who spent her early career reviewing video games before making the bold (or crazy) move into travel writing, despite suffering from terrible travel sickness.

In her spare time, she ran a successful lifestyle website aimed at teenage girls. She won the Jane Hayward Young Journalist of the Year award for her feature on girls in the games industry, and was named Editor's Choice in the industry trade magazine *MCV*.

Elizabeth lives in Buckinghamshire, England, with her husband.

www.officialelizabethrichards.com